FINGER OF FATE

by

Denise Jenkins

Dedicated to my family both past and present especially my husband David whose love and encouragement made this book possible, my sons Matthew and Adam for their support and daughter-in-law Alison.

<u>Preface</u>

It's April 1990 and Charlotte Stone gave up her life in a busy newspaper office to work for an elderly lady in rural Wales. It seemed like a challenge, but just how much of a challenge to Charlotte's mind and being was not evident until history began to unfold and envelop her to such an extent that her own life was under threat.

Finding herself thrust bodily back into pockets of time Charlotte witnesses the lives of predecessors as it all begins to form a pattern, a pattern of intrigue, happiness, despair and murderous intent.

Olivia Jones is her employer who has many secrets beneath her regal facade. Ralph Nicholls is the Estate Manager who also plays a double game which leads to fatal consequences. Thomas Blake, the favoured relation of Olivia who continually schemes and manipulates people for his own ulterior motives.

The characters of the small Welsh village dominated by Glas Fryn, the Manor House, all entwine so that history repeats itself with a malevolent effect on the current generation. They are exposed to an evil force which has survived the passage of time and threatens to destroy their future.

CONTENTS

CHAPTER 1

APRIL 1990

The Arrival

It was late afternoon in April and a dismal day with the natural light fading fast. Nature wreaked its fury against mankind with howling winds and a continual swaying curtain of rain. Mere mortals could not escape the weather's wrath.

Charlotte Stone could not take refuge indoors. She waited for her taxi feeling utterly wet and miserable. It had been a long day and an arduous journey which did nothing for her disposition. A train journey which meant several connections and the absolute boredom of waiting at so-called stations which were just a basic shelter with no facilities whatsoever. Then the transfer from rail to road. The bus seemed to meander endlessly through B roads, her vision impaired by steamed up windows and the blackness descending outside. Finally she had reached this place which was laughingly called a terminal. There were just two modern, vandal proof shelters which had not survived the onslaught of spray paint.

A few hundred yards away there was a telephone kiosk. Covering the ground to the phone box she got soaking wet despite making a dash for it, but it was a relief to find that the phone worked and there was a taxi firm advertised by a small sticker on the receiver. With a promise of a car available to pick her up within 10 minutes she ran back to the graffiti covered bus shelter and waited.

Huddled deep within her raincoat, Charlotte wondered why she had been lured to a remote Welsh village. The reputation of the Principality for its joyless climate was renowned and she should have considered the matter more seriously. Once again she read the timetable fixed to the shelter frame, but it only confirmed that the next bus was hours away so she had no alternative but to wait for the cab.

She also reflected the strain on her meagre purse and prayed that her final destination was not too many pounds away. She had bought a one-way ticket early this morning and the temptation to turn back was not financially viable.

Then she remembered. Gone back to what? There was nothing left. The only way was forward. A new start was the solution to her problems. God only knew what lay in front of her, but an offer of a job from a stranger was far more acceptable than the joyless past that she left behind. Half an hour later a car drew up alongside spraying water from an overloaded gutter onto the luckless visitor.

Enraged, Charlotte opened the rear door, flung her suitcase inside and swiftly dived in behind it. "You're the taxi, I presume?"

"If I'm not you're in trouble! Of course I am, love. Who else would be out in this weather?" The dark tousled haired man turned to face her and winked.

Gritting her teeth, Charlotte said as calmly as she could, "They said you would be 10 minutes, what kept you? What kind of taxi firm are you?"

Not in the least perturbed, the driver cheerfully explained his dilemma. "To tell the truth the only taxi firm around here! Sorry, love, but we only got two cars, see. Me and my brother used our redundancy money from the Pit to start the business and we manage alright until it rains. That's when we work flat out and make a bit of money. Oh yes, love, rain is a blessing to us!" Chuckling to himself he repeated, "It's a blessing to us, love! Where are you going then?".

Charlotte reminded herself that she was lucky that this dot on the map managed to boast a taxi firm of any kind. "Glas Fryn. Do you know it? Its near a village called ...."

A deep throated laugh issued forth as the driver spluttered his reply, "Everyone knows that house, love! Everyone!"

As the car lurched forward, the passenger leaned forward and asked, "It may be a stupid question, but does the place have such a thing as electricity, or even more important, indoor plumbing? We do seem to be out in the wilds."

The laughter continued much to the passenger's annoyance. "Oh yes, love! We're civilised now, we don't live in caves anymore! Mind you, the manners on some make you wonder!"

Charlotte sighed. "Sorry. That was a stupid question but walking into this hurricane in April put me off and I haven't seen a soul since I got off the bus. I know it's always supposed to rain in Wales but this! All I want is a hot bath."

The driver gurgled his last and became more subdued. "Don't worry, love. It comes as a shock to the system but you English can't say much. I remember once going to the game at Twickenham and .... oh ! Sorry, love, but if you came last month when the Rugby was on you would be in that bus shelter for the night! Anyway, you're soaked through and that's enough to make anyone feel miserable. Pity you came on a day like this because when the sun is out its like the Garden of Eden."

Sinking back in her seat, Charlotte sincerely hoped that the driver was right. As she pondered her decision to come for the hundredth time she watched the hypnotic swish of the wiper blades as they tried in vain to clear the windscreen. It seemed no time at all before the deep voice of the driver jerked her back to reality.

"Here we are, love! Glas Fryn." The car passed through the open arms of tall, black wrought-iron gates and crunched along a gravelled drive. "We heard that someone was coming, relative are you? Stopping long?"

"The village grapevine I suppose." Charlotte said flatly without answering either question.

"Aw, you'll get used to us, love. Mind you, she's a dragon that woman! Harder than nails and twice as sharp. But you must know that. Why else would you be here." The car had stopped and the driver faced her and winked yet again.

Charlotte smiled as she mused that her visit would probably arouse quite a lot of curiosity in the small community. It nestled in the heart of the rural countryside with awesome mountains rising in the distance to remind the occupants where they lived. Customs, practices, culture and folk-lore had basically remained intact from the outside world despite the advent of commercial media. At least, that was the impression she had from the tourist blurb! Recalling that the driver was waiting to be paid she fished around her handbag looking from her purse. "Don't worry, I'm pretty tough, you know. I don't know how long I'm staying as yet, but when I leave I'll just call you. Bush telegraph and all that."

Accepting the fare, the driver winked again. "You do that, love! Try picking better weather next time and I'll show you how good a firm we are by getting to you a lot quicker."

The passenger alighted dragging her suitcase behind her. There was no sign of the driver running the risk of getting wet by leaving his warm, dry car to assist. As she slammed the door he actually stuck his head out of the window and winked yet again. "Good luck, Miss. You'll need it in this place!"

As the taxi drove away with it's engine barely audible above the sound of the wind and rain, Charlotte muttered, 'So much for local support.'

Turning towards the doorway she felt a tremor of shock at the large, stone house which loomed before her. Pressing the highly-polished brass bell she waited with baited breath for 'Igor' to appear as happened in horror films, but the door was opened by a frail, wizened old man who was contrary to her expectations. An ill-fitting dark grey suit which has seen many years of service hung loosely, accentuating the bony frame.

"Good afternoon, Miss Stone. Please come in. May I take your coat?" The voice was clear and firm with just a hint of a Welsh lilt inflected in the tone.

As Charlotte stepped from the shadows into the light she removed her sodden garment. Handing the coat to him he took a sharp intake of breath and looked away quickly. "I know!" the guest nodded. "I look like something the cat dragged in."

Regaining his composure, the manservant hung up the dripping outer garment and nodded. "Madam is expecting you

10

for tea."

"You mean I don't even get to clean up! Great!" Charlotte ran her fingers through her long dark, wet hair and nodded. "I got a taxi because the bus service is so lousy but still managed to get wet. The driver kept winking at me. Do you know him? Dark haired chap with an annoying laugh. Has he got an eye affliction or is he just trying to be friendly?"

" Both." came the terse reply as the man turned to the left in the large square hall.

Charlotte obediently followed the little man but felt angry. She wanted a hot bath not an interview with a Dragon. She knew she looked dreadful with a creased skirt, damp blouse and long, straggling hair. Hardly the right impression to make, especially the first. The trail led into a room and through a maze of pot stands and occasional tables which also happened to be laden with leafy plant life. In the midst of all the greenery sat an elderly lady in a straight-backed Queen Anne armchair. Her light blue eyes scrutinised the tall, dripping guest with a strange and almost puzzled expression.

"So! You are Charlotte Stone. You are late. Sit down, young lady. Now that you've finally arrived we can have our tea. Late. See to it , Price."

The manservant disappeared as Charlotte edged her way around an aspidistra in order to sit opposite the grand old lady. Indeed, 'grand' was the only way to describe the elderly person who wore twin-set and pearls along with an immaculately toned hair-do. A plaid skirt and thick support stockings completed the picture of a retired country gentlewoman. Smiling as she recalled the taxi-driver's words, Charlotte knew what he meant by 'Dragon Lady'. The reception couldn't have been colder if another ice-age was on the doorstep.

The ability to start a conversation deserted the younger woman through sheer lack of confidence due to her dishevelled appearance whilst the elder was silent for a reason. In Olivia's opinion small talk was a futile exercise. Experience had taught her to forgo the banal remarks with regard to the weather conditions and such-like which only led to familiarity. Her method always placed her subjects at a disadvantage and gave her control of the situation. Silence remained supreme until the refreshments arrived.

Price expertly negotiated a laden trolley' through the mass of obstacles with the attention of both women riveted on his ability. The welcome sight of sandwiches, cakes and a large steaming pot of tea nearly brought tears to Charlotte's eyes. Realising that she was still in the civilised world she watched Price pour the elixir with rapt attention and admired the steady hand. Frail he may appear, but his nerve was certainly intact. Once his duty was done he left the room with a silent grace which one could only applaud.

"Well, Charlotte! For one of the modern generation you have little to say for yourself. I assume you have accepted my proposition?"

Revived by the hot brew, the young woman nodded. "I have, Mrs. Jones."

"I mentioned in my letter that we are distantly related, but I realise that you are unaware of the connection and it's too complicated to explain. I am your Great Aunt, for want of a better description, but it would prove more convenient if you were to address me as Aunt Olivia."

Laughing, Charlotte agreed. "Suits me, it may take some getting used to! As for your proposal, I must say that I was shocked at first, but considered the matter VERY carefully. There was my flat, my job and other little things which matter like friends, but at the end of the day I quite fancied the challenge, so, here I am!"

"Challenge!" boomed the imperious voice, "One would hardly call it a challenge! I consider the conquest of Everest a challenge."

A lop-sided grin from the visitor made her look as simple as she felt. Charlotte Stone had been hired by an unknown distant relation to compile a history of the House and locale. She had little doubt that her 'Great Aunt's' family would play the leading role as the story unfolded. Drawing a deep breath, she decided to put her cards on the table.

"Aunt Olivia ," Charlotte was surprised at how easily she used the term and, thus heartened, continued, "may I make my position clear? My previous employment was on a regional newspaper to write articles on local history or any other topical item with a historical slant. I am not a journalist, nor a historian and by no stretch of the imagination a budding author! I wonder if my limited experience qualifies me for your ambitions?"

When Olivia Jones smiled her face softened and transformed the vision into the romanticised ideal of a 'dear old lady'. "I know exactly what you have been up to! I selected you simply because you were not a sensation-seeking literary artist. I know that you will carry out the task through a love of history and do the job well, not to make a blockbuster out of local gossip and suchlike. Does that answer your question, child?"

"Almost," Charlotte nodded. "Just one more thing, how did you know about me, or to quote you, 'all about me'? Until your letter arrived I didn't know you existed."

Olivia rose and waved a dismissive hand. "My dear girl, one chooses carefully and does not enjoy having strangers taking up residence. I simply examined all branches of the family and you fitted the bill perfectly."

Charlotte stood up and moved to the side of the old lady's chair knowing she would tower over her and feel more in control of the strange situation. "Do you just happen to have a family tree handy just in case the odd appointment comes up? I didn't know I had any family living so you can imagine how much of a revelation this is to me."

"Now, now, Charlotte! In this day and age one cannot be too careful as you should know in your profession." The old lady rose and picked up her walking stick, walked to the bell-rope hanging besides the ornate mantle and tugged it once. "Price will show you to your room. We can discuss the project further at Dinner, although I scorn the practice of dinning and discussing business as ill-mannered under normal circumstances. However, in your case we will bend the rules. Dinner will be served at eight. Eight precisely." The interview was over. The newcomer had been dismissed.

Price magically materialised and indicated for the guest to follow which she did like an obedient dog. They ascended the wide staircase in the entrance hall then turned left. Charlotte noted that there was also a landing to the right and another straight ahead and would have loved to investigate, but her escort was standing besides the first doorway and with a sweeping hand indicated her room. "Miss Stone?" he said dryly in a surprisingly deep tone.

Nodding and doing as she was bid, Charlotte was surprised to see her battered suitcase lying open on the bed whilst a plump, middle-aged woman bustled around unpacking her belongings. "Oh!" the guest uttered, "there's really no need!"

Price spoke gravely as he followed her in. "You are a guest, Miss Stone. We consider it a privilege to serve you. Mrs. Jenkins has been assigned as your personal maid during your stay."

"My maid!" Charlotte laughed, "What kind of place is this?"

The dumpy woman stared at the guest in horror and answered quietly, but firmly, whilst casting a sidelong glance towards the manservant. "As Price says, Miss Stone, I'm here to look after you. All part and parcel of the treatment our guests receive at Glas Fryn."

Summing up the situation, Charlotte smiled, nodded and turned towards the man besides her. Her tone was light as she whispered, "Thank you, Price. I'm sure you don't want to hang around and see my undies being unpacked, do you?"

"Certainly not, Miss Stone!" With colour flooding into the drawn cheeks he turned and closed the door firmly behind him.

The maid was chuckling quietly as Charlotte walked over to the bed and flopped down in relief. "Now let me do my own unpacking!"

"Oh, you are wicked! Fancy saying that !" The laughter

continued to bubble as she spoke, "Old Price is good enough really, but he got old-fashioned ways and likes things done 'properly' and my life would have been a misery over the next day or so if he thought I was slacking. Mind you, he's like a kitten compared to Her Ladyship!" Clapping a hand over her mouth, the maid blushed. "Oh dear! There I go again! Me and my big mouth! Sorry, Miss Stone, I forgot that she's your Great Aunt. You must think I'm an awful woman!"

Charlotte smiled. "You're not, but she is! She's a complete stranger to me so feel free to say what you like. Would Price report you to her?"

"Oh no!" The small brown eyes twinkled. "He's got his own ways of doing things, but telling tales isn't one of them. Now, Miss Stone ....."

The young woman held up her hand in protest. "I can't stand being called that! It makes me seem like an old maid, call me Charlotte. What do I call you?"

"Well, to her Ladyship in a bad mood it's Mrs. Jenkins, but most of the time it's Cissie. Maid of all work and glad of the money!"

"Why do you think I'm here!" Charlotte retorted and both women broke into laughter. "Thirty, single and broke, that's me."

"Go on with you! I wish I was your age again. The world at your feet!"

"My feet have brought me to this place in the back of beyond during a howling gale! As for the social aspect, the welcome from the Ice-Queen was hardly inspiring so my 'new' life doesn't look very exciting so far. The only thing I would recommend would be the room service."

Laughing heartily, the stout maid clapped her hands in delight. "Oh, you're a tonic to listen to. You'll wake them all up around here!"

Charlotte felt oddly comforted by the words. "At least I'll fit in one way or another. What is she really like? Olivia, I mean."

Shaking her head, Cissie's expression said a lot more than

words. "A hard woman. I sometimes wonder if she's ever had any feelings for anyone, she was even distant with her hubby. Mind you, some people are like that aren't they, they just can't show their emotions. Still, when it suits her she can be the most gracious lady around these parts. She's well-respected, I'll say that for her! No scandal or anything like that, fair play."

"That must make life pretty dull," Charlotte teased bringing laughter to the merry face once more. Walking slowly around the room she nodded in approval. "I'm not complaining about the accommodation though, well-furnished and large, much better than my flat which was just a boring square box."

Shaking up the pillows on the bed, the maid answered carefully, "It's clean, well-aired and comfortable. Quiet too. This room is not too bad. Being a city girl I expect you'll find it strange. Don't look too hard though! It could all do with a lick of paint, the whole house. Cleaning the place is bad enough, but decorating it, well! You can imagine."

Standing over the short woman, Charlotte folded her arms and asked, "Are you trying to convince me that it's the best room out of a limited choice? How many rooms are there?"

Cissie shrugged and counted on her fingers. " Upstairs, you mean? Six bedrooms including the Master Bedroom. This is the main guest room and the other four are covered in dust-sheets most of the time. It saves a lot of work for me! Anyway, as I said, this one is well-aired."

"But?" Charlotte persisted as Cissie did not sound convinced of her own words.

"Well.......... nothing really. It's just that it's very old-fashioned for a young person. All this dark oak furniture which came out of the Ark. I find it depressing. I wouldn't like to stay here."

"I love Antique furniture, Cissie. It has character, just look at that bed! It looks so comfortable, even if you need a step-ladder to get into it!"

Cissie gurgled as she pressed her knuckles into the bed

16

cover. "It's got a feather mattress and beats the modern ones with springs, I can tell you!"

"Exactly!" Charlotte exclaimed as she flopped onto the item in question. "Wonderful! I can imagine snuggling into this and sleeping like a log. And the Bedspread! Beautiful! Patchwork and hand-made by the looks of it. Did my Great Aunt make it?"

"Not on your life, Miss! Work is a stranger to her hands. No. It was someone in her family back along. It's donkey's ears old! Anyway, if you feel the cold and strangers often do, they call it a damp cold, God Help us! Have you ever been up North? That's what I call cold - nine months of the year too!"

"If I get cold, Cissie?" prompted the younger woman.

"Oh yes! There I go again, getting carried away! There are some extra blankets in the bottom of the chest of drawers."

"Got that. Just one more question," Charlotte asked soberly, "was the headboard made to match the fireplace, or do they both just happen to be enormous?"

The maid looked from one item to the other before breaking into peals of laughter. "You're right! I never noticed it before! Dear, dear me! They were made to last, Miss, and your pillows will never slip through and that's a fact!" Mopping the tears from her eyes with her white pinafore, Cissie looked at her watch and gasped, "Gracious me! I'd better get down to the kitchen to help Mary. If you want anything, Miss........... Charlotte, just pull the bell rope by the bed there. I'll give you a knock about quarter to eight in time for Dinner." As she made to pull the door shut behind her, the maid turned sharply back and waved a hand in the air. "Oh! I nearly forgot the most important thing! The next door along on your right is your bathroom, all nice and private. There's plenty of hot water and towels."

"You're an angel, Cissie! Best news I've had all day. Thank you." Charlotte added gratefully.

Finally alone, Charlotte took stock of her surroundings which would be her retreat for the coming months. The walls were papered in a pale-green regency stripe which, judging by the fading corners, had a quality which stood the test of time. The floorboards were highly-polished with thick, cosy rugs scattered around the room. The large bay window was framed by green velvet curtains which had paled along the folds where they had been exposed to sunlight. Any view there might have been was obscured by the grey cloak of rain, but she remembered the taxi driver's words about the Garden of Eden and hoped the sun would produce an inspiring panorama when it finally filtered through.

Although the setting crowded her mind with questions about her new home, the physical need for a bath overpowered her mental activities. With great apprehension she made her way to the bathroom expecting the worse.

The room was huge and so was the bath. It was a Victorian relic mounted on cast-iron claw feet. Warm mahogany panelled walls contrasted well with the pure white porcelain of the furnishings and produced a bathroom which the modern generation tried to emulate.

Charlotte was relieved to discover that the plumbing was efficient as piping-hot water gushed out of the brass tap. After a long soak and a change of clothes, the guest considered the prospect of life with her imperious Great Aunt with less foreboding. Back in her bedroom she sat in front of the dressing-table, on what looked suspiciously like a piano stool, and rummaged amongst her make-up in order to make her face more presentable than a boiled beetroot.

Her mind wandered as she rubbed cream into her skin and she wondered why she had never heard from Olivia Jones, or any other relation, before now. Her mother had died when she was just a toddler and her father had brought her up single-handedly until fate intervened. When she was 8 years old he died after a short illness. The painful memory of those years had been pushed to the back of her mind for many, many a long day.

She had been classified as an orphan despite attempts by the Welfare Officers to trace her family and placed in a Children's Home where she remained for three long years. It

18

was clean, but Matron was distant towards her charges and the other Helpers followed her lead. They were sterile years, a nightmare after a loving childhood with her Dad.

Escape came at the age of eleven when she won a Scholarship to a Girls' Boarding School. It was a refuge where the atmosphere was caring and friendly, where both pupils and staff worked in harmony and achieved results. At 18 she gained entrance to University and tackled the outside world with confidence and vigour, life was better when you had control of your circumstances.

Where had Olivia been for the last twenty two years? Why didn't the authorities trace her all those years ago? Charlotte summed up the situation quickly. A child was a burden. The Ice Queen had only contacted her great-niece when an ulterior motive made it necessary.

Could she bear to work for an ancient woman whose standards belonged to the Victoria & Albert Museum? Perhaps the old girl was an animated waxwork kidnapped from Madame Tussauds! Maybe the whole business was a hoax! Returning to rational thought, she sighed. As long as it lasted this place was sheer luxury compared to her small, barely habitable flat. She would exploit the opportunity. Olivia Jones being a stranger made things easier. Not having any relations they would be an unfamiliar factor to deal with, but this way it was simply a matter of dealing with Olivia Jones in practical terms.

'Yes!' Charlotte announced to her mirror-image, 'we can all be selfish! I can bear to live in luxury for a few months, albeit antiquated luxury! Once my war paint is on I'll be prepared for battle!'

Her make-up producing a presentable countenance, she turned her attention to clearing away the jumble of items which had spilled out onto the dressing table. 'Good Lord! How did I ever get all this into that little bag?' she mused, then examined the space available. Three small drawers rested along the vanity table which also served as a mounting for the swivel mirror. 'Ideal for toiletries and my jewellery!'

she smiled happily.

On each side of the vanity table were deep drawers which were down to the floor. 'More like a desk!' she laughed as she gathered up some nightshirts which lay on the floor, then opened the top left-hand drawer to put them away. A wonderful, flowery aroma exuded from a scented liner and Charlotte giggled with delight at the thoughtful touch.

'Right! Underwear next. I've never been so organised!' As she opened the top right-hand drawer she gasped in surprise. Someone else had the same idea. It was full of neatly folded clothing and the delicate smell of Lily-of-the-Valley wafted around her. She checked the drawer below and found the same. Picking up an item she confirmed her suspicions, they were all made of fine silk.

The urge to touch the shiny fabric was irresistible, and so Charlotte examined the articles which felt like sheer elegance in her hands. Camisoles, nightgowns, long petticoats and impractical handkerchiefs were shaded in pastel colours of pinks, lilacs, blues, peach and the purest white. Each item was hand-embroidered with exquisite expertise in complimenting silk thread.

Guilt washed over her as she rummaged amongst such personal possessions, but it was quickly followed by amusement as she tried to imagine her matronly Great Aunt wearing such seductive underwear in her hey-day. Even though the shades and texture remained in pristine condition the styles belied their age.

'Wow, Olivia!' Charlotte exclaimed aloud, 'You must have been a very sexy lady in your day!'

Just before eight Cissie tapped on the bedroom door and opened it at the same time. She looked impeccable wearing a black dress with a starched white apron glowing over it. Hurrying her charge out of the room and down the stairs she stressed the urgency. "Her Ladyship is waiting. Nobody, and I mean nobody, keeps her waiting!"

The guest bit her tongue from replying 'To hell with the old bat!' and donned an apologetic expression as she entered the dinning-room. "Am I late? I'm so sorry but I'm afraid I dozed off. The long journey followed by the hot bath must have lulled my senses. It's never happened to me before!"

"Apology accepted." Olivia nodded in the most regal fashion. "It is your first evening at Glas Fryn, but in future I expect you to be seated by 7.55 in readiness for Dinner. Modern eating habits are deplorable and will not be tolerated in this house."

Charlotte rebelled. "Really? It's just like Boarding School! Does one have to be up at the crack of dawn and go through a fitness regime before breakfast? Does one have to 'dress' for dinner? Damn! I'm afraid I forgot to bring my evening gowns."

Olivia remained unperturbed. "Sarcasm does not become you Charlotte. I will make myself quite clear. You are in my employ, but also a guest. A family guest I might add. I am merely informing you of the household routine and trust that you have the good manners to comply."

Charlotte fought her natural instinct to retaliate and disciplined herself into humouring the old girl considering it was her first night under her roof, she had probably overreacted anyway. Besides which, she was starving and the change of tack would at least enable her to digest the long awaited meal. Principles were all very well, but the delicious aroma of home cooking to a hungry body was more than pride could bear. "OK. Point taken, Aunt Olivia. I will try my best to become a well-oiled cog in the smooth running of the household. When in Rome, and all that!"

The first course arrived with Cissie and Price. The young woman couldn't resist throwing a small barb at the armour-plated relation. "Oh dear! So much cutlery! Which spoon should I use for the soup?"

Hearty laughter burst forth from the elderly lady. "Touché, my dear, touché !"

Even Price gave a brief smile, or the guest mused, was it merely wind?

The meal was a credit to any culinary talent and Olivia

explained that the cook was none other than Price's daughter, Mary. She had taken the post over after her mother's death some years ago. "A dynasty of the Lower Orders, you might say."

"Of the Lower Orders!" Charlotte gasped. "You really do live in the past! This is the 1990's not the 1890's. There's no such thing as 'Upstairs, Downstairs' these days!"

"Oh, but there is. You have a lot to learn, child. I suppose one could put your ignorance down to a working-class upbringing." Rising from the table with dramatic effect, Olivia added condescendingly, "but we shall initiate you into the social graces of the modern world. Just the basics to start with, of course."

Charlotte was on her feet before she knew it. "Save it! If I'd been born in your era I would have been standing alongside Emeline Pankhurst! Under your terms I would have been a rebel!"

"Without a cause." Olivia retorted calmly.

"As I recall the cause was 'Votes for Women' and eventually successful."

"Yes, yes, on the face of it. But come along, coffee is always served in the lounge and we can resume the conversation in comfort." The elderly lady then strode from the room with a great theatrical flourish.

Shaking her head in exasperation, the young woman flung her napkin on the table and followed. One thing she had to admit, her distant Aunt was certainly one hell of a Lady! Crossing the hall she held her breath and counted to ten in order to control the urge to scream as the arguments crowded her mind, but her temper was dispelled as she entered the room. Her mind forgot their disagreements as she gazed in astonishment at the chamber.

The lounge was a mixture of modern design influenced by the classical. Shell-pink walls were decorated with white plaster-work mouldings creating a warm, but stylish setting for the furniture. The deep piled fitted carpet was also pale pink along with the luxurious silky curtains which were draped to take advantage of the natural light from the large windows. The two settees and pair of armchairs were covered in cream fabric adorned with delicate flowers which brightened the room through their subtle colours. The whole was bathed in a gentle glow from the globe wall lights with shiny brass fittings.

"Wow! My compliments, Aunt! I admire your taste. Superb!"

"I had a small, er........ windfall last summer and decided to have the decorators in. I gave them carte blanche with the decor and furnishings and trusted their reputation would produce a satisfactory result. Most of my evenings are spent in this room, hence the reason why I allowed myself the luxury of a complete renovation."

"Tasteful!" Charlotte smiled. "Almost as tasteful as ...."

As the young woman's voice trailed off the older one barked with impatience. "As what, pray? Another sarcastic remark?"

The guest reddened and squirmed with embarrassment. "No! No! It's nothing really."

"My dear child, one should never leave a sentence unfinished. It's extremely bad manners."

Wishing she had learned to curb her tongue, Charlotte felt obliged to explain. "Well, I hate to appear rude, especially since it's my first night here, but how does one admit to the crime of prying?"

Olivia shook her head in exasperation. "The more you say the less sense you are making, child! Prying? I think you should explain - preferably from the beginning."

Taking a deep breath, the younger woman spoke hurriedly. "I happened to open the drawers and there they were! I couldn't resist a peek. They looked so beautiful so I just had to take a closer look!"

"Charlotte! What are you drivelling about? Which drawers? Which room?"

"Why my room of course! Did you really think I'd be snooping in any other room in this house? If that's the case then I'll ring up the one and only taxi firm in this Godforsaken place and go tonight!"

Olivia tut-tutted and sank into a chair. "I didn't think for one minute........ I only wanted..........this is ridiculous! We are obviously at cross-purposes and I didn't intend phrasing my question in such an accusing manner. Now, back to the subject in hand. What did you discover in your room?"

"I'm sorry." Charlotte smiled as she sat on the edge of a settee. "I think guilt made me so touchy. I found some silk lingerie in the dressing-table drawers. They are beautiful, but quite old-fashioned in style which is why I assumed they were yours."

Springing from her chair with an agility which shocked the guest, Olivia tugged the bell-rope hanging besides the Adam fireplace. Moments later Cissie rushed into the room looking anxious.

"Yes, Ma'am? Anything wrong?"

"I gave you strict instructions to prepare the main guest room for Charlotte, but it seems you have neglected to clean out the dressing-table drawers. It's disgraceful and most embarrassing! Go up and do it properly - NOW !" The final word was yelled in a most unladylike way.

Murmuring assent, the maid turned to leave the room but stopped in her tracks, frowning. "But Ma'am! With respect, I turned that room out from top to bottom. There was only bed linen in the chest of drawers and I know that I took everything out to air them and..............."

"Mrs. Jenkins!" barked her mistress. "No excuses. Go up to the room immediately!"

As Cissie stormed off, Charlotte felt dreadful and blubbered, "It doesn't matter, I don't really need that much space, I can manage quite well!"

"What matters is the incompetence which has been brought to light! I will not tolerate slip-shod work."

Minutes ticked by until Cissie returned looking triumphant. "There's only Miss Charlotte's things in the room, Ma'am!"

The young woman jumped to her feet and patted the maid's arm. "I'm not doubting you, Cissie, but I'll show you where I found them, maybe you thought they were my things."

Olivia took charge of the situation. "We'll all go up. If you are trying to cover your tracks, Celia Jenkins, I'll take a dim view of this incident."

Speaking firmly in order to quell her overbearing Aunt and appease her only ally in the house, Charlotte added, "Yes! All three of us will take a look bearing in mind that Cissie didn't have time to clear anything away."

Not another word was spoken until they had made their way to the bedroom and examined the drawers in question. They were empty.

"There you are!" Cissie said triumphantly. "Nothing there, that's how I left them when I cleaned the room. Never was anything in any of those drawers anyway, only in the chest like I said .... "

"Enough, Celia!" dictated her employer. "You have made your point."

"The smell!" Charlotte uttered, "even the smell has gone!"

Olivia looked around the room and sniffed the air. "Nothing here. Come along, child, back downstairs. Run along, Cissie, Mary must be wondering where you are."

The maid led the way muttering under her breath as she headed for the kitchen, whilst Olivia made straight for a cabinet in the lounge and poured two generous brandies with her own fair hand. "Sit down and drink this," she ordered her young relative. "You look very pale, overwrought by the day I suspect."

As if in a trance, Charlotte took the drink and sipped it automatically. As the fiery liquid burned her throat she coughed and shook her head as if to regain some sense of thought. "They were there. Delicate, pretty silks. I handled them! They smelt so nice and the embroidery .... but of course!" Coming vividly to life she exclaimed, "They all had initials on them! They weren't yours after all."

A strange look fell on the older woman's face. "What were

the initials, child?"

"C.A.A. - on everything. The same initials .... "

"You said something about a smell, could you define it?"

"Yes, yes, I can. It was so fresh that you couldn't mistake it. Lily-of-the-Valley without a shadow of doubt!"

Olivia gulped her brandy with alarming speed, closed her eyes then opened them again laughing. "A hoax! That's it! A silly hoax. My dear girl, I'm afraid that you have been the victim of a silly prank. Servants are known to enjoy that sort of vulgar humour, you know."

Charlotte smiled, but not with warmth. "Really, Aunt! Underwear in a drawer is hardly funny." Giggles bubbled up inside her and she wondered if it was hysteria or brandy. "I mean, if I hadn't mentioned it to you then the 'joke' would have fallen flat. It doesn't make sense!"

"Think, child! As soon as Celia was told to check the room it disappeared. Plain as day! Treat you to a 'mystery' on you first day."

Now giggling between talking, the guest spoke haltingly. "It gives the expression .... 'naughty nighties'........a new.. meaning!"

A stern gaze quenched the flame of gaiety. "Country folk are a different breed, Charlotte. I will find the culprit and stop this foolish nonsense."

Fear of reprisals against Cissie forced Charlotte to think quickly. "Just forget it, Aunt. If this got out they would have a field-day in the villages around! The stranger who thought she was seeing things on her first night at Glas Fryn! Knickers at that!"

Olivia relented and even smiled a little. "Your foresight surprises me child. Yes. You may be right."

Feeling that the 'lower orders' had been saved, the young woman turned her questions to the strange incident. "Was there such a person as C.A.A.? Someone who lived here?"

Waving a hand dismissively, the elder woman answered nonchalantly, "No doubt there was. A lot of people have lived in this house, stayed in this house and even lodged here in days gone by."

Charlotte frowned. "Whoever they belonged to wore clothes of quality. You'd think she'd be remembered, and so many items! Strange about the smell too, why did you ask me what it was?"

"Curiosity, my dear, idle curiosity."

Charlotte knew that Olivia Jones was holding back, but she could hardly wheedle the information out of her when she had just arrived on the doorstep. There would be plenty of time to root out the explanation, plenty of time to solve the little mystery.

When Charlotte retired for the night she checked the drawers again, but they remained empty. Maybe it was a prank. Instinct told her it wasn't. Washed and dressed for bed she sat in front of the dressing-table to brush out her long, straight hair when she noticed a small silver key in the lock of the middle compartment below the mirror. It hadn't been there earlier, it was the only small drawer which was locked.

Assuming that Cissie must have found the key and left it for her she retrieved her own jewellery out of the end compartment to transfer it. The monetary value of her items were not great, but their sentimental worth were beyond price. Refusing to dwell on her past life she examined the contents revealed by the locked cavity only to find a jumble of old sewing-items littering the small drawer. Charlotte was fascinated with the bone crochet hooks, button hooks and a selection of buttons in leather, mother-of-pearl and glass. A thimble lay amongst the assortment and she examined the well-worn silver item which had tarnished with age.

Placing it on her index finger she gasped in shock as a sudden spine-chilling coldness swept through her body. Whirling blackness surrounded her as she closed her eyes tight, then her physical being felt as though she was floating through time and space leaving the real world behind.

Gradually the spinning slowed to a halt and the blackness faded to light. Her bodily senses returned and she cautiously opened her eyes. She was still sitting at the dressing-table but a weightlessness invaded her body. Looking in the mirror to see if she looked as odd as she felt, Charlotte let out a yelp of terror.

A child was standing behind her. A child who was admiring her long, golden ringlets and looking straight through her. Charlotte rose and spun around in one fluid motion to face the girl. "Who are you?" she whispered in shock. "What are you doing in my room? Nobody mentioned a child!"

The girl continued to gaze into the mirror admiring her face, a face which did not register reaction of any kind. Charlotte looked around the room in paralysed fear. It was her room, but different somehow. The girl who seemed oblivious to her presence was dressed in the Victorian style complete with starched white pinafore over a long, grey dress.

What was happening? All she had done was to look in ...... the thimble....... it was still on her finger.

CHAPTER 2

The First Journey

Realisation dawned on Charlotte that by wearing the silver thimble she had travelled through a void of time, the only explanation. The same place, a different time. The idea was far too incredible to consider, she had to be dreaming, but the smell of Lily-of-the-Valley pervaded her senses as if to confirm that she was not.

The door opened so suddenly that both Charlotte and the young girl jumped. "There you are, child! I've been looking all over the house for you. I might have known you'd be up here preening yourself and helping yourself to my toilet water. I've told you often enough that vanity is a sin!" The intruder was a small woman dressed in a long, black gown with a white lace collar, all topped by a white cotton bonnet on her head.

Looking very sheepish, but standing erect with her hands clasped behind her back, the young girl apologised. "Sorry, Grandmother. I love this room and just wish I had one to myself! Is that sinful too? "

The stern face of the old woman softened. "Work hard, child, then time will improve matters. Wanting what other possess generates both jealousy and greed, especially in girls your age!"

"I am not jealous or greedy!" the young voice trembled. "I work harder than all the rest, even the boys! I never complain when my sisters have pretty dresses and special lessons!" The voice grew stronger, but not petulant.

"You are the eldest. You are duty bound to help your parents whilst your brothers attend to their studies, as for your baby sisters they have to be brought up like young ladies in order to make their way in the world. You know full well what is expected of you."

"Yes, Grandmother," sighed the crestfallen girl. "I know

all that, but will I ever have a room of my own? That's not too much to ask, is it?"

"This is only a farmhouse, Charlotte, albeit a large one. We are a big family and would all like to have our own rooms. Be content with a roof over your head, there's many a poor soul would be grateful for that let alone regular meals and plenty to eat! Now, come along. Sunday tea has to be prepared."

"Yes, Grandmother." The girl hung her head and dutifully followed the old woman out of the room, but as she turned to close the door she looked straight at Charlotte and smiled impishly, then softly shut the door.

Feeling cold with fear, Charlotte was compelled to gaze at the thimble wedged on her finger. The sides and top were indented as normal, but a plain oval on one side was etched with scrolled initials.

'Oh my God! It can't be!' she gasped as she read the elegantly entwined letters. Snatching at the sewing implement and tugging it off in shock the world turned black once again, but the three letters danced and spun around her mind. Three letters. C.A.A..

When Charlotte gingerly opened her eyes it was to find herself standing in the bedroom with her own belongings scattered around her. 'I'm back!' she gasped in relief. ' The same place - just a different time. Present and past. People present and past.'

Her train of thought made her shiver involuntarily and gaze at the silver object clutched in her hand. The silk underwear and the thimble bore the same initials, they had taken her back to the past. Who was connected to the items? The young girl or the Grandmother? Judging by the size of the underwear it must have been the child she reasoned.

Pinching herself and speaking aloud for the sake of sanity, Charlotte walked to the bed and back to the dressing-table. 'Did it really happen or was I dreaming? If it was a dream I would have been lying on the bed, not sitting at the dressing-table. Yes. It did happen. The lingerie was true as well, not a hoax.'

She had witnessed a scene from the past when she herself had become a ghost of the future. She had been invisible to them except for the moment when the child left the room. Charlotte shook her head and reasoned that the child was probably catching a last glimpse of her own reflection after the lecture about vanity and sin!

'I wonder what Olivia would make of it? One minute she breathes fire and brimstone, the next she can be cold and uncompromising. No doubt she would commit me to an asylum! Perhaps it happens to everyone who stays in this room, in this house. It's old enough to carry a few haunting tales.'

No. She would keep the experience to herself. Her Aunt would only question her sanity and waive aside such incredible happenings as day-dreams, nightmares or hallucinations from an over-excited imagination. It would be better to try and dig around for information, something to substantiate her vision. As her course of action became clear, Charlotte had a feeling that even Great Aunt Olivia would approve of her discreet attitude!

Jumping into bed, she snuggled in amongst the warm folds of the surprisingly familiar patchwork quilt. Within moments she had fallen into a deep, relaxed sleep.

The following morning Charlotte donned jeans and sweatshirt and went downstairs in search of Olivia. Sticking her head around the door of the morning-room she saw the back of a tall, thin wiry figure busy dusting her way through the forest of furniture with precise efficiency. So engrossed was she in the work that she jumped at the sound of the guest's voice.

"Good morning! Any idea where I'd find my Aunt?"

The black, glossy bobbed hair swished around to reveal the face of a young woman in her early thirties. There was no doubting her identity as the strong, plain face mirrored the features of her father. The voice was melodious and contrary to the austere gaze. "Out in the garden I expect, she doesn't have any appointments today."

"Thank you." Charlotte lingered, "Are you Mary Price? The butler's daughter?"

"Yes, but he is not a Butler."

"Well, whatever! My compliments on the meal last night. I have problems boiling an egg!"

"Really?" came the bland reply whilst the dark eyebrows were raised in surprise.

"Yes. Really. Well, I'd better find Olivia. Sorry I disturbed you." Charlotte beat a hasty retreat .

Olivia appeared from the lounge and looked her guest up and down. "I thought I heard you. You have missed breakfast. Come along! I'll show you around the house so that you can get your bearings. Places to go, or not to go in some cases. Who were you talking to?"

"Mary Price. I did most of the talking. She's obviously not a socialite, she must follow her father."

"Servants are not paid to socialise. In every other respect they carry out their duties to the letter. I do not ask, or expect, anything more."

"Here we go with the 'them and us' claptrap again! I see people, not efficient robots put here to give you an easy ride through life!"

Olivia waved a handkerchief in the air. "I only allow such opinions because you have just arrived. In time you will understand and accept my doctrine."

"God Forbid!" Charlotte muttered, incensed by the argument. "Are you going to show me around or just wave that hankie and preach? Most unhygienic, Aunt."

Olivia actually laughed. "Your views are most refreshing, child. With you around there's little danger of my mind becoming idle!"

"If arguing prevents senile dementia then so be it! You will be one extremely sane old lady going by our record so far." Even though the ideals were alien to her, Charlotte couldn't help liking the old stick. Basically she loved characters, and nobody could deny that Olivia Jones qualified on that score.

The tour began and they stormed through the ground floor

which consisted of Lounge and disused Games Room on the right side of the hall from the front door, Morning Room, Dining Room and disused Library on the left. The latter was to be used exclusively for Charlotte whilst she compiled the proposed historical record.

The upper floor confirmed Cissie's description of the four rooms shrouded with dust sheets whilst only Charlotte's and Olivia's rooms were in use. There were several linen cupboards which were nearly the size of a typical box bedroom in a traditional semi-detached house.

"I have an en-suite bathroom." Olivia explained, "It was originally situated next to my room, but we blocked the landing door and had the entrance directly into my bedroom instead. An inexpensive but wonderful alteration! A modern innovation of which I thoroughly approve." Turning back to the stairs, she beckoned her guest to follow. "Now the garden. It's large and mostly neglected I'm afraid. One just cannot get the staff to maintain the standards required."

Charlotte smiled as she followed. "Are you saying that you can't afford gardeners'?"

"On the contrary!" Olivia exploded. "Even with a generous budget one simply cannot find suitable recruits in the area. If you look further afield then accommodation is expected to be provided and that IS far beyond my means. Please, Charlotte, don't have any illusions of grandeur, you have no idea how difficult it can be to live in a house this size."

"It must be a problem," Charlotte agreed, "but you live comfortably enough from what I have seen. Things can't be that tough, take me for example. You'd be crackers to employ me for an idiosyncrasy concerning your family record."

"Quite right, dear girl." Olivia beamed with pleasure as they made their way through the front door of the house and followed a path around the side. "My income is adequate. My financial affairs run along smoothly enough with the aid of an Advisor." Moments of silence ensued as they strolled through a Rose Garden. "Let us sit here for a while. I adore sitting here, especially when they are all in full bloom. You just wait until the summer!"

Charlotte complied and sat besides her Aunt on a stone bench. "Well, gardener or not, someone has been pruning the rose bushes, not to mention keeping the weeds down."

"Mary Price. Her hobby is gardening so she cuts the lawns, does a little weeding and cares for the plants. Of course, the Kitchen Garden has suffered, but one has to make allowances."

"Oh, my God!" Charlotte uttered. "I can't believe I'm hearing this. On top of being housekeeper and cook she's the gardener as well! How much do you pay her? Three wages? Huh! I doubt she gets one that meets the poverty level!"

Olivia banged her walking-stick on the ground with vehemence, whilst her compressed lips indicated that enough was enough. "My servants' wages are none of your business, girl, nor are their duties, pastimes or anything else! We all live quite happily here and don't need the opinions of an upstart to disrupt our lives. Take us as you find us, Charlotte, or there's only one alternative."

Hunching her shoulders against the stark truth, the young woman replied, "Or I can pack my bags and go? Under normal circumstances being called an 'upstart' would be enough to make me do just that. However," pausing to sit up straight and salvage some pride, she added, "in this instance I may have been too quick to criticise."

"Hardly an apology! One night under my roof and you think you can throw insults around willy-nilly!" Olivia said firmly, her lips returning to a solid line.

"O.K, O.K! I'm sorry. Is that enough or do you want blood as well? Just understand that I'm not the mousy type who sits in the corner taking whatever life throws at her. I question things, all answers are knowledge gained, an insight into the theatre of life. Can you live with that?"

A smile broke over the hardened features and light twinkled in the blue eyes once more. "I can live with it. I never did like 'yes-men'. You are a new breed, Charlotte. The 'liberated woman' I suppose."

"Mrs. Pankhurst did have a cause, Aunt Olivia."

"Oh yes! But there's always been outspoken women around. More often than not they cause trouble." Looking her young relative squarely in the face she gave a subdued ultimatum. "If you accept our way of life, then we can accept you, child."

Nodding with understanding, Charlotte felt moved. "Fair deal. I think we might learn a lot from each other."

"Very true, my dear." Olivia rose and pointed to the house. "Count Glas Fryn as your home whilst you are here. As I've already told you the Library will be at your disposal. If you need anything just ask Price."

Standing besides the old woman, Charlotte tried her luck. "I found some items in the dressing-table drawer .... oh! Don't look so alarmed! Just old buttons and things. The most interesting item was a silver thimble, very small, like a child's."

"What on earth could be so interesting about a thimble?" queried the elder woman as she made her way down an overgrown path.

"The initials engraved on it. C.A.A. again. Who was she?"

"I can't possibly identify an item like that! This house is full of bric-a-brac and suchlike! Good gracious me! It could have belonged to anyone!"

"Like the silk underwear? The same initials? Rather a co-incidence, isn't it?"

Olivia waved her stick as if fencing with an invisible opponent. "Please refrain from mentioning that ridiculous prank again! Now, if you wish to be more constructive and familiarise yourself with the community I suggest you visit the local villages. Pantmawr is the nearest. I belong to several committees there, and elsewhere, of course, but the observation of local colour would be a sound basis for the proposed thesis."

"Not to mention a good diversion for my inquisitive mind?" ventured Charlotte, but her words fell on deaf ears as her aged Aunt walked briskly ahead. Her new found relation certainly knew how to change the subject. It was a skill which had probably served her well over the years and left her subjects speechless, wondering where they had gone wrong. No doubt her fellow-committee members were victims of such tactics, but they didn't have the advantage of time. Patience will repay my efforts, she mused, I'll find out who C.A.A. was by the time I leave. I didn't work in a newspaper office for nothing.

A week had passed by and Charlotte Stone found that she was enjoying life, basking in the select tranquillity, accepting the order of routine and learning about her Aunt. The House and gardens were indeed a Garden of Eden to be savoured after a life of dormitories, cities and airless flats.

From the taxi-driver who had deposited her on the doorstep of Glas Fryn with promises of such delightful surroundings she knew that her presence would be known to the locals before she stepped foot in the village, but was still amused to be greeted with respect and an aloof curiosity. Olivia Jones was a status symbol to the nearby village and few communities in the district enjoyed such wealthy residents who bestowed generous gifts to worthy suits.

Manorial Lords were part of history, affluent newcomers treated with distrust, but local dignitaries like Olivia would suffice as a figurehead giving respectable credence to charitable causes. Consequently, a stranger with the sponsorship of an elite member to their credit was guaranteed acceptability within the indigenous society.

Charlotte mused that if she lacked company a walk to the village would prove entertaining. Folk chatted to her in a familiar manner, their dry humour so refreshing and naive. It would, as Olivia predicted, prove an invaluable asset by providing an impartial slant to the task ahead. Local history was best discovered at the source, and many older members of the small community had very long, clear memories about the past, even when they found the present confusing!

Her destination on this fine Spring day was the Post Office. It was run by a middle-aged woman who had been jilted in her prime and never looked at another man since, at least, so went the gospel according to Cissie and her words were not to be doubted. She was known by the nick-name of 'P.M.' which not only stood for Post Mistress but also alluded to a famous woman politician who made it to the highest office and was also renowned for breathing fire and brimstone when crossed.

Charlotte joined the snake of customers who all shrank when confronted by the 'PM'. Requests were meekly whispered and customers quivered in their shoes when they queried anything as the tongue behind the glass plated counter flickered with venom. When her turn came, the newcomer handed a Registered Letter over the highly-polished surface slipping it through the gap under the glass.

"A Registered packet? It must be important for you to pay all that postage. Miss Stone, isn't it? Stopping up at Glas Fryn? Staying long are you?"

"How much?" Charlotte asked abruptly whilst counting to ten in her head.

"Nearly two pounds, very expensive! Is it THAT important? What does the packet contain?"

The battle-cry rang out in the young woman's heart and suppressed annoyance sallied forth. "When I request a service I expect it to be carried out without question. You are merely a servant of Her Majesty's Royal Mail, so I'd appreciate it if you just did you job and stop prying Miss........ whatever!"

Sniggers grew in volume behind her as the Postmistress's eyes bulged and her nostrils flared. She stamped the packet with unleashed ferocity then pushed the change under the security glass with such force that it would master a shove-halfpenny competition. In Draconian tones she announced, "Kemp. Miss Kemp. It's easy to see whose blood runs through your veins! She won't listen to anyone either! We don't have the money to throw around like you lot. Next!"

"The glass between us must be armour-plated otherwise I'm sure I would have fried on the spot by now! Good day, Madam." Charlotte had the satisfaction of the last word and turned to leave the premises. Passing the queue they winked and nodded in appreciation of her valiant stand against the viper of their postal institution.

Still smiling and enjoying the warm glow of victory as she meandered down the lane towards Glas Fryn, Charlotte decided that it was time the place had a shake up! Just the stuff that heroines were made of. The village of Pantmawr ruled by dictatorial spinsters like Miss Kemp was just ripe for someone to stand up against them, wage war and free the poor villagers from oppression!

There again, perhaps she should be more tolerant as Olivia had suggested. One person could not change the centuries of habits and customs which forged the pattern of their lives. No. Observation was the key for the moment, to use her trained eye to watch the present ..... and the past?

Would she go back in time again? Like everything else, it was up to the individual to decide the course with fate playing a leading role.

Charlotte Stone concluded that life had become very pleasant, contrary to her expectations. A champion for the villagers' cause, deluxe accommodation, regular meals and an exciting new experience, not to mention her new-found relation, Olivia. Despite the old girl's antiquated ideals she had already found a place in her affections.

Glas Fryn bathed in the early May sunshine which spilled into the hallway as Charlotte walked though the open doorway. Olivia was just replacing the telephone receiver and seemed to be in an equally light-hearted mood. "Ah! There you are, my dear! We have a visitor. Come along to the Morning Room and I'll introduce you."

Dutifully obeying her Aunt's command, the young woman entered the room which appealed simply because it was so very disorganised. There was a man about her own age sitting with his legs crossed and looking very relaxed. He was reasonably attractive with fair hair and green eyes, but Charlotte felt strangely uncomfortable under his gaze.

"This is the young lady I was telling you about, Thomas.

Charlotte Stone." Turning from one guest to another with accomplished ease, Olivia continued with her introductions. "This is Thomas Blake, a great-nephew of mine, though not related to you, who is also my business advisor. He is a Financial Consultant by profession and I value his opinions highly."

"Hello, Thomas," Charlotte said mechanically, not at all impressed. "Aunt Olivia seems to have relatives springing up from everywhere."

"Charlotte!" the elderly voice snapped. "Thomas has been coming here for years, so kindly control your sarcastic remarks and have the grace to be civil to my guest."

Steaming within, the young woman was determined not to be reprimanded like an errant child. "I'm so sorry, Aunt! I find it difficult adjusting to the ways of my 'long-lost' family."

"You were not 'long-lost' as far as I was concerned, how else would I have contacted you? However, I can see we must verse you in the qualities of grace."

Charlotte ignored the last remark but questioned the first. "Funny that. It took you thirty years to get in touch. However, I must remember that up until a week ago I didn't know you existed. Ignorance is bliss, as they say!"

Thomas coughed in nervous anticipation as his elderly relative raised her walking-stick with menace. "Please, Aunt! You must admit that discovering such a formidable old harridan like you must be a shock to the dear girl!"

The stick fell to her side and Olivia smiled. "Of course, Thomas. You are quite right. Charlotte, my dear, I fear that we are too much alike, kindred spirits! I forgive you for your impertinence and apologise for mine. Now run along as Thomas and I have matters to discuss. We'll dine together at the usual time."

As the old lady stalked off to the lounge, Thomas saluted, clicked his heels and marched after her. Despite her indignation, Charlotte giggled at the light-hearted antics and realised that his interruption had avoided a full-scale argument with her impossible Aunt. Maybe her initial feeling of distrust was misplaced as far as Thomas Blake was concerned. One thing was clear, he had the old girl wrapped around his little finger.

Charlotte went to her bedroom and, with hours to kill before Dinner, she felt a great temptation to leave the present and try to travel back into time. Would it work again? Picking up the silver thimble she knew there was only one way of finding out. Maybe she would get some answers, find out who C.A.A. was.

The minute she slipped it onto her finger the spinning void of darkness consumed her, but this time she was not afraid. Gradually the world steadied and she opened her eyes. She had gone back as before, but this time noises drifted from behind the closed bedroom door, from downstairs. She followed the sounds without hesitation.

The hall seemed to be full of large pot plants and dark drapes which covered doorways making the large area appear gloomy with dust motes dancing in the air. Charlotte noted that the furniture was the same, even stood in the same places. The commotion came from the Morning-room so she gingerly peeped around the open door to find a scene which was enchanting.

A man was sitting on a high-backed chair holding a pair of crutches in his left hand whilst on his right, sitting as straight as a ramrod, was a woman dressed completely in black. Gathered around the couple were children, the girl from the bedroom on her last journey stood besides the couple whilst five smaller children were kneeling at their feet all facing forward.

Opposite the family group, on a chaise-lounge, sat an elderly couple who were flanked by two women whom Charlotte gauged to be in their forties. The sombre clothing did little to flatter their sallow skin, so age could be deceiving.

The man with the crutches was speaking in a deep, pleasant voice. "John, my dear brother, your visit is a tonic and we must hear that tale again! It seems a grand story for simple folk like us to digest."

Nodding gravely, the other man agreed in sombre tones. "I am also a simple man, Ivor, but I'll swear on the Good Book that it's the truth!"

The woman sitting next to him patted his hand and smiled. "John, my dear husband, we all know what a devout and honest man you are, nobody doubts your word!"

"No, indeed!" Ivor agreed. "You lead a very exciting life by all accounts!" His merry laughter rang out and the young children began to titter shyly. "See how impatient the children become with our talk! What do you say, Sarah?" he asked the lady besides him.

Smiling and nodding, Sarah agreed. "It's such a lovely day and I think they should be out in the garden." She addressed the younger of the women on the chaise-lounge. "Margaret, my dear, would you like to go with them? I expect you would be glad of the fresh air too."

Readily agreeing Margaret ushered the group of delighted children from the room. Charlotte followed them eagerly. The gardens had the same layout but were amazingly well-cultivated, especially the Rose Garden where Margaret sat on the stone bench with the children scattered at her feet.

"Do you want to hear the story again, children?"

"Yes!" came the unified chorus of young voices.

Sitting with her hands folded on her lap and her face enlivened by the rapt audience Charlotte saw a kind, homely person who enjoyed her role as storyteller. "As you know," she began, "I'm quite an old lady," quiet chuckles rippled through the beaming faces, "but the story begins before I was born!"

The girl from the bedroom smiled, but the shrill voice of a young boy asked, "Was that a very, very long time ago, cousin Maggie?"

With a tinkling laugh which transformed the middle-aged female into an attractive woman , she replied modestly, "Yes, Tom. Many, many years ago! 1831 to be exact."

Tom gasped in wonder. "But it's 1895 now! You are really

old!"

Margaret nodded patiently. "Ancient. Do you want to hear the story or not?" A babble of voices made her clap her hands to bring order. "Very well. Your Uncle John, my father of course, was a Carpenter at a large Hall. It was much bigger than Glas Fryn and miles and miles away from here in England. One day he found a young girl wandering in the Shrubbery. She was quite lost, crying and very hungry, so he took her to his cottage where my mother gave her tea and amused her whilst Father went to the Hall to make enquiries. Mother said that her clothes were beautiful, a fine ivory silk dress with bows and ruffles everywhere and the most dainty slippers you ever did see! She spoke and acted like a little Lady and Mother was quite taken with her.'

'Papa soon returned with a maid and a posh gentleman. The maid scolded the girl and they took her away immediately. Mother thought them very rude people to leave without a word of explanation or a 'Thank You', but Papa said that's how the Gentry acted.'

'Anyway, that happened over 64 years ago, and as Tom said, a long, long time past. But my parents never forgot the child and told us the story as we grew up because that little girl was a delightful memory of their early years together."

The audience sat in rapt attention as they listened to the story, and Charlotte wondered if the modern child would enjoy the tale as much. Technology may have brought new and wonderful amusements, but the simple art of story-telling was entertainment enough in bygone days. The excitement on the face of little Tom was charming as he urged Margaret to continue. "Who was she? A captured Princess? I bet she was!"

"Not quite." Margaret replied winking. "On a Summer's day in 1871, that's 24 years ago, there was a knock on our cottage door. It was a small woman dressed in black and she carried a strange plant. She said it was a gift and the exotic present was called a Cactus which needed special care, and since my parents had been so kind to rescue her when she was

42

a little girl it seemed the best way to say 'Thank You' for the deed. It was just like a fairy-tale because the woman was a very special person. It was not a captured Princess, Tom, but none other that Her Majesty the Queen. A lost Princess!"

Gasps came from the children and the eldest girl spoke in raptures. "Was it really her? Queen Victoria? How did a busy lady like her remember where you lived?"

Margaret laughed. "Yes, Annie. Mother said that she was boasting about being a Princess whilst she was entertaining her, but since most young girls dream of such things she didn't take any notice! She was only twelve at the time, but had never returned to the House until 1871. By that time she had been crowned Queen, married, bore nine children and finally widowed. On a tour of the nation she had once more returned to the House and remembered my parents. She asked the servants where to find the cottage where she had spent such a wonderful afternoon without her guardians!"

Annie spoke excitedly, "We had a big party on the garden when I was 8 because she had been Queen for so long! All the village joined in the party."

"The Golden Jubilee Celebrations were enjoyed throughout the country, even by Queen Victoria herself. My Father is too old to work now so we have time to visit you at last. We even brought a slip of the Cactus for you so that the whole family may share in the Royal honour! Look after it, children, and it will flourish as you grow up into young men and ladies. You'll always have a tale to boast about however rich or poor you may become."

"Are you coming to live with us?" Tom asked with a frown.

"No, we have a lovely little house to rent just a few miles away from the big Hall. My sister and I are working as seamstresses so we can look after our parents and all afford to live happily ever after!"

Charlotte left the happy, chattering group and returned to the house. There in the hallway was an earthenware pot placed on a large mahogany sideboard. One single blade of cactus was proof enough of Margaret's story. Removing the thimble jammed on her finger, Charlotte gripped the sideboard until the spinning, black void passed. Opening her eyes she stared at the large, healthy plant before her.

Cissie appeared from the lounge carrying a tray. She stopped as she passed Charlotte and asked, "Are you alright, love? You look as though you've seen a ghost or something!"

By suppressing the urge to laugh hysterically, her voice sounded strained and distant as she asked fearfully, "Do you know where this plant came from, Cissie?"

"Oh ,that thing! Her Ladyship calls it 'Queen Victoria' because it was supposed to have come from the old Queen herself! I ask you!"

"Don't you think so?" Charlotte asked seriously.

Placing the tray on the sideboard, Cissie folded her arms and spoke quietly while she glanced towards the lounge. "She reckons it was a gift to her Uncle for doing the old Queen a service. As if she's give a monstrosity like that! It's not even pretty, except when it flowers, and they don't last long. Called a Christmas Cactus 'cos that's when it's supposed to flower."

"It would have been rare in those days." Charlotte said defensively.

"Oh, it's rare alright!" Cissie laughed as she picked up her tray. "The whole story is rare! The old Uncle was from England, God Knows where - so who's to know if it's true or false? Anyway, I reckon it's just the old girl trying to be clever. Even her plants got to have Royal connections!"

Cissie carried on with her journey to the kitchen area whilst chuckling at her own wit. Charlotte smiled and touched the long, smooth leaves of the plant knowing the story to be true. It really was a Royal Cactus, descended from the original gift, a gift which had flourished through care and respect as a treasured family heirloom.

Dinner that evening was livelier for the presence of Thomas Blake. He had a charming and relaxed manner and knew exactly how to handle his Great Aunt, but his patience was getting thin as Olivia eagerly complied with Charlotte's request to tell the story of the cactus. The tale remained unchanged since the day that Cousin Margaret came to visit and entertained the children by telling about the brush with Royalty.

Thomas jeered, "Oh, really, Aunt! You are a total snob! A plant from Queen Victoria? It was probably pinched from Kew Gardens - the nearest it ever got to Royalty!"

"Thomas!" the raised voice of an indignant Olivia shrilled, "If you find the story incredible then keep your doubts to yourself. I can always request you to find alternative accommodation!" Turning to her female guest she added, "I should mention that Thomas plans to stay here for a while. He aims to compile a thesis on financial tactics in the modern world."

"In other words," Charlotte translated, "another book on 'how to get rich quick'."

"Not quite, dear girl." Thomas drawled while he looked at the ceiling. "I won't bother to explain since it would be above you head."

"As modesty is above yours?" Charlotte asked innocently, then turned her attention to Olivia who was enjoying the discomfort of her great-nephew. "Now, Aunt, back to more earthly facts and figures. I've been wondering how old this house is. Have you got any idea?"

"What a grasshopper mind you have, child!" Despite her remark Olivia looked pleased to take the chair. "Glas Fryn was originally a farmhouse. They say it goes back about two hundred years, but several extensions have been added since then as the family grew more affluent."

"Which part would be original?"

Olivia shook her head. "I'm not certain, but no doubt you'll find something or other in the Library to help you."

"What about the Deeds?" Charlotte persisted, "You must have the Deed of Property?"

Thomas interceded so quickly that he startled both women. "They are under lock and key in a safety deposit box.

45

I thought they were far too valuable to leave around here, our dear Aunt doesn't realise that you can't be too careful in this day and age. Even in this backwater."

Charlotte frowned, but tried to sound nonchalant. "It must give her peace of mind to have someone like you to look after her affairs."

"Only some of them," Olivia said quietly, "I have an Estate Manager who is extremely capable."

"Oh!" Charlotte said in mock surprise, "does he happen to be a relative too?"

The old woman coughed with discomfiture. "Yes, but the connection is so distant that it's irrelevant. I employed him as a young man who has since gained a good reputation and first-class qualifications. He has worked hard over the years both in practical and managerial areas. The result is that I have given him total control over the Estate."

Thomas rose from the table with impatience. "Miss Stone, Olivia doesn't have to explain anything to you, so I suggest you let the matter drop and get on with the business you are paid to do."

"Thomas!" shouted Olivia in outrage. "Charlotte is not just my hired help any more than you! Don't forget your position as my financial advisor, not to mention your generous fee!"

Fists resting on the table so that he could lean closer to the elderly woman he said through clenched teeth, "But you don't need to explain anything to her! Your finances, your staff or anything else!"

"No, I don't have to," Olivia stated calmly, "but I WANT to."

Thomas left the room and showed his disgust by slamming the door behind him. Olivia smiled. "He resents you, Charlotte. He has to share the limelight now. He thinks he's my favourite, and to a certain extent he is, so he considers you as one of my more eccentric ideas to be tolerated to a limited extent. I think he's afraid of fortune-hunters."

"But you asked me to come here! I didn't turn up in the doorstep with a sad story or begging bowl!"

"Quite. I intend to emphasis that point with him."

"In that case I'm off to my room. The sooner you put him straight the better! Goodnight, Aunt. I've had enough cut and thrust for one night. Jealous relations are not my forte."

Laughter creasing the lined face, Olivia clapped her hands and exclaimed with delight, "I'm quite enjoying this! Glas Fryn will ring with voices yet again! Goodnight, my dear. Thomas will come round, have no fear."

"On the contrary, I don't care less how he feels! However, Aunt, I do care and worry about you. Does he stop here very often?"

"Once every blue moon. He's very charming." The elderly woman frowned the rephrased her statement. "Normally very charming. Perhaps he's been under a lot of pressure lately, these financial people work under a lot of stress I understand."

Shrugging her shoulders, the younger woman pulled a face. "I doubt your theory, but if that really is the case a few days in this 'backwater' will soon solve that!" Holding up a hand to prevent protest, Charlotte continued, "his words, Aunt Olivia, not mine. Goodnight."

Charlotte lay on her high double-bed and considered the situation. Thomas Blake certainly resented her beneath his glossy facade, whilst Olivia was enjoying the undercurrents with a youthful vivacity.

Besides the emotional aspects there were other facts which emerged such as Glas Fryn itself. Whilst trying to establish the age of the building Thomas was quick to say that the Deeds were locked away. Was it merely because he was concerned with the security aspect of having important documents lying around? Or was it some sort of insurance against the eventual demise of his Great Aunt? Possession was nine points of the law, isn't that how the saying went?

Remembering her journey that afternoon to a Glas Fryn of another age, she thought of the children who listened to Margaret with rapt attention. The girl from the bedroom was called Annie, could one of the other little girls be Olivia? Was the old Dragon ever a child, she mused! No. Margaret had said the year was 1895 which made Olivia at least 100 years old now.

In the early hours of the morning, Charlotte woke with a heart-thudding start. What was that noise? A creaking floorboard? Lying still, she strained her ears for any sound which broke the still night air. Minutes ticked by in silence and she sobered herself with the thought that old houses always creaked and moaned like an aging person with drying joints. However, this was the first night she had spent under this roof with Thomas as guest. Giving up the idea of sleep she reached for the lamp on the bedside cabinet.

Lying in the comforting glow of lamplight, she reasoned with herself out loud. 'Now then, Lottie!' she giggled at the use of her school nickname. 'Do you really think that Thomas would consider rape or murder with Olivia just down the corridor! It sounds more like wishful thinking 'old girl' as he would say!' Laughing at herself, she reached for a book in order to induce sleep through reading, but her mind refused to register the words so she tossed it aside in frustration.

Getting out of bed with single purpose she sat on the dressing-table stool, hesitated for a second, then slipped the silver thimble onto her finger.

The bedroom was dimly lit by an oil-lamp burning low on the bedside table. A woman sat on the bed gently wiping the brow of a person who laboured to breathe. Charlotte recognised the patient as Ivor, the man with the crutches. He was trying to talk to his nurse, but each word was a painful task.

"Sarah......... stay.......don't.......... "

"I'll be here, my dear. Try to rest." As she continued to bathe his face with a damp cloth the soothing action helped him fall into a fitful doze.

Minutes passed before the door opened and the girl, Annie, tip-toed in wearing a long, white nightgown. She looked taller and older, but still an innocent child. "Mam? Do you need anything? Shall I make you a cup of tea?"

"No, my child. It's time you were asleep."

Shaking her long, fair hair she whispered, "All the others are sleeping, but I just............ " She looked at the sleeping form then to her Mother. "Dad is really bad this time, isn't he."

Sarah rose and placed her arms around Annie, then tenderly kissed the young forehead. "Yes, Charlotte Anne. For his sake go to bed and pray, then God will bless you both with a dreamless sleep. You have to be up early for milking."

"Will you call me if ...... if you need anything?"

"Yes, dear. I promise."

The young girl tip-toed to the bed and carefully kissed her father's cheek, "I've nearly finished the quilt, Dad. It will be lovely and warm for you, keep out the winter chill. Then you won't be ill again. Goodnight and God Bless." With tears glistening on her cheeks the girl kissed her Mother then left the room.

Sarah returned to her vigil by her husband's side. She whispered continuously as she cradled the lifeless hand. 'God, let him live!' whilst silent sobs racked her body causing her shoulders to heave in order to control the sound of her grief.

Charlotte snatched the thimble from her finger. She was an intruder in every sense of the word. An intruder in time, love, emotion and maybe death. One mystery had been solved. Sarah had used her eldest child's full name as a token of tenderness and love. Charlotte Anne. The thimble must have belonged to the young girl who shouldered such a heavy burden. Charlotte of the present felt honoured to witness the moving scene which took place in this very bedroom.

She looked at the quilt on the bed. Was it the one that Annie had lovingly stitched to prevent her father's illness? Was that why it felt so comforting and familiar?

She would have to return. The consequences of breaking through physical barriers didn't occur to Charlotte Stone. She was enchanted and bound to the family of the past. It was her special privilege. Her visits would continue. There was no turning back.

CHAPTER 3

Times Past

Charlotte always skipped breakfast much to her Aunt's annoyance, but was particularly thankful that she didn't have to face the other two residents on this specific morning. Going straight to the Library she welcomed the isolation of the shabby, neglected room. Time passed quickly as she examined the shelves for books on local history and so engrossed had she become in the dusty tomes that she was startled when the door was suddenly flung open.

"Here she is, Cissie! I told you she'd be hiding somewhere in this mausoleum." Thomas was grinning from ear to ear, aware that he was intruding.

Cissie followed bearing a tray. "There you are, Miss. Time for coffee and Thomas is here to make sure you take a break!"

"Oh," Charlotte mumbled despondently, "very nice, I'm sure. Thank you, Cissie."

The maid disappeared with the impression that she had done a good turn whilst Thomas gestured towards one of the leather armchairs. "Sit down, dear girl. Even bookworms need refreshment!"

Charlotte smiled sweetly. "You want to sit with me? An interloper? The hired help who asks too many questions? Maybe you are a hypocrite as well as a pompous ass."

Nonplussed, Thomas continued to grin. "Olivia has put me right on that score. I misunderstood the reason for your presence." Pouring coffee from the large, stainless steel pot he continued to grin. "Sugar and milk?"

Shrugging her shoulders resignedly and flopping into the vacant chair she accepted the cup which was thrust in her direction. "I get the feeling that I've just had the nearest thing to an apology that you could manage."

Thomas leaned back in the chair, his manner casual. "I'm

sure we'll get used to each others ways."

"There's always hope!" Charlotte retorted dismally. She became fascinated by the smarmy grin which was still worn on the fair-complexioned face. Even when he spoke it remained fixed. Perhaps he's had a mishap with 'super-glue' she mused. Her smothered smile only gave encouragement to the victim of her imagination.

"Isn't this cosy?" Looking around him as he spoke he added, "not the room, the company. Can I see a glimmer of a smile on that pale face? Yes? How long have you been here? Just over a week? You must find life pretty dull after the city. Where was it? Bath? You should be out enjoying yourself, the high life!"

Charlotte yawned. "I've tried it. I much prefer the quiet life."

"Shame, shame! Still, if you ever feel like painting the town red then I'm your man. Know all the high spots within the County!"

Sighing, the young woman could stand no more. "Lay off, Thomas. Your attempt at chatting me up is becoming boring."

Not a flicker of emotion showed on the man's face. "Very well, if you want to become a recluse then this is the place to do it. As to the cause which brought you here in the first place? Well I don't think you've made much progress so it could be a long stay. In which case, my offer may become more attractive." His voice sounded reasonable and sincere. "How are you making out with Olivia's brainwave, by the way?"

Charlotte replied gloomily, "Not very well. Information seems limited. You may be useful in that direction, you must know all about Olivia's family. After all, you are a branch of it."

"A branch from a tree which died out years ago. As for the rest of the clan, well..... you know how it is. Over the years I've been hearing the same stories over and over, but I can't say I ever listened properly. The old girl can ramble on a bit at times."

"I doubt that Olivia ever rambles! Incidentally, do you know her age?"

"Now you've stumbled on the best kept family secret! Unlock that mystery and you've cracked it."

Charlotte noted that the false smile never reached Thomas's eyes and felt repulsed by the dormant aggression which lay beneath the veneered surface. "On the subject of projects, how is your thesis going? I've not seen you put pen to paper yet, you just seem to amble around. That is the reason for your visit, isn't it? Seclusion to write a best-seller directed towards a deluded middle-class readership who are always waiting for the winning scoop?"

"Just taking a few days to relax, dear girl. Finance is a complicated subject and it takes a clear mind to consider all the intricacies of dealing."

Charlotte laughed. "It shouldn't take long to empty your mind, dear boy!"

Thomas stood up and shook his head. "What makes you so bitter, lady? Crossed in love? Feminist? Maybe you just hate men. Favour your own sex, maybe?"

Refusing to rise to such outrageous implications, Charlotte returned to the bookshelves. "You're disgusting, Thomas Blake. Just because I haven't fallen at your feet - or into your bed! Kindly shut the door on your way out."

The sound of the heavy door slamming was the sweetest sound Charlotte had heard for many a long day. She had seen off quite a few abusive men during her years at work, but none of them were as contemptible as Thomas Blake.

Lunch was an informal meal taken with Olivia. Charlotte noticed that the old lady seemed to be in a strange mood with little to say other than the usual polite exchanges. "Is anything wrong, Aunt?" the young woman ventured to ask during the dessert.

"Wrong? Why should there be?" Olivia barked.

"You don't seem yourself. You know, overbearing, inquisitive and always nagging about table manners!"

The old lady smiled. "Count yourself lucky that I've got

other matters to occupy me, Charlotte, otherwise I would be offended by your criticism."

"I'm merely concerned," Charlotte said softly, "I'm not used to you being so quiet. Is it Thomas?"

Coughing discreetly behind a napkin, Olivia nodded. "Indirectly, I suppose so. Nothing to give you cause for concern, and not particularly important. I'll thank you to respect my privacy in financial matters, child."

Charlotte was prevented from replying since she was choking on her food. Olivia rose from the table then picked up her walking-stick and ignored the spluttering guest. "I beg to be excused, child. I've ordered a taxi and want to make sure I'm ready when it arrives. They even charge 'waiting-time' these days, can you credit it? The world has become greedy, very greedy."

"Bring back the horse and trap, it would only cost you a handful of hay!" the young woman chortled.

"I'll thank you not to be so patronising, Charlotte!" There was a haughty set to her shoulders as Olivia left the room. Her great-niece smiled and wondered the nature of the financial obstacle which so preoccupied her. Thomas was the instigator, of that there was no doubt.

After her meal, Charlotte went to her room with the explicit intention of entering he portals of times past. Glas Fryn had proved to be a lonely place with only Cissie to talk to. Mary Price and her father remained aloof, distant, whereas Olivia was always on her guard and finding fault. Her only 'friends' were in the past.

It never entered her head that the supernatural experiences may affect her being. The fact was that she was fascinated, becoming obsessed with her inexplicable ability to delve into the lives of the past, convincing herself it was necessary in order to gather information for Olivia's project. Without realising it, the adventure was becoming an addiction.

With the thimble on her finger she waited for the dark void to pass. The tunnel of time was becoming an easier path to travel. Awareness returned and she was in the bedroom of olden days. There was no-one present but sounds invaded the room, sounds of people shouting which drifted up the stairs. Charlotte ran out to the landing.

Sarah was standing in the open doorway of the hall whilst a shabbily dressed young boy ran towards her gasping. "We found her, Missus!" A young freckled face blurted in triumph. "In the woods! Out for the count - and soaked through she is. Must have been there all the time!"

Sarah clutched the boy anxiously. "All night! Has she been there all night! Glory be! My poor child." Regaining her composure, she stooped and held the boy's shoulders gently. "Thank you, Joseph. You did well. Go to the kitchen and have some food while I wait here."

Looking behind him he pointed down the driveway. "Here they are, Missus! I wonder what happened to her? "

Sarah stood to full height to receive the party. "I expect she fell or something, now go on lad! Get something hot inside you before the rest beat you to it!"

The boy scurried off with the promise of a meal whilst Sarah ran up the stairs two at a time. Charlotte followed her to the Main Bedroom which was to be Olivia's in the future. "Ivor! Ivor! They've found her, my dear! In the woods, unconscious but in one piece."

"Thanks be to God," Ivor uttered. Pain etched on his lined face as he sank back against the pillows of the bed. "I can rest now. Take care of her, lass. Make sure she doesn't catch a chill, the nights can be cold."

Giving her husband a quick peck on the cheek she reassured him. "Sleep, my love. I'll see to our Annie, don't you fear. She's a tough one and I bet she's none the worse for wear."

As Sarah flew back down to the Hall a band of roughly dressed workmen were just carrying the makeshift stretcher in through the front door. A few followers with hands free doffed their caps with both respect and sympathy whilst one stepped forward.

"Down in Church Woods she was, Ma'am." The

spokesman was a tall, gaunt individual with a dropping moustache. "Must have tumbled or something we reckon. Anyhow, she seems to be alright apart from a few cuts and bruises. Shall we go over to get Doctor Sam?"

Sarah went to the side of her daughter and felt her brow. As flesh touched flesh, Annie's eyes sprung open and she smiled on seeing her Mother's face. "Mam! Oh, Mam! Am I home?"

"Yes, my child. You're safe now." Turning to the bearers she asked them to carry the patient up to the bedroom. They did so and an entourage followed the procession with sombre reverence.

Once Annie was laid on the bed they removed the precious stretcher which was a rough blanket much needed by the owner. Sarah stood in front of the gathering and spoke sincerely. "I thank you all from the bottom of my heart, hopefully the Doctor won't be needed. I know most of you have searched all night, others of you have come straight from night shift, but only one thing I can offer you and that's a meal. If you go down to the kitchen it will be ready for you."

The spokesman found his way to the front and nodded. "It's more than we expected, Ma'am. You have come to most of us at any time of day and night when we have asked," a murmur of assent went through the crowd, "so there's no need to thank us. We'll not eat you out of house and home, neither, just a mug of tea will do." Looking at the inert form on the bed he added, "You get well soon, little lady! Your Mam can't run the farm without you!"

As the men left, Charlotte looked at Annie and realised she was no longer a girl. How many years had passed? First she had been a child, then an adolescent, now a young woman. She was watching Charlotte Anne grow up!

Sarah stripped, washed and changed her daughter who lay deathly pale and silent until the ablutions were over. "Mam?" she asked in a clear voice, "I feel strange. Why is that?"

"Charlotte Anne, I want you to try and explain how you

feel," Sarah frowned then asked , "Are you in pain? I can only see superficial marks such as scratches on your face and hands, a few bruises elsewhere. You must tell me where you hurt."

"I just feel sore everywhere and .... and as if I'm floating. Does that make sense, Mam?"

Sarah shook her head. "Concussion, I expect. Did you fall?"

Lines creased the young brow as she tried to recall the previous afternoon. "Church Farm. I was going to Church Farm to collect the eggs."

"That's right, Annie. Your usual Friday errand."

Starting to cry, Annie became distressed and laboured with her breathing. "Oh, Mam! I can't....... can't remember anything! Did I get to the farm? Why was ...... was I in the woods? There was...... there was someone......... a queer smell. I'm hurting. Oh, Mam! I'm frightened!"

As Sarah comforted her daughter she wore a sad expression. She had seen the marks on her child's body, the scratches and bruises indicated that she had been violated. She waited until the distraught young woman lay drowsily on her pillow and went downstairs.

Charlotte followed her to the kitchen where a fresh-faced young man in his thirties with a shock of blonde hair was eating at the table. His clothes were creased and spattered with mud, but they were of a finer quality than the workmen's rough garb.

"Tom! Oh, thank goodness it's you!" Sarah cried gratefully.

"Someone had to see to the animals, big sister! None of your other children would do Annie's work. Young ladies and gentlemen, or so they think! Good thing they are with Mama for the day with the types that's been trooping through here. The servants have been run off their feet. I gave them a few hours off since our girl has been found." Looking for the first time at the stricken face before him, he apologised. "Sorry, sis. How is she? They said there were no bones broken, no

56

need for the Doctor."

Staring into the distance, Sarah stood ramrod straight and spoke quietly. "She's my first child. I have five other children but I've always loved her more than the rest. Sinful, but true."

To Charlotte's shock, the capable woman began to cry copiously.

Her startled brother rushed to her side and settled her in a chair by the range. "Come on, Sarah. The men who found her said she was alright, just wet and cold. You've spent a long night worrying and running between the searchers and Ivor, this is a natural reaction. You're exhausted, lass. Get it out your system, have a damned good cry."

"Oh, Tom, Tom!" Sarah sobbed, "You're wrong! I'm crying for Annie, my dear sweet Annie. I fear the worse. She's been raped, Tom! I'm sure of it." The tide of misery flowed from the depths of her soul whilst her brother held her in his arms and stroked the greying hair.

"Pull yourself together, Sarah. Did Annie tell you exactly what happened? She's eighteen and knows what life's about. Maybe she let a lad take advantage of her then got frightened. Too frightened to come home."

"No! No!" Sarah wailed vehemently. "She doesn't know Tom! I have seen the bruises and scratches, they're all over her legs, hips and breasts." Screwing her eyes shut against the unthinkable she continued, "She said that there was a queer smell and remembers nothing after that. I suspect the use of ether to knock her out first, the feeling she describes matches the after-effects. I know exactly what I'm talking about, Tom, especially due to my calling. My poor girl doesn't even know she's been attacked!"

Tom's face was grave as he knelt by his sister's side. "I've never known you to be wrong, Sarah. Did she see anyone at all?"

"No, at least not now. It may come back to her later."

"What if she's............................ " Tom's voice trailed off as he thought of the possible consequences. His fair head shook with anger. "Leave it to me. I'll get to the bottom of this. A stranger would be noticed in a place like this so I'll ask around" He held Sarah's tear-stained face in his large, roughened hands and asked, "We must be certain about this. The marks. Is there any chance she'd have got them through falling or something? I know you're a midwife but what makes you so sure?"

Sarah stopped weeping and looked her brother squarely in the face. "Her private parts are bloodied and black and blue, and the bruises are not just normal marks but in the form of finger-marks. I've seen it all before. Young girls have come to me in that condition. The Gentry are none to gentle when they take a servant girl! No, Tom. Our dear Annie has been raped, she's a ruined woman." She took a deep breath before adding in a trembling voice, "If Annie is with child it will kill Ivor. He worships her."

Kissing Sarah's cheek with great tenderness, Tom vowed, "We all love her and we'll all stand by her, that's after I've caught the evil bastard who defiled her!"

"Language, Tom, language!" Sarah admonished feebly. "Perhaps we ought to call Sgt. Hopkins."

"What! And have everyone in the area gossiping about our Annie! She'll have enough without that. No, Sarah. We will see that justice is done without a county scandal. Now, pull yourself together before the rest of your brood returns!"

Charlotte left the kitchen to return upstairs and noticed a newspaper on the sideboard in the hall. It was the South Wales Daily News dated 12th March,1903. Back in the bedroom Annie lay sleeping peacefully.

Charlotte removed the thimble and returned to the present. It was hard to believe such a thing could happen all those years ago, but Evil had existed since the Garden of Eden and continued to manifest itself through the ages. Charlotte Anne was the innocent victim of a man's lust, a victim who may have to pay dearly if the seeds of that evil bore fruit.

One thing was certain, Charlotte mused, the young woman's Uncle Tom would do his utmost to avenge the crime. A defender of his kith and kin and ready to find the violator and make him pay for the despicable act without the protection of judicial law.

Dinner that evening was far more pleasant due to the absence of Thomas. Since the old woman looked less agitated than she had during the morning, Charlotte asked, "How did your meeting go this morning?"

"Very well, thank you!" came the curt reply.

"So, no problems then?"

"No."

Charlotte was thankful that Thomas was not present, a comfort she welcomed, but it also gave her an opportunity to broach the subject of Charlotte Anne with her Aunt. Olivia became stone-faced when questioned but reluctantly parted with some information. "Well, if you MUST know she was my sister. Many years older than I, you understand. How did you learn about her?"

Floundering at the unexpected question, Charlotte tried to think of a plausible answer. "Oh! I can't quite remember. Perhaps Thomas mentioned something."

"Hardly. He doesn't listen when you tell him anything and I haven't reached the stage when I recall the past with tedious regularity."

The young woman recalled Thomas's remark about his Great Aunt rambling. "I'd be the first to agree that you have an extremely sharp mind for a person of your .... er,..... advancing years? Bearing that in mind I can't understand why you didn't tell me who C.A.A. was when I asked you the first time, or even the second time! You didn't even admit to her existence, your own sister for God's sake!"

Olivia closed her eyes and shook her head. "It's none of your business, Charlotte."

"Then why the bloody hell am I here? You want me to write a historical record based on your family and yet you hold back on your own sister! Did she commit some dark and shameful act? Was she disowned by the family, or by you in particular? I need to know for background."

"She's irrelevant. Kindly curb your language, Charlotte. You sound quite common."

"Take me as you find me. You still haven't answered my questions."

Olivia placed her hands on the table in exasperation. "If only I'd been able to mould you as a child then you'd be a lot more respectful towards your elders."

Taking a deep breath, Charlotte refused to be fobbed off. "Then I respectfully ask you about your sister, namely Charlotte Anne. As author of the history of Glas Fryn I will decide which material to use, just give me a brief description."

Gazing at her wrinkled, lily-white hands, the old woman finally nodded and conceded. "Very well. There's little to tell. She was the eldest and married before I was born. She was known as Annie. Due to the age gap a gulf was created between us so we were not close. I always think of her as the plump, homely type who doted on her brood of children. She lived in poverty and was quite unremarkable. I think that answers your question sufficiently."

Unable to defend the person whom Olivia dismissed so tersely, Charlotte knew she needed more concrete facts before she could interrogate her Aunt further. "How come she had silk underwear, then?"

"We still dispute the existence of such items as I recall."

"We agreed to differ in order to keep the peace, that's all. Can you explain them?"

Olivia nodded. "As the first grandchild Annie was treated favourably by her Grandparents as she grew up. That's my Father's parents, the Armstrongs. They were not rich by modern standards, but this house was their property and that should confirm their status."

"What about your parents? Did they inherit the wealth? Sarah and Ivor, wasn't it?"

"They inherited the house and land, but it needed to be worked to provide income. People didn't discuss money in those days, especially with their children!"

"They did if there wasn't any!" Charlotte retorted sharply. "Or if you were the eldest and had to slave whilst your brothers and sisters were educated!"

"Socialist talk!" Olivia snorted. "Enough of that. I am still waiting to hear an answer to my question. How did you learn of Annie, or my parents. You even know their names."

By now Charlotte had worked out an answer and responded cheerfully, "Oh, just talking to the old villagers and bits and pieces I found in the Library and my brilliant deductive mind, of course! Yes, Aunt. That Library is a Wonderland to me, full of surprises."

"Dusty and drear. I never liked the place. I wonder you found anything in the muddle."

"It'll take time to sort out, I agree. Tell me, who made the patchwork quilt on my bed? It's a work of art, so well made."

"I find your line of thought most annoying, Charlotte! It flits from one thing to another without rhyme nor reason. As for the quilt I haven't a clue what is on your bed and find such details of no consequence. As long as Cissie and Mary keep the house running smoothly I have far more important things to occupy my mind."

"It must be nice to a 'Lady'." Charlotte remarked sarcastically.

"It's a shame you're not more like Thomas. Very thoughtful boy. Are you two getting on any better?"

"Oh, yes. I think we understand one another now." Hoping her lie would go undetected, Charlotte asked, "Where is he tonight?"

Olivia laughed indulgently. "When he stays here he often goes out for the evening and stays with friends, especially when he imbibes. A very sensible young man."

"He's got friends?" Charlotte asked innocently. "He's lucky they let him slide under their table and sleep it off!"

Olivia was far from amused and bade her great-niece a rather frosty goodnight. Thomas's nocturnal habits were of no concern to the younger woman, they were a blessing in disguise. Instead her thoughts dwelt on Annie. She would return tonight, she had to know the outcome of the tragic assault.

Late that night Charlotte heard the definite sounds of creaking floorboards. If someone was prowling around the house they were not being very subtle, she giggled. Maybe Thomas was having a nocturnal rendezvous with one of the staff. Cissie seemed out of the question, so the only other resident female was Price's daughter. So the distant Mary had some passion behind that cool look, she thought ungraciously. Reprimanding herself for making such assumptions, Charlotte reminded herself of her personal record with men which was hardly anything to boast about.

Jamming a chair under the knob of her bedroom door Charlotte returned to the past with avid curiosity and unquestionable faith that it was physically possible. Once the void passed she opened her eyes to a scene which shocked her, it was the scene of a birth.

The young woman labouring in the bed was Annie, whilst her Mother, Sarah, bustled about the room with organised efficiency. Mesmerised, Charlotte suffered with each pain that Annie fought against with quiet dignity until the birth was imminent. Encouraged by Sarah, the new life was delivered into the world safely followed by the shrill cry of the child which pierced the air to announce it's arrival. Exhausted and bedraggled, Annie moaned with relief that the ordeal was over.

"What is it, Mam?" she gasped impatiently.

Busying herself with the newborn infant, Sarah answered quietly, "You have a healthy Daughter, Annie! Here. See for yourself ." Placing the swathed baby into the mother's arms, she announced delightedly, "Be careful, she's my first grandchild!"

Smiling in awe at the product of her pain, Annie nodded. "She's so beautiful! A Gift from God."

"For her sake, it's as well you think like that, child."

Annie's face was beaming with happiness. "How could I blame a little thing like this, Mam! She's part of me and I love

62

her. I'll call her Daisy. A delicate flower which grows freely and brings pleasure to the eye of the beholder."

Tears ran down Sarah's face as she nodded in agreement. "She'll bring more joy to this household than sorrow. Cherish her, Charlotte Anne. She may have been conceived though an abominable act, but delivered into our hands with the blessing of love."

Annie frowned. "She'll never know her father, especially after Uncle Tom found out and told his family. Where do you think they sent him, Mama? Does he know I was left with child?"

"So many questions! Knowing the family he was sent to some foreign land where his behaviour will be beyond their concern. As for the child, I'm not certain if he knew or not, but I doubt it."

"Uncle Tom told me he would never return."

Sarah nodded. "If he does he won't look very handsome! Your Uncle taught him a lesson he would never forget - and the boy's Father approved let me tell you!"

"I know we should forgive, Mam," Annie smiled, "but I'm so glad Uncle Tom caught him."

Her Mother nodded approval. "I promise you, child, he made sure that young man would never sire again. Tom said when human behaviour dropped to such immoral standards then it was unfair to castrate animals for less. Fair judgement, daughter?"

"Uncle Tom........did he really .... ?" Annie looked at the baby then nodded. "He was evil, but justice has been done because this child is not injured or deformed. She is a gift, an atonement for my grief. Good always prevails, and Daisy will prove that."

Returning to the present, Charlotte climbed back into her bed and felt a deep contentment. Annie's cruel rape had not left her bitter and rejected. Sarah, her Mother, was a tower of strength not given to soft words or loving touch, yet in her brusque way was totally devoted and understanding to her family.

63

Nearly two weeks she had been at Glas Fryn and during that short period she had seen Annie as a young child in her Grandmother's bedroom, a growing girl in the garden listening to her cousin's tale of Queen Victoria, as a teenager in the bedroom whilst her Father lay desperately ill, as a young woman who had been defiled and finally, at the birth of her first child.

Charlotte asked herself, 'Am I to see the life span of this Charlotte Anne known as Annie? Who was she? Olivia's sister, yes, but there must be another reason why I'm drawn to her. There must be a reason.' With that question repeating itself in her mind, Charlotte Stone finally drifted off to sleep.

Rising at six the following morning, Charlotte left the house for an early morning walk around the gardens. It was May and the temperature was starting to rise towards its summer crescendo, the air was fresh and scented with dew-laden blossoms. In the sheltered vale nature was protected to a degree that encouraged cultivated plants to bloom early whilst wild flowers grew in joyous abandon. The mingled scents were a heady brew to the city girl.

After walking and exploring all the paths and neglected segments of the grounds, Charlotte still couldn't clear her head of last night's vision and the consequence of Annie's misfortune. What kind of life lay in store for an unmarried mother in the early twentieth century?

Going back to the house she saw the kitchen door open and slipped in hoping to make herself a cup of coffee before the household stirred, but to her amazement Cissie and Mary Price were bustling around like demons. "Oh!" she exclaimed sharply, "I didn't think anyone would be up yet!"

Mary Price turned her long, lean body around with her arms akimbo. "You have no idea how much work is involved in a house this size! We have to be up at six and work like mad to be ready for Mrs. Jones when she comes down to breakfast at 8.30 precisely. Not for us the luxury of getting up when we please."

Charlotte resented her tone. "That's your problem. If it's

that bad why don't you pack it in?"

Mary was unrepentant. "Have you ever heard of 'loyalty', Miss Stone?"

Taking a seat by the large kitchen table, the guest laughed contemptuously. "Loyalty is one thing, slavery is another! Still, I don't suppose there is much scope in a place like this, better than no work at all."

"Generations of my family have lived and worked here and not because there was nowhere else to go. I'll thank you to leave my kitchen, Miss Stone. Even Madam doesn't come in here. It's my domain."

Cissie intervened by placing herself between the two young women and wagging a finger at each in turn. "I know it's early, but there's no need to go on at each other like this. Mary! I've never known you to lose your temper before. You, Miss Charlotte, did you get out of the wrong side of the bed this morning, or what? Now, sit down the pair of you and we'll have a cup of tea. No more arguing or I'll bang your heads together!"

"But Cissie!" Mary gasped, "We've so much to do. You know what happens when breakfast is late. She plays war all day."

"Blow her!" Cissie shouted as she made the tea. "Sit down, girl. Do as you're told for once."

Like a lamb, Mary Price did as she was bid. "Dad will go spare. She'll take it out on him too."

"No she won't," Charlotte announced positively. "It seems obvious to me that this house is run through a reign of terror. I'll have breakfast with the old girl and tell her that I ordered it for nine, then give her a few sharp words on the way she treats you all. Happy?"

"Good enough for me!" Cissie answered. "Here we are, a nice hot cup of tea. Come on, Mary. Drink up. You look like a hypnotised rabbit."

"This will never do!" Mary remarked scornfully. "Do you realise how much you've upset our routine, Miss Stone?"

"High time someone did." Charlotte retorted. "Relax! If

you're that bothered I'll give you a hand once I've had my tea."

Mary's hand flew to her throat. "Oh, no! That would never do. Of all the things! One of the Family working in the kitchen! Oh, no!"

"Stop being such a wet blanket!" Cissie said amongst her giggles. "Charlotte is alright, didn't I tell you?"

Taking the situation in hand, Charlotte spoke plainly. "Listen, Miss Price. I'm nothing more than a very distant relative of Her Nibs upstairs. All my life I've struggled for money and I've had to do everything for myself. I've never been waited on before or had lily-white hands like this!" Holding her hands up to prove the issue, she continued, "So there will be no more arguments. I'm quite ordinary and even employed by Olivia Jones just like you and would be quite insulted if you treated me as anything else. Clear?"

A smile played on Mary's face. "Cissie said that you wouldn't let her unpack for you. I thought it was an act, but she's right. You are different. We're not used to people like you."

"What do you mean, 'people like me'?"

Mary hesitated, then spoke slowly and deliberately. "Well, I suppose 'forward' is the best word to describe it. We expected you to have .... well.......... well, like the Mistress I suppose."

"Have breeding, you mean!" laughed Charlotte. "She's so far distant that the blood has run pretty thin by the time it got to me. I'm a liberated woman, Mary Price, I refuse to be the mirror image of the Dragon Lady!"

Cissie laughed heartily. "Didn't I tell you, Mary! Didn't I say that you would like her!"

"Yes." Mary admitted. "Come on then, let's get back to work. We'll not be laughing if we loiter much longer."

With an extra pair of hands breakfast was ready at it's usual time. Charlotte was already seated before Olivia appeared dressed to kill. She looked very smart in a pale grey suit and flattering pink blouse.

"Civic duties to perform, I'm afraid. I'll be away for most of the day but hope to be home in time for Dinner. Where's Thomas? Have you seen him this morning? Oh! Silly question. No doubt you have just fallen out of bed."

"That's where you are wrong, Aunt. I've been up for hours. I walked around the grounds and then helped out in the kitchen."

Olivia froze in the act of buttering toast. "What did you say? In the kitchen?"

"Yes. In the kitchen. Before you start blasting me with the rights and wrongs I did it to help your overworked staff. Mary Price protested most vehemently, but I insisted. You know how stubborn I can be."

"Indeed!" Olivia confirmed. "I trust it won't happen again."

"Oh, but it will!" Charlotte drove her point home. "If you say one word to the staff or make them suffer in any way then I'm going. My God! They're frightened to death of you and I can't sit by and watch them worry about the mood you're in. So, in future I expect you to be more tolerant and consider them as well as yourself."

Shaking her head in dismay, the old woman rubbed her hands together then dabbed her mouth with a napkin. "You are an odd creature. I want you to stay so I'll ignore the episode. Please respect my wishes and refrain from partaking of menial tasks. I'd better be going. Where is Thomas? He promised me a lift!"

Charlotte felt incensed. "Did you hear a word I said? Will you listen for once in your life?"

"How tiresome!" Olivia muttered, "Very well, child. I will try to be more tolerant. If I fail then I'm sure you'll tell me! Where is Thomas?"

Placated by the vague promise, Charlotte answered happily, "I don't think he came home last night. Where DOES he go?"

"None of our business, my girl. His friends are not our concern," Olivia replied as she rang the bell on the table. Price appeared and she issued orders. "Call a taxi. I want one outside the door in ten minutes. Accept no excuses, Price. Remind then that I am involved with the Council who control their licenses."

As Olivia swept from the room, Charlotte looked at the manservant's face. It remained impassive. "Does she always act like that?"

"Only when necessary, Miss."

"But to threaten a taxi firm? That didn't seem necessary."

Price smiled. "It is when they have let her down in the past. Once is excusable, twice is unforgivable, three times is fatal!" He was chuckling to himself as he left the room to telephone.

The morning dragged and the house seemed to echo with emptiness. The Library seemed like a prison, it had started raining which meant the garden was out of the question and Pantmawr seemed a long, wet walk away. Charlotte questioned the fact that she was actually missing her impossible elderly relation. Even though she deplored her tactics and Victorian attitude she couldn't help but admire the old girl. A character of substance who fascinated her.

She went to her room with a purpose. She would delve into her 'other' world, see Annie and the baby, watch the family whom she considered as friends, join in their lives in silent companionship. The silver thimble soon whirled her through the time barrier to the bedroom of old, but it was empty. Venturing to the top of the stairs she saw a maid enter the lounge, so scuttled after her laughing softly.

The room looked drab when compared with Olivia's modern decor, but despite the flock wallpaper and dark, cumbersome furniture it looked comfortable with a chaise-lounge and brocade covered armchairs and a large Aspidistra placed in the window. There were three people present. Annie and her parents, Sarah and Ivor.

Ivor, his crutches resting against his chair, was speaking. "So! This lad wants to marry you, my little maid! Didn't he have the nerve to ask me himself? That's the proper thing do."

Standing before him, Annie looked at her father directly.

"I'm not a normal woman, Dad. I have a two year old daughter and considered a fallen woman by most."

Sarah jumped up from her chair and stood besides her husband. "No, child. Everyone knows what happened. It wasn't your fault and I've never heard anyone direct blame towards you."

Annie nodded. "People have been kind, but despite that I'm 20 years of age, unmarried and a mother. Please, Mam! Dad! Face up to it, I'm no catch. Now I've met someone who loves me and accepts me for what I am. Your approval means so much to me."

"Do you love him or are you just taking a husband?" her mother asked sharply, "And what about Daisy? Have you thought about her?"

"I have always put my daughter first, you both know that! I'm no youngster given to flights of fancy. We love one another and when we are married Daisy will have proper parents and grow up like other children."

Ivor nodded, looked at his wife and caught her hand. "What say you, Sarah, my love? We know Annie well enough to trust her decision. What do you think?"

Annie knew her battle was won by the glances her parents exchanged. "Would you like to meet him? You'll have no doubts once you've seen him."

Her father nodded, a twinkle in his eyes as he spoke. "Aye, if he dare face me!"

Annie pulled the bell-rope besides the large, cast-iron grate which held a veritable furnace of a fire. Returning to face her parents, she explained, "I told him to wait in the kitchen." There was a short rap on the door to announce his arrival. "His name is James."

Ivor bid him enter and tried not to smile at the young man's appearance. The fresh complexion shone with cleanliness whilst his ill-fitting black suit shone for different reasons. His white shirt was immaculate, but the black tie vied with the suit for wear and tear. A mop of fair hair had been carefully greased and parted into tameness whilst a moustache let nature take its course. Charlotte saw the merry, sparkling blue eyes and knew he was the right man for Annie.

Pointing to a chair, Ivor waited until the young man was seated then asked innocently, "Are you on your way to a funeral, boy?"

Stunned, the suitor shook his head and answered politely, "No, sir Why should you think that, Mr. Armstrong?"

"You looked dressed for one!" Ivor chortled .

Gripping a cap in his strong hands, the young man replied firmly, "It's the only suit I have, sir. I'm not a rich man, but can live comfortably enough. I came to ask you if you'd let me wed your daughter and I didn't see the need of a new suit for that."

Sarah stiffened with shock at the reply. "Did you not! Have you an income? Could you support a wife and child?"

"I am a coal miner, Ma'am. I can keep them on my wages."

"A coal-miner! Oh, I see." Sarah looked shocked. "I hear that their wages are poor. Where would you live?"

James smiled. "I rent a cottage a mile or so away. It's got two rooms up and down. Plenty of room for little Daisy. They wouldn't be far away, Mrs. Armstrong."

Ivor laughed loudly, much to the amazement of the family. When he had regained sufficient breath, he said happily. "You have my permission, James. You seem to have everything worked out, and besides, Annie could have just run off with you. She's old enough!"

Taking Annie's hand, James nodded. "Your Charlotte Anne and Daisy will be happy, I promise you."

"Good enough!" Ivor agreed whole-heartedly looking around for his wife, but she was standing by the window deep in thought. "What say you, Sarah?"

A deep frown furrowed her brow when she turned around to face them. "What is your name? Your full name?" Her question was directed at James and he looked shaken.

"James Edward Nicholls, Ma'am."

"I thought your face was familiar!" Sarah gasped. "Your brother must be William. The man my younger sister eloped with!"

"Aye. Let that be no reflection on myself, Mrs. Armstrong, else I wouldn't be here."

Ivor laughed anew. "You can't deny that, Mother! That was years ago. Besides, they married in haste and now repent at leisure by all accounts. Serves them right."

Annie knelt by the father's side and announced, "We are getting married on New Year's Day. It's all arranged."

"Damn it all, girl! You're making sure you get him before he changes his mind." Ivor patted his daughter's head.

James stood ramrod straight in front of the older couple and announced, "It was an arrangement I made, sir. If it does not suit then it can be changed. All I ask is that you grace our wedding by being present."

"No fear of that, lad! We will bless the union and pray that 1906 will be the first year of a long and happy marriage. Be off with you now! Go and do your courting and leave us old ones in peace."

The couple left the room looking ecstatically happy. Charlotte could see the love shine from their eyes and felt deeply happy for Annie. "What's up, Mother?" Ivor asked his wife, jerking her back to the situation.

"Oh," Sarah sighed as she sat besides her husband. "I just hope that Annie will be happier than my sister, that's all. The Nicholls family have their problems. This James is just a working-man and our family will think Annie's demeaning herself."

"I like him. Annie's a good judge, Sarah. Besides, you've worked as a midwife all your life and there's a lot respect you for that. Just look at me. I might be an Armstrong whose family owned this house in better days, but a lot of good that's done me. Crippled most of my life and useless to one and all. I have to stand by and see my wife work her hands to the bone to keep food in our mouths, it's a bitter pill to swallow, my love. A bitter pill."

Sarah dropped to her knees and clutched Ivor's hand. "It was a farming accident, if you hadn't been out working with the field-hands then it wouldn't have happened. The people hereabouts respect you for that, you never played the idle landlord."

"I couldn't afford to! All my father ever left me was this farmhouse and the land. The money had gone, gambled away. We've always struggled because of it, so the Armstrongs and Nicholls have a lot in common!"

"Annie will struggle. At least she's used to hard work, unlike the others. How will we manage without her?"

"We'll find a way. The other children will have to start earning their keep and get their hands dirty, God Forbid!" Ivor smiled.

"But what about Daisy? We are to lose her too!"

"She's Annie's child when all is said and done. Hush now, woman! She'll only be a stone's throw away and able to visit as often as she likes."

Brightening at the thought, Sarah smiled at last. "Yes. You're right. All will be well. They'll both be nearby. Charlotte Anne is so different from the others, so very different."

"Never have two the same, girl! Being a midwife you should know that. Come on, help me up to bed. All this excitement is too much for an old man."

Charlotte Stone went back to the bedroom and removed the thimble. Returning to the present she felt rather odd for a short while, but it soon passed.

Another chapter in the life of Annie had been unveiled, another momentous occasion in the life of C.A.A.. Charlotte felt a thrill of excitement as the story unfolded before her very eyes, felt part of something special although she had no idea why.

CHAPTER 4

The Return

It was the first week of June and the sun shone to prove that summer was present. A Land Rover travelled through the lane past Glas Fryn and the driver smiled with pleasure of returning. Five minutes later he turned onto the concrete hardstand at the foot of a cottage garden.

'Cottage' was a deceptive title as the original building of his forefathers had been modernised and extended to provide space and comfort enjoyed in the modern age. Only one thing remained the same as it did over a hundred years ago, the charm of the place. Both the architect and builder had been wise enough to retain the vital character of the house which had stood the test of time.

As the homecomer slammed the door of his vehicle shut a figure emerged from the back door. The woman's smile lit up her plain face. "Welcome home, Ralph! Kettle's on the boil."

"That's what I call a welcome, Mary!" As he entered the kitchen he pecked Mary Price on the cheek. "How is everybody? Your father?"

Mary busied herself brewing tea and hoping that the blush on her cheeks didn't notice too much. "Oh, he's fine. I swear that the minute he gives up work he'll become a vegetable! Mrs. Jones is her usual caustic self and your cousin Thomas has taken up residence again."

"Why the hell does she put up with that waster! Have you noticed if anything is missing yet? He only comes here when he's short of money or desperate to hide for a while."

Mary poured the tea and laughed. "You don't know that! Come on, drink this up and tell me about your travels."

Frowning with concentration, he ignored her request. "Has he bothered you since? Has he been here often over the last six months?"

Mary Price shook her head. "No on both counts. Anyway," she said folding her arms, "he's got someone else to bother now."

"Oh? Let's have the gossip. Cissie's tongue been wagging again by the sound of it!"

"Not at all!" Mary exclaimed indignantly. "We've got a girl staying now. Well, I say girl but she's our age. Olivia hired her to write some sort of history about the family."

"Carry on, this sounds interesting. Who is she?"

"Charlotte Stone. Belonging to Mrs. Jones by all accounts."

Ralph sighed. "Aren't we all! I bet she's an amazon who is captivated by our friend Thomas Blake. I expect she creeps around her paymaster and has all the public school grooming required to suit Olivia's demands. Am I right?"

"No. Wrong about everything." Mary tried to define the woman she never expected to like. "She's always disagreeing with Mrs. Jones and Dad says that she's quite rude at times! The strange thing is, the old lady is enjoying every minute of it. I think they like each other despite their differences. Charlotte even helped us in the kitchen one day and there were sharp words with the mistress after, I can tell you!"

Ralph began to relax. "How is she with Thomas?"

"I think he's been trying his hand but she's brushed him off. I like her, Ralph. Cissie does too. Even my Dad has laughed over her altercations with Mrs. Jones and keeps mumbling 'she's back !'. God knows what he's on about."

"She sounds like the dose of medicine that house needs."

"Yes, grant you that, except.... except there's something wrong. Not with her as such, but.......... oh! I don't know. Sometimes she looks as though she's in another world. Do you know what I mean?"

" No," came the terse reply. "You're looking too hard, Mary."

Hanging her head with discomfiture, Mary closed her eyes. Ralph could be right. Despite her misgivings when Olivia

Jones announced that Charlotte was coming the newcomer had been everything Mary Price ever wanted to be. Confident, independent, able to choose her life's path, if only she had the chance .... Charlotte's words in the kitchen had been too close for comfort.

"Come on," Ralph said as he patted her arm. "I'll take you back and see for myself. No doubt the old girl will want a report."

Charlotte was immersed in the jig-saw of stories laid out on the Library desk. The only conclusion she had reached with the information supplied by Olivia was that her Aunt's commentary would result in a biased record which would be unworthy of publication. The task was becoming formidable.

Admitting to herself that with her training she should be able to separate the chaff from the grain, she knew the reasons why her mind was clouded. One issue was her time travel. Problems of the past should not worry her, she reasoned. You are merely a spectator, it has all happened and been forgotten long ago. The reason why she should experience it all will be proved with time.

The other issue was Thomas. Instinct warned her to be on her guard with the man of two faces. One face was charming enough to woo her austere Aunt, whilst the other face was sinister. Why did she feel such a deep-rooted hatred of the man? It was not a physical fear, it formed the substance of emotional turmoil existing in her sub-conscious. It would be worthwhile to make enquiries about him, she mused. She still had contacts, all she had to do was to pick up the phone.

The door opened and Charlotte's heart stopped as she expected the man she had been thinking about personified. "Sorry!" a deep voice barked as the door slammed shut.

Intrigued, Charlotte went into the hall. It was empty. She peeped in lounge and dinning room to find them unoccupied. She smiled to herself, don't tell me that my ghosts open doors as well - not to mention speak to me! Glancing at her watch she decided it was time for a coffee break anyway and hopefully a chat with Cissie. Talking to myself is becoming a habit, she mused.

Charlotte swung open the heavy kitchen door to find a stranger sitting at the large, scrubbed table. Mary, Cissie and Price were all talking at once, but stopped as she entered.

Mary got up from the table in a fluster. "Oh, Lord! I forgot about your coffee, Miss. I'll see to it straight away."

Charlotte felt like an intruder stumbling across a secret meeting. "It's OK, Mary. I'll make my own. You carry on, just don't tell the old lady that I dared to cross your threshold!"

The stranger at the table rose and extended a hand in one fluid movement. "Ralph Nicholls. Estate Manager." Friendship emanated from the relaxed handshake and she felt at ease with the generous smile which broke through the sun-tanned, weather beaten face.

"Charlotte Stone. Paid guest." Her remark was enjoyed by the man. Returning the smile she said, "So you're the reason why I was forgotten." The look of horror on Price's face was distressing. "Only joking, Price!" she added.

As she made a mug of instant coffee in the hush that followed, Ralph broke the silence. "What do you think of the place, Miss Stone? "

"Call me Charlotte, please! I love the house. I expect you have been told why I'm here. From what I've gathered you've been abroad, right?"

"Scotland, actually. That's abroad to folks around here."

Laughter erupted from the servants and Charlotte realised that she had never seen old Price even smile before.

Cissie giggled. "He's not far wrong, Miss! But he's having you on, he also spent a month in Africa."

Charlotte couldn't resist. "I thought you didn't get that tan in Scotland. Bit of a contrast though. Was there any connection, Mr. Nicholls?"

Shaking his head he replied, "No. Scotland was business. Africa was pure pleasure and a trip of a lifetime I'd always promised myself."

Mary looked radiant. "You were telling us about your holiday, Ralph. Carry on, Miss Charlotte makes no difference."

"Mary!" Price rebuked.

Charlotte laughed as she settled herself by the table. "Oh, get on with it Mr. Nicholls ....Ralph. Before we have a family feud!"

The atmosphere was light-hearted as the party listened to tales of a Safari in the African Bush which was entertaining, if not entirely credible. Price was undergoing a metamorphosis in Charlotte's eyes. With Olivia out for lunch he didn't have any pressing duties to perform and consequently became a person instead of a staid old servant ruling the house with his dour superiority.

Half an hour later the convivial atmosphere was instantly dispelled with the entrance of Thomas. "Well, well, well! The Wanderer returns! Looking very sun-tanned, Ralph. Scotland sunny, was it?"

The tension was strung as taut as a bow as the two men glared at each other. "You should know," Ralph drawled as he leaned back on the kitchen chair. "You were there recently."

Nonplussed, Thomas smirked. "You must be suffering from sun-stroke, old boy! Heathen soil as far as I'm concerned. Not where the action is. Besides, the reputation of the natives would be contrary to my line of work, the frugal Scot does not gamble with his finances!"

Ralph stood and slowly walked over to his distant cousin. His extra height added weight to his words. "On the contrary, old boy! There's no place on earth where I could mistake you. You smell like the proverbial rat and bring as much trouble. Jarvis agrees with me. There was no mistake. I saw you, Thomas. Plain as day."

For a split second Thomas seemed flustered as his face reddened and his mouth gaped. "Ah!" he announced as his composure returned, "Jarvis. But of course. I was checking out our dear old Aunt's investment. Making sure you were doing your job properly. Does she know how WELL it's doing?"

The face of the Estate Manager was dark and forbidding. "Check up on me and I may return the compliment. I'm sure Olivia wouldn't object."

Waving a hand in the air, Thomas slipped back into his usual casual persona. "Carry on, old boy! I've got nothing to hide. I only hope that you've learned something from your travels at home and abroad." Turning to the gaping audience he said evenly, "A light lunch, Price. I'll be in the Morning Room."

As Thomas left Charlotte heard the sighs of relief from the staff. Ralph merely nodded towards them and left via the back door without another word.

"I take it they don't get on!" Charlotte remarked feebly.

Cissie smiled. "At least you know how the land lies, Miss. You make your own judgments, but I know who I'd put my money on."

"Enough, Cissie!" admonished Price. "Family affairs are none of our concern. Will you be taking lunch, Miss Charlotte?"

"Yes, please. In the Library I think! Is there a key for the door? I'm sick of Thomas strolling in all the time." The reply was negative. Cissie suggested a barricade but Price decided that it was time to get back to work not gossip.

Ralph drove home over the short distance to his cottage in a blind fury. Damn him! Damn the man! There were few things in the world which would cause him to lose his self-control, it was unfortunate that Thomas was one of them.

After a quick snack for lunch Ralph turned to unpacking. As he emptied his suitcases he thought about the newcomer to Glas Fryn. Who was she in relation to Olivia Jones? Tall, slim with long dark hair, outgoing personality from what he'd seen and heard ....

Dashing downstairs into the study he pulled a box file out from a shelf laden with the same. He burrowed through old photographs until he found the one he wanted. It was her! Not as Charlotte Stone, but a reincarnation of a mystery.

The phone rang. Sitting at his desk and still holding the photograph he reached for the receiver.

"Is that you, Ralph?" asked the voice with a strong Scottish accent.

"Yes, Jarvis. Any news?"

"Nothing concrete. He was here though. Left a week or so ago."

"I know. He came hot foot to Glas Fryn. Keep checking, he's jumpy. The more I can do to shake him the better. Keep me posted but be careful, he's got powerful friends."

The voice at the end of the phone laughed. "Trust me, Ralph! It takes a lot to shake an ex-Scots Guardsman, you know."

As he replaced the receiver, Ralph felt uncomfortable. His desk. Something was wrong. He checked the drawers and knew that they had been disturbed. Mary would dust around when he was away for a while, but never touch anything else. Of that he was certain.

He rang Glas Fryn and Price answered. "Price, have you kept an eye on Thomas since he turned up?"

"As far as I can. You know how difficult..........."

Ralph asked , "Yes, I know. Impossible to keep track of him. Where does Mary keep the key to my cottage?"

"In her room, why? Anything wrong?"

Ralph sighed. "No, Price. Nothing wrong."

"Oh! By the way, Madam was sorry she missed you this morning and has invited you to Dinner tonight."

"Will HE be there?"

"Yes, as far as I know."

"Then you know the answer. I'm sure you'll think of an excuse for me."

"Part of the job, Ralph! Part of the job."

Deep within herself, Charlotte was convinced that the Library held secrets about the past residents. The shelves were a mess, but they would also be a perfect place for clues. It was a labour of love as far as she was concerned. Since she couldn't work in such shabbiness and disorder she would sort everything out and hopefully discover useful books or documents along the way.

She surveyed the room before her. Basically a large room split in half with the bookshelves at one end and desk and chairs at the other. Whoever had the shelves installed had tried to emulate a public library with two double-sided cases jutting into the room to form three separate oblong sections of shelves crammed with books. Unlike a traditional library where books would be categorised and ordered this version was particularly haphazard.

Even the other half of the room did not lend itself to study as the leather-topped desk had become torn and shabby with an ancient typewriter on top whilst the chairs were decidedly uncomfortable with cracked upholstery and lumpy seats. In better times the light from the French Window would have been beneficial to the student, not to mention the vista of a rolling green lawn and distant woodland to encourage serenity and concentration.

Concentration, she mused. How could one concentrate when you travelled through time, lived with an overbearing Aunt and a repulsive fellow-guest. Not to mention the latter's outright hatred of the Estate Manager. Life was certainly not dull at Glas Fryn.

First things first. The desk. Her notes were just bundles of paper held together with an elastic band so hardly qualified as a manuscript so the sooner the desk drawers were cleared the better. On inspection they were crammed full of old papers and documents so it would be wiser to consult Olivia before removing them.

Turning her energies to the bookshelves she worked for

two hours before realising what a momentous task she had taken on. For weeks she had tried to make headway getting as grimy as the items she had been handling. Inhaling the dust made breathing uncomfortable so she took an old Bible from the top shelf and sat by the window to take a break. If it was a family Bible they were always an invaluable source of information.

The old black leather-bound volume had been much used judging by the expansion and condition of the pages. The fly-leaf was stuck to the cover so Charlotte gingerly parted the fragile, yellowed paper. Gasping with delight she saw the initials at the foot of the page. C.A.A..

There was an inscription scrawled over the pages, the ink faded with age :-

To my First Grandchild on her 10th Birthday. December 25th, 1895
Read this Good Book and live by its Word.
Do not be Vain or Envious.
Be Humble and enjoy what the Lord has Given.
May the Lord Bless and Keep you.

The Bible was a gift from the old lady whom Charlotte had seen on her first journey back in time! Underneath the inscription the initials C.A.A. had been written in childish hand. On the opposite page was another entry in a firm, flowery hand.

Daisy 1903

A piece of paper slipped out from the book. It was a letter. Charlotte read the yellowed and tattered scrap with fascination.

June 5th, 1920.
Just a note to say that Daisy will be staying with me for a

*few days to help me look after my Grandmother. I am
pleased to say she is getting better by the hour and will be up
and about by the end of next week.*

*Your potion certainly did the trick, Mrs. Nicholls . I wrote
to my Father as you advised but we have not heard a word as
yet. I doubt we will. He has forgotten he ever had a
daughter. By the way, the mystery man has not appeared for
the last two days. David is trying to find out who he is and
promised to guard us with his life! Rest assured he will.*

Daisy sends her love and my regards to you all.
God be with you, Emily.

Charlotte shuddered. The date was June 5th! Today's date!
Pure coincidence or some unearthly plan? A knock on the
door caused her to jump up and give a shriek of fright.

Cissie rushed into the room with alarm. "What's up, Miss?
Good Lord! You're as white as a sheet. Sit down girl, before
you fall down!"

Regaining her confidence, Charlotte patted Cissie's arm.
"No, no! Really, Cissie, I'm fine. I was so engrossed in my
reading that you startled me, that's all."

"Humph!" Cissie barked. "You scholarly people are all the
same, get into things too deep." Staring hard at the young
woman she spoke like a worried mother. "How did you get in
that state? Have you looked in the mirror? If I were you I'd
go and have a bath before Dinner, those old books are so
dusty."

"Is that the time?" Charlotte gasped. "I'm off! Can't
possibly turn up for Dinner looking like a common old
chimney sweep, can I!"

After bathing, Charlotte laid on her bed still wearing her
bathrobe and examined the Bible and letter once more. It was
the only tangible proof of Daisy's birth and the incident in her
bedroom when Annie's Grandmother warned her not to be
vain! But who was Emily? A friend of Daisy's obviously, in
1920 Daisy would have been 17. Who was the 'mystery

man'? Who was David? The thimble. If she went back now perhaps she would arrive at the date on the letter.

The thimble took her through the tunnel of time. When the void cleared she was not in the bedroom but in the open countryside facing a row of three small cottages. Children played in the garden. The girls wore long dresses with white pinafores with one boy wearing a knitted suit.

"Mam! Mam!" The tallest girl shouted. Her long black hair flowed in a glossy sheet. "Come and see, Mam! Horses all dressed up!"

A woman appeared at the end doorway. Plump with shinning brown hair knotted into a bun, Charlotte gasped. The smooth, creamy skin and features were unmistakable. It was Annie, older, but with the same merry twinkling eyes.

Looking across the fields to see two large horses wearing black plumes on their proud, tossing heads, she turned on the children. "Go out the back, children. Stay there until I call you."

A pretty fair-headed girl about ten years old questioned her Mother. "Can't we stay and see the horses, Mam? We've never seen any like that before. What's that big box they're pulling?"

"Eleanor! Go and feed the hens! Mary, you watch over them."

Mary, the tallest, persisted, "But, Mam .... "

"Do as you are told!" A deep voice growled from behind the hedge. "Else I'll lock you all up! Get along now!"

Annie turned a grave face towards the voice. "Sgt. Hopkins! You're too late. Bread all sold out to the Gypsies down on Bottom Field."

A large man dismounted from his bicycle. "No, Annie. I'm here officially so as to speak. It's......."

Annie pointed towards the nearing horses and cart. "You're too late for that too, Sgt. Hopkins. That's the ambulance and since my Jim is the only miner around here I know he's been hurt."

Tucking his helmet underneath his arm, the balding man nodded. "I heard your Jimmy had an accident on my way here. I came from your Mother's side."

Annie shook her head. "Father?"

"I'm afraid so, Annie love. Passed away this morning. Your Mam asked me to tell you before anyone else did. Now this!" he indicated towards the oncoming vehicle.

"Yes, the hearse which also serves as an ambulance. Seems my family have need of both today. Still, my Father has been so sick this last year it's a blessing for him. Mother too, if the truth be told. Thank you, Mr. Hopkins. Now be off with you before you frighten my children to death!" Tears glistened in her eyes as she spoke.

The Police Officer smiled. "Do them good!" Then his face reverted to its solemn appearance as he replaced his helmet. "I'll call in tomorrow, just to see how things are."

The 'ambulance' drew alongside as the policeman left. Two men with blackened faces clambered out of the covered cart and began to pull a crude stretcher out. The driver climbed down to help and spoke as he did so. "He fell down the Drift, Missus. Thanks to Sam Lewis here he's alive. Grabbed him thinking he was a bundle of rags or something."

Annie turned pale as she saw the bloodied, broken body of her husband. "Thank you, Mr. Lewis. How bad is he? Didn't they even clean him up? You can't tell the wounds from the coal-dust!"

One of the men with a sooty face answered as they gently carried the patient into the cottage. "It was lucky we could get the ambulance, Missus. In small mines like ours we usually borrow a trap, the mine-owners care little for safety. Since the war ended two year ago there's plenty of labour to choose from. If a man falls there are plenty more queuing up to take his place."

They placed Jim on the sofa and Annie tenderly unbuttoned his waistcoat. "Well, I thank you men. God spared him his life and I'll do the rest. You got twins, Sam Lewis.

Am I right?"

Surprised by the question, Sam Lewis stammered in reply. "Aye...............aye, I have that. Your Mm..mm..mam delivered them. The....they....they are ten now."

Annie smiled as she continued to undress her husband. "Then they'll be eating you out of house and home then. I'll send some bread down tomorrow."

"No...no..no need, Missus! No need. It..it..it could have been anyone of us f-f-falling down that s-s-shaft. No! Y-y-you just look after our m-m-mate Jim, y-y-y-you'll have little time for b-b-baking."

The three men doffed their caps and as they turned to leave the driver spoke softly, "The Doctor will be here soon. These men got to get back to work and I have a ....well, you know why the horses are dressed, Missus. Our deepest sympathies. Old Ivor Armstrong was a good man. God be with you. Goodbye, Mrs. Nicholls."

As Annie attended to her husband a loud scream pierced the air. The children! They were peering through the back window. Beckoning them inside, Annie squared her shoulders and gave no quarter. "What was that noise all about? You can see your Dad's been hurt and I need to see to him. Now, all go off to Grandma's and stay with her for a while. Daisy will look after you and young Olivia will be glad of the company." Taking a deep breath, she added quietly, "Granddad died this morning and she'll be missing her Papa."

Eleanor gasped. "Granddad dead? Oh, Mam! Why are these terrible things happening? What about Dad? Will he be alright, Mam? Little Isobel was the one who screamed when we hitched her up to the window and she saw the blood. We're all frightened, Mam."

Annie held out her arms to her children and managed to encompass them all. The cuddle reassured them as did her words. "We'll all look after him and make sure he gets better. Now, you behave for your Grandmother, you must remember to be quiet. Eleanor will look after you all since she's the eldest, but Mary, you take special care of Isobel because we all know what a little rascal she can be! Run along now."

The four children with sad faces obeyed in silence.

Charlotte Stone watched as Annie waved her children goodbye and admired the courage and love which was housed within her small frame. As Annie returned to her husband's side a well-dressed man strode in through the front door without knocking. "How is he, lass?" Striding over to the sofa he examined the patient in silence. After much shaking of his head and tutting he announced his diagnosis. "Jim's in bad shape, Annie. Broken limbs which we can heal, but the signs are he's had a nasty bump on the head which could lead to more serious problems. Still, one thing at a time. Let us set those broken bones and make sure he will walk again."

They worked together quietly until Jim looked like a mummified body, still unconscious. Between them they dragged a mattress down the narrow, stone stairs and placed the heavy body on a makeshift bed in the warm kitchen. Once this was done they gratefully sat besides the range to drink a much needed cup of tea.

Annie spoke for the first time. "Thank you, Doctor Sam. You got here quickly and I appreciate that."

"No quicker than your Mother would have got to a birth." The large, bewhiskered man laughed. "Many a time she beat me to it!" A frown creased the broad brow. "It's down to you now, my girl. He'll need a lot of nursing. Keep him warm and well nourished and let time repair the damage. The children are still a bit too young to help, but Daisy is a good girl. She'll be a comfort to you and your Mother now that..........."

"Now that Father has passed away?"

"I wasn't sure you knew. I was afraid I would be the one to break the news on top of this." He nodded in Jim's direction.

"Sgt. Hopkins came up and told me straight away, he's a good man. As for the children, Eleanor's nine now, Mary is five and works wonders with two-year old Isobel! Yes, Mary is a natural mother even at her age so she will look after

Owain for me, he's a year old now. They'll all help me with the washing and baking. Daisy has her studies and Mother will need her company even more now."

"How will you manage for money? You've all those mouths to feed."

Rising with dignity, Annie replied with absolute faith, "God will provide. He spared Jim so he'll not see us starve. We grow our own vegetables and there's the hens to provide eggs. My baking brings in pennies enough for needle and thread to clothe us. Send you bill, Doctor Sam. It will be paid."

The mild-mannered physician rolled down his shirt-sleeves and gave a rueful glance at the spirited woman before him. "I owe your Mother far to much .... " seeing the scowl on Annie's face he changed tack. "Besides, I seem to be months behind with the bills. Months! Paperwork is not my province, waste of time when I could be out doctoring - which reminds me. I'll have to consider the case of Emily's Grandmother in my calculations. God knows what concoction you sent that woman but the old witch has fully recovered! Deadly Nightshade was it?"

Annie giggled. "Even our Daisy's patience was tried with that woman. If it wasn't for Emily being her bosom pal she would have left her to suffer! At least they were safe under one roof."

"What do you mean, girl? Safe? From what?"

Shaking her head and turning aside to pick up the Doctor's overcoat she replied, "Nothing, nothing at all. Just a saying. Nothing more."

Donning his coat and picking up his bag the kindly man gave his final instructions. "You fuss too much over your brood. Now, watch Jim carefully, Annie. Shock could set in. I'm passing this way tomorrow so I'll drop in. By the way, don't try lifting him with that babe on the way. It will be your last child, make sure it will be born for Jim's sake."

Charlotte's vision turned black. She had returned to the

present. Feeling emotionally drained and utterly sad over the plight of Annie she dressed for Dinner.   Tears coursed down her cheeks for the family she left behind. A broken husband, children to feed and care for and the added burden of pregnancy - not to mention the death of her father, Ivor. Poor Annie. If only she could help physically and not be a helpless onlooker - a ghost from the future! Time would not let her cross that barrier.

Life was very cruel for Annie, but she had to remember it was in the past. There was nothing she could do to change history.

CHAPTER 5

Confidences & Conflict

Charlotte went down to Dinner feeling depressed and couldn't help being affected by the past scenes she had witnessed. Matters were not helped by the situation downstairs. Thomas was in the Dining-Room and ordering Cissie to fetch him a drink. "Madam doesn't like it before a meal is served, Thomas. You know that as well as anyone."

"Damn you woman!" he shouted, "get me a large whisky. NOW!"

"Go on, Cissie." Charlotte said softly as she entered the room. "Make that two, please. We'll tell Olivia that we forced you, so don't worry."

Mouth agape, the servant scurried away. Thomas smirked in victory. "Well, well! The paragon of virtue addicted to the bottle. I'd never have guessed."

"Stop trying to be so clever, Thomas. There was no need to yell at Cissie like that, she has her job to consider."

"Frightened to death of her, the lot of them! Who is she, anyway? Just a wealthy widow when it comes down to it."

"Wealthy being the operative word as far as you are concerned." Charlotte retorted. The drinks arrived with a sour faced Cissie who dumped the tray on the table and quickly retreated.

"Don't forget, dear girl, you wouldn't be here if she wasn't paying. We are all mercenaries when it comes down to it."

Charlotte gulped the fiery liquid in earnest. "With a difference. Some of us care. What do you get out of it?"

Thomas swirled his glass and gazed into the amber liquid. "You are the one earning money under false pretences, Charlotte. Haven't even started writing yet, have you."

Alcohol always had a sedating effect on Charlotte, thus she was able to keep her temper at bay. "It's rather difficult when everyone is so tight-lipped!" Sidling up to him she smiled sweetly, "For instance, what do you know about Charlotte Anne?"

Frowning for a second, Thomas probed his memory. "Oh! As I recall she was the one who had an illegitimate child. She made matters worse by marrying a peasant of some kind."

"Thomas!" the young woman exploded. "Peasant? What era do you live in for goodness sake."

"Well as far as I can gather you've stumbled upon the skeleton in the cupboard. Ask Olivia about her, all I know is your namesake brought disgrace to the family name."

"Your name is Blake, not Armstrong. How ARE you related?"

"Ah! Good evening, my dears." Olivia swooped into the room. "I apologise for being late but .... drinks? At this hour? Thomas - yes, but you Charlotte?"

Charlotte gave a guileful glance at her counterpart and replied, "Sorry, Aunt. I just couldn't let Thomas drink alone. It would have been very rude."

"You're learning, child. However, Ladies do not always follow suit in order to be sociable. Let us be seated. I invited Ralph but it seems he has a lot to catch up on. Did you meet him, Charlotte?"

"Yes. Thomas enjoyed chatting with him, didn't you, Thomas?" she asked innocently.

Spears of hatred shot from his eyes as he replied, "Odious man."

Charlotte couldn't resist a jibe. "It seems that whilst Ralph was in Scotland he saw Thomas there too. Isn't that right, Thomas?"

"Scotland!" Olivia queried. "What's this about Scotland?"

The glance Thomas cast was enough to turn milk sour as he adopted a placating tone towards his elderly relative. "I popped up there a while back for a few days for a short break and check up on things. Merely protecting your interests, no harm in that is there?"

Olivia was outraged. "On the face of it quite an innocent story, but you have no right to interfere in my affairs up there. I have absolute faith in Ralph Nicholls and I expect you to honour that trust. Never, I repeat, never, check up on him again. Is that understood?"

"Perfectly. I just hope that your trust is well placed." Thomas replied as he tugged at his necktie.

Charlotte intervened to avoid further friction even though she has sparked it all off. It was not for the sake of the brash young man, but to prevent her Great Aunt becoming stubborn and unreceptive. "Aunt Olivia. May I ask you something?"

"What is it?" snapped the old woman.

"The old desk in the library. I wanted to use the drawers to file my material but they are crammed with old papers. Could I remove them? Are they important?"

Smiling at the request, Olivia felt important once again and so her good humour was restored. "My dear child! I've no idea what they could be. My late husband used that desk and he died some thirty years ago. Find a corner for them as they can't be of any use now."

Thomas jumped in with alacrity. "Ah! You may be wrong there, perhaps I should go through them."

Olivia shook her head. "Pointless. Just bundle them in a box and get Price to put them in the attic, Charlotte."

As Price arrived with the main course, Thomas coughed and spluttered as he tried to talk quicker than his tongue would allow. Price gave a derisive glance at the young man who threatened to spoil the appetite with his unsavoury behaviour. The words which Thomas was battling to utter finally made comprehensible speech. "No! Not the attic! Far too damp for papers and documents. Good grief, Aunt, they would just turn to pulp or worse up there." Feeling that he had the benefit of Olivia's attention he continued in his usual suave tone. "How about the old Games Room? At least it has the benefit of heating and you could go through them when the whim takes you, just to make sure there's nothing important amongst them."

Charlotte took the opportunity to plunge headlong for her own selfish reasons. "Thomas could be right! There could be significant papers amongst them like ..... like..., " pausing for effect she burst forth, "like Birth Certificates or the like."

"Ha!" Olivia exploded with mirth, "The only certificates you'd find in his desk would be of canine pedigree!"

Puzzled, Charlotte asked for an explanation whilst the horrible sound of Thomas laughing rang in her ears. "The late Mr. Jones bred Spaniels, dear Charlotte!" Olivia proudly announced. "His dogs were highly regarded by the Hunting fraternity. Fox hounds are all very well for chasing the fox in packs, but when it comes to a Gun Dog you can't beat the faithful old Cocker Spaniel. Mr. Jones enjoyed both sports and was very knowledgeable about such things. The birds he used to bag on a Shoot! It would put the rest of the Gentlemen to shame."

Foiled again, thought Charlotte. She tried to conjure up a different approach as they retired to the lounge, but decided to wait for an opportunity, it was her best chance. Thomas quickly drank his coffee aided by a generous measure of brandy and then excused himself with vague politeness. Charlotte was happy to see him go and hoped her Aunt would feel less inhibited and thus receptive.

"Aunt," she began positively, "I'm not getting very far with this historical record scheme of yours. I think you should hire an expert and make better use of your money."

Her ego in top gear, Olivia beamed with benevolence. "I know you can do it. You just need a guiding hand, a different perspective."

Pausing for effect, Charlotte gazed at the print of Glas Fryn which hung above the fireplace. "Perhaps. If only I had a few basic facts such as dates, names, places and so forth, then I could build from there. Rather like a pyramid in reverse."

"That's the ticket, child. Be more positive!" rallied Olivia Jones. "Now, the guiding hand I spoke of, well, I could be of help."

"Of course! You help would be invaluable." Charlotte feigned surprise, "We could start with your parents, or anything else you can think of ."

Looking smug, Olivia settled into her armchair. "I have neglected you, child. Well, my parents were Ivor and Sarah Armstrong. Mother was a midwife and worked to bring us up like young ladies. For as long as I can remember my father was a cripple and died when I was fifteen, but whilst he was alive we all obeyed him without question. He was a kind man who never raised his voice as far as I can recall. I think they came to live here when his parents found it too much work and retired to a smaller residence in Pantmawr. When they died he inherited it. Glas Fryn was just a large farmhouse originally with additions over the years."

"Dates?" Charlotte asked hopefully.

"Mother died in 1935 at the age of seventy, father died in 1920, but his age was always a mystery to me then. Now I know he was about 60. What else can I tell you?"

"What about your brothers and sisters? I assume there were others besides Charlotte Anne?"

Sipping her brandy, Olivia nodded. "Oh, yes! Annie was the eldest, of course. Thomas and John were killed in the First World War and young Ivor survived the Great War but as a cripple. Seven years after Ivor came Isobel then Elizabeth with me some 16 years behind her! My mother had me when she was 40, during the 'change of life' apparently."

"Quite common in those days, I understand," Charlotte confirmed. "I should imagine you were quite spoiled being so much younger than the others!"

Olivia smiled . "Not really. You see, both Isobel and Elizabeth remained spinsters and considered me as an embarrassment. Isobel died five years ago of starvation. That through her own frugal ways as she left thousands of pounds! Elizabeth died last year leaving a fair amount of money and hence the windfall which paid for this room.' Taking another sip of the alcoholic refreshment she continued.

'Now my brothers, that was another story. Before they went to war I remember them as wonderful friends who were always ready to take me out somewhere or play a game. They were 28, 29 and 30 when they took the King's shilling. They were all farmers and healthy, robust lads. I'll never forget the day the news came, Poor Mother. Two sons killed and the third near to death in some makeshift hospital in France. On top of that she heard that her brother had been killed in action in the same week. A terrible, terrible time. You could hear a pin drop in this house. Charlotte? Are you well, child? You look uncomfortably pale."

The young woman was remembering the past when Olivia's mother turned to her brother for help in the kitchen of this very house. The fresh-faced young man who vowed vengeance on Annie's attacker. Fighting to regain control of her senses she reached for her drink and gulped the fiery liquid. "Oh, dear! Sorry, Aunt. I just find it so sad. Your Uncle? What was his name?"

"Tom. Hale and hearty Tom. Mother wore black to the end of her days. For nigh on twenty years she wore nothing but black. Bit like the old Queen."

"War destroys so much more than men on the battlefield, doesn't it. Such a waste."

Olivia barked, "Are you a Pacifist?"

The sharp question jolted Charlotte into a train of logical thought. She had always believed that one should fight for the cause of freedom, vanquish all that is evil, each person a free spirit, but her personal life had been shadowed by the slaughter of war and the facts which Olivia laid before her was opening old wounds.

"No, Aunt. I just feel that any life lost under such circumstances is tragic. I'm afraid that people take freedom too much for granted these days."

"I agree with your reasoning, child. Patriotism is all very well until it claims the lives of those nearest and dearest. We tend to let life pass us by until it affects us. Grief is hard to bear when death occurs. Both expected or sudden. You never married, Charlotte?"

Surprised by the question, the young woman answered sharply. "No. My fiancé got killed before we could make it to the altar. Do you know anyone who wants to buy a cut-price wedding gown? Brand new, one careful owner." Charlotte paused and admonished herself for being so sarcastic. "Sorry. It's just that................."

Olivia clapped her hands. "Then you will understand. I want to show you something special." Rising with stately grace she went to the bureau in the corner, dropped down the top and unlocked a small drawer which she then removed. "There's a secret compartment behind this drawer," she explained. "Here! My most treasured possession."

Olivia handed her great-niece a small velvet covered box. Charlotte opened it and gasped at its content. Nestled on a bed of red velvet was a ring, a very large opal surrounded by a double row of diamonds and mounted on an elaborate gold shoulder. "Oh, it's......... it's beautiful!"

The bright blue eyes of the older woman brimmed with tears as she nodded in agreement. "It does take your breath away. That was my Engagement Ring, not from Mr. Jones I hasten to add. No, this was from the man I loved who on February 8th, 1927 got killed in a train collision at Hull whilst on a business trip for his father. I was twenty two and thought the world had come to a standstill. My Mother was most supportive, Annie too. There's an old saying - 'Opals and Pearls mean tears' - it proved to be true for me."

Charlotte nodded. "The strange thing is that my ring was similar, half the size of this one with fewer diamonds of course, but too close for comfort."

"One cannot buy such quality these days. Mine is now an antique whereas yours would be a modern ring."

"Right," Charlotte retorted snappily, "but who's talking money?"

Looking unhappy, Olivia nodded. "How ungracious of me. I beg your pardon, but I didn't mean .... Did you keep your ring as well as the wedding gown?"

"No. Just the dress, why I don't know. My fiancé was killed in Ireland nine years ago. The Unseen Enemy. A Sniper's bullet. Not all 'wars' are in the dim and distant past, Aunt. We have a lot in common, don't we! Similar rings, similar fates with our fiancés, really. You did get married eventually though."

Waving a hand dismissively she retorted, "When my Mother died in 1935 we had little to live on. Mr. Jones made an offer for Glas Fryn and the family accepted. He offered me a post of Housekeeper as I knew the ropes or, if I preferred, marriage. The latter seemed more respectable."

"A marriage of convenience!" Charlotte exclaimed. "Surely such a thing was rare by 1935!"

"Perhaps. Mr. Jones was a good man and allowed me to live as I wished. He made no demands upon me and my virginity remained intact."

Aghast at the admission, Charlotte knew by the regal tilt of the head that Olivia's words were true. She was actually proud that she had remained faithful to the memory of her dead fiancé, but was it really a deep emotional problem which prohibited normal physical desire? Returning the precious ring to the elderly woman, Charlotte spoke softly, "Better to have loved and lost.......... so they say."

Pity surged through her as Olivia gently cradled the ring in her hand. "Indeed!" the abrupt tone returned. "I consider myself fortunate to have known both love and companionship."

Charlotte nodded. "Your story is ideal for the project. Full of human interest and compassion! I could ...."

"No!" growled the outraged woman. "I forbid you."

"But I thought the whole idea of this conversation was to know your past? I know it must be painful for you, but if you want me to write an accurate history of this family then you must be prepared to include some personal details."

Olivia placed her ring on her marriage finger. "It still fits! I always had thick fingers. Mother said they were not 'Ladies Fingers', not like ...." her voice trailed off as memories took over.

"Aunt?" Charlotte asked quietly then kneeling besides the old woman. "I'm sorry. Of course it's a private thing. I was heartless. I had my ring buried with my fiancé. It seems we both lost the ones we loved more than any other."

Olivia sighed and removed the ring. "I only told you because I want you to have this. Not now. Not while I'm still alive. You know where it's hidden and when I pass away I want you to have it. Nobody else knows the story, nobody else would understand like you."

Moved to hear such words from her stern Aunt, the young woman stroked the mottled hand. "Then I am privileged. I promise not to mention it to anyone, let alone print it. So please forgive me for ever thinking about it. Thank you for sharing your secret with me."

"Humph!" grunted Olivia whilst she smiled. "I wasn't wrong! Understand, Charlotte, I have numerous relations whom I consider with civility however far removed, but you are different. That is why you are here. A woman after my own heart."

Such a deep feeling of compassion churned inside Charlotte Stone that she felt unable to utter a word. Annie of the past and Olivia of the present were bringing her soul to life after many years of detached indifference.

Olivia took the slender young hand and patted it. "Come along, child. It's time we went to our beds. Goodness knows what Thomas is up to, no doubt he'll return in the early hours." She rose from her chair and looked down on the dark head. "You are so like....... so like a very dear person I knew years ago. Her qualities have been passed on to you but with a sharper edge! One day I may tell you another story, when the time is right. Goodnight, Charlotte."

Responding to the last words, Charlotte bade goodnight and made her way upstairs. Who was that person? Was it Daisy? It was haunting her.

In her room the words of Olivia raced through her mind and played with her senses. She had to return. After preparing for bed and waiting for the house to settle she slipped the thimble onto her finger and travelled the void without reservation.

She was still in the bedroom but the 'old' bedroom and magical sounds drifted up the stairs. It was music. Someone was playing the piano. Did Olivia have a piano? Charlotte followed the sound downstairs to the Morning-room where a young girl sat before a Grand Piano playing it with a rapt expression whilst an elderly lady listened. A lady dressed in black. The pianist had jet black hair plaited around her head and a sylph-like figure which swayed like a reed.

When the music finished the old lady clapped her hands in appreciation. "Oh, Daisy! My dear child. You play like a professional. It MUST be your career. Emily said that her mother knows the right people and .... "

Daisy gracefully fled to the old lady's side. "I know that Emily's mother would have all the right contacts, after all she has played all over the country and even abroad during the War. I also know that she was no mother to Emily. Up until the day she died she was rarely home and that left Emily in a right pickle, didn't it! No, Grandmother, I have decided my future and Monday can't come soon enough."

"But Daisy, such talent going to waste. Nursing is so ....well, do you realise what it involves? It's certainly nothing like the romantic novels you read!"

Daisy smoothed the wrinkled hand which was clutching a walking-stick. "My Grandmother a midwife and you ask me if I know what I'm doing! I've seen babies being born and that's hardly romantic. I've seen my father after his accident and helped Mother bathe his wounds all those months. To me, all that is far more rewarding than playing a piano, performing just to satisfy a rich audience's whims is not for me."

Shaking her head, Sarah Armstrong pleaded, "But what about your Mother? She wouldn't want you to take such a menial job. Annie always wanted the best for you."

"Mother is pleased, so is Dad. I know he's not really fit yet, it seems his nerves have gone, but Mam says that his body has healed and time will help with the mental problems."

Wiping the tears from her eyes, Sarah spoke with a tremulous voice, "But Daisy! You know about your birth? Jim is not your natural Father."

Daisy nodded and stood up clasping her hands together. "I know that he loves me. I know he married my mother aware of the circumstances. I know they adore one another and are still like young sweethearts. I have no other father."

"You HAVE!" came the terse reply, "and he's back! Did they tell you that?"

Daisy gulped. "No. Nobody told me that. I wonder if it's the man who's been watching Emily and myself? David is trying to track him down."

"Your father's nephew, David? Your cousin?" Sarah Armstrong asked smiling. "I heard that he's making up to Emily! Her family will never agree to the match you know. They are very wealthy and her grandmother would never let her go."

"But David is a kind and gentle person, Grandma! He may be rather serious but he's hard-working. Why should they object?"

The old woman screwed up her eyes and explained her reasons. "David has been brought up in our Church. Emily's family are Catholic, albeit passive worshippers. In their eyes David is a Protestant and they will forbid a marriage on religious grounds alone."

Daisy smiled sweetly. "Emily knows that. It's 1921 now and times are changing. Her family have threatened to disown her, but she is determined to marry David. Anyway, she never sees a penny so the money makes little difference to her."

Sarah twisted her lace handkerchief in her gnarled hands. "My child, we stray from the subject. You say a man has been hanging around, can you describe him?"

Frowning, Daisy nodded. "I've never seen him close up, but he's fair and stockily built. I should say about average height and in his middle age. Why, Grandma?"

Sarah rose slowly from her chair as she answered. "Oh, nothing. I just wondered .... " Standing as straight as she could, she changed her tone. "Your parents are right, child . Do what you will but the truth is that I will miss you. You have been such a comfort to me over they years, now Olivia will take your place. The other two are like old maids already."

"Come along, Grandmother!" Daisy laughed as she took her arm. "Let's have tea."

" Just remember this, Daisy. Of all my children Charlotte Anne suffered the most, but praise God she found a strong and lasting love despite the difficulties. I delivered you into this world and knew you were special. Take your gift to others and be dedicated to your chosen cause."

"You never know, I may return as a qualified Midwife and follow in your footsteps!"

Sarah laughed quietly. "If you do make sure you get paid! I only received goods in kind to help me feed my growing family. I learned my trade by experience so the knowledge cost nothing. Your life will be better than that."

Charlotte returned to her own time leaving an old woman holding on to the arm of her beautiful granddaughter. The face of Daisy seemed familiar, yet strange. It haunted her as she finally fell into a deep and dreamless sleep.

It was two in the morning when Charlotte was awoken by a noise.

Emerging from her deep slumber she was barely aware of

it's source. Flicking on the bedside lamp she sat up in bed and listened. The silence was broken by the hooting of an owl in the dark, velvety night. She clambered out of bed and ran to the window to throw the curtains open wide. Instead of the inky blackness of the garden there were two patches of light on the lawn. One was a dim light with her own silhouette, but another much brighter light shone above it.

Charlotte figured it came from the floor above which were the attic rooms. Rubbing the sleep from her eyes she threw on her dressing-gown and went out of her room to investigate, but realised that she didn't know how to get up to the next floor. Creeping past Olivia's door she held her breath but a loud thud startled her.

"Who's there?" a shrill voice uttered as Olivia blundered out of her room and straight into her guest.

"It's OK, Aunt! It's only me!" the young woman reassured as she tried to stifle her amusement. Olivia was wearing a thick, pink hairnet which had fallen askew thus making her look comically dishevelled.

"Good grief, girl, what are you doing out here? Was it you who made that noise?"

Charlotte whispered, "You heard it too? I think it came from above but don't know how to get up there."

"Oh, my goodness!" the ashen faced lady replied. "Hang on, I'll show you. Just wait a minute." Dashing back to her room with remarkable speed she re-emerged wielding a hockey-stick. "I always keep this handy. Got my walking stick too. Come along!"

Olivia led the way in the opposite direction and opened a door at the far end of the east wing. "There's half a dozen steps up to the landing," Olivia whispered conspiratorially, "from there you can see all the attic rooms. I'll just put the light on to flush the devil out."

As the light flickered into life an almighty roar sounded whilst a figure came hurtling down the stairs. Olivia gasped whilst Charlotte grabbed the hockey-stick and pushed her

Aunt out of the demon's path. With the stick above her head she took a sideways swing at the assailant and heard the dull thud as the stout weapon made contact. The figure sprawled at her feet with a horrible moan.

Olivia looked dazed but clung to the open door and shouted, "Hurrah! Well done, girl! That showed the fiend!"

"Hold on, Aunt," Charlotte said as she knelt by the inert form. "I think we may have been a bit hasty."

"Don't be ridiculous, child. That man was trying to murder us!"

Charlotte shook her head as the body groaned into life. "Hardly. It's Thomas."

The injured man regained his senses and manoeuvred his body into a sitting position, but yelped in pain with each movement. "My God!" he gasped, "Here was me..........thinking.........thinking that I was............ was defending two..........two helpless women!" As he tried to laugh he coughed and spluttered in agony.

Charlotte was unmoved. "What were you playing at, Thomas? Why were you up there in the first place? It is the early hours of the morning, after all!"

Olivia intervened. "He must have heard the noises too. Come along, Charlotte. Thomas was only trying to protect us. It's unfortunate that he suffered for his pains."

"Oh yes?" Charlotte queried. "Then why is he fully dressed? We didn't stop to put our clothes on, did we."

"Ah!" Thomas interjected, "I can explain that. I'm afraid that ...." moans issued forth, "My God, woman! You certainly pack a punch ! I think my arm is broken."

Standing aloft like a glorious victor, the young woman was relentless. "Finish your story and then I'll call a doctor."

"God! Were you ever in the SAS?" Thomas moaned. "What I was.......... was trying to say was that I'd only............. only just come home when.......... I heard a.......noise."

"That's enough!" Olivia barked in her normal tone of voice. The hairnet spoiled the effect in Charlotte's opinion.

"Call the doctor, girl, and then make some hot, sweet tea. We could all do with reviving, I'm sure."

"What?" the young woman asked in mock indignation, "Me in the kitchen! How can you suggest such a thing."

"This is an emergency and poor Thomas needs something for the shock. Run along, child."

Charlotte left before she wielded the hockey-stick at another. You just couldn't go bashing poor old deluded women.

The Doctor duly arrived and ferried the patient off to hospital whilst the two women returned to their beds and slept soundly. In the morning Thomas returned with his arm in plaster and sling. He looked ashen and the bristles sprouted from the unshaved face. The fixed grin was absent. He went to his room without saying a word to anyone.

Olivia entered the library where her great-niece was working to tell her about the patient's return. "I know your intentions were good, Charlotte, but did you need to hit him quite so hard?"

"You wouldn't have said that if he was a stranger. I resent your remark."

"Apparently his arm was broken. You must have realised it was Thomas."

Standing in front of her Aunt, the young woman took umbrage. "All I saw was a figure hurtling down on us. He could have been the mad axe-man for all I knew and I reacted with all the strength I had to save you! In fact, I seem to remember you congratulating me at the time. Anyway, have you stopped to wonder why Thomas should throw himself down the stairs like he did? He must have known it was us or the Price family."

Shaking an immaculate head, the elderly woman muttered as she turned to leave the room, "But such force! Really! Really!"

Charlotte called after her, "Next time I'll stand aside and wait for the introductions shall I?" Then to herself whispered, 'and if it's Thomas then I'll hit him harder where it really hurts.'

CHAPTER 6

Old Enemies

Charlotte felt angry at Olivia's attitude and went to the kitchen in search of lighter company. Price was snoozing in the chair by the fireside with a newspaper falling off his lap. The back door was open so she went out into the glorious June sun.

Mary and Cissie were busy weeding a flower-bed. "Good Lord!" Charlotte uttered. "Don't you two ever stop?"

Mary straightened her reed-like body, "It's lovely out here, Miss. Anyway, it gives my Dad a bit of peace."

"I should say!" Cissie exclaimed. "All hell broke loose last night, didn't it ? Well done, Charlotte, well done!"

"Her Ladyship doesn't see it that way, blast her."

Mary shook her head. "Don't you take no notice of her. That scoundrel is up to something and no mistake. We'd love the chance to go after him with a hockey-stick, wouldn't we Cissie!"

All three laughed in a united cause and Charlotte felt less miserable. "I'm off for a walk. Blow the cobwebs away. Dare I ask if you want to come along or is the lure of the trowel too much for you."

Mary smiled happily. "Go on with you! Believe it or not we are enjoying ourselves so you go and do the same. Put some Welsh country air in those city lungs and it will do you the power of good."

Taking the opposite direction to Pantmawr, Charlotte felt relaxed as she wandered through the quiet, rambling lane and enjoyed the scenery. Rolling green fields with clusters of woodland were visible when the hedgerows dipped or thinned out. Some cottages were scattered around and had been converted from their original basic accommodation of a century ago into idyllic country retreats.

The road inclined gently and became shaded within a copse. The smell was fresh, damp and wonderful to a city-bred woman and she closed her eyes to savour the refreshing drop in temperature. When she opened her eyes again it was to see a man standing in her path.

"Bit far from home, aren't you?" he said with heavy sarcasm.

"Am I trespassing or something?" Charlotte frowned.

"No. Would you care if you were?"

"On this particular day, Mr. Nicholls, no!"

Ralph took in the vision before him. Tall with long dark hair and a reasonably pleasant face. The features were strikingly similar to that photograph. What was it Mary Price had said? In another world at times? Realising she was drained of colour he was forced to ask, "Are you alright? You look very pale."

"How nice of you to be concerned, Mr. Nicholls. I'm flattered, but just because I don't have the rosy cheeks of a country girl there's no need to worry."

Taking a deep breath to control his temper, Ralph replied as evenly as he could, "I'm as worried about you as I would be about any injured animal. Come on. I live near here and you should have something to drink before you trek the three miles back to Glas Fryn." Turning he walked towards his home.

Forgetting her indignation, the young woman ran after him. "Three miles! Have I really walked that far? Doesn't feel like it."

On reaching the cottage Ralph made straight for the kitchen to make a pot of tea whilst his visitor looked around in astonishment. Placing a steaming mug of laced brew on the table he motioned to a chair. "Sit down and drink it."

As she did so, Charlotte asked, "It only looks like a whitewashed cottage from the front but surely this is not the original kitchen!"

"Of course not. When my ancestors lived here they were

grateful for a dry roof and the convenience of a nearby spring for water, not to mention a garden large enough to feed their brood. Their priorities are not mine so the building has been extended in keeping with its style." Ralph paused then asked once more, "Now will you tell me what's wrong with you?"

On the defensive again she drew her shoulders back proudly. "Nothing. Not with me anyway."

Ralph was puzzled. " No riddles, please Miss Stone. I'm not Thomas."

Galvanised into action, Charlotte stood up so quickly that her chair went flying. "If you were then you'd get the same! Cousins, aren't you? Well let me tell you this, Mr. High and Mighty Nicholls! I'm the wrong one to tangle with!"

Stunned at the volatile reaction, Ralph spoke harshly. "Before you vandalise my furniture I assure you that I loathe the person in question and wish him to the Devil! Have you murdered him or something?"

A grin broke through the young woman's strained features and she picked up the chair. "Not quite." Sitting down again and drinking the soothing tea she continued, "He's just got a broken arm, compliments of Olivia's hockey-stick and my killer instinct!"

"Shame. You could have done better than that. How did it happen?"

Charlotte related the events of the previous night to the serious man. His expression remained passive throughout and only asked questions when she had finished. "Are you sure it was him making the noise in the attic rooms? He could have been checking like he said."

"Burglars don't put lights on. It was a chance in a thousand that someone would see the light from the back of the house. I've heard noises before and thought it was the staff moving around or something. I even wondered if Thomas was having an affair with Mary Price!"

"Not for the lack of trying," Ralph commented. "Give me your opinion of him."

Clasping her hands together she nodded. "I wouldn't trust him an inch. I think he's using Olivia for a bolt-hole or something. She was very agitated one day soon after Thomas arrived at Glas Fryn, but she went off somewhere and came back a lot happier. When I asked her if it was anything to do with Thomas she said it was 'indirectly linked' to him. By the way, what was all that business between you and him about Scotland? Olivia wasn't best pleased when she found out."

The sun-burned face grinned. "A bluff. It shook him though, but not as much as your onslaught, I dare say!"

"That's another thing," Charlotte retorted, "Olivia had the nerve to say I was too impulsive this morning."

"Check the attic rooms. You've got access," Ralph watched as the young woman became agitated. "What's wrong? Afraid of ghosts? You don't seem the type."

"Ghosts?" whispered Charlotte. "What made you say that? Just because it's an old house someone has to invent a ghost! I would have thought you were above all that nonsense."

"No," Ralph replied with all seriousness. "I would be the last one to question local folklore. You could be a ghost of the here and now, a reincarnation of a past being. Have you ever considered that theory?"

Shuddering, Charlotte shook her head. "Absolute rubbish! There was me thinking you were the sensible one. Time I was going home."

Feeling a strange sense of unease about her reaction, Ralph picked up the car keys from the worktop. "Come on, I'll run you back."

"No. I'll walk."

"I'm going that way anyway." Without another word he led the way to the Land Rover and jumped inside. As he started the engine his passenger got inside reluctantly and he drove her to Glas Fryn without another word being spoken. As she alighted at the gates of the House he grinned, "Remember, anytime you're passing the cottage and feel like an argument I'll be happy to oblige. See you, Lottie."

As the vehicle drove away, Charlotte began walking up the drive feeling startled by the use of her nickname. The sound of crunching gravel heralded Thomas's approach and interrupted all thought.

"It didn't take you long, dear girl . I hope you are more gentle with your boyfriends than you are with your fellow inmates!"

"That you will never know, Thomas." She left him standing on the driveway looking evil. It certainly didn't take him long to recover, she thought to herself.

Dinner that evening was very entertaining for Charlotte. Thomas was the focus of her amusement as he attempted to eat with one hand whilst cursing and apologising to Olivia in the same breath.

"We should have asked Mary to chop up Master Thomas's food, Aunt. How thoughtless of us!"

"Is it true that you went to some private girl's school?" he barked with venom in his tone. "Gym teacher an ex-marine by any chance? Butch and aggressive type if your hockey swing is anything to go by."

Charlotte laughed. "You obviously went to a school for creeping wimps."

Olivia clapped her hands. "You are both reverting to your childhood days by the sound of it! My Mother would take a boiler-stick to anyone who uttered a word at the table."

"So violence is inherent!" Thomas remarked with heavy sarcasm.

"Thomas." declared Olivia, "What were you doing up there last night? I doubt your story about an intruder."

Colour flooded into his fair complexioned face as he tugged at his shirt collar with the only good hand. "It's the truth. The house could be haunted for all I know!"

Giggling, the young woman persisted, "You were the only supernatural being up there! The light was on for ages."

"Rubbish! I only had a torch."

"No, Thomas." Charlotte argued solemnly, "I know the light was on because I saw it from my bedroom window."

"Ah !" he uttered whilst his eyes twitched nervously. "That proves it !" Thomas declared as he reached a solution. "I would hardly go switching all the lights on if I was looking for a burglar, would I? The light you saw could have been the culprit."

Olivia nodded. "That would explain it."

Charlotte sprang from the table in disbelief. "Come off it! He's lying through his teeth, Aunt! What the hell is up there anyway? Junk? Unwanted bits and pieces? Any self-respecting burglar would look down here, or even the bedrooms, not a dusty old attic!"

"That's how much you know, Charlotte dear." Thomas smirked. "The antique trade would kill for genuine articles and an old house stuck in the country is an ideal target. Our Aunt could have a small fortune collecting dust up there." He ignored the younger woman who was stalking around the table with arms folded and directed his remarks to his elderly ally. "You really should install an alarm system, Aunt. You could well own priceless antiques without realising it."

"Judging by last night," Olivia snorted, "I consider Charlotte as worth far more than bells ringing or electrical gadgets buzzing!"

The remark helped to ease Charlotte's temper as she stood still and faced her enemy. "Don't worry, Thomas. If any of those nasty people break in here I'll have the old hockey-stick handy. You may rest easy in your bed - that is, when you are in it . Besides, from your apparently expert knowledge of the crooked underworld I'm certain that I'm looking at the only threat to this house!"

"One small incident and you think you can handle anything!" muttered Thomas. "One day......one day......."

"Are you threatening me, Thomas? You seem peeved because we are realistic, not two women quivering with fright."

"Enough!" Olivia ordered. "Charlotte, refrain from adding insult to injury. Thomas has his physical pain to contend with and I think you should be more considerate."

"He should be using more consideration, not me! I don't go creeping around in the dead of night."

"Charlotte!" gasped the older woman. "We've been through all that. I forbid the matter to go any further."

Thomas nodded and patted Olivia's hand. "I'm quite prepared to call a truce. We are under your roof and subject to your rules. I have no wish to offend you, dear Aunt."

Feeling nauseous at the words dripping like syrup from the devious tongue, Charlotte spoke abruptly. "Since I was disturbed last night I'm very tired and in no mood to compromise. Goodnight, Aunt. Let me know if you are bothered by any one-arm bandits!"

That night, when the house fell quiet, Charlotte slipped back in time with the aid of the little silver thimble. She had become so engrossed in the past because the people were becoming part of her, they were so different from the present.

She was outside Annie's cottage again where the children were playing outside. A baby was being carried by Mary whilst two girls and a small boy were tossing a ball to each other. The boy missed his turn and began to wail. "Where's Mam? I want Mam!"

Mary cradled the sleeping babe and smiled. "Hush now, Owain. Go and play. Mam is waiting for Doctor Sam."

Charlotte caught her breath as the smallest girl with scruffy hair and dishevelled clothes asked her big sister, "Is Dad ill, again? I saw him go out and he hasn't come back. Has he fallen down a big hole again?" As she spoke the child kicked the doorstep instead of the ball.

"Isobel! Look at the state of your shoes!" the eldest girl admonished. "Mam will go spare! Go and play round the back out of the way."

Mary intervened before the threatened tears gave vent.

"Dad's well enough, Isobel, but he can't afford new shoes yet! Do as Eleanor says, Mam will call us when she's ready."

As the children ran out of the gate happily, Eleanor scowled at her sister. "Stop rocking, Mary! Baby's asleep. If you want to be a Nanny you'd better stop being so soft with children." Raising her head and shoulders she sounded as haughty as she looked. "Come on, we'd better follow them. Mam put me in charge, after all."

Charlotte smiled as she watched them go. So Annie's last child had been born and was thriving. The sudden appearance of the Doctor startled her, but as he opened the door she followed. Invisible she might be, but she was not able to go through doors.

A young man was lying face down on the scrubbed-top table with a blanket over him whilst Annie held a young woman in her arms. "Here's Doctor Sam. You see to the bowls of hot water my girl, I'll help the doctor."

As the Doctor removed the blanket from the patient the young woman screamed. "No! No! I couldn't! Daisy is the nurse, not me. Oh, my God!"

Looking over his half-moon spectacles, the Doctor frowned upon the scene. "Your fiancé is lying here with his backside peppered with shot and all you can do is swoon and feel sorry for yourself! I hope David knows what he's marrying."

Annie was bolting between the table and the kettle looking thunderous. "Sit down and keep out the way if you won't help, Emily!"

The impromptu operation began and Charlotte had to turn away. She sympathised with the girl Emily as ....Emily? The name rang in her head and she stared at the snivelling figure. Emily! Daisy's friend.

"What happened, girl?" the Doctor asked. "Someone thought they were shooting at rabbits by the look of it. You should take more care where you do your courting girl."

"No! No! No! " Emily shouted. "It wasn't like that! It was

done deliberately, Dr. Sam."

As she spoke the words Jim came through the door with the policeman in tow. "If that's true, Emily, here's the person to tell." He then went over to the patient his voice concerned. "How is David?"

The Doctor grunted. "Your nephew will live to tell the tale."

"Well, he's the only one I got," Jim sighed. "More like a son since his father's bedridden. The war has a lot to answer for even though its been over for 3 years."

Annie agreed. "As for his mother, she may be my sister-in-law but she's no wife or mother and that's a fact! Same with Emily's mother, always gadding about."

The Sgt. sat opposite Emily and took out his notebook whilst still listening. "She's a fine pianist, by all accounts Annie. They tell me your Daisy is too."

The Doctor spoke softly, "Daisy has a level head on her shoulders and will do better as a nurse than a pianist. There, all done. Ready for a cup of tea, Annie."

"Now then, Emily," the policeman said briskly. "Enough chit-chat. Let's hear what happened."

Calmer now, the young woman nodded and spoke evenly. "We came out of the woods in the bottom field and a man was walking towards us with a gun. It was the man who has been following me for months, Daisy too. He just aimed at us! David pushed me back into the trees and the next thing I heard was the gun going off. David was lying on the ground and I thought .... I thought ....he was...dead!" Tears fell from the passive face.

"Did you recognise this man?" the official voice asked.

"No. I'm afraid not."

Leaning forward in his chair, the Sgt. prompted, "Well can you describe him?"

"Oh! Fair, well-built and ..... oh! I'm not sure! Ask Daisy, she's seen him!"

Licking the nib of his pencil, the policeman drew a deep

breath. "Daisy's in London, Emily. How long has this been going on? Does he follow you all the time? Everywhere?"

"No, not all the time." The tears were now flowing freely as Emily grew more distressed. "Please take me home, sir! I....I....... Oh, dear! If my Grandmother heard about this she would ......"

Annie rushed to the distraught young woman and comforted her. "It will never reach her ears if I can help it! Sgt. Hopkins here will take you home, Emily. David will be staying here for a few days to get over his wounds. You can visit when you like."

Reluctantly the policeman agreed to Annie's demands to keep the incident quiet but vowed to get to the bottom of things. He then left the cottage to escort Emily home.

Dr. Sam looked worried. He accepted a cup of tea and sat by the fire. "I don't like it. There's something sinister about this. Any ideas, Jim?"

"Yes." James Nicholls nodded. "I have my own ideas."

Banging his cup into the saucer, the Doctor asked, "Well? Who is it for God's sake? We can't let a madman roam around the countryside taking pot shots as people. Someone will get killed!"

Annie shook her head. "God will protect the innocent."

"Humph!" the elderly man replied. "Well God must have been napping this afternoon when David got his rear end blasted!"

"God never sleeps," Annie stated quietly. "David will be up and about in a few hours. His pride will hurt the most."

"Blake!" The Doctor slapped his knee as truth dawned. "Fred Blake! It must be. Emily's family would stop at nothing to get David out of the way!" Another thought occurred to the Doctor as he train of logic proceeded in his head. "Oh, no. Annie, lass. Forgive me."

Jim was standing with his back to the fire and hands dug into his pockets. "I mind you to keep your thoughts to yourself for a while, Dr. Sam. There are others to consider."

Annie sat down wearily and nodded. "It's alright, Dr. Sam. My Jim knows. If Daisy's natural father has returned then she's out of harm's way. He probably has a few scores to settle including my Uncle Tom who sorted him out all those years ago, but the war claimed Tom's life so he is beyond that scoundrel's revenge."

Charlotte gasped. So Daisy's biological father had returned. He had attacked Emily and David. Was Daisy next? The cruel rapist had come back with vengeance on his mind.

The vision was fading, the room was swirling around, she had to go back to the house........to her room......... she had to get back.............

She opened her eyes. The light was grey. She was damp and shivering with cold. Her hands touched the strange, furry surface she was lying on. It was grass. Glistening dew-laden grass. Sitting up she found herself in the middle of a field with the dawn mists shrouding everything with a foggy mantle. Her nightdress was thin and her feet bare. Charlotte began to feel frightened. Where was she?

Emptying her mind of her experience in Annie's house she concentrated on getting her bearings and returning to Glas Fryn before anyone knew she was missing. What would Olivia think of her! What a meal Thomas would make of it!

A gate. She could see a gate looming up ahead. Charlotte tried to reach it but her body would not react properly. She tottered and felt dizzy, then summoning up all her willpower she crawled on all fours until she could grasp the wooden crossbar of the gate in relief. A lane on the other side gave her fresh hope, but, unable to stand she rested as the skies grew lighter and nature lifted the misty mantle. It was the dawn of a new day.

"Well, well! What 'ave we 'ere then?" An old man on a bicycle stopped besides the strange figure leaning on the field gate. "For a minute there I thought I was seeing a ghost! Who are you? What you doing out 'ere?"

"Oh, help me, please!" Charlotte pleaded. "I want to go

home but I'm lost. Where am I?"

"In top field, that's where you are, Miss!" The toothless grin was friendly and curious. "You're a new face, where do you call 'ome then? Eh ! You wouldn't be 'er Ladyship's girl would you? What the 'ell are you doing out 'ere? The old girl kicked you out, 'as she? Didn't give you chance to put your clothes on neither!"

"No! No!" wailed the distraught young woman. "Just tell me the way back, I beg of you!"

"You're in no fit state to go that distance, Miss. Just you wait there while I fetch 'elp." Hesitating for a moment, the old man delved into his overcoat pocket. " 'Ere. Take this to keep you going."

Taking the proffered hip flask, Charlotte drank it without question. The fiery liquid brought her senses back to some sort of reason. "How long will you be?"

"Two shakes of a lamb's tale, love! Before you finish that flask, anyway!" The old man chuckled as he mounted his bike and left her. Continuing to sup the alcohol, whisky or brandy she couldn't tell, but it was warming her from the inside out. An age seemed to pass before a vehicle screamed to a halt in the lane.

"Bloody hell! Charlotte? What are you doing out here? Why are you wearing a nightdress?"

Despite the tone she was grateful to see a familiar face. "Mr. Nicholls! Ralph. Oh, please, take me home. Please!"

As he opened the gate and helped her to drag her feet to the Land Rover he talked. "I thought old Ted Skinner had been hitting the bottle again! Knocking my door at six in the morning with this tale. Oh, I see you've had the benefit of his constant companion."

The urge to cry was overpowering, but Charlotte fought back the tears in the presence of the Estate Manager. He might see her in this incredible state but she would not bare her emotions to add more spice to the story. No doubt this incident would be bandied around his local pub so the less dramatics the better.

They were outside his cottage within minutes. "Come on. Can you make it or ...." Ralph sighed. Charlotte was fast asleep.

With a struggle he carried the lifeless body into the cottage and put her on the settee and covered her with a blanket. What the hell was going on? Glas Fryn. He must phone Glas Fryn.

Price answered the telephone. "Ralph here, Price. You've lost a guest, Charlotte. She's with me. Keep it quiet if you can, I'll explain later."

"As you say, sir. I understand."

"Send Mary over with some clothes for her, will you? She's in her nightclothes and can hardly return in that state."

Price paused. "In her night clothes? Strange. What ......"

Ralph sighed. "Just do as I ask, please! It's for her sake, not mine."

As Ralph replaced the receiver he turned to see Charlotte in the doorway clinging onto the pillar for support. "Where am I? Why are you here? Oh God! I feel terrible!"

"Wandering in the fields at dawn has that effect. Can you make it to the bathroom? A hot shower then breakfast. I think Ted Skinner's tipple did the most damage!"

Ralph guided Charlotte to the bathroom, ran the shower and left towels and bathrobe within easy reach. She understood his sharp commands and responded with a glazed expression. The sound of the doorbell was welcome. It was Mary.

"What's going on, Ralph? Dad said that Miss Stone was here. Is she alright? Why hasn't she got clothes?"

"She's going to be OK. She's in the bathroom and rather the worse for wear. Go and help her, Mary. Make sure she doesn't drown herself or something."

Mary Price looked questionably. "It's not for me to ask, but ...."

"Just go and see to her!" Ralph barked. "She didn't spend

the night here, if that's what you're thinking."

As Mary smiled and went on her errand, Ralph returned to the kitchen to cook breakfast. Damn them all! How did he get into this situation?

Twenty minutes later Mary entered the kitchen looking happier.

"I'll have to get back, Ralph. Charlotte will be down in a minute. She said she must have been sleep-walking, but I can't understand how she left the house. It was all locked up! I'll swear to it."

"What about Thomas? He comes home all hours of the night and could have left a door unlocked."

Mary nodded. "Like as not that fool left the front door unlatched, he's too drunk to notice half the time. Anyway, I'll tell Madam that she went out for an early morning walk. She's done it before."

Ralph smiled. "Thank you, Mary. The less the old girl knows the better."

Mary left and Ralph returned to the cooker. As he turned the bacon which spat and sizzled in the pan he thought about the morning's events. Something strange was happening to Charlotte Stone. He would get to the bottom of it, but he had to be subtle. For once in his life he must suppress the urge to demand answers and learn to be more persuasive.

Time. Time would reveal answers. He would be patient. The strangest thing of all had been the small silver thimble on her right hand......

CHAPTER 7

The Dawn of Truth

As Charlotte dressed in her jeans and sweater which Mary had brought over from Glas Fryn she considered the events of the night. How could she explain them away? Up until now she had worn the thimble to travel back into time and always returned to Glas Fryn when she wished to. This time was different. Mary believed the tale of sleep-walking, but Ralph Nicholls was not such a gullible person. Had he noticed the thimble jammed on her finger? She prayed he hadn't and slipped the precious possession into her trouser pocket.

She made her way downstairs with trepidation. The smell of the food was ambrosia to her weary body. As she entered the kitchen her host pointed to a chair and she obeyed the silent command. A laden plate was put before her and they both ate in silence.

"Thank you." Charlotte said with genuine pleasure. "I didn't realise how hungry I was."

"Coffee?" Ralph asked as he cleared the plates away. "I'll make it strong as Ted was a bit too generous with his flask, am I right?"

Charlotte laughed with relief. "I must admit that I took advantage of his generosity! I was frozen to the bone ...."

Ralph placed an aromatic, steaming mug before her. "The crack of dawn is not the time to go crawling around fields in your nightwear." The mud and grass stains on her legs and clothing was evidence of that.

Forcing a light-hearted laugh, Charlotte felt helpless to defend herself. "I think I ought to go back home now. Olivia will be asking questions. She'll only take it out on Cissie and Mary."

"She thinks you took an early morning stroll. Mary will

make sure of that." Ralph sipped his drink and felt unable to contain his curiosity any longer. "What happened? And you can forget the fairy tales."

Her adrenalin started to flow and give strength to her mind and body. Her secret must remain so. "If you don't believe me then tough! Sleep walking is recognised as a medical condition. Nothing strange about it. Surely a practical man like you can understand the syndrome."

"The distance you covered would make the Guinness Book of Records. Where you were found was odd. There used to be cottages there years ago. The ruins were still there when Ted Skinner was a boy. They were burnt out."

Charlotte felt her life-blood drain. Burnt out? Annie and Jim? The children? Dear God! The children! Why was everything dancing in front of her eyes? The table. The ceiling. The man's face. All whirling and merging into one.

"Charlotte? Lottie!" Ralph yelled as he shook the thin frame of the stunned woman. Her eyes were blank. Was it a fit? Shock? His medical knowledge was limited but his next action was out of pure instinct. He slapped the white face hard. As a red weal stained the pale skin the eyes began to focus. It worked. "Back with the living, are we? Come on."

He led the unresisting young woman into the study and sat her on the leather settee. "Put your feet up," he commanded as he poured brandy into a glass. "Drink this. Straight down. That's it. OK, now?"

Charlotte spluttered and coughed after drinking the liquid and her senses returned. "At this rate I'll be an alcoholic! Oh, my God! What the hell do I look like?"

Ralph smiled. "Typical female reaction, what do I look like! You are going to be alright. Want some more coffee? Put your feet up. I'll ring Price so that he can tell Olivia I'm showing you around the Estate so that will give you a few hours breathing space. You are certainly not fit to face the world yet."

Charlotte nodded. "If you would, please. As for the coffee,

make it black, sweet and hot if you don't mind."

As Ralph left the room Charlotte let out a deep sigh. What had he said? The cottages burnt out? She had to find out more and prayed that the cottage was spared. What year was it then? Emily's letter was dated 1920. Daisy was nursing so she must have gone back to the early twenties.

Ralph returned with a tray. "I phoned the House. Apparently Olivia didn't even ask where you were. She went out after breakfast and assumed you were still in bed. Here. Drink this."

Doing as she was bid, Charlotte began to giggle. "You're not exactly the nursing type, are you!"

A glimmer of a smile broke over the weather-beaten face. "The livestock never complain, but I usually smack their rumps not their faces. I hope you realise that it's 8.30 and I haven't started work yet because of you."

Distracted, Charlotte asked, "Olivia went out early, didn't she? Very unusual."

"Not when you consider she was going to London. Catch the 9 o'clock train. She goes twice a year but nobody knows why." Ralph sat on the edge of his chair and clasped his hands together trying to think of the best way to ask questions. His normal bluntness was not easy to override. "You went into another orbit when I told you about those cottages. Why?"

Charlotte wanted so much to tell someone about her travel into the past, about the people she had come to know, about their hardships and happiness. She couldn't. Ralph Nicholls was not exactly the kind of person who would understand. "I....I have this fear of fire. I don't know why. The contents of that old man's flask must have laid bare my phobia."

Eyes narrowing, Ralph shook his head. "Nonsense. You're trying to hide something."

"Like what?" she shouted feeling vulnerable. "I've always been terrified of being trapped in a burning building. I have recurring nightmares about it, even had therapy as a child." Feeling foolish at her outburst she muttered, "Why the hell am I telling you this!"

Ralph rose from his chair and poured himself a brandy. His action puzzled his own mind as he never drank very much, certainly not in the morning. "What about your family? Maybe your mother instilled the fear in you without realising it."

Frowning, she replied quietly, "I doubt it. My mother died when I was two. That just left Dad who died six years later. Why?"

"Just bear with me. Who brought you up? "

"Children's homes until I was eleven, then I passed a Scholarship and entered Girls' School where I stayed until I was 18. My own person from then on."

Ralph sat besides her and looked grave. "Has your problem ever been explained? What about the therapy?"

Feeling embarrassed at using her real phobia as an excuse to explain her behaviour, Charlotte felt cornered. Shaking her head in reply she was afraid of getting in too deep. "The therapy was short-lived. They just said that I had an over-active imagination."

"Well I think I know why you have that fear," the man stated flatly.

"Oh!" the young woman gasped in surprise. "Psychology your hobby is it? Two brief meetings and you can diagnose the cause of my nightmares? Really, Mr. Nicholls. You are wasted as a farm hand."

Looking insulted, Ralph glared at his guest. "Just try listening for once in your life, damn you!" His words had the desired effect as Charlotte slumped back against the arm of the settee and nodded meekly.

"One of the cottages I told you about was home to my Great Uncle, his wife and children. They narrowly escaped with their lives. The eldest girl was staying with her Grandmother but saved them all because she came home on impulse, some unexplained sense of danger. The point is, Lottie, one of the children saved that night was your mother."

122

"What!" Charlotte whispered. "How do you know that? My mother's maiden name was ....was..........Dear God! I don't know her maiden name!"

"Mary Nicholls. She was the daughter of Charlotte Anne Armstrong and James Nicholls. She was trapped by the fire because she was hampered by carrying a baby, her youngest brother. They came to live here after. I know that because I have a personal interest. My Grandfather was James Nicholls's nephew, David, who was also caught up in the fire."

"Annie my Grandmother! They lived here? David was your Grandfather? Well, damn me! Olivia told me that you had looked into the family history but didn't explain why. Another thing she didn't tell me that her sister Charlotte Anne was my Grandmother! Why is she so secretive?"

"Because she likes to have power over people. Leaving you in the dark is her idea of controlling your mind as far as her biased idea of a book goes. Don't you have a Birth Certificate? That would show your mother's maiden name."

"I only got a copy certificate which shows date, name and sex. I can't believe it. Annie and Jim my Grandparents!" Noticing the enquiring look on Ralph's face she covered her familiarity of the ancestors. "Olivia gave me some information when pressed, but it took a while to sort out relationships, at least, I thought I'd sorted them out."

"So," Ralph persisted, "back to last night. Why were you at the site of your Grandparent's home?"

Charlotte's confidence returned with her new-found knowledge. "Like I said, sleep-walking. Perhaps some ghostly force led me there, or to be more realistic it was sheer coincidence. Who knows."

"You do. Ghosts of the past are not to be taken lightly. Be careful, Lottie. Thomas is not the only threat as far as I can see."

"Stop being so melodramatic!" she jeered. "You have solved my irrational fear of fire, told me who my

Grandparents were and generally saved me from an embarrassing situation. Thank you, Ralph. Now I want to go home. Most of my pride has vanished this morning, I will now swallow the last remnants of my pride and ask for a lift home."

Ralph Nicholls took her to Glas Fryn in silence. A curtain had fallen between them. Both knew that more trust was needed before questions would be answered, before they crossed the barrier of true friendship.

The House was quiet. Charlotte went to the kitchen to tell someone she was back. At least she would be left to her own devices, left to think about her outstanding travels and Ralph's revelations. Annie and Jim her Grandparents! Little Mary who nursed the baby was her Mother! It was wonderful yet sad at the same time. It all fitted as she knew her mother was in her mid forties when she was born.

"There you are, Miss Charlotte!" Cissie beamed. "You're getting as bad as that Thomas out at odd hours. Early morning walks are all very well, but the mornings can still be damp. Even in July! It's the mountains, you see, they attract the moisture which seeps down into the valley. You're not used to it, Miss."

Charlotte laughed at the clucking hen. "I'm fine, Cissie. Mind if I make a cuppa? Would you like one?"

Cissie put the kettle on. "Any excuse for me! I'll make it. Even though the old girl is in London for the day I feel her evil eye watching me!"

"Why has she gone to London? Any ideas?"

"No. Wish I had! She's always done it." Cissie commented as she poured the tea, "Got fingers in pies we'll never know about. Here, Miss. Drink this. We're on our own. Mary and Price have gone to town to get the monthly groceries and Thomas hasn't been here since Dinner last night. Even with his arm in plaster he's up to the same tricks."

Charlotte sipped her tea. "What about local gossip? Somebody must know something in a community like this."

Frowning, the plump woman answered. "That's the funny part. Nobody mentions him. He can't be playing about in the village or they'd know. He's devious, but not enough to fleece the local people. No. I think he must have a love-nest somewhere. There's lots of places in the middle of nowhere being rented out in the countryside around. Now with his arm in plaster he'd soon be noticed!"

"Any likely candidates amongst them? Single women, divorced, married even? I doubt he has any moral scruples."

Cissie folded her arms. "Most of them are retired people. Mind you, there's quite a few places called 'holiday homes' in the district. Empty most of the year round and making the locals angry because they can't afford to buy one."

"Oh! I see." Charlotte exclaimed. "You mean Nationalists and the like? Yes. I can see their point, but I don't think raising properties to the ground is the solution." She shivered at the thought. "Arson is a criminal action whatever the reason."

"No! No!" Cissie protested. "That doesn't happen around here! That sort of thing used to go on up North, but they have always been more ....more.......well, fiery - if you pardon the expression!"

"Very witty!" Charlotte laughed. "Still, back to Thomas. Keep your ear to the ground, Cissie."

"Oh, you know me," Cissie giggled. "Always ready for a bit of gossip!"

As Cissie busied herself with her duties Charlotte went to her room hoping to have a nap. That was until she lay on the bed and thought about the knowledge she had gained from Ralph Nicholls. Why didn't Olivia tell her that Annie was her Grandmother? Come to that, why hadn't she ever questioned Olivia on how she was related? Such an obvious question which she'd never pursued. Her mind was in turmoil. Drifting into sleep her body felt as though it was floating. She was not alone in the room. Women were talking, the voices became clearer as did her vision.

"Feeling better today, are we?" the older woman asked brightly.

"Oh yes!" the younger one replied as she sat in front of the dressing-table brushing her long, dark hair. Charlotte knew it was Daisy. Her face was thin with a fine bone structure, her beauty came from within, from the essence of being which radiated an inner serenity. "I think I'll go into the garden this morning. It looks such a lovely day. Have I your permission, Grandmother?" she asked with an impish grin.

The kindly smile which came from the older woman brought her identity to Charlotte in a flash. Sarah Armstrong, Annie and Olivia's mother, her very own Great Grandmother. "I don't see why you can't enjoy this fine weather the Lord bestowed on us. Just as long as you wrap up warm."

Walking to the window, Sarah's face became sad. "How long have you had consumption, child?"

The young face fell. "I should have known better than to come here. I could have gone to a Rest Home and then you wouldn't be any the wiser. Mother and Father have troubles enough at the moment. What happened to Emily and David?"

Sarah frowned. "How did you hear about that in London?"

Daisy laughed. "Believe it or not, one of the patients had a visitor from these parts, a long lost Uncle or something! Anyway, he seemed to know me, I had the strange feeling of knowing him from somewhere, but just can't pinpoint it."

"What was his name? I know most folk around here. I brought most of them into the world!"

Faltering, Daisy replied, "Strange. I haven't got a clue! He just asked my name and we got into conversation. He didn't even ask about his nephew now I come to think about it." She shook her head. "How very odd."

"How did he know your name? What did he look like? The nephew, what was his name?"

Looking perplexed, the young woman dropped her hairbrush and turned to her Grandmother. "I suppose he could have asked any of the nurses or patients what my name was.

As for his nephew, well Peter Drayton was so ill that he was unable to recognise his parents or anyone else. Don't you think it's strange too, Grandmother? It's funny how he told me about Emily, he KNEW we were friends!"

"Sinister would be a better word, dear child. Was he fair, sunburned with a gruff voice?"

"You DO know him!" Daisy exclaimed.

"I'm afraid I do. He's not the class of person you should be associated with. Please, child, if he approaches you again don't have anything to do with him. Would you promise me that?"

"As you say, Grandmother. I..........." the young, luminous face turned white as realisation dawned on her. "He is the man who was watching Emily when we were nursing her Grandma, the man David tried to track down." Her voice dropping to a whisper she concluded, "He must be the man who tried to shoot David. He must be my father."

Sarah waved a dismissive hand. "You are right, my child, but didn't you tell me that Jim was your real father? He was the one who brought you up and loved you? Forget this other person, Daisy. He's trouble. The most important issue is your health. I trust you to keep your promise and leave the Devil to his own!"

"I will," Daisy nodded. "He had such........such......well, his eyes....... " Shuddering, the young woman smiled. "I'll keep my promise Grandmother, never fear."

Taking her granddaughter by the shoulders, Sarah spoke briskly. "What do the doctors' say about your illness? Truth now."

"They said that I was over the worse, but every few months it recurs and I have to rest. I'm strong enough to fight it, Grandmother. It must be the country air I was brought up on! Two of the other girls...........well, they didn't manage to get over it."

"It can be fatal, but it sounds as though you've survived the worse. Does your mother know?"

"No. There's no reason why she should. Dad's on the mend at last and baby Arthur is very demanding! Please, don't add to her burden, please!"

Sarah smiled. "No, child. That I would never do. She's a proud woman and I know how much she has struggled to keep her family fed this last year. For all that the children are a credit to her. Make sure that you get over this, Daisy. We are all very proud of our nurse!"

"I will," Daisy vowed. "Some fresh air would be marvellous! Oh! Could you send young Price over to Emily? If she could visit it would be good to hear the news!"

"Emily's working until 6, but the boy could take the message there though I doubt her Grandmother would pass it on. How the poor girl puts up with that woman I'll never know. When she comes into her inheritance there'll be a different story to tell, mark my words."

"Oh, Grandmother!" Daisy teased. "I do believe you are becoming a gossip!"

"Young lady, if you don't show some respect I'll forbid you going outside this bedroom door for a month!" The gentle smile playing around the lined mouth discounted the threat.

Charlotte opened her eyes to find the room bright with sunlight. It was only twelve and lunch would be ready soon. Better get up and freshen her appearance. As she left the room, Charlotte felt her scalp tingle. She turned to the dressing-table. The thimble. She had travelled back without the thimble. Was time and fate playing tricks with her? Had the strange void of travel overtaken her mind and body to claim her at will?

"Oh, there you are Miss Charlotte." Cissie interrupted her speculation. "Ready for lunch?"

"Yes. Just give me five minutes, please."

Cissie put an arm around the young woman. "What's wrong, love? You look awful. Are you ill? Shall I call the Doctor?"

128

Tears threatened to fall upon the kind words. "No. Thank you, Cissie. I always look dreadful after a nap. Nothing to worry about."

"If you say so. Come down when you're ready." Cissie turned to leave. "I've seen better corpses, and that's a fact!"

As Charlotte washed her face she was shocked when she looked in the mirror. Her face had become gaunt, haunted. Her physical being was affected. Considering the years she'd travelled it was only to be expected, she reasoned. It wouldn't stop her, or judging by the last experience it couldn't be stopped. The past lured her. Her ancestors lured her. For as long as it lasted she would be easy prey.

Lunch was taken with Thomas which certainly didn't help the digestion. Charlotte tried to sound natural, tried to keep her revulsion hidden, but it was the most difficult piece of acting she had to perform in her life. "How is the arm, Thomas? When does the plaster come off?"

"Several weeks yet as a clever girl like you would know." He smiled ingratiatingly. "How is Ralph?"

"Fine," she answered calmly. "Not that you really care."

Thomas laughed. "How could you accuse me of not caring about my own flesh and blood. We share the same grandparents. My mother and his father were brother and sister. First cousins, old Ralphy and I."

"You wouldn't think so!" Charlotte retorted, then changed tack to avoid argument. "How long do you intend staying here? The thesis coming along, is it?"

Thomas wiped his mouth with a napkin whilst glancing slyly at his fellow diner. "I can't possibly work with an arm in plaster, dear girl! I'll be here a while longer thanks to you. Why? Anyone would think you wanted to get rid of me."

Charlotte ignored the jibe. "As long as Olivia doesn't mind you sponging off her, you mean. Where do you go at nights, Thomas?"

The grin faded. "Come with me and find out. As for 'sponging' what about you? Taking a wage off Olivia for the last few months and how far have you got? Nowhere! It sounds as if we have a lot in common, dear girl. Quite a lot! Fate has thrown us together."

"Often fantasise, do you?" Charlotte said as she left the table. "I'm warning you, Thomas Blake, if you try anything with Olivia I'll make sure the whole world knows what kind of swine you are!"

As Charlotte went to her room the bells started ringing in her head. Blake. Blake. Blake! Of course! Daisy's father was Fred Blake, the exiled rapist! The man who returned. Possibly the man who had taken a shot at David and Emily. Fair hair and stockily built. Thomas was the same. Was there a link? Ralph would know, he had traced the family. There was a quicker way. Go back. Return to the past and see the man for herself.

As she reached the top of the stairs the world turned upside down and Charlotte found herself in the garden of Glas Fryn. It was different, yet the same. It was neat, orderly and abundant with colour. She could hear screams.

People were racing past her and she followed. They stopped outside a small pavilion and two men fell out of the door. They were fighting and the small gathering shouted encouragement. One of the men fighting was Jim and he managed to knock his adversary to the ground shouting as he did so. "You dare touch that girl again, and by God I'll kill you Blake!"

The defeated man rose slowly, his nose and mouth bloodied from the affray. "I'll be back, Nicholls, I'll be back! First I'll get your wife then I'll claim my daughter. Hear that? MY DAUGHTER!" With amazing speed he fled but with an entourage led by Jim in hot pursuit.

Charlotte felt sick. The man called Blake was the image of Thomas. He must be an ancestor, must be. With trepidation she watched as Annie led a young girl out of the pavilion holding her tight and trying to comfort her. The victim was Daisy.

Jim returned, red-faced and wheezing. "Got away, Annie love. Daisy, did he hurt you?"

The ashen faced young woman turned to her adoptive father and smiled as best she could. "No, Dad. Thanks to you. He dragged me in there and tried to strangle me, but I've got a good pair of lungs!"

Her grandmother, Sarah, pushed her way through the clutch of servants. "My darling child! What is going on? Annie! Take her to bed. She's just getting over that illness."

Annie cuddled her eldest daughter close. "Can you make it to the house, Daisy? All this after that bout of bronchitis, poor child."

A young girl ran to help. "Auntie Daisy! What happened to you? I only went to get some lemonade, I'm sorry!"

The weak and scratched victim smiled. "It's alright, Livvy. It wasn't your fault. You can take the lemonade up to my room instead."

Jim shook his head as he watched his wife take Daisy back to her room. Turning to his mother-in-law he said quietly, "I'll have a word with Sgt. Hopkins. They need protecting from that madman. He'll not give up."

Sarah Armstrong patted his arm. "You do that, Jim. You do that."

A misty veil clouded Charlotte's sight, the pavilion blurred as did the people. When her vision cleared she was staring at a ruin in the garden. It was in the same spot, but in a different time. Her own time. She was completely alone.

It had happened again. Transported through time without the aid of the little silver thimble. Going back without premeditation. The past was warning her. Fred Blake and Thomas Blake were one and the same person. Danger lurked in the past and still existed in present.

Olivia returned late in the evening with little to say. Thomas stayed home within arm's reach of the brandy decanter in the Lounge whilst Charlotte went to bed to have an early night, but sleep eluded her and the hours dragged as her mind tried to make sense of past and present events.

The clock's illuminated face showed three and Charlotte became aware of a presence in the room. A shape appeared at the side of her bed, it had no substance, it was all grey. An arm reached out as if to touch Charlotte's face, it seemed so near, yet far away. There was no face, just a form. Trying to touch her...... icy slivers ran along her cheek and cold enveloped Charlotte's entire body and froze her very being. Then the vision faded into the cold, dim light of dawn.

Pins and needles scourged her body as she reached for the bedside lamp. She felt no fear. The apparition was not malevolent. The lamp brought a soft, comforting glow to the room as the shadows dispelled and normality returned. Could the ghosts of the past travel to her time? If so, why? A warning? Charlotte found that sleep eluded her as her mind was in turmoil .

Mary came up just before eight with an early morning brew. "Here's your tea, Miss Charlotte. Drink it while it's hot. I thought you might like a lie in after the night before."

"Thanks, Mary. That's very kind of you. Where is Cissie today?"

"Day off. Gone to Eastbridge to her daughter's." Mary sat on the bed as she chatted. "Pity that. She only goes four times a year then they treat her like dirt."

Charlotte raised her eyebrows at the statement. "Why? Cissie is a lovely person!"

Mary nodded. "Very motherly, our Cissie. Trouble is that her daughter married a lawyer and is so busy mixing with the Gentry that she's ashamed of her mother. They got a daughter, twelve she is, takes riding lessons and goes to private school, talks and acts like a right little madam, but Cissie thinks she's wonderful."

"Poor Cissie." Charlotte remarked sympathetically.

Sighing, Mary continued, "She knows that she's an embarrassment to her daughter but nothing will stop her from seeing her only grandchild. Cissie reckons for all the kid's airs and graces she loves her Grandmother. I hope she's right. Cissie was widowed young and worked here ever since. She's got rooms in the far wing. She scrimped and saved to put her girl through University, but after all that her daughter just thinks of her as a skivvy."

"That's dreadful!" Charlotte remarked forcefully. "Is this place Eastbridge far away?"

"No!" answered Mary. "That's the trouble. It's the next village to the east, well it's more like a town now. They bought this cottage and renovated it until it looks more like a modern Manor house now and Cissie is so proud of it! Poor thing." Mary looked downcast for a moment before she asked casually, "By the way, Miss. Were you alright last night? I mean, no more sleep-walking or anything?"

Non-plussed at the change of subject, Charlotte rallied to the question. "Oh! No. What must you think of me? It must be the changes in my life taking their toll or something. I'm sorry if I put you to any trouble, Mary. I appreciated you covering up with Olivia. Thanks for fetching my clothes over too."

"Forget it," Mary replied absently. "Oh yes, the reason I came up. Ralph is downstairs. Do you want to see him? Shall I tell him to hang on?"

"Please. I'll be down in ten minutes."

As the housekeeper left the room Charlotte grabbed her clothes and dressed. Why she hurried she didn't know, but for some strange reason she was happy that Ralph had called. Dashing on a little make-up she made herself presentable before going down.

As she entered the kitchen Ralph and Price were deep in conversation at the table. "They call women gossips," she teased, "just look at the pair of you!"

Price rose from the table looking guilty. "Breakfast, Miss Charlotte?"

Ralph answered for her. "Do some tea and toast for her."

Charlotte rebelled. "How dare you! I never eat breakfast but perfectly able to ask for myself if I need anything."

"Get some food inside you before we go. Next meal will be hours away."

"Go?" the young woman asked. "Go where?"

Looking condescending as he replied, Ralph explained. "I have to go to Cardiff. The Archives Department, interested?"

Despite herself, Charlotte was charged with enthusiasm. "You bet! How long will it take to get there?"

"Under an hour, depending on traffic."

Twenty minutes later they were on their way taking the A roads on their way to the Welsh Capitol. Charlotte enjoyed seeing the rich countryside and villages which were a mixture of quaint and crowded settlements. Rural life and industry swept through the Principality with an amazing degree of versatility which evoked feelings of appreciation, sometimes revulsion, in the young woman.

"Impressed?" Ralph asked breaking the silence as they reached the suburbs.

"Yes. A diverse landscape."

"Farming and heavy industry, both vital to the life-blood of our ancestral land. Somehow they manage to exist side by side. Progress is changing the face of the industrial side to produce a cleaner and safer source of employment in this age of technology. Some old areas have been developed into attractive environments. I suppose we should be grateful."

"You sound resentful?"

"Not really. In the last twenty years some of the changes have been radical, it takes some getting used to. Of course, I could have taken the motorway where there are fewer scars to be seen, but this way is much more interesting."

"From what I can gather the values of the populace are still the same. Take the inhabitants of Pantmawr, they're still a suspicious bunch!"

"The eyes of a stranger sees the truth."

Charlotte frowned. "Is that a quotation?"

Laughter erupted from the sober driver. "Yes. A very famous one! A Ralph Nicholls original."

Appreciating the joke, Charlotte smiled. "So you have got a sense of humour lurking in there somewhere. Is it far now?"

"No. Just through this traffic." His good humour subsided as he glanced at his passenger. "We're making this journey for your sake. Advice from the good servants of Glas Fryn."

"What?"

"They are worried about you. Price was amazed that you didn't know who your family were and suggested a visit to Cardiff. Hopefully we can prove your lineage. A friend of mine is expecting us."

Shaking her head, Charlotte smiled. "Incredible! You discuss me with the servants! Olivia would not be amused or approve of this venture."

"They care. They asked me for help. You look terrible and your condition gets worse by the day. Be gracious enough to accept their kindness, Lottie."

Tears threatened as Charlotte let the words sink in. Had her appearance caused fears for her health? She had been dragged back to the past over the last three months, it must be having an affect on her well-being. Price, Mary and Cissie had noticed. Nobody had ever worried about her before.

Not true. Her father had cared for the short time she had him. Her fiancé had cared but there no-one there to be concerned when she lost her beloved in that distant land. Just a week of compassionate leave to grieve and then return to the harsh world. The words of her colleagues were mere sympathetic noises, polite sentences devoid of feeling. It was an emotional shock to learn that people REALLY cared about you.

CHAPTER 8

Accidents & Designs

A young man greeted Ralph with an easy familiarity as they entered the impressive city Archives department. "Hello there! Come through. I've put all the relevant documents on the desk to save you time. How are things in Eastbridge these days? Same as usual?"

Ralph chatted with social ease as they were led to a quiet office. Ensconced with files and plastic coffee cups they were left to peruse at their leisure. Ralph was worried about the pinched face sitting besides him, but detached himself and turned to the matter in hand. "That's all the documentary evidence on record about Glas Fryn. Not quite your ancestry on a plate but it should help."

"I thought you said you had business here?"

"I have. The business of proving your forbearers. There's a photocopier over there, take copies and study them at your own pace. Parents, grandparents, whatever. If you need anything else just give Paul a shout."

"Why are you doing this?" Charlotte asked bemused.

Ralph shrugged. "It seems scandalous that you came here blind to your family ties. Olivia might had held back for ulterior motives, perhaps out of shame, who knows? Whatever the reasons you should be acquainted with the facts. I'll leave you here for an hour or so," he nodded, "I really do have some business whilst I'm in the city."

"Suits me. I won't even notice you've gone with this lot to go through!"

As Ralph left he had a quick word with Paul to stay close to Charlotte then made his way to a solicitor's office where he was received warmly. "Ralph! Good to see you! You look fit and well, travel must suit you."

"How is that sister of mine? Still spending all your money?

It's the reason Jo married you, do you know that!"

"Oh yes, she has proved the fact often enough. She's in York for the week with an old University friend and staying in the most expensive hotel, of course." The words were spoken light-heartedly by the solicitor.

Ralph smiled. His sister enjoyed life to the full with no expense spared whilst her husband revelled in his work. The result was a very happy marriage between two people who understood and tolerated each other to extremes through love and trust. "You should have gone with her, you could do with a break, or is such a suggestion heresy?"

"At the moment it would spell ruin," came the sober reply. "My partner has decided to emigrate to America. He spent a holiday there and reckons he could make a fortune out of libel suites and retire within five years! Anyway, enough of my problems, what about you? I've hit a brick wall so far. Any further developments your end?"

Ralph sat in the chair opposite his brother-in-law and became thoughtful. "When I got back someone had been through my Study. Mary Price had a key at Glas Fryn and our friend happened to be on the scene a week before me. I think his timing was more than chance. You know Mary, she's frightened of taking so much as a biscuit for fear of being branded a thief, so she is out of the picture." the Estate Manager paused, clasped his hands together and continued in a lower tone. "Olivia has taken on a young woman to write up the local history of Glas Fryn. Not just anyone, one of Olivia's ideas and a strange co-incidence."

Brian, the solicitor, frowned. "A likely candidate for the Estate?"

Nodding, Ralph looked grave. "The only candidate in terms of family connection. Annie's granddaughter, no less!" A smile crept across the lean features as he recounted the incident which resulted in Thomas's injured arm. "She stands up to the old lady too! In fact, Olivia revels in the situation by taking Thomas's side and causing friction. It could have repercussions, dangerous consequences."

The solicitor leaned forward over the cluttered desk. "What about Jarvis? Has he come up with anything?"

"Nothing. I've got Price on the look-out at Glas Fryn but he says that Lottie is guarded as far as he's concerned, but there again she's the same with me. Wary of everyone. Do you know, Brian, she didn't even know her mother's maiden name or how she was related to Olivia. She acts strangely at times."

"Well, one thing I know," Brian smiled. "She's caught your interest. The way you are talking about her. Personal feelings clouding the issue maybe?"

Ignoring the innuendo, Ralph wavered before replying. "Something is wrong, Brian. She looks.. looks...... haunted for want of a better word. My senses tell me that she's in danger. Not only that but she's the image of .... " Ralph stopped short and hunched his angular shoulders. "Forget it. As for personal feelings you can tell that sister of mine that once bitten twice shy! Never again. I'm a bachelor for life, that I promise."

"Pity," Brian replied despondently. "If Jo thought that there was a sniff of romance in the air she would be back like a shot."

"I know," Ralph confirmed with humour. "Not to mention spending even more of your money! Back to the matter in hand, Brian. Keep digging, time is our only ally in this. We have to protect out interests."

Charlotte was delighted that she had documentary evidence of her ancestry. A good background to the story of the House and a collection of certificates which answered some questions. By the time Ralph returned she was hungry and feeling good. By agreement they stopped for Fish and Chips on the return journey. "Great! Oh, how I've missed this!" Charlotte exclaimed as they ate their lunch in the Land Rover. "Mary's cooking is really good, but I've missed the simple things like this."

"Did you live on your own before you came here?"

"Yes. Why?"

"No reason."

"Every question has a reason," Charlotte retorted. "Do you know who Emily was? Any ideas?"

Ralph looked shocked and asked tersely, "Where did you pick that name up?"

Smiling, the young woman read his reaction. "You DO know who she is! Tell me and I'll tell you if it makes sense."

"Childish!" Ralph denounced.

"So you never play games, I suppose? Even verbal sparring is a game and you played that one with Thomas. You won, as I remember."

The Estate Manager conceded. "Ok, Ok, clever lady. Emily was the name of my Grandmother. Her maiden name was Blake, does that make any sense?"

"Did she live locally?"

"Yes, in Eastbridge. Now tell me how you found the name. It wouldn't come up in research you did today."

"A letter in a Bible. My grandmother's Bible to be exact but I didn't realise that at the time, of course. It was presented to her, Charlotte Anne also known as Annie, by her grandmother. I found it in the library."

"What did the letter say?"

"Oh, it was just a sort of 'Thank You' message really. It also mentioned a David and something about a mystery man. Fascinating, isn't it!"

Ralph nodded. "David was the name of my Grandfather. Could I see this letter? It's becoming very personal."

Charlotte hesitated. For some strange reason she wanted to keep everything to herself, all the characters, the incidents and drama. How could she tell the man besides her she had actually seen his grandparents? That she had seen the Doctor dress the wounds of David whilst Emily was accusing a long-lost Uncle of attempted murder? No. She could never tell anyone about her travels into those past lives. It was too late to cover up the letter, but very little could be gained from that scrap of paper. "Yes, yes of course. It would be far more interesting to you because of your family connections."

"So why the big decision?"

"Sorry?"

Ralph hit the steering wheel with his hand. "Goddammit, woman! Something is going on! I could see your brain ticking over, what are you into?"

The young woman's eyes grew dark, the brown turning to the black of her hair. "Just take me home and I'll give you the letter. You know damn well that I'm trying to do some research for Olivia and I was wondering if the letter would be vital to the work, that's all! Have you got nothing better to do than look behind every word, every sentence?"

Ralph started the vehicle and lurched the Land Rover into motion. "You got a problem, lady! Only guilty people analyse every question or remark."

Charlotte felt the truth hit home. He was right. She was becoming neurotic and feeling threatened by innocent remarks. Were these the first sign of madness?

Ralph dropped her at the gates of Glas Fryn looking murderous, his austere face a mask of loathing. As soon as the passenger alighted and slammed the door shut the vehicle screeched off. "Pompous ass!" she shouted after the cloud of dust. "Very macho! Tearing off like a petulant youth!" Realising that talking to herself confirmed her suspicions she scurried into the house for sanctuary.

It was already four in the afternoon and Charlotte actually relished the idea of afternoon tea with Olivia. At least that old lady brought you to your senses, she smiled. As she reached the stairs Mary Price rushed through the hall from the kitchen. "Miss Charlotte! Wait a minute." Mary approached looking grave and twisting her hands in nervous anticipation. "I'm afraid we had a little accident whilst you were out. It's Madam. She fell."

"Is she alright?" gasped Charlotte in alarm, "What happened?"

Mary rushed to put a hand on the guest's arm. "Don't worry, Charlotte. She's only twisted her ankle but at her age we can't be too careful."

"Quite," Charlotte affirmed. "Where did she fall?"

"In the garden. The Doctor's been, we called him straight away. Good thing Thomas was there at the time, she could have been there for a while!"

"Thomas!" Charlotte barked. "What has he got to do with this?"

Mary looked pleadingly at her inquisitor. "They were walking in the garden together, down by the old Summer House. She slipped on the steps apparently."

"And he just happened to be around! Huh!" Charlotte shouted, "Don't you find that a strange coincidence, Mary? The old girl may use a walking-stick for effect, but her pins are sound!"

Mary shook her head. "We can all slip and fall. Please, calm down or she'll hear you. Nothing wrong with her ears, we know that!"

Sighing deeply to regain her composure, the guest agreed. "Right. Is she in bed?"

"Yes. Go on up and I'll bring tea for both of you."

As the housekeeper turned away Charlotte felt guilty at her outburst. "Mary, sorry I yelled. It wasn't you I was getting at."

"I know that," Mary answered softly and left.

Charlotte climbed the stairs feeling concerned and anxious over the welfare of the old lady. Was her reaction a statement of emotion? Psychiatrists would say so without doubt. She entered the darkened bedroom tentatively.

"Come in, child. Open those dammed curtains will you! It's like the Black Hole of Calcutta in here!"

Laughing with relief, the young woman did as she was bid. "I think you were supposed to be resting, Aunt! Been falling for a younger man from what I hear?"

The July sun streamed into the room and accentuated the white face of Olivia. "Sit down and stop being so ridiculous! Where have you been? I didn't see you this morning."

"Out with Ralph. I want to know what happened to you before you start pumping me. Come on, truth!"

Olivia let her head drop back on the pillows. "I merely slipped on the step by the old Summer House. So stupid! I walk round that way every day and know the garden blindfold, it's only a shallow step and I was just about to.................. " a puzzled expression left her with words hanging in the air until she shook her head and resumed talking. "I tell you what, young lady, lying on the grass at my age is neither comfortable nor elegant!"

"Thomas was with you. Did he....well, distract you?"

"Odd." Olivia muttered as a thought suddenly struck her. "Very odd. Years ago........ " she trailed off much to her audience's frustration.

Charlotte persisted. "What was odd? You look perplexed. Did something happen there before? Think back, perhaps when you were a child?"

Mary arrived with the tea and Olivia took full advantage of the intrusion. "At last. Just because I'm confined to bed for a few days there will be no malingering, girl! Do you hear me?"

Mary Price smiled. "We wouldn't dare, Madam! Try and eat something."

Olivia laughed aloud. "I could eat a horse! Fancy sandwiches, eh! I hope you got something decent for Dinner because these will hardly fatten me. I missed lunch through that half-soaked Doctor. The time he took you'd think I'd suffered multiple fractures not a twisted ankle."

As Mary left, her face impassive, Charlotte reprimanded her Aunt. "It's a wonder they put up with you. Your difficult enough at the best of times, as an invalid you're unbearable!"

Olivia smiled mischievously. "In that case nobody will keep me here longer than necessary, will they."

"Wicked woman!" Charlotte laughed. "I bet you were hell

as a child! Speaking of which, I asked you a question. You can't distract me, I've been trained to notice the slightest details such as the raising of an eyebrow, the twitch of an eye and deliberate attempts to change the subject. The Summer House, was it used when you were young?"

"I think so. Can't really remember. It was just a vague recollection of something happening years ago, but it's gone. Very odd. I expect it was because my Mother always told us to keep away from there as it would be an ideal hiding place for travellers and tramps." The wrinkled face set into a picture of stubbornness. "You know, I think this is all a ruse to prevent me from asking where you have been today! You should feel guilty leaving your frail old Aunt without notice."

Laughing, Charlotte remarked, "Frail, my foot! I'll tell you where I've been today. Cardiff. Ralph took me to the Archives Department and I learned some very interesting facts."

"Oh!" Olivia uttered in surprise. "I hope it will contribute to the book. You haven't got very far, have you."

"Probably because you've been hiding the truth, Aunt. Why didn't you tell me that Charlotte Anne, the sister you scorned, was my Grandmother?"

The old woman looked visibly shaken. "Ralph told you, no doubt. I thought it strange that you appeared to be ignorant of your relationship within the family, but thought it wise to leave skeletons in cupboards."

Amazed at her assumptions, Charlotte stood up and folded her arms. Pacing the room to control her temper, she spoke sharply. "I am not a skeleton am I? I think it's more a case of shame as far as you're concerned! I was an orphan at the tender age of eight, but you buried my existence until you needed me for your own ends. You reasoned that a poor relation would obey your every command and consider it a privilege to live in this dusty old place under your regime. You hoped that paying me a salary would quell any rebellion against your outdated life style and also ease your conscience in the bargain. Sorry, Olivia, but years of neglect cannot be bought and paid for like one of your charities."

"Huh!" the elder woman exclaimed as she sat upright in her bed. "Neglect, eh! That's how little you know, Charlotte. Just like your Grandmother, jumping to your own version of the truth."

Standing still, the young woman looked sceptical. "So give me your story then. Tell me how you tried to find me for over twenty years before you stumbled across my whereabouts just when you needed someone to work for you! This should be good."

"Right!" Olivia nodded. "Sit down, please." Once the deed was done she continued, "When your mother died I offered your father a home here where you could grow up with your Grandmother. She was an invalid and blind, but we nursed her until her death. Your father refused. He said he had plans to emigrate and give you both a new start and refused point blank to even let you have a holiday here. It was two years before I learned of his death, so I found out where you were and made sure you went to the private school for girls. It was agreed that they cared for you in every way."

It was Charlotte's turn to be shaken. "But I won a scholarship!"

"An arranged scholarship, yes. I was pleased to hear that you passed their standard regardless. Where do you think the money for the uniform came from? The trips abroad? Your upkeep during the school holidays? It was not a charitable institution, child."

"My God!" the young woman gasped, "you've engineered my life! Why didn't you make yourself known to me?"

"Because you had very proud parents. I respected your father's wishes to leave you alone. He cut himself off from the outside world once your mother had passed away. Your Grandmother asked me to watch over you, nothing more. Just watch over you."

Arms clutched around her body, the great-niece was dumbstruck. "I just can't believe I'm hearing this. My life being observed, reported back to you. It's incredible."

Shaking her head, Olivia looked sad. " No, no, no! It wasn't like that. The Solicitors took care of the finance and I only heard brief details and actually lost track when you left college. It was quite a task finding you again." The light blue eyes were watery as she said softly, "I confess that had you been settled with a family of your own you wouldn't have heard from me. I would have been content to let you go."

"It's still cruel, you would have denied me the knowledge of my roots. To know where you belong counts for a lot."

Olivia smiled warmly. "You really feel that? That you belong here at Glas Fryn?"

Pausing for serious consideration, Charlotte felt her anger dispel. "Yes. I think I do." Sitting on the edge of the bed she clasped her Aunt's hand. "Why did you put Annie down when I asked about her before?"

"Truth? She was happy, as simple as that. I suppose I've always been a jealous old cat! She had her man, I didn't get the chance because fate took mine away from me. Annie knew all that and still she always forgave me for my behaviour." Falling back onto the pillows, she sighed deeply. "Enough now, child. I'm very tired. Come and see me in the morning. Please?"

"Of course, it will give me chance to digest things. Do you need anything?"

"Not now. There are errands I wish you to carry out tomorrow if you would. Goodnight child."

As Charlotte went to her room many thoughts crowded her head. All her life she had managed to struggle and gain her freedom and independence through hard work and determination. She had never questioned the fact that everything was provided in the school. She had assumed that the holidays were earned through merit, the clothes by a scholarship grant. Her life had been a lie, she had been financed by a woman who provided everything except the obvious. Loneliness was the hardest thing to cope with.

It was 7.30 in the evening before Charlotte emerged from her room and went down to the kitchen only to interrupt the preparation of the evening meal. Price, Mary and Cissie stopped their chores as if struck by lightning. "What's wrong with you lot?"

Cissie looked at the Prices' before speaking. "Is Madam alright? She hasn't taken a turn for the worse has she?"

"You must be joking! Starving, yes! Better put your skates on, slackness will not be tolerated, you know!"

Mary Price nodded solemnly and pointed to a tray which had been set for the invalid. "It will be served at eight o'clock prompt, Miss. Would you like to dine with her?"

Charlotte laughed, "Hell's Bells! I was only joking, but you are serious, aren't you. Why are you calling me 'Miss' again? I thought we sorted that out!" The perplexed look on their faces was amusing.

Price gave a slight bow before coming to the defence of his daughter. "It's only proper, Miss Charlotte. In Madam's absence we will now take instruction from you. We respect your position."

"Position? What 'position'? I'm paid like the rest of you! I was hoping that I could eat with you tonight."

"Cissie!" Mary took command, "Finish the tray and take it upstairs while I lay an extra place at the kitchen table."

The order was carried out by a very happy, bouncing Cissie. It was Price who had the strangest reaction. He grinned and nodded as he watched the two young women, muttered and clucked as he opened the bottle of wine. Charlotte was fascinated and utterly foxed.

The meal was eaten around the scrubbed top table in an enjoyable atmosphere. Cissie prattled on about the people they knew whilst Price interjected with dry, amusing remarks. As they ended their meal and Cissie cleared the table she continued to talk, "Now for a nice cup of tea. I wonder where that scoundrel has got to? He soon shot off, didn't he! I find the whole thing suspicious. Didn't I tell you so, Mary? The old girl is as firm as a rock on her legs, she walks that way nearly every day in the fine weather."

"Accidents can happen anytime," Mary reasoned. "I'm always tripping over things and I'm only thirty!"

Price nodded and reached for his jacket hanging over the back of his chair. He took out a packet of cigarettes and lit one with immense relief. "That's right. Trip over a matchstick would Mary ever since she was walking."

Charlotte clapped her hands with joy. "You're smoking, Price! I've been here months and never knew!"

"Oh dear!" the manservant sighed. "Sorry, Miss............ Charlotte. If it offends you......"

"Only if you don't give me one!"

"You smoke?" Mary asked incredulously.

"Yes, occasionally, that is when under stress. Today has been very trying."

"So Ralph told you then?" Price asked as he offered the packet and struck a match.

"Yes." Charlotte confirmed as she paused to light the cigarette. "You knew? Of course. Servants hear and know everything, don't they."

Cissie plonked a tea-tray down on the table and frowned. "Excuse me for being so dim, but what is going on?"

Price stood and waved a hand towards Lottie. "Something you don't know, Mrs. Jenkins! This is the granddaughter of Charlotte Anne Nicholls, nee Armstrong who was Olivia's sister nonetheless! I said she was back and I was right!"

"So that's what you've been rambling on about!" Mary said surprised. "You and Ralph knew? That's why you suggested the trip to Cardiff?"

"Yes." Price smiled. "I didn't have any facts but once I seen her I just knew that Annie was back!"

Charlotte felt frightened but couldn't explain why. "What do you mean, 'she's back'? I don't look like her, I'm not even like her in my ways so what made you say that?"

Price blanched. "How do you know ...... has Ralph shown

you the photographs?"

Realising she had said too much about Annie, Charlotte covered herself. "Olivia has shown me some snaps......... what photographs?"

"Oh, I've never seen them myself," Price looked sheepish, "but I remember Annie. You have her ways and stand up to Olivia like she did, that's a fact."

Charlotte was captivated. "Did you know my parents?"

"Your mother as a child, yes. She went to London into service, most girls did in those days. She married and stayed away. After your mother died Annie sent word to fetch you back, but your father never answered a letter or ever came near here. A broken man, by all accounts."

"He didn't last long," Charlotte said quietly, "I wish he had brought me back here. From the records Annie died in 1970, so I could have known her. My Grandmother, that is."

Price shook his head. "She went a few months before your father. She died here."

"Which was her room?" Charlotte asked .

"The one you are sleeping in, Miss."

A shudder ran through her body as the connection between her and the past became clear. "Tell me, was she sound in her mind when she died?"

"As lively as ever! At 85 she could think things out quicker than Olivia who was 20 years younger." Price laughed pleasantly. "She would tell us stories about her life as if things happened only yesterday, an amazing memory. Her spirit never wavered and it was her strength which carried her through the hard times, some very hard times."

Mary nodded. "Ralph could tell you about the lean years, about families starving and men fighting through hunger and frustration. No industry, you see."

"Not everyone suffered!" Cissie snorted, "The likes of Her Ladyship always had butter on their bread."

Price waved a hand. "Now, now! Our Lady up there merely followed the path life set for her. Annie took her own direction but became far richer in her way. She had love and happiness deep in her soul."

Charlotte felt moved. "What a lovely thing to say!"

Price patted the young woman's hand, his skeletal face glowing as he recounted the woman of the past. "My father idolised her and I grew up doing the same. In her younger days she loved riding and if she heard the hunting-horn she'd drop everything and follow the Hunt. She even took one of her babies once wrapped Welsh Fashion in a shawl!"

"Is that really true or are you embroidering fact?" Charlotte asked flippantly.

Chuckling to himself, Price challenged, "Ask Olivia! She was disgusted."

Cissie laughed. "Well I never! She'd be had up for cruelty these days. Mind you, Welsh Fashion the baby would be safe as houses, pity they don't do that these days."

Before Cissie carried on with her opinions, Mary shot her a glance which stopped the flow. Charlotte didn't notice as she was spellbound with this man who knew the people she had seen in the past. "Do you remember her mother? Sarah?"

"Oh, yes! Even though I was just a lad when she died, mind. Been a midwife all her life and never took a penny for her services. Old Dr. Sam would tease her about it. Annie learned a lot from her mother about herbs and suchlike, the old Doctor often found his patient cured before he got there!"

Mary was watching Charlotte and felt uneasy at the look on her face. Her eyes were glowing out of a stark white face and it didn't seem natural. "You didn't know anything until today?" she asked quietly.

Charlotte didn't hear the question. Her Grandmother had drawn her back through her spirit which had never left the house. Price had known her, talked to her, a tangible link. "You must remember my Grandfather, James."

Whilst Cissie and Mary exchanged worried glances, Price was only too ready to continue his nostalgic trip. "Yes, he died five or six years before her. They were devoted. He was quiet and gentle and always had time for people. Like a Pied Piper to children he was. Annie reckoned he had never grown up himself!"

The plump servant patted Charlotte's hand, "Are you alright, love? You're white as a sheet. Have another cup of tea, it must be the shock of hearing about your family, I suppose."

Making a great effort to quell her eagerness for information, Charlotte nodded. "Yes, its been quite a surprising day. Olivia told me this afternoon that she paid for all my education and kept track of me all those years and there was me thinking I'd done it all on my own. I would like another cup of tea, please Cissie."

Mary frowned, "You mean she knew about you and never contacted you until a few months ago? Huh ! Pity she didn't leave Thomas where he was! He's not even directly related to her."

"What IS his connection?" the young woman asked intrigued.

"Well Ralph could best explain that, but I gather the Blake family fortune should have been his Grandmother's but she was cheated out of it by her Uncle. Whatever, it ended up with Thomas's side instead."

"Ralph's Grandmother?" Charlotte asked feeling elated, "That must have been Emily. He told me that today."

Shaking her head, Mary replied, "I haven't got a clue! Why? Do you know the story?"

"Oh no!" Charlotte said airily as she thought of a reason, "Just pieces of a jig-saw. Olivia drops snippets of information here and there and I'm trying to make a complete picture."

Cissie looked towards Price, "Wasn't there something funny about Thomas as a boy? I know her Ladyship took him in because all his family had died."

Price nodded. "He was one of twins. I remember their mother fell from a cliff when the family were on holiday, she died two weeks later without ever regaining her senses. Madam was most upset."

Charlotte gasped, "You mean there's two of him! God help us!"

"Was." Price said grimly. "His brother Charles died six months after the mother, he was sick and choked in bed. A week or so after that his father had a fatal heart attack so Thomas lost his entire family in six months."

"Somehow I can't find any sympathy for him," the young woman stated coldly. "How old was he when all this happened?"

"Oh, I remember that alright. He was twelve and Olivia brought him here after his father's funeral. He was a right little trouble-maker but we were told to be lenient with him due to the loss of his parents and brother."

"So, Olivia took him under her wing at that tender age." Charlotte remarked cynically.

"No!" Price said emphatically. "His Uncle Alan turned up, his mother's brother, he's a Doctor with a practice in Cumbria. Although he was single he said that he had made arrangements to look after the boy and would make sure he had a decent education."

"Was this Uncle after the family fortune?" Charlotte asked.

Price looked surprised. "Certainly not. Alan Nicholls is a genuine man, even Olivia liked him. No. He took the boy on as a sense of duty. The only other family were Ralph's parents and they were struggling to make ends meet."

"This Alan Nicholls," Charlotte questioned, "Is he still alive?"

"Yes. Must be in his sixties now. He used to come here occasionally, but it's been years now."

"But Thomas kept turning up like a bad penny! Shame." Pausing as her mind worked, the guest wondered, "Are you sure Thomas didn't bump his family off to get the inheritance?"

Price compressed his lips, then shrugged his shoulders. "I'll tell you this, Miss Lottie, its crossed my mind often enough, Ralph's too. Don't forget, they were his family as well and he can remember it all."

"This conversation is becoming sinister." Mary said quietly. "We know Thomas is no saint, but heaven forbid! A murderer at the age of twelve! Dad, you should know better than to go saying such things."

Charlotte agreed. "You're right, Mary. Sorry, my imagination making much out of nothing. Still.............." she mused, "funny about Olivia slipping........."

Cissie rose from the table and groaned. "I know one thing, age is the biggest enemy of all! My legs are playing me up something rotten. The sooner Her Ladyship's out of her bed the better."

"Can I help you with the dishes?" Charlotte volunteered.

"No, indeed!" Mary ordered. "Cissie, you can finish now and go and put your feet up. It's won't take me long to clear up. You go on up to bed, Miss............. I mean, Charlotte. No sleepwalking!"

Charlotte smiled and nodded. "Ok. I'll check Olivia before I turn in. Goodnight all."

Olivia was sleeping soundly, so Charlotte gratefully crept to her room. After a token wash she hastily changed into her night-shirt and snuggled into the comfortable bed. As she put off the lamp she smiled and stroked the quilt. Annie had made it. Her Grandmother had painstakingly stitched the colourful design which now comforted her unknown grandchild.

Time had a funny way of transmitting hope and affection. Mulling over the chat that evening she wondered at the strange tale of Thomas. Perhaps losing his family so quick at the tender age of twelve had turned his mind. There again, it might have been his desire to become undisputed heir to the Blake family fortune. How much of a fortune was there? She must ask Ralph, he would have clear ideas on the subject. Trouble was, it would also cloud his judgement having a personal tie. Sleep stole upon her with death and innuendo playing on her mind.

CHAPTER 9

The Long Dark Hours

Sleep came quickly and deeply. Charlotte had been utterly weary, her body feeling strained and aged. There was no urge to travel back, nothing calling her into the past, just a physical and mental need for rest and contemplation.

A sound woke her up with a start in the dark, velvety night. It sounded very close. The luminous hands of the clock showed the time as 2 am and she turned achingly in her bed trying to shut out the outside world.

Scraping. Something was being dragged across the floor above her head. Giving up the comforting warmth of the bed she went to the window. A light shone from the upper floor to throw its glare onto the garden as it did before.

'I'll catch you this time, old boy!' she whispered to herself as she slipped on her dressing-gown and grabbed the hockey stick. This time she knew where the attic entrance was so she gingerly crept along the corridor praying that Olivia wouldn't hear her. Reaching the door to the upper floor she fumbled for the knob and cursed herself for not having a torch. Locating the knob, she turned it carefully but as she pulled the door towards her the old hinges squeaked and sounded like high-pitched screams in the silent house.

Listening with baited breath, Charlotte hesitated. Nothing happened. A black void lay ahead. With one hand she held her defensive weapon in readiness whilst the other clung to the left-hand wall. Shuffling slowly forward until her slipper came against the first riser of the stairs she said a silent prayer.

Tentatively, she began her ascent. The stairs creaked and it was icy cold. The intruder must be able to hear her, she reasoned, but all around was silence and complete darkness. She reached the landing area and smiled as the cloudy sky relented and moonlight illuminated her surroundings. Watching and listening she paused. Nothing. No sign of an intruder. He must have heard her coming and switched the light off. Perhaps there was another way out ....

Her contemplation was sharply interrupted by a door on her right swinging open. Gasping in shock, Charlotte waited. Something human had pushed the door, not some ghastly spectre, so she clenched the hockey stick with both hands in readiness. Silence.

Getting impatient with the game she held her weapon high and charged through the open doorway yelling as she did so. Something hit her across the lower abdomen and she thrashed wildly with her weapon. The door slammed shut and a click echoed in the night. As her eyes became accustomed to the natural moonlight shining through the large windows she saw that she had been attacking a large table.

She had run straight into the table whilst the human element has escaped through the door. To confirm her fears, Charlotte threw herself at the exit with all her strength to gain freedom, but the stout door was locked. She had fallen into a trap. She could hear footsteps walking across the landing and down the stairs to confirm her foolhardy escapade. "Thomas!" she yelled, "I know its you. Thomas!" Silence.

'Bloody hell! I'm an idiot!' she chided herself. Coming up here alone, a totally stupid thing to do. Thomas's veiled threats when they had confrontations were ringing in her ears and brought her to stark reality. It must have been him. Noises right above her room, luring her up here knowing full well she would rise to the bait. How could she prove it? No. He was too clever for that.

Taking stock of her situation she knew it would be daylight before she could possibly gain freedom. Looking around the room all she could make out was the dark shapes of furniture against the walls. Sitting on the bare boards she leaned against a wall and buried her face in her hands. It would be a long, cold night. Why, oh why, didn't she stay in her cosy bed?

"You know Grandmother Sarah sent us up here out of the way whilst she entertains her dear, stuck-up daughters! Honestly, the way they act you would think it was 1824 not 1924!"

Blinking and shaking her head, Charlotte looked up to see an orderly room with two young women sitting at the table. It was daytime and sunlight streamed through the window.

"Don't be like that, Daisy. Your Grandmother is very proud of you, and they are your Aunts after all. Anyway, I'd rather be up here out of the way than sit drinking tea and trying to be polite."

Daisy smiled. "Yes. You're so right, Emily. I'm being spared the third degree, I suppose. Aunt Elizabeth and Aunt Isobel are so stuck-up! Same old questions and remarks. 'What have you been doing, Daisy? Isn't nursing such hard work, and one has to perform tasks which must be extremely offensive to one.' "

Both girls fell into fits of laughter as Daisy had mimicked her relations. "I should be grateful really. They are always very nice to me, even if they look down their noses at my mother. Olivia is very sweet, maybe because she is only two years younger than me. We are more like sisters. She's courting now, by the way."

The fair headed girl nodded. "Yes, it's quite serious so I hear! Like David and myself. I can't bear to think if I had lost David when .... well, when he was shot. I know that was 3 years ago in 1921 and Uncle Fred disappeared after that because Sgt. Hopkins was looking for him but I heard he has returned again now."

Daisy banged the table with her fist. "Oh, Emily! I feel so frightened. Why did he have to come back?"

"Your father? Natural father I should say." Emily shrugged her shoulders. "I wish I knew the answer to that. I think he's broke and only came back to get money from my father again. That's why he wants me out of the way so he can inherit the lot."

"Never!" Daisy answered incredulously. "Your Grandmother would protect you surely? You father's business can't be worth that much anyway can it?"

"Oh no?" Emily retorted. "What about my mother's dowry? The money and property which amounted to twenty five thousand pounds? None of it has been touched! My father owns hotels and his business is thriving," she paused looking sad, "as for my Grandmother, she's always favoured her eldest son. He can do no wrong in her eyes."

"What! The fact he's a rapist and an exile who has the gall to return and try to shoot you. Is she blind to all that!"

"She doesn't believe my story, she says that I'm the wicked one by trying to turn everyone against him."

Daisy looked incredulously at her friend. "Your father must have made a Will so you're bound to get everything when he dies. What has he got to say about all this?"

Shaking her fair head, Emily confided in her counterpart. "My father is a drunkard, Daisy. It started when my mother died as he felt she had betrayed him. I'm the image of her and he hates me, says that I will betray him too. Grandmother says that she'd put me out on the street if I didn't work for a living. Do you know what, Daisy? I am waiting at tables and serving men who my parents entertained as guests! I know them by name, sat with them at the Dinner Table as a child!"

Daisy gasped in horror. "Do any of them recognise you?"

"No! Waitress are like servants, they never have faces, not counted as people. So, at least I am spared the humiliation of being known."

"Oh, poor Emily!" Taking her friend's hand, Daisy said softly, "You have David, he loves you. If he follows my Dad, and I mean Jim Nicholls, the man I call my proper Dad, you'll do well to marry him. Have faith, dear Emily. All will be well."

Emily laughed loud and harshly. "If I marry David then I am in breach of my Faith. I am a Catholic, don't forget, David is a Protestant. I will be completely disowned."

"Things are different now, it's 1924!"

"My Grandmother would use that to play on my father and make certain that I am exiled and her dear Fredrick inherit. Since Papa is drunk most of the time I know he would go along with her."

"But this is dreadful!" Daisy condemned. "You must fight it. Fredrick Blake has attacked both of us, remember, besides his earlier crimes something must be done!"

Emily looked resigned. "There's no proof, is there? No, Daisy. I'll marry David Nicholls, money or not, Faith or not. Your mother married Jim who was penniless and they have never regretted it. Neither will I. I love him. There has been little love in my life to date, so it is worth forsaking everything to be happy."

The dark-haired young woman let the tears slide down her cheeks. "That's what counts, Emily. Marry my cousin, David. Find joy. You are both very dear to me."

The vision faded and darkness clouded the scene. Daisy and Emily had returned to their time, their problems, their loves and lives. Charlotte Stone was trapped in the attic of Glas Fryn.

The creaks and strains of the old house echoed through the cold and dusty attic rooms, draughts came from every direction whining eerily as they crept through cracks and crevices. It was July, but even so a biting chill emanated from the thick stone walls in the deep of the night.

Shivering in her cotton dressing-gown she paced the room and huddled her arms about her body to keep the warmth from escaping. Even though she had travelled back to the past without any dread, the cheerless room made her skin prickle with ghostly fear.

'I wonder what time it is?' she asked aloud, 'must be about three by now. What time does Price get up? Six thirty, seven?' At the thought of at least three and a half to four hours stranded in the attic Charlotte felt close to tears.

She slumped on the floor facing the windows so that she would catch the first sight of a welcome dawn, watching as the moon dipped in and out of clouds like a mischievous being. One minute it would shine fully into the room to give relief to the deserted soul only to disappear instantly and thus alarm and perturb the mind.

Charlotte tried to be logical. How would they know where to find her? Who would dream of looking up here? If Cissie or Mary found her room empty they would assume she gone for an early morning walk, there would be no hue and cry. They might even wonder if she had gone sleep walking again, but a search would not lead them to the top of the house.

Fighting back the despair, she let her mind wander over events since she came to this place, the place where her family began, the place where they lived and died. Died. Her mind raced. Where were they buried? She would have to visit the graveyard. Ralph would take her there.

What about Thomas? What did he hope to gain by locking her up? It must have been him! Was she asking him too many questions? What did he get up to around these parts? Out all hours, it must be some scam to keep him at Glas Fryn. When she got out of here she would investigate with more determination than ever, dig up the dirt on him. She had watched the methods of her journalistic friends target someone who appeared respectable and legitimate, but a careless word or deed would open a crack in the watertight reputation, a crack which would be examined deeper and deeper to reveal a scoundrel of some degree.

'I can do it! I will do it!' she chanted to herself and other words spilled out as though she were delirious. 'Fredrick Blake terrorised Annie and Daisy, even his own flesh and blood, Emily. His descendant will not do the same to me and Olivia. The line of evil must be stopped.' Her eyelids grew heavy and gratefully she yielded to a fitful sleep.

Bright sunlight streaming through the large, grimy

windows aroused Charlotte. The sheer joy of surviving the night restored her energy and she rushed to the windows ignoring the pains of cramp and hoping to call for help, but to her dismay the frames were nailed down. Looking around the room she could find nothing that would help, just the table and two empty wardrobes. The only tool she had was the hockey-stick, it would hardly prise a window open and even if she broke the glass it would probably be a futile gesture because she was trapped in the back end of the house. An idea struck her. If she made a loud enough noise she was bound to attract attention in the floors below.

The wardrobes! They were both empty with doors askew, abandoned long ago. With a great effort she pushed and pulled the smaller of the two from the wall. Dust travelled into her nose and mouth making it a very uncomfortable process, but finally inch by inch she managed to make enough of a gap to get behind the smaller wardrobe. Bracing herself against the wall she pushed with all her ebbing strength. The giant wooden structure tumbled and crashed to the floor in a cloud of dust.

Wasting no time she worked on the second wardrobe which was heavier and far more difficult to manoeuvre. She was getting desperate so slid behind the monster grazing her legs and arms but caring little for the pain, just pushed from the wall and imagined the unyielding lump of wood to be Thomas. Her adrenalin flowed as she grappled and pushed until it finally toppled and fell to the floor with a wonderful, resounding crash.

She waited. It seemed an age before a dull, thumping noise rang in her ears. Someone was running up the stairs! There was a good deal of clattering as footsteps echoed on bare boards. Charlotte flung herself at the door and beat upon it with her fists.

She could hear muffled voices before one spoke clearly. "Are you OK, Lottie?" the deep tones of Ralph demanded.

"Yes!" she shrieked in response, "get me out of here!"

"Stand back. We're forcing the door." There was the crack of splintering wood, an agonising time before the lock gave way and the door flung open. The room was invaded. Price, Mary and Cissie were fussing around but stopped when Ralph strode in carrying a crowbar and smirking. "We can see she's alright. Just a bit dirty and bedraggled. Go and run a bath for her, Cissie. We can ask questions over a good cooked breakfast."

Temper and humiliation blinded Charlotte to her state. "I was locked in here by some maniac! Now, if you'll excuse me it's been a long, cold night and I can run my own bath!" She stalked from the room with her head held high, but her legs like jelly.

When Charlotte looked at herself in the mirror she couldn't help but laugh. Dirty, dishevelled and grazed she looked like something the cat dragged in. After her bath she slid into her jeans and sweater and felt ready to face the world, besides, the smells wafting from downstairs promised a hearty breakfast.

Sitting at the kitchen table she was presented immediately with a steaming mug of tea. "Great," she sipped the brew, "so how is Olivia this morning, folks?"

"Fighting fit!" Mary replied sharply. "It's been murder trying to explain about you, but we told her you had gone for an early-morning walk. It would be wise to keep up the pretence."

Ralph had been sitting silently with his coffee mug clenched between his large, work-worn hands. "What happened, Lottie?"

Looking him straight in the eye, she told the truth. "There was a lot of thuds and bumps above my room about two this morning, so I went up to investigate. Whoever it was trapped me in that room and locked the door. Simple as that."

Ralph clenched his fist even tighter. "What a damn stupid thing to do! The intruder could have been violent!"

"I had my hockey-stick! That reminds me, I must get a

torch, it would have been useful last night."

Cissie who had been bustling about stopped and flapped her pinafore. "That wouldn't have done you much good, Lottie! You only got to read the newspapers these days to hear about attacks and suchlike. Your stick wouldn't have helped if he'd had a knife or something, would it?"

Price admonished the imaginative maid. "Enough, Cissie! Go and see to Madam. She'll be waiting for her second cup of tea." As the plump little woman followed out the orders she muttered under her breath as she left the kitchen. Price then turned to the guest and said conspiratorially, "We knew there was something wrong after Cissie found you room empty. We searched the grounds then rang Ralph just in case you'd walked in your sleep again. We're glad that you are alright. We'd never have looked up there if we hadn't heard that noise."

"Yes, well that was one of her better ideas." Ralph remarked as he turned his gaze from Price to Charlotte. "You were a fool to go up there in the first place."

"It was Thomas, I'm sure of it! Did you see him last night, Price?"

Shaking his head, the old gentleman replied, "If he was around he made sure we didn't see him. Why should he lock you up there?"

"Spite!" Charlotte answered fired with her ideas. "He thought he'd frighten me to death by imprisoning me up there for the night, but he's only made me more determined! I'll go and see Olivia now, she said she had some errands for me to run this morning."

As Charlotte left the room silence descended. Price smiled and shook his head unable to bear his memories. "I told you, Ralph! She's back. Annie would have done the same."

Rising from his chair with impatience, the Estate Manager walked to the back door and paused. "I hope she can stay the course," then squaring his angular shoulders he said flatly, "if it was Thomas then she'd better watch her back. The Blake family are pretty determined as well. You're wrong about one thing, Price. She may have Annie's spirit, but her face belongs to another."

"So there you are!" Olivia said sternly to Charlotte as she entered her bedroom. "You are very inconsiderate going off without a word."

"Thomas does it all the time."

"That's different," Olivia announced without explanation. "I have some letters to be sent recorded delivery so I hope you have enough energy left to carry out the task? Dear, dear me. What a start to the day! I was woken by some strange crashing sounds this morning. It seems something fell over in the attic, at least that's what Mary told me, but it's very upsetting. Then after I instructed you to be here early you have gone for a walk at such an ungodly hour! Really!"

"You're complaining better, Aunt. Shall we synchronise watches? I'll be leaving at 9am precisely. Now, how long does it take to walk to Pantmawr and back, add five minutes in the post office .... "

Olivia chuckled. "Minx!" As she handed the letters over she paused, "You are so like her, you know. Your ways. Be proud, Charlotte. I only wish I had known you sooner."

A strange, choking feeling welled up in the young woman's throat. Why should she feel like this? Olivia was a strange character who could conjure up emotion without warning. "I'm proud of my ancestors, Aunt Olivia. You too." She left the room without looking back.

As Charlotte walked down the drive of the old house she turned and looked up at the topmost windows. Hours before she had been imprisoned within the thick, cold walls. Yet another aspect of time had evolved before her eyes during those long, dark hours. She would never be alone, her friends of the past and present always seemed to be around. Ralph was standing by the ever-open gates. "Want a lift?"

About to refuse, Charlotte thought better of it due to her

feeling of tiredness. "Yes. Pantmawr, please."

"Land Rover's parked in the lane. I've got a lot of work on today, but would you like to come over this evening? Can I pick you up at eight?"

"For dinner at your house? Don't tell me, it's etiquette for the damsel in distress to repay her Knight by dinning with him? Old Welsh custom?"

"You are an idiot!" Ralph replied lightly. "Yes, dinner in my house but simply because I have some old photographs you might like to see."

Charlotte smiled as they climbed into the Land Rover and moved off. "Beats etchings! OK. I'll bring the letter, the one your Grandmother Emily wrote."

A slow smile creased his thin weather-beaten face. "I think we could help each other, Lottie."

Pantmawr lay before them. The words penetrated her skull like a soothing balm. "Perhaps we can. Thanks for the lift." she called as she alighted from the vehicle feeling surprisingly happy but not knowing why.

As she approached the Post Office she saw a figure slip out of the side door from the corner of her eye. Taking little notice she entered the shop to find it empty both of customers and Postmistress. Miss Kemp appeared from the back looking flushed and made up like a painted doll.

"Two for Recorded Delivery, please." Charlotte asked politely.

Taking the letters the Postmistress began to fill in the slips, but couldn't resist the temptation to make some remark. "I hear Mrs. Jones has injured herself in a fall. Can't be too careful at her age. Bones become very brittle."

"You should know," Charlotte replied with her sweetest smile. "But I'll tell her how concerned you are. I expect Thomas told you all about it."

Stamping the receipts with clenched fist, the woman completed her task before replying. "Thomas! Why should he tell me?"

164

"Good question, Miss Kemp. Good question."

Leaving the hostile premises, Charlotte browsed around the few shops and enjoyed the experience as the residents were friendly and polite in contrast to Miss Kemp. Sometimes they were just inquisitive, but in a bland fashion which offered no offence as the vendors were blessed with the warmth of humanity. The Bakery displayed a delicious array of fresh cream cakes so she bought an assortment as a treat for everyone much to the surprise of the assistant who remarked that shop-bought cakes never entered the doors of Glas Fryn.

In a tiny bookshop she found a few interesting items on local history and folklore, even an Archaeological study of the district which looked rather daunting and complicated, but could contain relevant information about the House.

At the Newsagents she found Thomas browsing through the magazines and for a few moment she felt repelled and almost turned away, but getting to the bottom of his schemes would mean facing him and feigning friendship. Enjoying the element of surprise she stood behind him and whispered, "I understand they put the Girlie magazines on the top shelf. Can you reach?"

Turning with a reddening face he looked shocked. "You! What are you doing here?"

"Shopping, what else? Oh! I see!" she giggled, "you thought I was tied up elsewhere, is that it?"

His face fell in astonishment for a split second then he regained his composure just as quickly. "Olivia can be rather demanding, especially when she's indisposed."

"Quite." Charlotte thought he covered up very well under the circumstances. Determined to be civil she continued to look cheerful. "I've been thinking what a good thing it was that you were with her when she fell. I'm sure it would have been far worse if she'd been lying there for any length of time."

"Absolutely. Well, I'd better be getting back. I haven't had chance to see her since it happened."

"You were out all night?" she asked innocently.

Thomas coughed and nodded in the same motion. "Yes. All night. Friend of mine stopped over."

"How nice! Where did you stay? Is there really a hotel in this little place?"

Looking uncomfortable, he shook his head. "There's not, only a pub with some rather basic rooms. Eastbridge is more civilised. My old pal was kind enough to drop me off here on his way through. I say, Charlotte, what is all this about?"

Smiling serenely, she managed to reply enthusiastically, "Just showing an interest, Thomas, that's all. So you'll be walking back then? Fine. We'll keep each other company. The exercise is welcome because Mary's cooking is wonderful but fatal to the figure. That is when you are there to eat it."

"Her scope is very limited in my opinion, I tend to have more exotic tastes, dear girl."

They were out of the shop and on the road to Glas Fryn. "Are we talking about her cooking or the person?" Charlotte goaded. "Perhaps you find Miss Kemp more exotic? Don't deny it Thomas, I saw you leaving the side door of the Post Office earlier."

"You must be mistaken! It could have been anybody."

"Not with an arm in plaster. It's a dead giveaway, Thomas. Strange really, the other villagers treat you like a leper except for her."

A deep frown creased the pale brow whilst the grin was erased. "The place is populated by hillbillies. Interbreeding. Morons beget morons. Anything new and they make the sign of the evil eye."

"Hey! That's a bit strong! I'm new here and they treat me very well. You must have done something to upset them, after all, you've been coming here for years."

"Look here, old girl, I think you're letting a vivid imagination get the better of you. Keep your investigations confined to the field you are paid to discover."

166

"Why?" Charlotte asked in mock amazement. "Have you got something to hide? Some dark and disgusting secret? Miss Kemp the tip of the iceberg, is she?"

The face turned puce with rage. "You've been warned! Stay out of my affairs! If I had two good arms I'd strangle you here and now, but I can wait. This plaster will be off soon. Beware, dear Charlotte, beware!"

Shrugging her shoulders nonchalantly in order to hide the shiver which ran down her spine she continued, "Or you may resort to locking me in the attic? Or perhaps you'll wait until I'm old and defenceless and push me down the stairs."

Throbbing temples betrayed the volcano which was erupting inside her opponent. His eyes glared as they threatened to pop out of their sockets and his voice took on a menacing timbre. "You play a dangerous game, lady. Did you concoct all this yourself or did you get some help from your bed mate? My God! He has even got you working for him."

Stunned by the hard slap which numbed his cheek, Thomas was left standing in the middle of the road whilst Charlotte marched on ahead. She was smiling. It was not the best of tactics, but perhaps she had pushed him into playing his hand. Whatever the outcome it was worth everything to hit him! She just had to watch every step of the way from now on, no holds barred.

Olivia asked her great-niece to join her for lunch. She had an occasional table placed by the large bay window of her bedroom and directed that it be set for two. With slow but steady steps and the aid of a crutch she gratefully left the confines of her bed.

"You can't imagine how wonderful it feels to be mobile again, child! I never was one for lounging around in bed."

"You've only been in bed for twenty-four hours." Charlotte smiled.

A scowl qualified the next statement. "At my age you welcome each day and be thankful for your faculties. Confinement makes you realise how worthless life must be without your health. I can understand how old people in homes go barmy! Treated like children they become such."

Cissie served lunch and beamed at the sight of her mistress. "Nice to see you up, Madam! Let's hope you are back to normal soon."

Olivia inclined her head regally. "No doubt it will mean an easier life for you, Cissie. Where's Thomas? He said he would join us for lunch."

"If I see him then I'll tell him, Madam." Cissie sighed then left the room.

It turned out that Thomas had eaten lunch in the dining room alone then promptly left without a word to anyone. Taking advantage of the opportunity to make a private phone call, Charlotte rang an old colleague. After exchanging pleasantries and office gossip she explained the reason for ringing and the response was exactly what she expected. Bill would make enquiries about Thomas Armstrong and get back to her as soon as anything came to light.

Feeling very pleased with her contact, Charlotte decided to snatch some sleep after her uncomfortable and traumatic night. As she entered her bedroom a force materialised from the dark shadows to pin her against the wall. A plastered arm pressed against her throat and squeezed the breath from her body whilst the weight of the attacker held her immobile and defence impossible.

"Thought I'd gone out, didn't you!" rasped the excited voice of her assailant. "You fell for my little ruse and thought the coast was clear to use the phone."

Charlotte's mind raced as the implication of the words sunk in. Thomas must have overheard her asking Bill to dig into his background. How could she be so stupid! Why didn't she use the public telephone in Pantmawr?

"Lost for words for once! What are you after Miss Prim and Proper Stone! I've been digging around too. Your past is not exactly squeaky clean, is it! Olivia might be interested to hear about your dirty little affair with a married man, not to mention the abortion he paid for! Your teacher, wasn't he? What a sordid past you have. Take my advice, ring that friend of yours again and tell him you've changed your mind, or I'll have to tell our dear Aunt the truth about you. Maybe Ralph would enjoy the story too, see what kind of whore he's taken to his bed!'

Pure venom laced the laughter as the torturer enjoyed his moment of glory. 'Who would have thought it? Still, perhaps we can come to some sort of arrangement to make sure I don't let things slip. Female company is rather scarce around here ...."

All the while gasping and wheezing, Charlotte tried to fight back. "I'm not playing your evil game! Distorted gossip. Dubious sources and ..... " she spluttered each word like a drowning woman. Finally, an inner surge flowed through her body to give her enough strength to free a leg and with primeval hatred brought it up between her assailant's legs full force.

It sent him reeling and muttering obscenities between clenched teeth. Taking the chance Charlotte rushed to the bed and grabbed the hockey-stick. "If you want another broken arm just try it! I'll break every bone in your miserable body!" Yelling in a frenzy she hit him across the back as he tried to get up. "Get out! OUT! Crawl back to the cesspit you came from!"

Footsteps sounded outside on the landing and Price was the first to arrive. His jaw dropped as he saw the crouching figure of Thomas stumble towards him. "What's going on?" he asked, "We heard shouting."

Tossing her weapon to one side, Charlotte pointed towards the culprit. "Ask him! Ask him! Rapist! Blackmailer! Just ask him!"

Trying to straighten himself and stop clutching his private parts, Thomas spoke quietly hoping to impress his audience. "The girl's hysterical. One tries to be friendly towards her and the vixen turns on you! I think Olivia should know just what kind of a shrew she's harbouring."

Mary pushed past the crippled man and comforted the victim. "I know who I believe! Dad, call the Police."

Thomas turned deathly pale at the suggestion and thought quickly. "What are you going to say? One person's word against another? No. I don't think you need them."

"They may decide you warrant investigation and you wouldn't like that, would you Blake?" Charlotte gloated.

"What on earth is all this rumpus about?" The high, demanding voice of Olivia shook them all. Above the shouting and arguing they hadn't heard her approach. She stamped her crutch on the floor in anger. "Someone speak!"

Cissie took the lead. "Your wonderful Thomas just attacked our Lottie. Not only that, but he'd have murdered her if she hadn't got the better of him! Thank God he still got one arm in plaster or she wouldn't have had a chance, that's all I can say."

"Is this true, Thomas?" Olivia asked sternly.

Grinning sheepishly, the man clung to the doorpost as he replied evenly, "As if I would, dear Aunt! She gave me the impression that my attentions would be welcomed, then out of the blue she went berserk. I think she needs help, Aunt. Medical help."

"You bastard!" Charlotte screamed like a banshee as Price and Mary held her back. "You stinking liar! Rotten blood runs true!"

"Charlotte!" Olivia boomed. "Disgraceful behaviour I must say, and such language! I think Thomas is right. You misunderstood his intentions. Young ladies these days don't seem to realise how they can incite a man. Cissie, Mary, see to my great-niece and make sure she gets some rest, she's obviously overwrought. Price, you can help me back to my room. I will consider which Doctor will best serve in this case."

"I don't believe it!" Charlotte yelled, "She thinks I'm cracking up! Dear God!"

Cissie patted the young woman's arm as the party dispersed. "Come on, love. We know what he's like, that's what counts. He's the devil on earth, that one. Isn't that right, Mary?"

Turning down the bed, the housekeeper nodded in agreement. "He's tried it on me in years past but not so forceful I must admit. At least you hit him where it hurts, Lottie. Did you notice the way he walked off? Sort of bandy-like!"

Laughter is said to be the best cure and Mary's remark sparked off the remedy which brought Charlotte to her senses. "Oh, Mary! You're a tonic."

"Me?" she asked surprised. "That I DON'T believe!"

Fresh laughter broke the tension and the three women sat on the bed like schoolgirls. Cissie mocked Olivia, "Mary, my dear, perhaps we should check the linen cupboard for a strait jacket. I'm sure I had one years ago!"

"That's right, Madam," Mary parried, "we put your husband in it to make sure he married you!" They fell about holding their abdomens like three fairground puppets.

"You two are wicked," Charlotte chortled, "but we shouldn't laugh, poor old dear thinks I'm a femme fatale." Mopping the tears from her face she sobered a little. "Ralph asked me to dinner this evening. I think I'll go now, get out of the way before Olivia gets the funny farm collect me! What time is it?"

"Only three, he won't be home yet." Mary answered. Feeling guilty, she gave hope to her luckless contemporary. "I've got a key, though. He wouldn't mind if you used it, especially under the circumstances."

Charlotte frowned then sprang to her feet. "Oh dear! I should have seen it before. I am so stupid! You have something going with Ralph, haven't you. I'm sorry, Mary. I hope I haven't trodden on your toes or caused a problem between you both."

Mary grunted. "Chance would be a fine thing! We're

friends, Lottie. Just good friends, and that's the truth. I look after his cottage when he's away, that's all. We grew up together and he treats me just like a sister, well, better than his sister actually."

"He has a sister? Where?"

"She lives in Cardiff somewhere. Married a Solicitor."

"Even he has got ulterior motives." Charlotte denounced. "He fitted me in with a visit to his family when we went to Cardiff. Other business, indeed!"

"What about the cream cakes you bought for tea? Do you want to take them with you?" Mary asked practical as ever.

"No. Treat yourselves girls. Be naughty, eat the lot!"

With the key in her hand, Charlotte walked to Ralph's cottage with an air of freedom. The physical aspect of Thomas's reaction hadn't be unexpected, but she had touched a nerve that was certain. Now to surprise the patronising Nicholls, he would never expect to find her 'in situ'.

CHAPTER 10

Truth Will Out

The cottage looked like something out of a dream as it bathed in the bright sunlight with flowers adorning its garden and walls. Charlotte sat on the lush green lawn to enjoy the quiet and nature's sound. Birds sang, butterflies danced, bees hummed, all inducing contemplation and peace. Bathing in the normality of it all she tried to put Thomas's attack out of her mind. It had been her own fault, she had pushed him too far. Now she had to pay for the consequences. Her throat was sore and her body ached, but the afternoon sun bathed the wounds and calmed the mind.

Voices filtered through her brain and she opened her eyes expecting to see Ralph, but the scene was different. She was sitting amongst a vegetable patch which reached up to the front door. At the door was a man dressed in black and talking to someone in the shadows, she rose and brushed the dirt off her jeans as she scampered to the open doorway.

She entered. A vicar was sitting before the fire talking to a young girl who was lying on a settee wrapped in blankets. "How are you today, Mary?"

The young chest heaved and gasped as she tried to reply. "Better sir, lots better."

Annie appeared with a tea-tray. "We Thank God that she's still alive, Vicar. She nearly perished in that fire, but He spared our child. It has brought her asthma on, but that will go with rest."

"This is very cosy, Annie!" the Vicar said as he looked around the room. "You were lucky it was vacant. I'm surprised you didn't go to Glas Fryn, plenty of room there especially now your father has passed away."

Annie shook her head. "Not as long as my sisters Elizabeth and Isobel are there. They don't like children and I know they would never make me welcome. Olivia is different, she is young yet."

Taking a cup of tea he coughed before continuing. "I understand. Actually, I am here by request of the school. They wanted me to have a chat with you. It seems there's a problem with little Isobel."

Annie froze. "What's wrong with her? Has he met with an accident?"

"No! No! Nothing like that! Sit down and drink your tea, girl."

Doing as she was bid, Annie pressed the gentleman. "What kind of problem? She's a livewire and been worse since her Dad had that accident. The house fire didn't help, she's taken to screaming and kicking everyone. Now she's in school and learned to read and write we hoped she was growing out of it."

Chuckling to himself, the man of the cloth nodded, "That's the problem, Annie. It's what she's written all around the school yard and the Chapel walls!" Puzzled at the Vicar's behaviour, the worried mother urged to explain. He continued, "She has chalked everywhere as far as she can reach. I'm afraid she will be late home since she has to scrub off the offensive abominations as punishment."

"What was it? What did she write?"

"Annie, to save the blushes of young Mary here, all the swear words you can think of! No doubt she was egged on by the boys."

Annie dropped her cup, her face aghast. "What! When that little devil gets home she'll get her father's strap and no mistake! Oh, my goodness me! How will I ever face the village again? The Church! Oh, Lord help me!" Throwing her hands over her face in horror, she found it strange that the vicar was laughing. Mary had been giggling which started another attack and a child began crying upstairs. Shaking a finger at the Vicar she said sharply, "Now look what you've done! It was a nice peaceful afternoon before you turned up!"

"In your home, Annie? Never! See you on Sunday." Still laughing and holding his sides the vicar left.

Charlotte watched as Annie attended to her daughter, the daughter who was to become her own mother. How she longed to have been cuddled and loved through her childhood. There was no doubt she came from a very loving family.

Without warning the world went black.

She found herself lying on the floor of Ralph's lounge. Carefully she got to her feet and listened. All was quiet. Feeling dizzy she went through to the kitchen and put the kettle on to make herself a strong cup of black coffee just as the lock turned in the back door.

"How the hell did you get in here?" Ralph asked in complete surprise.

"Oh! Er, Mary gave me the key. I hope you don't mind. You did ask me over for Dinner. I'm a bit early I'm afraid."

Leaning against the kitchen unit he frowned. "My door was still locked."

"Yes, well........ yes. I must have locked it behind me without thinking. You have to do that when you live in the city, you know."

Shaking his head, Ralph threw his car keys on the table. "Want something to go with that? There's biscuits somewhere. What made you .... " The light from the window fell on the young woman's face to reveal the bruised face and arms. "What happened to you?"

Following his gaze and seeing her arms marked, Charlotte shrugged. "Thomas. We had a difference of opinion." Thinking of her Grandmother comforting her daughter in this very cottage she felt her reserve break. Tears trickled down her pale, scratched face much to her embarrassment.

Ralph felt totally lost. Her face was drawn and pinched with dark shadows under her eyes. Every time he saw her she was getting worse. Her long, dark hair had lost it's shine and her clothes looked far too big for her slight figure. Something was radically wrong with the woman and she needed help.

"Come on." he encouraged folding his arms, "Is this the same person who takes on the world with a hockey stick? Who flings wardrobes around in attics? That person wouldn't crack up after a row with a wimp like Thomas Blake."

"It was more than a battle of words," she whispered wiping her face as she did so. "But you are right. I won't let it get the better of me. I'm sorry."

Taking her arm, Ralph led her into the lounge. "Make yourself comfortable while.............. Lottie? Are you going to faint or something?" She had turned so white that he wondered if she was going into a fit.

"Where is the door? The front door?"

Ralph felt strangely cold. "There used to be a door just there, to the left of the window, but it was blocked up during the last war." He waited for her reaction.

"Could......... could we go into the study? Please?"

How this woman could possibly know about the door was a mystery, but he decided that the only way to find out was to humour her. Wait for the right moment. In the study he poured a drink which she accepted and drank without question. "What did Thomas do to you?" he asked flatly.

Shaking her head she drained the fiery liquid and held the glass up for more. "I asked for it. We walked back from the village together this morning and I was an absolute bitch to him. After lunch I thought he'd gone out so rang an old contact and asked him to investigate Thomas Blake, but it seems he overheard the conversation. My side of it anyway. When I went up to my room he was waiting for me." A slow smile spread over the gaunt face. "He didn't get off unscathed. Let's just say he had trouble walking away!"

Ralph felt an evil force well up inside him. It took him by surprise to feel such a strong emotion, but he controlled his voice to cover his feelings. "What did Olivia have to say about it? I hope she kicked the waster out!"

"You must be joking! Her poor Thomas must have been

misled. I shouldn't have led him on!"

"Dear God! The woman's demented!"

"No," Charlotte replied sadly, "She's just totally naive. Did you know she paid for my education? No? It shook me I can tell you. She said she carried out my father's wishes to stay away, not to make contact."

Ralph went to his desk and unlocked a drawer. "Take a look at these. Your long-lost family!" He watched her pick up the old photographs and gaze at them slowly, longingly. Sitting besides her on the leather settee he took them from her. "Let me introduce you. This family groups is one of the oldest, Sarah and Ivor were your great-grandparents and the baby in arms is Olivia. Hard to believe she was ever that helpless! Oh yes, the young woman standing behind is Charlotte Anne, your grandmother. You must be following your father's side because she was short and plump."

"Oh yes!" the face became animated, "she was!"

Taking each sepia print he named the images which were mostly the Armstrong family through the years. Most of them featured Olivia.

"I'm afraid there isn't any of your grandparents or their children. I think a lot of things were destroyed when their home burned down. Ah! Just a minute, though!" He returned to the desk and shuffled amongst papers and documents. "I know it's here, yes! Take a look at this."

Charlotte had followed him and took the large studio print from him eagerly. "Daisy! Where did this come from?"

"You know who she is?" he asked astonished, but the rapt look on the young woman's face told him to play the strange game. "Just look at that Grand Piano she's standing by, do you think she could play it?"

"Very well indeed! She could have made a career out of it but became a nurse instead." Silence fell. Charlotte held on to the photo and poured herself a generous drink without asking or thinking.

Ralph took the glass out of her hand. "That's not the

answer. Tell me what's happening to you? You know all those people in the photos, don't you? Not just recognise them, but KNOW them. Especially Daisy. She was a love child and I know that Olivia would never tell you about her."

"A love-child she was not!" screamed the young woman as she glared into his face. "Annie was raped whilst she was unconscious, a child begotten by violence, not love!"

Summoning up all his strength to remain calm and reasonable, he spoke softly, "Do you have visions? Dreams? See the ghosts of the past? I won't think you're mad, Lottie. I can accept other planes, physic powers or whatever. Just tell me how you know so much."

The tear-stained face looked anguished. She wanted to give in but was afraid of the consequences. "I don't know. How do I know I can trust you?"

"I'm not Thomas. My grandmother may have been a Blake by name but she was ostracised by her family for marrying a Protestant. David Nicholls, that is, who was the nephew of your Grandfather James Edward Nicholls, known as Jim. What better qualifications do I need?"

"None." She sighed deeply and fell quiet as the Estate Manager waited with baited breath for her to open her mind. Finally she spoke. "Could...could you tell me where the bathroom is? I feel a bit queasy."

"Upstairs to the left, same place as last time you were here." Ralph groaned as she ran off in haste. He knew that it would be no good pressurising the woman who held some secret, a secret he would have to be patient with. Realising that neither of them had eaten he made his way to the kitchen to cook the promised meal. If he could get her to relax, gain her trust, then maybe Charlotte would confide in him. Despite the questions which crowded his mind, when his guest finally reappeared he was dishing up the food and whistling nonchalantly.

"I'm so sorry! You must think I'm a right idiot." Although her complexion was colourless her eyes looked brighter.

"Sit down. You need a decent meal inside you. Steak and chips are my speciality. In fact," he looked over his shoulder as he served, "the only thing I can cook properly."

Keeping the atmosphere light Ralph knew that any sudden move, word or remark would send her scurrying away in fright. Polite conversation about the village, the area, even his job had a soothing effect and he was happy to see a clean plate and a healthier tone return to Charlotte's cheeks by the end of the meal. He accepted her help to wash the dishes and noticed that the angular shoulders became more relaxed as she went about her task with pleasure.

"Right!" he announced, "All done. Coffee percolated, a fire crackling away in the lounge just waiting for company."

"The lounge?"

"Yes. The summer nights tend to get chilly in these old cottages, come on!"

They settled down in comfortable chairs each side of the fire with the logs sparking and coffee and brandy to hand. Ralph had decided that truth was the best course to take and so he talked gently. "Lottie, you have made a few friends since you've been here. Price, Mary and Cissie in the house, Ted Skinner outside. He came back to ask about you, you know. We care, Lottie. You look dreadful, a changed woman since you came here and it's causing concern. If it's a personal health problem then we can seek medical help."

Close to tears again, Charlotte exploded. "You mean a psychiatrist! I'm not mad, Ralph, no way!"

Jumping out of his chair, Ralph felt frustrated at not being able to get through the barrier which surrounded the woman before him. He paced the room then stood in front of her. "Nobody thinks you're mad, for God's sake! I was talking in physical terms, not mental."

He watched her taking a deep breath and reach for the brandy glass. Sipping it slowly then replacing it she nodded. "I'm becoming neurotic. Sorry." Pausing for a moment then smiling she said, "Good grief! I can't remember when I apologised so much. To tell you the truth, I've had some strange experiences since I came to Glas Fryn and I don't count Thomas amongst them." She looked up at her host, her dark eyes veiled in mist. "I think perhaps I should trust someone, you seem the best candidate."

Ralph flopped back into his seat sighing with relief, knowing the battle was won. "I am. Tell me how you know these people from the past, how you knew there had been a front door into this room."

"Well," she hesitated before she could find the right words, "I'm not sure if.......... if the past is haunting me...... or if I am being haunted. My minds slips back ....NO! My whole being goes back. I can move but no-one sees or hears me. I am a spectator, an invisible spectator."

"How often has this happened? Once, twice?"

Resting her forehead on her hand she frowned, "I'm not sure, perhaps a dozen times? The last time was this afternoon. I came in here by the front door. Annie was living here and Mary was sick. She had Asthma."

Ralph sat bolt upright. "You saw your Mother as a child?"

"Yes! Yes I did!" Charlotte paused and looked at the stunned expression. "You believe me? You're not laughing at me?"

"No. Why should I? What you saw bears true. I just find it incredible. Is that how you knew Daisy from the photo? From seeing her in the past?"

The words blurted out before she realised. "Yes! I was present at her birth and have seen her growing up. I've heard her playing the piano and her Grandmother Sarah begging her to take it up professionally. Daisy said that she wanted to be a nurse so went to a London hospital where she trained."

Ralph was on the edge of his seat. "Where did you see all these things happen?"

"Glas Fryn. At least, that's where it starts but you know where I ended up the other day, at the site of Annie's cottage."

"My God! This is spectacular! You really are travelling

back in time! No wonder you look ill. Have you thought about the consequences, Lottie? It's having an affect on your physical being, you have to stop!"

"If it was you, would you stop?" she asked defiantly. "Besides," her voice dropped with an inflection of fear, "I can't control it anymore. At first it was happening when I put a small silver thimble on my finger, but now it just happens."

Ralph stood and leaned his elbow on the mantle. "A thimble? You put a thimble on your finger and .... you had that on your finger the morning Ted found you! I thought it was peculiar, but it slipped my mind. You were in a state and I was worried." Drumming his fingers on the mantelpiece, he asked, "Would it work with anyone else? Why you?"

"It all began with the silk underwear in the drawers of my room, visible only to me with the initials C.A.A. embroidered on them. Now I know it was my Grandmother's initials, her maiden name that is. Apparently I'm in the room she last occupied and I'm also her namesake and apparently when my Mother died Annie pleaded with my father to come and live at Glas Fryn. Obviously, he refused. The thimble was engraved C.A.A. as well, it must be her spirit drawing me back to tell me about my family, the family I never knew."

"This is so incredible! You could probably tell me more than I have learned in years of study. Is that how you knew about, Emily, my Grandmother?"

Gaining confidence, she nodded. "Emily and Daisy were great friends. Oh yes! I've brought the letter. Here." Producing the old paper from her pocket she watched him read it and shake his head. "You can keep it, Ralph."

He nodded his thanks and placed the letter on the mantelpiece. "Going back to the other morning when Ted found you......... well, as I said you were in a terrible state. What had you seen, Lottie?"

"Well," she thought carefully, "in a nutshell it was about your Grandparents, Emily and David. They were not married then, of course, but David had been shot and Emily said it was her Uncle Fredrick who aimed at her. It seems this man was also the one who had raped Annie, so he was actually Daisy's natural father."

"The Blakes! Dear God!" Ralph shouted, "Do you realise that he was the man who cheated Emily out of a fortune? She was ostracised because she married David, a Protestant. Her share of the inheritance all went to her brother Albert who sired a son. Thomas's father, no less. I don't know what happened to Fredrick but he didn't get a share according to the records."

"So she really did lose everything?" Charlotte asked quietly.

"Everything. Emily and David lived in poverty all their lives. They had three children Jinny, Alan and Jack who was my father. Jinny rubbed salt in old wounds when she ran off and married Albert Blake's son. This disgusted the family because he was her first cousin and the family feud over the lost inheritance was still fresh in my Grandparent's minds. Anyway, Jinny had twins but she died when they were about twelve."

Charlotte nodded. "That's where our Thomas comes in! He was one of the twins. I know what happened after that, Price told me. His mother, his twin brother and his father all died within died six months of each other."

Ralph sank back into the armchair. "Uncle Alan took him in under his wing, but Thomas caused so much trouble at home and in school that even Alan washed his hands of him."

"He's always been a doubtful character then."

"Yes," Ralph answered distantly, "Always."

"I think I want to go home now, Ralph. I'm feeling exhausted."

"But there's so much to talk about! I want to know .... " he stopped himself. The guest's eyelids were fighting with gravity and he realised he was being selfish. There was so much he wanted to know, if only he could step into her shoes and travel back in time. "Come on," he said abruptly, "let's get you home."

Struggling out of the chair, Charlotte followed him wearily to the Land Rover. He started the engine up, but before they moved off he turned to face her and gripped her hand. "You could always stay here, you know."

Taken aback, she answered shakily, "I.....I don't think so!"

Ralph laughed as he realised the implication of his suggestion. "I promise not to take advantage of you. There's three bedrooms so you could take your pick." His amusement subsided, "What if Thomas tries something else? He'll never give in. He's dangerous and I don't like the thought of you under the same roof after today."

Charlotte patted his cheek. "I can handle it. Thanks for being so considerate, but I want to keep an eye on Olivia. If he tries anything with her she won't be able to fight back."

"Promise me two things, Lottie. If there's anything, and I mean anything, that causes you concern you'll phone me."

"OK. That's one thing, what is the other?"

"This time travel business. Stop it. I know it's incredible, fascinating and even addictive, but it's harming your being. There are bound to be physical consequences. Just stick to the here and now, please?"

Charlotte sighed deeply. "Since it's you and you haven't laughed at me then I promise not to willingly travel for the time being. If the spirits want me to be drawn back then there's nothing I can do."

"I can't believe I'm having this conversation. I suppose I'll have to be satisfied with your answer." As they moved off he said lightly, "I wonder if our Thomas is home? I could have a chat with him."

"Stay out of it, please Ralph!"

Reluctantly he agreed, but still went inside Glas Fryn with her to make sure all was well. Mary told them that Thomas had left about six with an overnight bag, but no explanations.

As Ralph left, Mary placed a steaming cup in front of

Charlotte and ordered her to drink it. "It will make sure you have a good night's rest. I've seen to her Ladyship so you can go straight up."

"What do you mean, 'seen to her'? Have you drugged her or something?"

Mary looked down at the table. "Well, just a little something in her tea. Just herbs. It will keep her quiet until the morning with a bit of luck!"

Laughing, Charlotte felt the liquid relax her body. "If it was anything like this stuff she'll be out like a light! I can feel the aches and pains easing already. You could make a fortune with this, Mary. Solve the drug problem overnight!"

"Plants and herbs can be just as addictive if they are misused, Lottie. Most drugs start off as plants. Think about it."

"Of course, I guess I'm not thinking straight. I'm off to bed, Goodnight, Mary."

The stairs seemed like a never-ending obstacle as he body became so relaxed she wondered if her bones were melting. The bed was the most welcome sight she had ever gazed upon, she sank into it's downy softness and yielded to an all enveloping slumber.

Charlotte woke the next morning feeling completely refreshed in body and mind. She threw open her bedroom window to let in the sunshine and birdsong and revelled in being alive and well. 'It must have been that elixir that Mary gave me as a nightcap. Wow! She should bottle it and sell it! '.

Laughing to herself she jumped when a voice came out of the blue. "My goodness, Lottie! You look full of the joys of Spring this morning, or should I say joys of summer." Cissie had bustled into the room and began making the bed. "After yesterday I didn't expect you to be washed, dressed and smiling!"

"Don't tell the Drug Squad, but it was Mary's special brew!"

Cissie laughed. "Oh, that! God Knows what's in it but it never fails to work. Well, most of the time, anyway. Nothing would put a smile on Her Ladyship's face."

"How is she this morning?"

"Ready to see her subjects," Cissie giggled, "when you're fit. I could make excuses if you like. Going on at you like that after her precious Thomas attacked you, it's not only him got a twisted mind if you ask me."

"Oh, I'll go and see her now. Don't think too bad of her, Cissie. She's known him for years, a lot longer than she's known me."

"Huh! All the more reason to see through the devil! Run along then, ten minutes then breakfast. You need filling out, getting scrawny you are."

Bobbing a curtsey, "As you say, Ma'am!" Charlotte left the maid shaking her head and laughing.

Olivia was sitting by the bay-window of her bedroom from which point she could survey the front gardens.

"Morning, Aunt. You look better, soon be running around the house again."

"Not soon enough. You don't look any the worse for wear, despite your little disagreement with Thomas." Pausing for breath before continuing in a gruff voice she asked, "What is going on between you two? He was never aggressive before you came here."

Feeling offended, Charlotte barked her reply. "Then his true colours have come to light." She stood with her arms folded and legs apart.

"Don't stand like that, child! You look like a common-washer woman. Sit down."

Enraged by the elderly autocrat she paced the room ignoring the command. "It must be the genes I've inherited, a family trait! After all, my Grandmother married below her station, didn't she. At least she had pride, enough pride to marry the man she loved not to be bought as part and package along with the house. You all looked down on her, but she didn't sell herself for bricks and mortar! Thomas must follow your devious side of the family hence the reason why you stick by him. You'd sell your soul to the Devil to get your own way!"

Olivia looked grim. "Finished, Charlotte? Feel any better after your bout of verbal diarrhoea?"

Astounded at the reaction, Charlotte felt her pent-up anger evaporate. Begrudgingly she sat down opposite Olivia but continued to fold her arms as a last protest. "You were wrong. You cast me as instigator of HIS evil actions."

Olivia shook her head. "Why should he attack you? What reason would he have? He has got a broken arm so he is the one who has a positive disadvantage."

It was not possible to tell Olivia about the attic episode, about the long, dark hours locked up in the cold upper rooms. Pointless telling her about the incident with the Postmistress, his threats and blackmail. "Perhaps he resents my presence because I ask too many questions. Why does he have the Deeds of Glas Fryn, for instance? I suspect his motives. He hasn't put pen to paper since he's been here yet his excuse was to write a thesis. All very suspicious."

Tilting her head at an angle, Olivia bit her bottom lip before replying. "He may be jealous of you, and you must admit you both antagonise one another, and I think a physical outburst was inevitable. You broke his arm remember, purely by accident, perhaps, but a man can only take so much, child. I'll have a word with him and I'm sure his behaviour will become impeachable once more."

Charlotte shook her head at the deluded woman. "What about the Deeds? What has he done with them?"

"Not that it's any of your concern, but I sorted that out with my Solicitor last month. They are quite safe. Now run along, child. Get some fresh air, you're looking rather peaky."

"I wonder why!" Charlotte slung the remark over her shoulder as she left the room.

During breakfast in the kitchen the telephone rang. It was

for Charlotte. "Hello, Charlotte! Did I wake you?" the cheerful voice of Bill, her old work colleague asked.

"We get up at dawn in the country, Bill. Not like you townies!"

"This Townie has been up very early to catch the worm, kid! This fella you asked about, is he any relation?"

"No. What have you got, Bill?"

"Two years ago he was sacked from a big financial firm in the City. Nothing concrete to charge him with, but the story is 'insider dealing'. He'll never work in that line again, I promise you. His name stinks. They think he blackmailed clients when they were in dire straits and advised them where to put their money. He had some very happy investors under his wing until they found half their profits creamed off. There was no proof, of course, he's a sharp character and they don't know where or how the money went. Enough for you?"

"Sharp he is. Thanks, Bill. I owe you."

"Next time you're in town you can buy the drinks, love. Take care, kid. Whatever you do, don't give that guy you're life savings!"

A feeling of elation soared inside Charlotte as she returned to the kitchen to finish off her breakfast. The phone rang a second time. It was Ralph. He wanted to see her straight away and would pick her up in five minutes.

When he arrived he barely said a word and once she was sitting in the Land Rover he drove off with impatience. He careered through the lanes in silence and she saw the Eastbridge sign flash past. Thirty minutes later they were parked on a deserted, grassy verge overlooking a calm, slate grey sea.

Charlotte was happy despite the odd behaviour of her companion. Turning to Ralph and laughing she spoke cheerfully. "You look very stern for such a romantic spot like this! Shall we get out? I didn't realise we were so close to the sea. It's wonderful, natural and impressive. You can imagine smugglers waiting on the rocks to lure a ship to the shore, brilliant!"

A nod was the only form of reply. They went down a channelled path between grassy banks to a rocky shore interspersed with sandy patches. The rocks gradually gave way to sand and shingle, to the beach where the water lapped gently at the edge. Throwing pebbles into the sea, Ralph finally spoke. "Thomas paid me a visit last night. Late last night."

"Oh dear! I hope he lived to tell the tale!" Charlotte smiled.

"He had a tale alright. He told me about you. I know he's a bastard, but it knocked the wind out of my sails, I can tell you. Is it true?"

Charlotte realised that the story Thomas had tried to blackmailed her with had been passed to the man besides her. "You mean to tell me that you believed him?" she asked incredulously. "You listened to him and have the gall to ask me if it's true?"

Ralph turned and gripped her arms. She winced. "I need to know the truth, Lottie." He was shaking her like a rag doll. "Tell me!"

"Hey, back off!" Charlotte held back her tears as he relaxed his fierce grip. "A distortion of facts. He picked up idle gossip."

Dropping his hands and digging them into his jeans pockets as if to control them, Ralph looked out to the distant stretch of water. "So tell me the facts. If you want my trust I need yours."

"Ok. I was working in a Newspaper office before I came here and it's the ideal place to misconstrue facts! I started going out with a person who'd been a student-teacher during my last year in school, but what everyone fails to remember is that he bunked college and joined the army. He served two years before we met. He loved his regiment, it was his life.

'To cut a long story short we were engaged to be married. Three months off the wedding I was rushed into hospital with a severe haemorrhage which required emergency surgery. It was an internal rupture of some kind and I was warned that it would be unlikely that I would bear children. Naturally, people assumed the worse. I must have been pregnant, an abortion gone wrong, wasn't he her teacher or something? My close friends knew the truth and said it didn't matter what others thought, but if you sling mud some of it tends to stick. I had enemies, it was that kind of cut-throat career, anything to climb the promotional ladder and make a name for yourself. I hated it. Office gossip can destroy a person."

"What happened to your fiancé?" Ralph asked gruffly.

Charlotte let the tears trickle down her cheeks as her emotions ran riot. "Killed in the line of service on that lyrical Emerald Isle. Nobody recalls the blood spilled. He never knew I was ill, never knew that we wouldn't have been able to have children." Wiping her face with the back of her hand she sniffed, "That was years ago and a closed chapter. A treasured memory. Just like Olivia and her lost love, really."

Ralph turned and held her in his arms once more, but gently this time. "Thomas got hold of the gossip then. But how?"

Pushing him away and not daring to look him in the face, Charlotte gazed at the water lapping around their feet. "The same way I found out about him, I suppose. Contacts. It's not hard to dig the dirt if you know the right people."

"What was that?" Ralph asked bewildered. "What did you find out about him?"

"He was sacked for 'insider dealing' and fleecing clients. Nothing was proved, of course."

Clasping Charlotte to him he laughed. "You're a bloody miracle!" Then holding her at arm's length, he gazed into her face. "I'm the culprit this time. Sorry. I had to know the truth. I .... " he hesitated, "we are all fond of you. The only way to combat such vicious accusations is to get to the truth from the victim. Don't let Thomas make you a victim."

The strange mixture of emotions welling up inside her made Charlotte smile and turn away. She walked the beach and clambered rocks knowing that he was behind her every step of the way. "There's the Postmistress too!" she shouted back.

"Which one? Do you mean Miss Kemp from Pantmawr?"

"I saw Thomas leaving there via the side door. I think he's using her as well."

"As well as what? Who?"

"As well as Olivia, of course! I asked her about the Deeds to Glas Fryn but she brushed me off. Thomas has them, but I wish I knew why. She assures me that they are quite safe."

"What!" yelled the tall, angry man. "He's got the Deeds! The stupid old bitch!"

Charlotte stopped to face him. "You obviously didn't know. It involved her Solicitor whatever it was. She's convinced that everything is legal and above board. What can we do?"

Ralph gazed into the worried face with tenderness. "You do nothing. You are not the only one with contacts. I'll pull a few strings."

"Oh!" Charlotte asked innocently. "Would your brother-in-law in Cardiff be one of them? He is a Solicitor isn't he? At the time I was surprised that you seemed to put yourself out for me, but you didn't, did you."

Shaking his head and laughing, he answered truthfully, "It was rather convenient . You have an uncanny knack of finding things out. I've never met anyone like you before, sharp and inquisitive but not maliciously so."

Charlotte frowned. "Well, as long as we are honest with one another we know where we stand. Thomas is our mutual target. Come on, time we got back."

They travelled back in silence each with their own thoughts and theories. One thing which was clear, they needed each other to combat any designs which Thomas Blake had in motion in order to protect Olivia.

CHAPTER 11

The Other Woman

When Charlotte returned to Glas Fryn she immediately made for the kitchen. Cissie was washing up dishes at the sink and welcomed the offer of help. "Mary is trying to make sense of the garden again and her father is down the cellar. I think he enjoys a smoke and a glass of brandy while he checks the supplies! Poor old thing, he ought to retire. His father dropped dead in this very kitchen, you know! Worked to death her was, worked to death!"

"Oh, Cissie! Don't be so morbid. Hurry up with those dishes, I'm catching up with you."

The plump body wobbled with amusement. "If Her Ladyship could see you now! Begging for dishes to wipe! Oh, Lord Above! She'd have a fit." The merry face turned towards the tall, thin woman besides her, "Ralph has put some colour in your cheeks, anyway."

Feeling a blush rise, Charlotte gently pushed Cissie's shoulder. "Forget it! Nothing going on so no gossip, promise?"

"In that case," Cissie smiled secretly, "You wouldn't be interested in what I heard."

"Come on, spit it out!"

"Well, I was over in Eastbridge yesterday and bumped into an old friend of mine. We've known each other since we were in school, but only see each other once in a blue moon. She 'does' for the people who own holiday homes now, she says that it's easy work and the pay is twice what I earn and ...."

"Cissie!" an exasperated Charlotte rang out. "Is there a point to all this?"

Chuckling in response, the maid continued, "Be patient, Lottie. I'll come to it when I'm ready." Wiping her hands on a towel she put the kettle on. "Now, where was I? Oh yes! Peggy. As I was telling you she goes round the holiday homes cleaning. I asked her what kind of visitors would come around these parts? There's nothing here for them. It's miles to any decent town and ...." she stopped herself as the kettle came to the boil and made a pot of tea. "Here we are, Lottie. Sit down and enjoy this."

"Thanks, Cissie. Now get on with your story, please."

"Right. Well I think Thomas is renting one of the cottages." She paused as her audience jumped to attention. "Peggy had been told not to go to this particular cottage because it was a private property and they didn't need the Cleaning Service anymore but she went there all the same. Very nosy woman is Peggy, mind! Always has been. Anyway, a woman answered the door and she got very nasty with Peg. Told her not to go there again."

"What has it got to do with Thomas?"

Taking a deep breath and narrowing her eyes Cissie explained. "As I said, Peggy is nosy and doesn't like being told. She made enquiries in the area, she knows everybody, see. It seems that a man goes there regularly and stays until the early hours, sometimes the night. The description fits our Thomas to a 'T'! In fact, they remember him because he's upset quite a few in the neighbourhood."

Charlotte tried to think rationally. "We suspected that he had a woman tucked away, didn't we? Well, if it is Thomas we can hardly hang him for having a woman friend within easy reach, can we."

"I know," persisted Cissie, "but it's very underhand and sly, don't you think? I wonder who she is? He's hiding her, that's for sure!"

"She could be a married woman and want to keep things quiet, keep herself to herself." Charlotte smiled, "The very behaviour which would set local tongues wagging overtime!"

Nodding in agreement, Cissie laughed. "Peggy's exactly like that! Sees innocent things and embroiders a mystery around them. My Goodness me, it got her into some trouble in her younger days."

"Where is this cottage, Cissie?"

"Somewhere between here and Eastbridge, that's all I know."

"A needle in a haystack! I've already seen an Ordinance Survey map of the area and it's a haphazard mass of minor roads and they all got clusters of houses along them."

"Right enough, Lottie. That's country life for you. I'd better get moving or else I'll have to go into hiding to escape from Missus up there!"

Charlotte laughed. "Speaking of work I think I'd better try and sort myself out in that direction. I'll be in the library is you want me."

Sitting at the desk in the library with a clean sheet of paper in front of her, Charlotte arranged her thoughts and noted the important points. Bill had given her Thomas's recent history and promised to get in touch if anything else transpired. Good old Bill had never made a top investigator, but whatever his assignment had been his results were always thorough and accurate. Therefore, she could rely on his information and jotted down the main points.

Thomas handled Olivia's financial investments by her own admission. Did he give all the profits to her, or cream off a generous percentage? More importantly, he had the Deeds to Glas Fryn. Why? Had he used them as security on something?

Where had the Blake fortune gone? If it was still intact he could live off the interest, so why swindle people? She considered Thomas's movements since he came to the house. She had caught him in the attic, why was he up there? The answer was to check it out.

As she passed through the hall the doorbell rang and she shouted through to the kitchen that she would answer it. Opening the door she was taken aback. "Miss Kemp. What do you want? Cutting down on postmen, are they?"

With a crestfallen face, the Postmistress delved into a

voluminous handbag to produce a packet. "I can't hand this to you. It's addressed to Mr Blake. Is he in? I would prefer to give it to him personally."

"A Registered Letter, eh? Why didn't the postman bring it with the morning mail, or even second post?" Folding her arms in determination, Charlotte watched the parchment coloured skin tighten with anger.

"He forgot it. I thought it must be urgent and came all this way to make sure our service was beyond criticism and this is the treatment I get! You're not 'Lady of the Manor' yet, Miss! I insist on handing this to the addressee."

"Then be prepared for a long wait, Miss Kemp. Thomas skives off nearly every day, not to mention the nights! The hours that man keeps! It wouldn't surprise me if he had a mistress tucked away somewhere. In one of those holiday cottages, maybe. Well, where else is there to go around here?"

Thrusting the envelope back into her shapeless handbag, the woman shook her head vigorously. "Tell Mr Blake he may collect it at the Post Office."

"You're not going to leave it?" Charlotte gasped feigning surprise. "Isn't that going to reflect rather badly on your service? I am here to receive it, willing to sign for it and yet you refuse to deliver. I doubt your superiors would look upon it kindly. You have a strange devotion to duty, Miss Kemp."

Wondering which way to turn, the woman hesitated for a moment before clamping her bag shut. "He can collect it."

"But Post Office hours are limited, you would be guilty of delaying the Mail, unless you are available to special clients at all hours?"

"Really! I have never been so insulted! You must be taking lessons from that old dragon in there!"

A car roared up the drive and pulled in with a crunch of gravel. Thomas jumped out looking dishevelled and his face a picture of apprehension as he took in the scene. Quickly recovering and fixing the inevitable smile he straightened his tie and strode towards the two women.

"Miss Kemp! What a pleasure to see you! Can I help in any way?"

The lined face creased as the bright red lipstick slashed a smile across the powdered countenance. "Mr Blake, I was trying to deliver this package to you but this, er........ person, was not helpful. One does not expect such insulting remarks when one tries to carry out one's duty. How you can suffer such a person I really don't know!"

"My dear, lady. I apologise for your reception. In appreciation of your kindness I'll run you home. It's the least I can do."

Charlotte leaned against the door and spoke encouragingly. "Go on, Miss Kemp. Take the chance you've been waiting for! Just keep an eye open for police cars. Thomas still has one arm in plaster and being seen with him could cast a slur on your reputation." As they turned from her she called out, "You know how he broke his arm, don't you? Fighting off another woman, that's how!"

Thomas gritted his teeth as he opened the car door. "You come out with the most ridiculous drivel, Charlotte. Come along, Miss Kemp."

"Taking her to your secret love-nest?" Charlotte called as Thomas got into the car. The gravel sprayed as he turned the car with wheels spinning and sped down the drive.

"You saw her off then?" a voice said behind her.

"Price! Were you eavesdropping? I'm surprised at you, what would Olivia say?"

Smirking, the manservant said quietly, "Probably ask me to repeat everything word for word!"

Laughter bubbled up inside Charlotte as she closed the door. "How do you put up with her, Price? All these years, too."

Holding his jacket lapels proudly he answered with confidence. "Because I'm part of everything. The House. The Family. All of it. Never known anything else except for the Army during the War. I will never forget how happy I felt to return in one piece, to find everything just as it was. I'm set in my ways and enjoy life just as it is. It would have been nice to have the wife with me, but Mary's a good girl and one day I might have grandchildren."

"Your wife? What happened to her?"

"Heart attack. Mary was ten. Madam was very good to us. She paid for the burial and everything, very understanding. She's a good woman, Lottie."

Tucking her arm under his she agreed. "Underneath the shell, you mean? I know, Price. I know." They walked towards the kitchen door and Charlotte patted his arm. "Did Cissie tell you about her 'gossip'?"

"Yes," he nodded slowly, "she never could keep anything to herself. It sounds plausible though and the Blake's owned a lot of cottages around Eastbridge years ago. I wonder who the woman is?"

Relaying the information from her old colleague, Bill, Charlotte asked Price for his opinion. "I'd say he's up to something other than a clandestine love affair. All the years he's been coming here I've watched him but there's nothing I can put my finger on. He attacked you, Lottie, why didn't you report him to the Police?"

"My word against his? No. Besides, a charge of Assault wouldn't bring everything else to light. Also, Olivia's assumptions were true up to a point, if the Police had asked if I encouraged him with any word or deed then I would feel the guilty party for taunting him. No. I'm going to get to the bottom of Thomas Blake and expose him for the crook he is."

"I'm always here, Lottie. You know that."

Pecking the wizened cheek she nodded and fled before her emotions broke through the surface. Price smiled and uttered softly, ' She's back. She's back'.

Escaping to the garden via the French Doors in the library, Charlotte dug her hands into her trouser pockets and strolled through the depleted flower-beds which once boasted a mass of colourful blooms. Thanks to Mary there was still some pride to be salvaged from the days of past glory.

The Summer-House stood before her. The paint was peeling off the rotting wood and the glass that once glazed the windows had long since disappeared. The path ran in front of it and three shallow steps in the shape of a crescent joined the path on a lower level which continued around to the Rose Garden. Olivia has walked this way every day, weather permitting, and it was here that she had slipped.

"Who are you, lass?" a voice asked besides her.

Jumping out of her skin she turned to face the man she had seen in the past. Jim Nicholls, her Grandfather. He had emerged from the Summer-House. A well maintained and freshly painted summer house. Jim's chubby face had grey whiskers and a heavy moustache with a pipe dangling from his mouth. Was he talking to her? Impossible! She looked around but there was nobody else in sight.

"Lost your tongue, lass?"

"Um........ me? Are you talking to me?"

"Of course I am! What's up with you, girl?" He held his pipe in the cup of his hand and puffed on it gratefully. "Old Sarah disagrees with smoking, that's why I'm out here! Are you one of Daisy's friends? You must be. Trousers! I don't hold with women wearing trousers, young lady, but Daisy says that it's fashionable in London."

Charlotte felt excited and frightened at the same time. "Is Daisy here? She told me to call in if I was passing." She lied without effort.

"Nay, lass. She left yesterday. Are you close friends? You look the spit of her, you know! What's your name?"

"Charlotte. Charlotte Stone. Yes. You could say we are pretty close."

Jim laughed and his kindly eyes shone with pride. "Charlotte! My wife's name, God Bless her! I can't recall Daisy mentioning you, though. Never mind." He took matches out of his pocket and re-lit his pipe. He blew out palls of aromatic blue smoke and nodded with pleasure.

"Where are you staying, young lady?"

"Oh! I've been invited to stay here. I've been made very welcome."

"Sarah is a good woman, I'm very fond of my mother-in-law. She practically brought our Daisy up, you know. They....." he stopped talking and held his head to one side. A blue uniform came along the path from the Rose Garden and Jim waved in greeting. "Hello, Sgt. Hopkins! What brings you here?"

"Who's this young thing, Jim? Another friend of Daisy's?"

Charlotte was astounded when the policeman took her hand and shook it firmly. His flesh was warm and quite normal, her presence taken for granted. "Pleased to meet you," she said automatically.

He frowned at the mode of dress then shook his head smiling. "Don't hold with trousers on women, but I fancy my wife had been wearing the pants in our house for years! What do you say, Jim!"

Both men broke into hearty laughter and Charlotte couldn't help but join in. "Next thing they'll be after our jobs! A woman policeman! By damn! It doesn't bear thinking about."

"When you two have finished, can I ask you about Daisy?" Taking a gamble, she spoke haughtily. "Have you made any progress, Sgt.? Daisy was attacked on this very spot but you don't seem to be very concerned about it. Perhaps women would do a better job than men?"

The jovial moustached face dropped in amazement. "We know who done it, it's catching the blighter, that's the trouble! Have you thought about my suggestion, Jim?"

Taking the pipe from his mouth, Jim nodded. "I've thought hard about it. If my Annie and Daisy are in danger then I'll do it. What about Emily?"

"She refuses protection. I can't do much about that."

"What are you going to do?" the young woman asked puzzled.

The policeman put his hands behind his back and rocked

on the balls of his feet. "Under certain circumstances I am authorised to issue arms for the purposes of protection and defence. Since Annie and Daisy have both received physical and verbal threats from a certain person I advised Jim to take advantage of the law."

Astounded, Charlotte asked, "Is it really legal?"

"Technically, Miss, yes, but it hasn't been known in my time. However, Fredrick Blake is a nasty character and will stop at nothing. He tried to shoot Emily and injured David back along, now he has attacked Daisy in this garden and threatened Annie with her life."

"So why haven't you arrested him?"

Jim spoke angrily, "Because he's crafty, that's why! He's always got an alibi and it's one word against another. We've got nothing concrete to take to the Justice, nothing!"

The Sgt. nodded. "Don't worry, Miss. We'll find a way. Meanwhile you could help by keeping an eye on Daisy for us. Down here she's amongst people who care but in London it's different. Would you do that? She wouldn't press charges when he had a go at her, next time it may be too late."

Feeling an absolute fraud she nodded and choked back the tears. She shut her eyes to control her emotions but the tears flowed unchecked. When she opened them again the two men had gone. Time had snatched them back. She was alone in front of a dilapidated Summer-House crying her eyes out.

Recovering she considered the scene and suddenly realised that she had travelled and been a living person in the past. She had spoken to her grandfather and even discussed Daisy with him. So great was the danger from Fredrick Blake that the policeman had advised the use of a gun as protection. She compared the past to the present and knew that it was a warning to herself and Olivia. Thomas would stop at nothing. Thomas was a descendant of Fredrick. Blood will out.

Olivia had managed to negotiate the stairs and demanded lunch in the dining-room. Thomas had returned and so his presence was also demanded. The trio sat down at the table in silence, a silence which was tangible.

Olivia sighed and grunted. "Well I didn't expect bunting or a brass band, but I thought my return to normality would cause some form of approval. I was obviously mistaken."

Forcing a smile to her thin face, Charlotte nodded. "I'm glad you're feeling better, Aunt. I really am." She glanced at Thomas. "A double celebration, I see! Thomas has had his plaster removed. Now he has both hands free to push you down the stairs."

"Charlotte!" barked Olivia. "That is quite uncalled for! I'm surprised at you."

Thomas revelled in the criticism and waved his hands in placation. "It's alright, dear Aunt. Charlotte must have her little joke."

"You're the joke, Thomas." Charlotte parried. "I wouldn't wave that lily-white appendage around if I were you, people might get the wrong idea."

"Bitch!" he snarled, "If it wasn't for you..........."

Olivia interrupted. "Enough, children. Ah! Price. Lunch never tasted the same upstairs. It must be dreadful to be a permanent invalid."

"Better stay clear of Thomas then." Charlotte quipped.

Rapping the table, the elderly woman threw a darting glance at her great-niece. "Whilst you are under my roof you will both remain civil to one another, is that clear?"

"As crystal." Thomas agreed. "Naturally I respect your wishes, I promise to treat your great niece with the respect she deserves."

Rising from the table, Charlotte threw her napkin on the white tablecloth. "Excuse me, Aunt Olivia, but I badly need some fresh air."

As she left the room she could hear Olivia calling after her, but she could no longer pretend to be polite in the presence of Thomas or make false promises just to please her Aunt.

Running to her room she threw herself onto the bed and

clutched the patchwork quilt and cried as though her heart would break. How could she pretend that everything was normal when Thomas had attacked her, blackmailed her and tried his best to turn Ralph against her. Why did that hurt most of all?

A hand patted her shoulder and she turned in alarm to see Cissie with a tray. "Come on, Lottie. You have to eat something." Placing the meal on the bedside table she took the young woman into her arms. "There, there, my lovely girl. Cry if you want. It drives more devils out than in! Old Cissie has got broad shoulders."

The pent-up rage and fear spilled out of Charlotte until she wept herself dry cradled in the loving arms. "Oh, Cissie! I'm sorry, but it all got on top of me. I just couldn't stay down there with him, I just couldn't!"

"I know that," the voice said gently as she rocked the distraught young woman, "come on, my lovely. Pull yourself together and have some lunch. I'll tell you what, I've got this afternoon off so why don't you come with me to Eastbridge? You haven't been there, have you?"

"No, no I haven't. Been through it, I think." Moping her face with a borrowed handkerchief she sighed, "Yes. I'll come with you. Just give me time to put my face right."

"That's my girl!" Cissie exclaimed. "You're stronger than him, just remember that."

Charlotte nodded. It was true. She had the strength of her ancestors flowing through her veins, the strength to fight off adversity in whatever shape or form. Thomas's antecedent was a maniac, a cold-blooded madman. Her life was running on a parallel with the past. The time travel was a forewarning for times present. She would heed that warning and defeat Thomas Blake.

As she left her bedroom to join Cissie she felt a cold hand on her arm, squeezing gently. Turning with fear gripping her stomach she saw no-one, but the terror left her body. She was not being haunted by recent events in this room, she was being comforted and encouraged by the past.

Taking the local bus service to Eastbridge, Charlotte enjoyed the ride as she could see over the hedges and find out what lay beyond. Lush green fields, scattered farms and woodland were revealed and she only half-listened to her companion. The small town boasted a large square with a War Memorial and it was obvious that this was the centre which attracted most attention. The main thoroughfare had light traffic but people were bustling from shop to shop and the area was pulsing with life. Joining the queue of passengers alighting at this point Cissie nudged her arm.

"Let's go to the tea-room. It's WI day but we'll squeeze in somewhere."

The tea-room was rustically cosy and full to the brim with chattering ladies who varied in age and appearance. Above the hubbub of female voices Cissie picked up the tones of her old school friend. Pushing her way amongst the small tables she called out, "Peggy! Peggy! Save us a seat, Peg!"

A small shrew-like woman stood up and waved an arm. "Ooh! Hello, Ciss! Fancy seeing you again so soon! Come on, there's spare seats over here."

Sitting at the table with a spotless red-checked tablecloth, Charlotte was introduced by the maid. "This is our Miss Charlotte, Peg. You know, the one I was telling you about. Mrs. Jones's great-niece."

"Pleased to meet you, Miss. What brings you here today? Come to see our Celia's daughter, have you? Oh no! Couldn't have. She's away for a few weeks and the girl is staying with some friends."

Cissie tut-tutted irritably. "You know more than me, Peggy. I only brought Lottie here to look around because she's only been to Pantmawr and there's more shops here."

Peg winked, "Not to mention a friendlier Post Office!" All three women laughed aloud causing frowns and berating glances from the ladies around. "Talking of hard women, how's your Aunt, my dear? By God! She's a tartar that one! I worked there once years ago but I only lasted two days. Told the old girl where to stick her job."

Laughing and enjoying the bald honesty of the little woman, Charlotte ordered tea and cakes as her treat. Cissie sighed as a plate of cream cakes was placed on the table. "Bang goes my diet! What a choice. Thank you, Lottie. You've got a heart of gold but I'll be cursing you next time I get on the bathroom scales." Turning to her friend she winked. "Not like that other one. He's a sponger amongst other things."

"Oh, I can believe that!" Peggy agreed. "Did Cissie tell you about that cottage? Yes? Well let me tell you that people thereabouts are fed-up with the pair of them. Coming and going all hours of the night with no thought for the noise they make."

Charlotte leaned forward. "What do you mean? Comings and goings? What are they up to?"

Screwing up her wrinkled face, Peggy shook her head. "There's been a big van thing back and fro at all hours. Country lanes are not made for vehicles that big, even cars have trouble in places, but they fly around like bats out of hell! They both got cars, too, him and the woman, and God Forbid anything that stands in their way!"

"Have the neighbours complained to them?" Charlotte asked.

"Well that's a bit difficult. Most of the cottages change hands regular as clockwork being holiday homes, but nobody knows who actually owns that one. I just get to hear things when I go cleaning. They've all been on about the lorry and cars saying that they came here to get away from things like that. They pay all that rent to find lunatics hurtling past their doors and it's always the same description so we can't blame it on youngsters, can we."

Cissie intervened. "Where is it exactly, Peg?"

"You know the old Llewellyn place? Remember we went to school with the boys Dai and Clew? Well that's it, their old

203

cottage on the Pantmawr lane."

Cissie nodded and a glint came into her eye as she looked at her watch. "Look at the time, Lottie! We'd better do our bit of shopping before we go back. 'Bye, Peg. Nice to see you again."

Peggy looked disgruntled. "So soon? Oh, what a shame. Well, thanks for the tea, my dear. Perhaps Cissie will bring you again soon."

As they left the tea-room, Cissie pointed the way to Pantmawr. "It's fair walk back, mind. Do you want to wait for the bus? Any shopping you want to do?"

"No shopping. You know very well what I want to do, Mrs. Jenkins! We could do with the exercise after those cream cakes, don't you think? Maybe a detour to that cottage would be a good idea, I saw the look in your eye!"

Giggling, Cissie took the young woman's arm. "Right enough. What are you going to do, though? You can hardly knock on the door."

Charlotte smiled. "Trust me, Cissie. Don't forget my former job on the newspaper, there are ways and means to get information."

They followed the road for a mile before turning off to the right and down a narrow, meandering lane which passed various houses and cottages en route. It was understandable that the noise of traffic would be a disturbance, especially at night when the silence echoed any sound.

Once over a small, hump backed bridge they had reached the building in question. "This is the one." Cissie announced. "Now what?"

Opening the gate, Charlotte ordered, "Follow me and look pious, like a typical canvasser. I'll do all the talking." Before her companion had chance to protest she had pressed the doorbell and they waited with baited breath. The door opened and Charlotte spoke to the bleached blonde woman who had seen the best of forty years. "Good afternoon, Madam. We are from the local Women's' Institute and are canvassing the surrounding district in order to gain an insight into family life in the nineties. It's a nationwide survey and should prove helpful in today's society. How much has the family changed over the last fifty years? How has the movement flourished in rural areas with dwindling populations? These are the questions we are hoping to answer by interviewing local people like yourself."

Drawing on a cigarette the woman snarled, "You're out of luck. I'm no local."

"Oh!" Charlotte feigned surprise, "What a shame You look like the type of person whose views would prove invaluable. Are you on holiday? What do you think of our little corner of the world? What attracted you to Wales? Where do you come from?"

Folding her arms in grim determination, the woman cocked her head to one side. "You're a bloody nosey lot around 'ere, I'll tell you that for free. Stick that on your report! Now, get lost and find some other poor sod to interrogate!" The door slammed with a dull thud as the woman retreated.

"I didn't handle that very well, did I." Charlotte said unhappily.

"Come on," Cissie directed as she put an arm through her ally's. "Whoever she is she's common as dirt! I didn't think Thomas would stoop that low. Queer kettle of fish if ever there was."

As they walked the rest of the way home in the July sun they pondered over the situation. A cottage in the middle of nowhere and a kept woman who was the very antithesis of a voluptuous mistress made the whole thing suspicious. Thomas was younger, educated and sophisticated in comparison to her which left a very odd situation indeed.

"You should be an actress, Lottie! The way you gabbled on about a survey and the WI left me wondering. I'll tell you what," Cissie announced, "I had a good look at the inside behind her while you were yapping away and it's full of old furniture. I don't mean crowded like Her Ladyship has it, but full and crammed into the room like a shop."

"Old as in antique?"

"Yes. Classy stuff. Things like Her Ladyship would have, from what I could see anyway."

Charlotte's mind worked overtime. Antique furniture, vans coming and going under cover of darkness, Thomas out nights on end, possibly a rented home with a woman as caretaker. It all added up to a very nasty, criminal picture.

CHAPTER 12

Distractions

Ralph found it difficult to concentrate on his Estate work and had never appreciated his staff as much as he did now. As a general rule the business was well managed by loyal and trustworthy overseers who knew that if they carried out their jobs efficiently they would benefit financially as well as the landowner. A few had tried to abuse their position over the years, but their dismissal served as a reminder to others that it wasn't worth losing their livelihood by taking such chances.

The Estate Manager was respected and knew each employee personally. If they had reason to complain they knew their case would be heard impartially and action taken if necessary. Compromise played a large part in settling disputes and Ralph Nicholls had the knack of finding a happy medium to suit all parties and thus, generally, peace prevailed.

Naturally, a lot of effort and planning was required to foresee problems, possible obstacles and always the fickle hand of nature which could destroy a harvest within days. As individual farms and breeding programmes they would run at a loss, but as a collective whole they made a profit through co-operation and labour sharing. Each worker was well-versed in the system and always willing to help a neighbour during busy periods or in times of crisis.

It was the end of July and everything was running smoothly. Harvesting had been arranged between the farms and all kinds of weather conditions taken into account. Ralph was on his way to his next call when he passed Charlotte and Cissie on the road from Eastbridge. Stopping the Land Rover he waited for them to get in.

"Is it alright for both of us to get in the front of this thing?" Cissie asked looking worried.

"For the sake of half a mile I'll break the law." Ralph said seriously. "Come on, Cissie, live dangerously!"

"Taking Lottie out for the afternoon is exciting enough, let alone getting into this contraption!" Cissie laughed. "Guess what she did? Only knocked on the door of the cottage, didn't she! Let on she was from the W.I. and spun a right yarn, I can tell you."

"What cottage?" Ralph snapped.

Cissie was in her element. "The one that Thomas has rented. Well, think he's rented but it's private not a holiday home. We found out about it and he's got a woman there, but you should see her! Ooh! Common as muck!"

"You're sounding like Olivia!" Charlotte laughed, "Common as muck and bold as brass, she'd say!" They had arrived at the front door of Glas Fryn.

As the two women clambered out of the vehicle, Ralph asked, "Got any plans, Lottie? Thought you might like to come with me on the next call."

Cissie pushed the young woman gently, "Go on, love! I've got work to do and it will do you good to get away from here for an hour or so."

Charlotte climbed back into the Land Rover and waved happily as they drove off. As they travelled along the road Ralph asked what Cissie had been talking about and Charlotte told him the story. "Interesting," Ralph commented, "I wonder who this woman is? How is Thomas tied in with her? Assuming she is not just a bit on the side."

"I have yet to get to the bottom of that, but I've got a nasty feeling that it's connected to his visits to the attic."

Ralph nodded but fell silent. The road was narrow and steep to the remote hill-farm and required concentration. After climbing for several miles they arrived at a plateau where the farm was situated commanding such a breathtaking view it was awesome. Rolling hills, rough grassland and in the distance a village which lay in a vale bathed in a blue haze. As they drove through the gates two sheepdogs ran around the slowly moving vehicle, barking until it was parked in the yard. Once the engine was turned off they were quiet, but continued to circle.

"Coming?" Ralph asked his passenger who was looking decidedly nervous.

"What about them?"

" Bill and Ben are harmless. They just don't like cars. Sheep are more their line."

Charlotte smiled and alighted. The top half of the farmhouse door opened and a shout rang out. "Mr. Nicholls! Well, I'll be damned!" The rest of the door swung open and a large, burly man with a ruddy complexion waved them in. "Here, Bess! Get the kettle on, we got visitors. Out! Out!" he shouted to the dogs as he closed the door behind them.

A large range dominated the kitchen which was old-fashioned but clean and cosy with the smell of home-baked bread. A small, wren-like woman patted her pinafore and dipped her head. "Hello, Mr. Nicholls. Brought a young lady with you, I see."

"I have that, Mrs. Pritchard. Meet Charlotte Stone, Olivia Jones's great-niece. I thought it would be a good idea for her to meet some of the tenants."

"Who was your mother, girl?" the farmer shouted.

"Umm.. Mary. Annie's daughter." Charlotte replied meekly.

"Did you hear that, Bess?" bellowed the farmer as he slapped his knee. "Annie's kin! You're welcome here, Miss. You're welcome in this house!"

Bess made the tea then fluttered about making sure everyone had a seat and a plate full of Welsh cakes fresh and still warm from the bakestone on the Aga. "Well I never!" she shrilled. "You don't look like Annie. We'd never have guessed. Is Mr. Nicholls looking after you properly?"

Ralph diverted the conversation to the purpose of his visit. "How are you managing up here? The sheep are thriving, the records prove that, and I know from the accounts that this is the most profitable of all the Estate properties. I also know that you are both over 65 now and deserve to take life easier. The winters are hard up here and the Estate cannot expect you to weather another year in this remote place. I've written to you several times about this matter, why haven't you answered any of my letters?"

"Those letters went straight into the fire, lad! Aye, they burned well and all. We're staying here until we're taken out in wooden boxes."

Ralph sat forward with his hands resting on his knees. "Mr. Pritchard, you are not being evicted, you do an excellent job. But think of the harder times when you are cut off for weeks at a time, even during the mildest of winters. If it's not snow and ice there's the hill-fog to contend with. Retirement isn't the end of the world."

"It is to us!" Mrs. Pritchard screeched. "There's been Pritchards here for longer than anyone can remember. Your precious records should tell you that! We might not have sons to carry on, Mr. Nicholls, but we are fit and well and can hold our own. We are practically self-sufficient up here, we've had to be and there's no reason why we can't carry on. It's the only life we've known."

Charlotte smiled, loving the characters who were part and parcel of the earth they lived off. "Excuse me, could I say something? I've listened to both sides and understand how Mr. & Mrs. Pritchard feel as this is their home. On the other hand the Estate have offered an alternative because of your advancing years and the harsh conditions," all eyes were trained on her as she paused for thought. "Perhaps the solution would be two extra hands? You could continue living here with all the knowledge and experience to train them, the farmhouse looks big enough to take two extra and if they paid lodgings it would save you both from working so hard to pay the rent. Does that sound plausible to you, Ralph? Mr. & Mrs. Pritchard?"

Ralph looked amused. "It's worth a try. Mr. Pritchard could

teach young lads more than any course we could put them on in Agricultural College. What do you think, Mr. Pritchard? Mrs. Pritchard?"

The farmer stood up looking very fierce. His bulk threatened to burst from his old tweed jacket whilst his braces looked as though they would snap. He moved to an old Welsh Dresser, took out glasses and a bottle and returned to the group. "Ever had Welsh Whisky, Miss? Your idea is better than any young Nicholls ever had! We'll do as you say, let's drink to it. Agreed, Bess?"

Her head nodding vigorously she took the proffered glass from her husband. "Wonderful idea! You may not look like your Grandmother, Miss, but you think like her! People used to go to her with their problems and she always had an answer. A wise, hard-working woman, she was. Indeed, very wise. Mind you, you have the look of someone.............. but I can't think who."

"If you are paying a compliment then I'm honoured, Mrs. Pritchard." Charlotte raised her glass, "Here's to your future, my first glass of Welsh Whisky with Sheep-Farmers Extraordinaire!" The Pritchard's laughter was so loud that the dogs began to bark again.

When they left the farm there was much waving of hands and promises to return soon. Ralph was laughing softly as he drove out of the yard. "Little Miss Clever Clogs! You don't happen to have two lads lined up for the job, do you?"

"No. I thought I'd better leave something to you. Will it work? Seriously?"

"Without doubt! It would have cost far more to give them a retirement cottage at a peppercorn rent, not to mention training a newcomer for years to reach the Pritchard's standards."

"I thought you agreed too readily! Anyway, this way everyone's happy. Even me. They are full of spirit and character, but why does Mr Pritchard have to shout all the time? My ears are ringing!"

"It's the sheep." Ralph explained with good humour. "He's out on the hills in the day and shouts to his flocks and the dogs, but the trouble is he takes his work home with him and his wife doesn't notice anymore." He glanced at his passenger and his laughter died. "You belong here, Lottie. Everyone knows it."

"Maybe," she nodded thoughtfully. "maybe I do belong."

When Ralph got home his phone was ringing . He picked up the receiver with a sense of dread. "Hello? Jarvis? Is everything alright? You sound worried."

"Yes, yes, I'm fine." the voice snapped back through the wire. "I'm not so sure about the business though. We've had a few accidents."

"Accidents? Explain, Jarvis."

"Nothing you can put your finger on. Unexplained fires, electrical problems, vehicles tampered with. I think we ought to start things rolling, Ralph."

"No. That's impossible at the moment. Take on extra men and keep watch around the clock. Anything else suspicious?"

"Not really, I'll keep you posted. Any developments that end?"

"Nothing firm. Look after yourself, Jarvis. Just in case."

Replacing the receiver Ralph stood stroking his chin, deep in thought. He picked up the handset again and dialled. The female voice that answered was unfamiliar. "Castle and Morris Solicitors. Good Afternoon. May I help you?"

"I'd like to speak to Mr. Castle, please."

"Whom shall I say is calling?" the efficient voice asked.

"Ralph. Just Ralph." The line clicked and hummed before the strange voice returned. "I'm afraid Mr. Castle has left for the day. May I take a message?"

"No message." Ralph cut off the call and dialled another number and a more familiar voice answered. "Hello, Jo. How's my little sister?"

"Ralph! Where have you been hiding yourself? I'd

forgotten I had a brother. Why don't you come to Dinner one evening?"

"Because I know you hate cooking! Is that husband of yours there?"

"Yes he is and don't you dare keep him talking! We're due to leave in fifteen minutes. Here he is, 'bye!"

"Brian. Sorry to bother you at home, but I did try the office first. Who's the new girl on reception? You've had the same staff forever and a day."

"She came highly recommended and seems to be efficient. What's up, Ralph? Anything happened?"

"There's problems with the Scottish venture and Jarvis sounds jumpy. He wanted to start the ball rolling but I don't think it would be very wise at the moment. Any suggestions?"

"Let me guess, the girl at Glas Fryn? Is that why you're holding off?"

"Yes. It's my battle, Brian, not hers. The trouble is she's found some dirt and isn't willing to let go despite repercussions. I don't want to let things slide, but it's tricky."

Brain paused. "Well,......... you can hold off until tomorrow by which time I can think of the best course to take. Knowing Jo's friends I'll have the whole evening to think things over, they tend to like the sound of their own voices so I just sit back with a smile on my face and they think I'm a good listener. You'd be surprised how many problems I have solved during our dinner dates!"

Ralph smiled at his brother-in-laws tactics. "You're OK, Brian. No panic, just me being over anxious. I'll wait for your call."

The next day after his usual morning rounds and checks Ralph showered and changed then drove over to Glas Fryn. It was mid afternoon by the time he arrived and entering through the back door he found Mary sitting at the kitchen table shelling peas.

"Ralph! Dad's just gone to ring you. Mrs. Jones wants to

213

see you. I must warn you, she's not in a good mood."

Nodding he sat opposite her. "How is Lottie behaving lately?"

Mary looked surprised. "What a funny question. You were with her yesterday afternoon so you should know."

"You know what I mean, Mary."

"Oh!" realisation dawned on the housekeeper. "You mean after the business with Thomas? Well, she gave him what for, I can tell you. Have you heard the latest about a cottage?"

"Yes. I wish she wouldn't take chances like that. Tell me, Mary, does she look ill to you?"

"No. Well, not ill exactly." Mary stopped her work and narrowed her eyes. "Like I told you before, she acts strange at times. Like she's somewhere else." Shrugging her narrow shoulders she continued, "apart from that I admire her. I wish I had half her courage."

"Where is she now?"

"In the library working like mad to try and make some headway. "Mary looked into his eyes and asked shyly, "You like her, don't you. More than like her, am I right?"

Looking astonished Ralph returned the gaze. "I'm worried about her, that's all. I'll go and see Olivia now. I take it she's mobile again?"

"Yes. She's in the lounge." Picking up another pea-pod she teased, "Admit it, Ralph Nicholls! You are very fond of our Lottie but too frightened to face facts."

"You have been reading too many romantic novels, Mary Price! Stick to shelling peas."

As Ralph made his was through to see Olivia he made a detour to the library. The dark head was bent over the desk engrossed in a book. "Get ready," he announced. "we're going for a meal in fifteen minutes."

Jumping at the sound of his voice she yelled back, "I'm busy. Go and pick up somebody else or better still take Mary. The cheek of it!"

Walking up to the desk and leaning on it's edge he said

smoothly, "No-one else will do. Please, Charlotte Stone, accompany me to dinner this evening. There, is that better?"

"An improvement, yes. Give me half an hour."

As Ralph left the library to cross to the lounge he passed Thomas on the phone. He stopped and listened to the conversation in order to antagonise his adversary.

"Er, yes," Thomas glared back as he tried to continue his call. "if you could arrange that Miss Aynsley, I would be very grateful. The last er........dispatch was very helpful indeed." He paused as the caller spoke. "Yes, quite! You will be well rewarded for you efforts, dear girl. Goodbye."

The two men faced each other with pure hatred in their eyes. Thomas smirked. "I put your ignorance down to being a village idiot. Olivia should select her hired help more carefully."

Hands thrust into his pockets, Ralph shook his head. "Talking of village idiots I heard you're knocking off the Postmistress. Is that HER reward for services rendered?"

"You really shouldn't listen to gossip, old boy."

"Oh, but I never do!" Standing close to his enemy, Ralph whispered, "Next time I want a bedtime fairy story I'll call you, the last one was better than fiction." He walked away before he gave in to the temptation to hit out. This was not the time or the place.

Olivia was sitting on the settee with her legs up on a stool when her Estate Manager walked in. "Ah!" she shouted, "About time! You are becoming very lax, Ralph. I haven't seen you for weeks. I want to know about the Pritchard business for one thing, have you got them out yet?"

"No." Ralph bluntly replied as he poured himself a drink and took the chair opposite her. "That problem was solved yesterday afternoon."

"Without my consent? What have you done? It had better be financially viable."

"The solution should prove advantageous to both parties. The Pritchard's' will remain. Mr. Pritchard will train two young men whilst Bessie will act as landlady and charge rent."

Inclining her head, the old lady approved. "Yes. Good idea. Employing two men will prove a lot cheaper than letting the Pritchards' have a retirement cottage at peppercorn rent. We really don't have to offer them housing at all with a tied property. I don't know any other landowners hereabouts who would be so benevolent."

"True. Anyway, it was Lottie's idea, not mine. I took her along and she assessed the situation and came up with the answer." Taking a sip of his drink, Ralph realised something was wrong. "Why are you so worried about the money? You've always left everything to me. The Estate is profitable and provides a regular income."

"Hard times, Ralph. We must watch the pennies."

"Olivia," Ralph said quietly, "The Estate accounts were healthy enough on the last audit, hardly making a fortune but enough to earn a decent living and keep you and this house going. Have you run into difficulties? Financial problems?"

"Minor irritations, not problems, and nothing at all to do with you, Ralph. Back to the reason I asked you here. The farm in Scotland. I want you to sell it."

Ralph's tanned face turned pale. "You ARE in trouble! Thomas. He has to be behind all this!"

"What are you so upset about?" Olivia snapped. "Thomas was kind enough to advise me which of my assets would be best disposed of. Would you prefer me to sell the Pritchard's farm from under their feet? I could do that."

The tall, lean man stood up and put his empty glass on a side table. He glared at the old woman and reached a decision. "I'll buy the land in Scotland off you. I'll pay the full market value and raise the funds somehow, don't worry about that. You can also accept my resignation. I'm sure Thomas will have someone lined up to step into my shoes."

"Ralph!" Olivia softened. "This is ridiculous. All over a plot of land a few hundred miles away."

"Next time it WILL be the Pritchards' farm, then Home Farm, then the rest of the farm cottages. With Thomas pulling the strings you'll be lucky to hang on to Glas Fryn!" Ralph stormed out of the room boiling with rage.

Making for his Land Rover he jumped in and started up the engine, his foot hard on the accelerator. He became aware of another noise. Lottie was banging on the door. He eased off the pedal and wound the window down.

"You asked me out, remember? Unlock the door! What is wrong with you?"

Reaching over he opened the passenger's door. As soon as his passenger was inside he drove off and careered through the drive gates and into the lane without stopping. An oncoming car was forced into the side and sounded its horn as the Land Rover sped away.

Approaching Pantmawr he continued his frantic pace ignoring yells and pleas from Charlotte until she screamed at the sight of a child crossing the road. Braking and swerving at the same time they missed the terrified boy and shot through a drive entrance, slewed across the lawn and finally came to a jerking halt.

A man came out of the house looking shocked. "What the 'ell is going on? Mr. Nicholls? What happened man? Are you drunk?"

"No, Mr Miles. I'm sorry. Problem with the steering." Ralph lied.

"You could have killed someone and just look at my lawn!"

"Send me the bill and I'll pay for the damage. It was a pure accident. I'd better take this thing to a garage straight away and get it seen to." Before the man had chance to reply he reversed back over the deep channels cut into the green swathe of grass and escaped.

The child had disappeared and the village quiet. At a far more moderate pace Ralph turned back and made for home. He glanced at Lottie but she sat stone-faced and silent.

Criticism enough. They had hardly walked into the kitchen when the phone rang.

It was his brother-in-law. "Our Dinner date was cancelled so I went back into the office to see what I could do. Nothing new to report, I'm afraid. All my leads have drawn a blank, every one of them. I must be losing my touch."

"I think I know why, Brian. What is the name of your new office girl?"

"Jill. Jill Aynsley. Why on earth do you want to know that?"

Ralph sighed. "She's on Thomas Blake's payroll. She's hoodwinked you, used the information to pass on to him."

"Bloody hell!" An embarrassed cough came down the line. "That explains it. She rushed off this afternoon to visit a sick Auntie, would you believe. God help me! I dread to think what she knows. I trusted her references."

Ralph sighed. "Too late now. I'll handle things from now on. You're going to need a new receptionist. Now she has the information she won't be back. Be a bit more careful with the next one, Brian."

Charlotte had made coffee and sat at the kitchen table waiting. Joining her he nodded. "Thanks. I behaved like an adolescent, sorry about that."

"You would have been even sorrier if that man had called the police! Still, it doesn't seem in character with you so I assume your meeting with Olivia was the cause?"

Tapping the table-top he replied blandly, "I don't really blame her, she's just a puppet. You know there's property in Scotland? Of course you do. Well, Olivia told me she wants to sell it. I can guess who put the idea in her mind."

"Is it that important?" Charlotte asked. "It's far away from here and she may be right to concentrate her investments in one place. Isn't it just a working farm?"

Getting up and walking to the window he answered lamely, "Something like that. What puzzles me is the fact that she seem so short of money. She even threatened to sell the Pritchard's' farm if I didn't make arrangements straight away. Thomas must be taking her for a fortune! I'm still trying to find out what he's done with the Deeds of Glas Fryn."

"She wouldn't dare throw that old couple off their farm! Did you tell her we came up with a solution? Did she actually say she needed the money?"

"That was her drift, yes. She approved of your 'rescue plan' for the Pritchard's in one breath then blackmailed me with its sale the next! That's why I have to do as she asks, I couldn't go back on my word. Our word."

Charlotte shrugged her thin shoulders. "The only answer is to do as she says, Scotland will have to go."

"But it can't!" Ralph exploded, "It's taken years of planning and .... Oh, hell!" The phone was ringing again.

As he answered Ralph felt a deep sense of foreboding. The soft Celtic lilt the other end was faint as she gave her message. Ralph felt physically sick and clenched the receiver through hatred and pain. "I'll come up straight away, Helen. I'll be there as soon as I can. Goodbye now."

"Ralph?" Charlotte asked tenderly as he turned to face her. "What's wrong?"

Taking a deep breath he answered using every ounce of his self-control to remain calm. "My right-hand man in Scotland, Jarvis, died two hours ago. He was involved in a road accident apparently. A car mowed him down last night and drove off. That was his wife on the phone."

"Dear God!" the young woman uttered. "I'm so sorry. Are you going up there tonight?"

"Yes. Sorry about the Dinner I promised you, but I have to go."

Charlotte stood besides him and kissed his cheek. "Are you alright to drive all that way?"

"Yes," he answered, touched by her concern. "Thanks for the thought."

"O.K. Just take your time. No more ploughing up lawns,

eh?"

Ralph's voice came out in guttural tones as he fought to keep his emotions in check. "You must promise me, Lottie, keep a low profile with Thomas. I want you to .... " It was difficult to voice his thoughts, "I have every reason to believe that Jarvis's death was no ordinary hit-and-run, so I'd feel happier if you had some form of protection. I don't want to leave you here with him around. He's already attacked you once and next time it could be far worse. Stay clear of him. Take one of my guns. Keep it by you at all times."

Struck dumb, the large dark eyes looked startled and worried by the suggestion. Charlotte shook her head vigorously and clasped her hands so tight the knuckles were white. "History repeats itself! No, Ralph. I'll take my chances. No idea how to handle one anyway."

"What do you mean? History repeats itself?"

"My Grandfather was issued with a gun by the police because Fredrick Blake had threatened his family."

"How do you know that?" he asked angrily, "Been back again?"

"Yes. In fact I had a conversation with Grandfather and the Sergeant. I wasn't a spectator anymore. I didn't try to go back, it just happened. They thought I was Daisy's friend from London. They laughed at my trousers, actually. Said it would never catch on!"

Ralph gripped her by the arms and held her so tight it brought tears to her eyes. "For God's sake, woman! What are you trying to prove? You'll kill yourself, it's just not possible!"

Remaining calm, the almost black eyes bored into his. "It is possible and I haven't got any control over it now. I think it's a warning. They'll protect me from the evils of Thomas Blake. I am protected. Not by guns, but by love. Love that crosses all barriers of time. They are with me, Ralph. Every step of the way they are with me and helping me. Go to Scotland and take care of things. I'll be here when you get back."

Releasing his hold, Ralph felt as though another being was speaking to him through Lottie. She looked distant and unreal and he suddenly understood what Mary Price had been trying to explain. "Come on, I'll run you home before I pack. Just make sure you are still in one piece when I get back. Ghosts and all!"

Charlotte smiled and broke the spell that bound her. The atmosphere returned to normal and she followed Ralph out to the Land Rover. The short drive home passed quickly and as she got out of the vehicle she walked round to the driver's window. Ralph wound it down and gazed in wonder at the strange being before him.

"Give me a ring when you get there. Let me know how things are going, it won't be very pleasant, I know."

Ralph nodded. "I'll ring you every day to make sure you are still alive and kicking. Tell Olivia about Jarvis, but just say it was an accident. Take care, Lottie."

Looking sad the young woman put on a brave smile. "Be careful. If Jarvis was killed on purpose........ well, just watch yourself. You owe me a meal!"

As she ran around the back of the house Ralph wistfully watched her slim body disappear. How he wished he could stay and look after things, look after her. Remembering his friend and companion lying dead in a mortuary forced him into action. He turned the vehicle and returned to his cottage to collect a few belongings. All the while his mind churned over recent events. What had Jarvis discovered to sign his death warrant? The answer lay many hours ahead.

Dinner was an ordeal. Olivia was in a quarrelsome mood and vented her feelings on her fellow diner. "So, Ralph let you down, did he! Really. That man is getting above his station. Estate Manager he may be, but he dared to question my judgement with regard to the dispersal of my property and I found his attitude quite objectionable."

Charlotte felt riled by the attack. "Serfs know the land better than their Masters. To translate, Aunt Olivia, Ralph knows the Estate better than you. If you've squandered the profits then it's your own fault."

"Squandered! How dare you girl! If I've squandered anything at all it has been on your education! Never been taught to respect your elders, that's a fact." Waving a napkin with a flourish she nodded for Price to serve.

"True." the young woman retorted, "we were taught that respect should be earned, by young and old alike. So you did waste money, didn't you! Mind you, I haven't been as big a drain on your resources as others I could mention."

"What do you mean by that?" Olivia asked calm again as she started eating.

"You introduced Thomas as your financial advisor. What happened to the investments he was supposed to have arranged? What has he done with the Deeds to this house? Why are you so broke?"

"You assume my financial situation, child. I merely wish to concentrate my resources to this area. The Scottish Estate was my husband's birthplace and I've only held on to it for sentimental reasons. I now wish to be rid of it."

Charlotte gave a harsh laugh. "You have never been sentimental! You're as hard as nails, hard enough to threaten the eviction of an old couple who have worked for you all their lives, hard enough to sell off your husband's birthright!"

Olivia wiped her mouth with the napkin. "Life can be hard, you should have learned that much. There are no children to inherit my late husband's property so I will dispose of it as necessary. He left me everything, there was no-one else." Looking old and sad, she smiled wanly, "Come to think of it, I could sell this place and retire to a villa in France or Spain, but never will. This house is MY birthright and I fought tooth and nail to keep it. I'll die here. I'll join the other ghosts."

This last remark dispelled all Charlotte's anger. "What do you mean, the other ghosts?"

Olivia smiled, "Just a figure of speech."

"No it wasn't. You meant it. Please explain to me. I promise not to laugh or belittle you, I'm curious."

Olivia waited until the dessert was served before she spoke. "I never feel alone. It's not just memories. They are all here with me. I used to see them and watch as they lived out their lives. I was invisible."

Food was the furthest thing from Charlotte's mind as she listened to her Aunt. "Who are they? When did this happen to you?"

"They were my parents, my brothers and sisters. When I got married I was so very unhappy. I felt that I'd sold myself for the sake of a house. I was very fortunate that Mr. Jones was a true Gentleman and treated me with kindness and respect. As I began to trust him and grow fond of him the visions disappeared, but I know they are still there and I have always found it a great comfort." Taking up her cake fork and spoon she tackled the dessert. "If you send for a psychiatrist my child, I'll know you are trying to commit me to an asylum."

Charlotte's smile was fragile. "Dear Aunt, you may be tough on the outside, but you are the most interesting character I've ever met! You are as sane as I." The young woman knew she was giving herself a clean bill of health at the same time, or were they both mad? "Anyway," she changed the subject to avoid being drawn, "Ralph will be away for a few days so things will have to be held in abeyance. He's travelling to Scotland tonight because of the accident."

"Accident? What accident?"

"Jarvis. He was killed in a road accident, a hit-and-run apparently."

Olivia dropped her cutlery and put a hand to her chest. "Dear old Jarvis? Dead? Oh dear, dear me!"

"Sorry, Aunt. I should have told you earlier. He must have been your employee thinking about it. Did you know him well?"

"Yes. Very well. He was my late husband's son, my stepson."

Charlotte was stunned.

CHAPTER 13

Risks & Mishaps

Olivia explained that Jarvis was the only child by Mr. Jones first marriage, but when his father re-married the son felt bitter and adopted his mother's maiden name. He joined the army and it was ten years before he got in touch and told them he had married.

"Did he finally accept you?" Charlotte asked.

"Yes. We became good friends. His father offered him the farm in Scotland but he refused saying he was a soldier, not a farmer. It was only five years ago that he left he Army and I suggested he retire to his birthplace. He made it quite clear that he only wished to rent the property as that would not oblige him to work the land.

' It suited us both and Ralph and I were quite happy to have someone living there we could trust to keep an eye on things." Olivia rested her chin on her hands. "Perhaps it's as well that I'm selling the place now."

"But that would have meant leaving Jarvis and his wife homeless!"

"Oh, no, child! I only wanted to sell the land, not the farmhouse. It wouldn't have made any difference to them."

Charlotte wondered why Ralph had reacted so strongly about the sale when the Jarvis's would be unaffected. Olivia echoed her thoughts. "I just can't understand why Ralph was so against it. He even told me to accept his resignation. I ask you!"

"He resigned over it?" the young woman was aghast. It was obvious that something far more important than a working farm was at stake, but Ralph wasn't telling anyone. Why was he so secretive?

Olivia rose from the table. "Naturally, I will defer such irrational threats under the circumstances. Oh dear! Poor

Jarvis. I was so pleased when he finally accepted me, he was the only person my husband and I shared. They never had children you see, but it would have been so nice to have had grandchildren, our only chance. It was not to be." Sighing shakily, she turned towards the door. "It's been a very tiring day and I wish to go to bed. Goodnight, Charlotte dear."

Charlotte was sure she could see tears in the rheumy eyes as she walked from the room. Her usual bounce had gone and her shoulders drooped. Suddenly, Olivia seemed like a very old woman.

The staff of Glas Fryn were shocked to hear of the death. Mary went straight up to see Olivia and returned within minutes to say that she was tucked up in bed crying her eyes out.

"Poor old thing!" Cissie said sympathetically. "She didn't see him often but he was her stepson when all's said and done."

"Where's Thomas?" Charlotte asked suddenly.

"Been out since Ralph had a go at him this afternoon." Mary supplied, "Why?"

Charlotte smiled and looked at Price with a wicked gleam in her eye. "Have you got such a thing as a bicycle around here?"

Startled by the change of subject, he nodded. "Yes, a rusty old thing. Why? What are you up to?"

Racing to the back door she laughed. "I fancy a ride. A lovely summer's evening shouldn't be wasted! Come on, let's get mobile."

Price took the lead muttering as he did so whilst Mary and Cissie followed the trail to the garage. The huge, cavernous building looked shabby and the doors creaked alarmingly as Price gained entry. The bicycle was a very rusty old model with flat tyres and wheels that squeaked with every turn.

"Wonderful!" Charlotte exclaimed. "Pump and oil-can, if you please."

Price grunted and rummaged around the garage with

difficulty as the single electric light bulb threw off more shadows than light. "You'll need a puncture repair kit too, not worth the bother. I had to use that pushbike and I can tell you, Miss, it's more push than bike!"

Blissfully disregarding the moans and groans, Charlotte set to work and managed to patch all punctures and oil all moving parts to make the transport roadworthy within an hour explaining she used to belong to a Cycling club years ago and restoring the bike was child's play.

Cissie and Mary left her to it, but once she was ready to set off Mary came running from the house. "You're not REALLY going out with that at this time of evening! I can guess what you're up to and you are just asking for trouble. Please, Lottie, stay home. If you want to enjoy the summer night we can get the garden furniture out and have a bottle of wine together, how's that sound?"

"Brilliant idea! You see to that and I'll be back to join you soon."

Charlotte winked as she wobbled off down the drive. She could hear the gasps as she fought to gain her balance, but her old instincts came to the fore and she soon rode in a reasonably straight line.

All the effort put into oiling the old machine paid off as she silently cycled past the rented cottage and stopped by the next farm gate. Propping the bike against a hedge she crept back and walked stealthily around the back of the building. A light shone from the downstairs window and she peered inside. Thomas was there along with another man and the blowsy woman. They were sitting down amongst a litter of furniture talking and drinking.

Charlotte watched and waited. It seemed an age before anyone moved, but the sound of a heavy vehicle galvanised the party into action. The woman opened the front door to admit another man and they began to take out articles of furniture. Thomas stood in the middle of the room and directed the operation without lifting a finger. Once several items were removed the engine roared into life and the two men left. Just Thomas and the woman remained. They laughed, threw their arms around one another and collapsed onto a settee.

Charlotte crept away. Curious she was, peeping-Tom she was not. Once in the lane she grabbed the bike and pedalled furiously to try and catch the vehicle she'd heard. Fate was on her side. It was stuck at the crossroads of the main road. She rode alongside the large van to find two cars blocking the way. They had collided at the junction causing minor damage but major irritation to the van driver who was shouting, cursing and sounding the horn.

Turning her bike she stopped alongside the van driver. "An accident, eh? Has anyone called the police out?"

The blaring stopped and the driver opened the window fully. He had a florid face with bulging pale blue eyes which threatened to pop out of their sockets. "There's no need of the law, lady. Just clear off and keep your nose out."

The gruff voice was menacing, but Charlotte stood her ground. "They are blocking the main road and could cause a more serious accident. I'll pop into the Station on my way back." Her heart stopped as the man lunged out of the lorry, the door missing her by inches.

The lumbering giant stood over her snarling, "We'll be here a lot longer if the pigs stick their noses in! I'm in a hurry and the likes of you aren't going to stop me. Neither are they!" With that he turned towards the cars and spoke with the drivers. It was only moments before the car owners got into their respective cars and started the engines.

The van driver returned to his vehicle, slammed the door and revved the engine to a monstrous pitch. Charlotte shouted over the roaring noise, "What did you say to them?"

Poking his head through the open window he laughed, an ugly sound which came from his stomach. "On yer bike, lady!" Another throaty laugh joined his as he wound up the window and drove off, his way clear.

They turned left towards Pantmawr and Charlotte followed. The bike had developed an ominous squeak which was not surprising due to its condition and sudden use, but it was only just over a mile to Glas Fryn so she prayed that it would make the distance.

As she neared the house she could see red tail lights ahead. To her horror it was the large van parked in a lay-by with its engine ticking over.

Were they waiting for her? Two men against one woman would prove to be difficult, she surmised. Charlotte pulled in and waited in the shadows. Some ten minutes passed and she felt impatient, there was no escape, just hedges each side of the road. Dusk was falling fast, it would soon be dark and that seemed a daunting prospect without a light on the bike. She reasoned to herself that she was nothing to the men in the lorry, just someone who had exchanged words with them back at the road junction. Maybe she was being paranoid. Taking a deep breath she decided to cycle on and reach the safety of Glas Fryn.

As she passed the vehicle she almost jumped out of her skin as the engine roared into life. Her adrenalin flowing she pedalled for her life as she heard the lumbering van start moving. It stayed behind her but with the engine racing in short bursts in order to spurt her into action. At last she saw the gateway of home and pedalled as though her heart would burst, her legs aching from sheer exertion. As the dark shape behind her gathered speed to mow her down she veered off through the open gateway of Glas Fryn, her lungs searing with pain. The gravel caused her to lose control and she went head first over the handlebars and landed with a sickening thud. The world turned black.

When she opened her eyes there was a sea of faces around her. She tried to get up and managed to rest on her elbows. "Cissie? Mary?" she whispered. Her lips wouldn't move properly.

"You're alright, love," Cissie answered. "The Doctor has

looked you over in case you broke anything, but he says you're in one piece. Can you manage to get up? We're here to help you, come on Lottie. That's the way my girl, up you come."

With hands coming from every direction she was aided to her feet. Tottering through dizziness she waited until her eyes focused properly. "Price? Is the bike O.K.?"

"You shook a lot of the rust off it! Trouble is, the front wheel has joined the back one." A dry snigger came from the wizened old man. "Come on, lass. We can replace that old thing, but not you."

A smartly dressed young man hovered as they led her into the house. "I think I'd better run her into the hospital. You never know. She's had a nasty bump on the head, we can't be too careful."

Cissie was making tea and giving orders. "Sit down, Doctor. We'll have a cuppa before anything else, the best thing in the world for shock."

Charlotte felt better once she drank a hot, sweet cup of laced tea. She smiled but it hurt. Touching her face gingerly she could feel rough skin and swelling. The young man frowned. "How do you feel, Miss..."

Mary had been busy with a large tin box and now brought a lotion and cotton wool over to the injured party. "This might sting a bit but it will heal the skin quickly. You've grazed your face but not too badly. No scars, I promise!"

Charlotte felt a lump come to her throat as Mary smiled at her. The plain face was transformed into an angelic countenance which nurses seem to be born with. The balm was soothing and made her face tingle, but not enough to cause discomfort. "It wasn't the bike, a van tried to mow me down," she explained, "I was lucky to be so close to home."

The Doctor frowned. "A van? Blue van? Was it the large box-type they use for carrying goods?"

"Yes," Charlotte confirmed, "Why?"

"There's been several incidents over the last few months. A

230

vehicle of that description has been reported for dangerous driving, especially through the village. The worst incident was two weeks ago when it careered past a kid on his bike and sent him flying. He was lucky to escape with a broken arm, but the boy was very distressed."

Charlotte looked at the fresh young face for the first time. "It might not be the same vehicle. It could be co-incidence."

"Several of the villagers confirm that it's the same blue van. Anyway, this ought to be reported to the police. Mr Price, would you be kind enough to ring the station?"

"I already have, sir."

"Why are you here, Doctor?" Charlotte asked. "I can't believe you got here that quickly!"

Price patted the Doctor on the back. "Her Ladyship called him out and he happened to be in the house when Cissie heard you scream. "Seeing the look of alarm on the young woman's face, the manservant added, "Don't worry, Lottie. It's only her ankle swollen again. She insisted on calling the Doctor out at this time of night."

The young man's face reddened. "I'm afraid she considered me too young to be a qualified practitioner, said I was wet behind the ears and wouldn't know measles from acne!"

"That's Aunt Olivia!" Charlotte smiled. "Anyone under the age of fifty would be unqualified in her book. She's had some bad news today, so tends to start looking for someone to shout at. Thank you for coming to my rescue, no doubt it proved a welcome diversion for you."

"Are you sure I can't run you to the hospital? Concussion should be checked out and you were knocked out for some ten minutes."

"I feel fine. I might not look very good, but my head just aches a little. Sorry you had to contend with Olivia, she's very trying."

"The whole village is trying!" the young man laughed. He was a handsome man with glossy black hair and a gentle manner. His confidence seemed low at the moment, but

Charlotte felt that time and his perseverance would change that.

"I feel like some fresh air." she said as her head began to float.

Mary nodded. "We set up the table and chairs in the garden so go and sit outside and I'll bring you a light supper. Are you in a rush, Doctor?"

"I'll wait for the Police. They seem to be taking their time."

Cissie laughed, "You will have plenty of time, old Tom is probably on duty which means you might be here for breakfast too!"

Before she realised it Lottie was sitting on the patio with the young doctor. She could feel his embarrassment and tried to dispel the atmosphere. "If you are on call shouldn't you get back? Don't let Mary and Cissie boss you around."

As he smiled his face relaxed. "I have a mobile phone, a vital piece of equipment in this area, when I can get a signal, that is. Actually, I'm starving so I hope that I'm not wanted for a while."

"We haven't been introduced properly, have we. I'm Charlotte Stone, Lottie to friends. Olivia Jones is my great-aunt but don't let that influence your opinion of me. I work for her and supposed to be researching a book for her. I used to work in a News Office so life here is pretty tame. What about you? It must be like trying to part the Red Sea when trying to handle people around here. A miracle if it works, bloody impossible if it doesn't!"

A deep laugh was her answer. "At last! I have come across a sane person. I can see that hospital is the last thing you need. My name is Paul. Paul Samuels. When I qualified I worked in Manchester for a few years but I threw fate to the winds and opted out of the rat-race. Now I discover the community regards me as a first-year student. The women tend to mother me whilst the men treat me with incredulity." He changed his voice to the local idiom, "This lad can't possible know how to cure a gammy leg, he has to be TOLD to give a sick note, nothing but a boy! The old Doc. understands, he knows I need a month off work with my old complaint!" Returning to his normal voice he grinned, "A regular handful don't come to the surgery for a cure, just for a legal excuse for a few weeks off work with pay."

Charlotte laughed at his mimicry of the locals. "I can imagine the obstacles you have to face."

Mary arrived with supper. "A hot-potato dip, tuck in. How are you feeling Lottie?"

"Entertained, actually! Thank you, Mary."

As they delved into the delicious snack, the young woman winced as she tried to eat. "Ouch! Bet I look worse than I feel. Tell me, Dr. Sam ......er, Samuels? Have you any connections with the area?"

"Yes. As a matter of fact my grandfather practised here. He died when my father was training, he's a Doctor too so I am the product of a line of medics. Dad settled down in London so I've never been here until this post became available."

Charlotte felt moved. "I'm sure he'd have been delighted so know his grandson took his place. He was a bit of a legend around these parts," to cover her statement she added, "at least, that's what I've heard."

"Well, I'm not going to get rich in a backwater like this, but I just felt that I had to come here. Not a problem as I was the only applicant anyway! Tell me, why did you call me Dr. Sam?"

"That's what they called your grandfather. If a name can be shortened then the people around here will take advantage."

Their conversation was interrupted by his mobile phone ringing. "Have to go I'm afraid." he announced after responding to the call, "a new arrival deciding to enter the world before time. When the police arrive would you ask them to see me tomorrow morning after surgery? Are you sure you're O.K.?"

"Yes to both questions. Goodbye, Dr. Samuels."

Shaking her hand he smiled warmly, "I like Dr. Sam better. It feels like I've come home. Does that sound absurd?"

"On the contrary, it sounds perfect. Just a tip, let it be known whose blood runs in your veins and you'll be surprised at the effect it will have."

"Patient curing the ills of the medic, eh? I'll take your advice, can't do any worse anyway! Bye, Lottie."

As he left she sat back in the chair and felt happy. The spirit of the old Doctor had returned to the village. Was it co-incidence that she herself had returned to her family home? It was as if fate was weaving a web from the new generation to build a thriving community despite the advance of time. If history was repeating itself then she would go with the tide, if she was the link then she would join the other factions. Ralph was also involved, he was Emily and David's grandson. All the elements were repeating the past. Even Thomas represented the evil side of things.

Price was a relic of past lives, Olivia too. What about Daisy? What happened to Daisy? Perhaps she was still alive somewhere, perhaps her children or grandchildren were living in the district. She must remember to ask Olivia, she would know.

The police arrived in the form of a large, burly Sergeant. They sat at the kitchen table and a statement of events taken down word for word. Accepting a cup of tea from Cissie's bottomless pot, the policeman laid down his notebook. "Very precise narrative of events, Miss Stone. No doubt your training has schooled you in describing events. Are you sure the driver could see you? Did you have lights on the bicycle? Were you in control of it as the vehicle approached or did you panic?"

Charlotte gasped, "I don't believe this! They tried to mow me down! No, I didn't need lights on the bike because it was still daylight. Just take a look at the mangled wreck left on the drive. They did it on purpose."

"Now, now, lass!" the policeman waved a large hand.

"Take it easy. I know you've had a shock, the state on your face tells me that, but it's my duty to explore all angles. Now then, this accident on the crossroads, can you tell me more about it? It hasn't been reported, you see."

"The van driver made sure of that!" Charlotte barked. "It looked to me as though one pulled out into the path of the other, it wasn't serious but the drivers were arguing the toss. I wish I'd taken their numbers as well then you might believe me."

"As well?"

"Yes! As well as the van ....oh, oh dear! Sorry. I should have told you." Charlotte gave the registration of the van and the policeman beamed.

"At last! We've had several reports of this vehicle but you're the first one to take the number. Well done, Miss Stone." The commendation was sincere.

The Sergeant left to make his report out and try to trace the van through the number. He doubted if anything could be proved due to a lack of witnesses, nevertheless, if the vehicle returned to the area it would be watched.

"Well, that was a waste of time." the injured party exclaimed when she sat around the table with the staff. Dropping her voice several octaves she continued, "We'll keep you informed, Miss. An appeal will be made for witnesses, but until then the complaint will be registered without further action."

Even Price laughed at the charade. "Hopkins is a good man. If he can do anything he will. Don't be too hard on him."

"Hopkins?" Charlotte trilled, "Was that Sergeant Hopkins?"

"Yes," Price answered evenly, "Why?"

Trying to cover her shock, Charlotte put a hand to her head. "Nothing! Sorry, I just.........well, it's been one hell of a day! How about a nightcap?"

"Coming right up!" Cissie replied setting a hot toddy in front of her. "Now tell us about tonight, my girl. I don't mean the accident, where did you go on that bike? You went to that cottage, didn't you?"

Mary settled herself with her father and urged Charlotte on. "Come on, Lottie. It won't go any further, I promise. So does Cissie!" she added casting a scathing glance at the plump maid.

"O.K., but the accident is relevant to the story. I could only see through the back window, not hear anything, but Thomas was there with that woman and another man, a big brutish type. Then a second man arrived in a large van thing and between them they loaded some furniture into it, the room was crammed with stuff! Anyway, I followed this van and it was held up at the crossroads. I offered to get the police but surprise, surprise! They didn't like the idea. Once it all cleared and the van turned left towards Pantmawr I pedalled for home knowing I could never keep up with it. But the van had stopped and parked just down the road from here, so I ended up making a bolt for it, that was when they tried to run me down. Thank God I was near home."

Mary asked in a worried voice, "You really think they tried to run you over?"

Charlotte nodded. "If they did it to frighten me they succeeded! I must admit I misjudged it a little. I thought I was nearer the house than I was." She paused her mind racing on, "still, Thomas doesn't know about it so don't say a word. I just fell off the bike, O.K.? I doubt if his henchmen would bother telling him about their little game with me."

Cissie clapped her hands. "My lips are sealed," as she looked around the table she felt uncomfortable, "Well they are! I promise!"

Price patted the plump hand. "I know we can count on you, Cissie."

Turning to Lottie he spoke gravely, "It's a dangerous game you're playing. I'm not happy about it, not happy at all."

Mary tried to lighten the mood. "Good thing the Doctor was here. You took a shine to him, Lottie."

"A bit young for me, Mary. Actually, he's Dr. Sam's grandson."

Price jolted upright in his chair. "Never! Good Lord above! They're all coming back!"

Mary looked up in the air in frustration. "What are you going on about, Dad? All coming back?"

"Lottie for one," he explained, "Dr. Sam's grandson for another. Then there's Sgt. Hopkins whose grandfather was a local bobby, Ralph's family goes way back and us, Mary! Even Thomas. All coming back from the past. It's uncanny."

"Dad!" Mary squealed. "You're giving me the creeps! I don't remember half of those people but you've talked about them often enough. Your imagination is beyond. Stop going back!"

"I'm not going back," he replied flatly, "the past is repeating itself."

Charlotte agreed. "You're father is right, Mary. Perhaps it happens in small communities like this, I don't know."

"I just hope that there's not two of me!" Cissie laughed aloud. "I'd better go up and check Her Ladyship, the bell is clanging like mad!"

Charlotte looked up at the row of antiquated bells attached to a board. Each one had been labelled in the dim and distant past. "Those things are Victorian! It's time they went."

Price smiled as he said sincerely, "Not as long as the last Victorian reigns!"

Charlotte volunteered to see Olivia on her way to bed, late though the hour was. She found the old lady in a state of agitation made worse by the sight of her great niece. "Charlotte! What have you done to your face? You look grotesque!"

"Kind words, indeed." Catching her reflection in the dressing-table mirror she was shocked at her swollen, grazed face. "You are right, but your choice of adjective is hardly consoling."

Getting out of bed and ringing the bell-rope vigorously the

old lady barked, "What has been going on? Where is that girl?"

Charlotte sighed. "On her way up, just give her chance! You should be asleep."

"I am not a child!" The door opened and Mary walked in with two glasses and a decanter. Olivia pointed to the table in the window bay. Mary did as she was bid and left the room with a silent grace. Her father had taught her well, Charlotte mused. Olivia walked over to the table without any aid or sign of limp. "Sit down, child. Pour. What happened to you?"

"I went for a bike ride and fell off. Gravel rash. Good job the doctor was at hand."

"He's no Doctor! We are better of with Mary's crackpot potions. Where did the bicycle come from?"

"The garage. A few punctures but serviceable. At least it was. It came off worse than me."

"Good! Then you will leave the confounded thing alone! Your face is a mess and it will take months for your skin to heal. You should remember that you're not getting any younger and act accordingly."

"I'm not ready for the twin-set and pearls brigade yet, Aunt. Besides, things are different these days, attitude to age had changed dramatically."

"Oh, yes!" Olivia grunted. "I've seen middle-aged men jogging around trying to look fit whilst the expression of agony on their faces is unmistakable. Women are just as bad. They pile on make-up and wear ridiculous clothes trying to look younger than their daughters. Things have changed, I agree, but for the worse."

Charlotte felt very tired and conceded defeat. "If you say so, Aunt. It's late and I'm ready for bed if you're not. By the way, Thomas is absent again, do you know where he goes?"

"Oh really, child. You have asked me that before and I keep telling you it's none of our business. You are positively hounding the boy!"

"ME! Hounding HIM! Dear God! You'll eat your words

one day, Aunt. He's a scheming con-man and the truth will come out if it kills me!"

Olivia rose and walked over to the young woman. "You are overwrought, child."   Patting her arm maternally she continued, "Go to bed and stop worrying about Thomas. You're letting your imagination run wild. I may be in the twilight of my life, but I'm not such a fool as some might think. Goodnight, Charlotte."

In the early hours Charlotte was woken by something unknown, no sound or movement broke the stillness of the night but the atmosphere made her skin prickle with fear. Peering cautiously over her blankets she could only see the grey glow of the coming dawn shedding a feeble light whilst the dark shapes of the furniture loomed like sentinels in a tomb.

Her fear was so great that she was afraid to reach out for the bedside lamp in case an icy coldness gripped her exposed limb. Burying herself beneath thc heavy bedspread which her grandmother Annie had made she fought the unseen enemy by lying still and begging for sleep to return.

Something was wrong. Something terrible was going to happen. It was a force which enveloped her mind leaving her powerless to resist, yet too vague to put into logical or reasonable thought. Were her ancestors warning her? The patchwork quilt was her sanctuary. Wrapped deep within the folds the night dissolved into harmless dreams.

"Come on, love! Nice cup of tea for you. Good gracious! You look like a loser in the boxing-ring. Poor girl, how do you feel?"

Charlotte felt relieved to wake and see Cissie by the bedside. Had last night been a dream? That terrible fear and dread which filled her being was the most frightening experience of her life. She sat up and drank the welcome brew and tried to smile. "Ouch! It hurts to move my face. I thought it would be better today."

"Get yourself up and Mary will see to you downstairs. She's got her hands full at the moment. That silly old bugger, pardon my Welsh, came in stone drunk last night and fell down the stairs!"

"What!" Despite the pain of using her facial muscles the news was like an antidote. "Thomas?"

"He's the only silly bugger I know!" Cissie chuckled and clapped her hands. "I beg your pardon, Lottie, I don't normally swear but to see that good-for-nothing go head over heels down the stairs made my day! Or should I say night? It was about two in the morning when he came in and made such a commotion that the Missus came out on the landing. He'd just made it up the stairs when Madam shouted at him and waved her walking-stick. He was laughing and pretending to fence with her but lost his balance and went down quicker than he came up!"

Through gritted teeth the young woman said, "Stop it, Cissie! It hurts to laugh! I hope he broke a few limbs, or better still, his neck."

"No such luck! So drunk he just passed out with the shock of his acrobatics! We called the Doctor out, that's twice he's been here in one night poor lad. Anyway, he helped us get him to bed and reckons there's no damage. Trust you to miss all the action. You must have slept like top. Mary's potions work like a charm, don't they."

As Cissie left the room, Charlotte wondered about Mary Price and her natural remedies. Had they caused her to hallucinate? Probably. Then she had nothing to worry about, those strange feelings of dread were merely a side-effect of nature's cures. She prayed that this was the case. Why else had she been so terrified?

CHAPTER 14

Old Wounds & New Suspicions

Price had agreed to accompany Charlotte to the attic during the afternoon when he had two hours spare. It was to be done without Olivia's knowledge because it was certain that she wouldn't approve. Until the allotted hour, Charlotte ambled around the gardens having failed to work in the library due to her reduced eyesight. Her eyes were two swollen slits like a punch-drunk pugilist, so she hid behind sunglasses.

After Mary's administrations it was easier to move her facial muscles. The soothing balm helped with the pain and as long as she didn't look in a mirror she felt a lot better. Going out and about was not advisable and she certainly didn't want the locals gazing at her, speculating and gossiping.

Thus confined to barracks, she found herself outside the ruin of the summer house yet again realising that she hadn't travelled in time for days. Her last encounter had been in this very place when she had been able to talk to her Grandfather. Would it happen again? She sat on the wooden steps and waited. Resting against the doorpost she listened to the sounds of a perfect summer day and closed her eyes to listen to the birds singing with the joy of life, giving herself up to the warmth of the sun and nature's melodious song.

A hand gripped her shoulder and she opened her eyes with hope. Had her ancestors come back? She turned to see the face of an old man looking at her intently. "You alright, Miss?"

Startled, Charlotte jumped to her feet. The face seemed familiar yet strange. "Do I know you? Are you from .... " she was about to say 'the past' but something stopped her.

"Pantmawr, aye," the old man answered. "Ted Skinner. I used to be the gardener here. Las' time I saw you was in a field at the crack of dawn dressed in your nightgown of all things!"

"Of course!" the truth dawned on Charlotte, "You were the one who found me and got Ralph."

"Thass right, Miss." The thin, sharp face peered at hers. "What happened to your face? Been fighting with 'er Ladyship?"

"Not quite, Ted! Fell off a bike to tell the truth. Thank you for helping me before, I remember your flask, it was ....well....intoxicating!"

"Should be! Best Welsh Whisky. Keeps out the nip during the night."

Charlotte was puzzled at the remark. "I tried it before at the Pritchard's' farm and it's very warming as you say. But why at night? Why should you need it at night?"

Ted Skinner winked. His kindly eyes sparkled from the tanned, dried skin like jewels in leather. "I can't sleep so good, besides, the missus snores something awful! I go out and about on my bike and enjoy the wildlife so to speak, especially the ones which look better on the dinner table next day. Rabbits have a habit of collapsing at my feet, you could say."

"I suppose trout jump out of the river, too!" Charlotte asked smiling.

Inclining his capped head he laughed softly. "It 'as been known, Miss. It 'as been known."

"Sit down, Ted, and tell me what else you see on your travels during the wee small hours. I bet you could write a book."

Settling down besides the young woman he nodded. "I could that, young Miss. I could that. The things that go on around here and it looks like a sleepy village by day. I daren't tell the Missus mind! Oh no, a right gossip she is! Good hearted though."

Charlotte liked the old man and felt easy in his company. "I bet you're glad that you have retired, eh Ted? This place must have been back-breaking work."

Lighting a pipe he answered slowly. "I grew up with it so it didn't seem like work at all. I'm the wrong side of 75 now so it's time I packed it in." He sucked his pipe speculatively. "'is Nibs made sure I was out of the way by causing trouble and the old girl trusted 'im more than me. I 'eard 'e fell down the stairs last night, pity he didn't break his neck. "

Amazed that he knew about Thomas's accident, Charlotte nudged the old man. "How did you know about that ? I know the grapevine travels fast but that defies the speed of sound!"

A quiet chuckle erupted, "Nay, girl! Now an' then old Cissie gives me a bacon butty, but she was out shopping today. Price kindly gave me a bite an' told me 'bout your trouble. Asked me if I knew anything. He got a woman you know."

"Price?" Charlotte asked astonished.

"Don't be daft! That poor ol' bugger still hankers after his wife. Thomas Armstrong, 'e's got a woman, but you know that, don't you girlie? Don't go creeping round there on your own, lovely girl. Did that van run you down?"

"Yes!" Charlotte gasped, "at least it tried to. DID you see anything?"

"No. First I 'eard about 'im 'aving a cottage like. Must be off my patch, else I'd know. That's where he must spend most of his nights, that Thomas. Leave 'im be, girl. Leave 'im be."

"But I'm sure he's robbing Olivia right, left and centre. I can't let him get away with it. I'm going to put a stop to his schemes with or without anyone's help."

Looking troubled, Ted Skinner rubbed his chin. "Leave that to Mr. Ralph. He'll find a way. By God! You're like Annie. Jim too, come to that. Your Grandpa Jim was a stubborn mule for all his quiet ways. Brave man, too. He had a terrible accident in the mine but went back once he was fit again. It takes some courage does that."

"I can imagine." Charlotte shuddered as she remembered the state on the broken body in the old cottage.

"Not only that," the old gardener continued, "he sought out his enemy and killed him!"

Charlotte felt as though a blow to her chest had knocked all the wind out of her lungs. "Jim? He killed................. did he kill Fredrick Blake?"

" 'ow come you know about Fred Blake, girl?"

"Oh, I .... well........... " Sighing with exasperation she patted the gnarled hand. "I just do. Tell me what happened, Ted."

Tapping his pipe on the path he refilled it as he spoke. "Only me and the ol' Sergeant knew what 'appened. It was kept very quiet 'cos Jim was innocent, a man driven out of his mind by the tricks of Fred Blake. I don't know the reasons behind it, I was only a lad, but I saw them fighting, Jim and Blake.

'There was two shots, the first one injured your Grandpa and the second one killed Blake. Jim sent me to fetch the police and made me promise not to talk to anyone else. When I came back with Sgt. Hopkins and he asked me what I saw an' he swore me to secrecy. You took such things to 'eart in them days, I've never told a soul. Not a living soul."

"You told me. Why?"

"You're 'ere to put things right, lovely girl. Why else were you in that field? It's close to where your grandparents lived before the fire, I know that much. Your Mam nearly died in that blaze."

Charlotte shivered. "I know, Ralph told me. I'm terrified of fire, Ted, but didn't know why until I came here. You seem to understand."

"Aye, I do that. I know I was young but I know who did it. Blake. I saw him."

Wondering if the old gardener was telling the truth she asked guardedly, "You seem to know a lot, Ted. Why didn't you tell the police at the time?"

A dry laugh rasped in his throat. "I did. The ol' Sergeant said I was a good boy but the Courts wouldn't believe any nipper. Blake had powerful friends and wealthy relatives. I think that's why ol' Hoppy covered up when Blake got killed. Everyone says it was an accident like, only I know better."

"Where did it happen?"

Getting up, Ted Skinner winked. " 'ere, Miss. Right 'ere. To the very day if I remember rightly, or the night to be exact, that would be last night, like. To tell the truth, Miss, I was out poaching for my Ma when I saw it so it didn't take much to shut me up!"

It dawned on Charlotte why she had the strange sensations the night before. Mary's potions were innocent. The past had invaded her innate being and the horror of the night long ago manifested itself into a fearful emotion.

Ted Skinner peered down at the young woman and spoke sharply. "You can believe me or not, Miss. I know what I saw. Your Grandfather put paid to an evil man an' that was justice. These days they'd call it rough justice, but Jim Nicholls was an 'onorable man and God was on his side. Take it easy, girlie, and heed my words. Stay clear of that Thomas. Blood flows through the lines whether it be good or evil." He walked down the path towards the house and Charlotte jumped up quickly.

"Ted!" she shouted as the old man halted in his tracks, "can you tell me anymore?"

"Next time, lovely girl. Next time. I'll be 'round."

As the man left Charlotte let the revelations sink in. Fred Blake, the natural father of Daisy, had tried to murder a whole family by burning them out of their humble cottage, he had shot at Emily his niece, injured David who was Jim's nephew. He had threatened Annie and stalked Daisy. No wonder her grandfather felt threatened.

Ted Skinner had seen it through the eyes of a child, placed his own conclusions to the facts before him, but the real facts ran deeper than he would ever know. The adult world was full of complications and hidden motives. Perhaps it was time she viewed the facts with the simple perspectives of an infant.

Good always triumphs over evil, the good live happily ever after. No. Real life didn't work out like that.

During the afternoon she went up to the attic rooms with Price as arranged. Their progress was quiet and slow, quietly for the sake of Olivia and slowly for Price's sake. Their footsteps sounded unnaturally loud as they stalked the bare floorboards which creaked and groaned in protest.

"Are you sure this house isn't riddled with dry rot?" Charlotte asked of the old man.

Coughing and wheezing, Price shook his head. "You never know. I reckon I am, and this house is far older than me!"

Charlotte put her arm around the bent shoulders and spoke softly. "I'm sorry, Price. Do you feel alright?"

A slow smile lit up the skeletal face and the glitter in the rheumy blue eyes belied his age. "Annie all over again! She cared too." Taking a deep breath he straightened a few degrees. "There's not many have bothered to ask me how I feel. Come on then, let's get started."

"We can forget the old nursery anyway. I've seen enough of that room to know exactly what's in it, just upturned wardrobes now! Let's try the others."

"Lottie?"

"Yes?" she asked with bated breath.

"Why are you whispering all the time? No-one will hear us up here as you know to your cost when you were trapped that night. That's why they put the nursery on this floor. Children were seen and not heard!"

A giggle erupted in the young woman's throat. "Poor kids, being stuck up here out of sight out of mind. Lead the way, Price. Let our investigation commence."

The pair began their scouting mission of the attic rooms. There was very little to see except the odd pieces of furniture such as broken chairs and heavy wardrobes. A few badly marked sideboards and blanket chests were dispersed amongst the rooms, their scars evident even through a thick layer of dust.

"Seen enough?" Price asked as he held a handkerchief to his nose and mouth.

"Yes, nothing worth bothering with. Thomas has made sure of that."

They left the third floor feeling dirty and disappointed, supposition was all very well but facts were harder to accept.

Charlotte sat at her dressing-table feeling very depressed. Proof was such an elusive commodity and she wished she's worked in the more investigative areas of her old newspaper office. Experience would have made up for inadequacy. Still, all was not lost. She could travel back in time, back to her family roots, back to the ones she had come to love. The thimble which first transported her into the world beyond was slipped onto her finger and she waited. Nothing happened. The magic had gone.

Close to tears, Charlotte flung the item down and went to the bathroom to wash the dust of the attic away. Just as she immersed herself in the bath of steaming aromatic water she heard Cissie's voice calling her. "In the bath, Cissie. What is it?"

"Ralph's on the 'phone." came the muffled reply through the locked door.

"Sod's Law!" Charlotte muttered. "You wait, and wait, and wait, then just as you get into a bath the 'phone goes!"

"Lottie? Did you hear me?" Cissie shouted.

"Yes. Tell him to ring later. I'm busy!"

The steam in the bathroom was not caused through the hot water alone. Charlotte had been anxious to hear from Ralph, because of Jarvis, because of the tale of Ted Skinner, because of the attic search, because........... despite her reluctance to admit it, she wanted to hear his voice. Yes. She was missing him.

Getting out of the bath she wrapped a large towel around her slim body and brushed her hair in front of the wall mirror. She gasped as a numbing coldness swept through her body and the room spun like a child's top. When it stopped she felt nauseous and gripped the shelf in front of her to regain her balance. Gingerly, she looked into the mirror. The reflection was not as it should be. It was not the bathroom and her image was not reflected in the glass.

It was a bedroom with heavy, dark drapes and large oak furniture. An old woman lay in the bed whilst another sat by her side. Sarah and Annie. Her grandmother and great-grandmother. Sarah looked frail and found breathing difficult.

"How are you feeling now, Mam? The pain any easier?"

Nodding, the old woman smiled. "Mrs Price's medicine will do the trick. It always has. Shingles are the curse of the Devil. Keeps coming back. How are the children, Annie?"

"Mary's poorly with asthma again, but the rest are fighting fit. The fire didn't help that girl's lungs at all."

"That man should be brought to justice. Jim keeping an eye out?"

Annie nodded then began to sob. "Oh, Mam! I've seen him watching the cottage and the children say that he's followed them home from school. Sgt. Hopkins says that he can't prove anything against him, but got Jim to keep a pistol handy just in case. Now our Daisy's missing!" Crying into a handkerchief she let her fear spill out.

Sarah had paled. "Have a good cry, Annie love. It must be hard to keep face in front of the children, I bet everyone said I shouldn't know either! Tell me about Daisy."

"The hospital rang Dr. Sam to see if she'd come home because she hadn't reported for duty for two days. They'd checked her room but her things are all there. Mam, do you think he would have ......"

"Stop it!" barked the voice from the bed. The effort forced her to wait before she could continue. "Do the police know?"

Nodding and trying to stop the flow of tears, Annie told her mother that Sgt. Hopkins was making enquiries in this area whilst her absence was reported to the London police force. "The first thing he was going to do was check on Fred

Blake, but we haven't heard back from him yet. If anything has happened to that girl...........

Sarah sounded sharp as she tried to bolster her daughter's worse fears. "Daisy has many friends. You'll find her with one of them, no doubt. Emily would be the person to help. Ask Jim to go over and see her."

"He's done that. Emily hasn't heard from Daisy for a few weeks."

Sarah took a deep breath and narrowed her eyes. "Annie! Stop fretting. That girl is nearly 30 years of age and she can well take care of herself. This Blake business is getting out of hand. Like as not he's gone to ground like the wily fox he is. This has been going on for years now." Sarah paused, "Where are the rest of my family? Are you keeping them away?"

Nodding, the stricken face of her daughter replied sadly, "Yes. I thought you should have rest. Dr. Sam said as much."

"Since when have we listened to doctors? I am not on my deathbed child, and my family are what I live for. Besides, they are so well-behaved in my presence it doesn't seem true!" As the old woman chuckled it started a fit of coughing.

Charlotte saw the pain on the face of her great-grandmother Sarah before the darkness descended and dragged her back to the present. She was still wrapped in a towel and felt unbearably cold. Rubbing herself briskly she realised the situation. Time travel wearing only a towel? If anyone knew she would be committed! It really was becoming quite inconvenient, the thimble didn't work anymore so the time warp was beyond her control - or was it possible to control it? Goose-pimples rippled through her flesh at the thought. If only she could talk to Ralph.

Going down for Dinner, Charlotte went into the kitchen to see if Ralph had left a message but was disappointed by Cissie's negative reply. The three staff members were putting the final touches to the meal with quiet efficiency and turned down her offer of help.

Olivia was down at 7.55 prompt dressed to the nines.

"How are you feeling, child? You still look dreadful."

"What a morale booster you are! I might ...." her words froze on her lips at the entrance of Thomas.

"Good Lord! What a sight. Enough to put one off one's food."

"Then eat elsewhere, Thomas." Charlotte retorted.

Olivia interceded. "We will all eat together and in harmony. As for you, Thomas, your behaviour last night leaves a lot to be desired. We will forget the episode but only on condition you treat others with the respect they deserve. Ah, Price! Come on, children, enjoy your meal."

Charlotte totally ignored the presence of her adversary and ate her meal with gusto. It was strange that the meals at Glas Fryn were plentiful and delicious yet she was losing weight. Many women would love to be in such a position, she mused.

As the dessert arrived Olivia tapped the table. "Take your time, child. A hearty appetite is all very well, but one must never concede to physical urges. Mind over matter, that's the key."

Feeling like an admonished child, Charlotte held back the physical urge to throw something at the smirking Thomas and adopted the dictate of her Aunt. "Mind over matter, eh? Well there's something on my mind, so perhaps the matter should be discussed. I've been up to the attic today, just out of curiosity you understand. A lot of wasted space up there, Aunt. Nothing much except dust and echoes."

"On the contrary," the indignant host replied, "the furniture up there is accumulating value, not to mention the paintings. Mr. Jones bought them as investments but I couldn't stand the things."

"There are no paintings up there, Aunt. What furniture there is looks of little value, just the odd wardrobe and sideboards which need major restoration." Pausing for effect, she turned the gaze to the man at the table. "You look quite pale, Thomas. Anything wrong?"

Olivia rang the small silver bell by her side. When Price

appeared she spoke harshly. "I want the inventory of the attic. Now!"

"Inventory?" the old servant asked in amazement.

"Yes, Price. A list. A record. Try not to look so vague, man!"

The frail shoulders mustered at the sharp tones of his mistress and he answered with a calm, unwavering voice. "I've been in this House man and boy, Madam. There has never been an inventory for any room in the house, least of all the attic. When an item is no longer required it is taken upstairs for storage and forgotten. You may recall an incident with the old furniture from the Lounge when you refurbished the room?"

Looking guilty, but setting her mouth in a stubborn line she answered haughtily, "I can remember that stupid woman from the village asking if she could have it all! What was it she said? Oh, yes! Some excuse about using it in the community centre. The very thought of it! All and sundry sitting on my furniture, quite degrading!"

Price nodded to confirm the story as Charlotte banged the table with her fist. "How selfish can you get! You'd rather put it up there to rot than donate it to a worthwhile cause! Well it serves you right because there's nothing up there now. No furniture, no paintings or anything else worth a light!"

The colour had drained from the old lady's face. "You must be mistaken, must be! I'm going up to see for myself."

"No!" Charlotte yelled as she stood up. "We'll go into the lounge and talk. That includes you, Thomas."

"I....... I have to use the bathroom. Back in a jiffy!"

As Olivia left the room leaning heavily on her walking-stick, Thomas fled with the speed of light. Charlotte stationed Price in the hall to make sure that the culprit didn't leave the house. "When he comes down drag him in if necessary, O.K.?"

"Oh, yes, Lottie! You can rely on me. About time he faced the music. He looked guilty enough."

Charlotte went into the lounge and poured two large brandies. Handing one to her aged Aunt who was slumped in her favourite chair she sat on the floor by her side. "It's true. There's nothing up there. I have no reason to lie to you."

A shaking hand put the glass to her lips and gulped the liquid courage. "Price was right about the attic. It's always been treated as a dumping ground for unwanted articles. Out of sight, out of mind. You were right too. I have been selfish and now fate repays me with its own form of justice. I have been robbed."

"Aunt, I've got my own ideas about the subject. Are you willing to listen now?"

"No need. It must be Thomas. How on earth did he get it out of here? There's always someone around. Where did he take it?"

"He has rented a cottage in the Eastbridge area and it's stored there before being transported to more lucrative markets. He's assisted by a woman, a coarse type with a foul mouth."

"Terrible! Terrible!" muttered the stunned Olivia. "I trusted that boy. Perhaps we are mistaken. There must be an explanation for all this."

Hearing mumbled voices in the hall outside, Charlotte went to the door and opened it wide. "Let's ask him. Come on, Thomas. Join the party. We could do with a good fairy-tale."

Passing her he grinned into her face and uttered "Bitch!" under his breath. Helping himself to the brandy decanter he turned to Olivia still with his fixed smile. "Now then, dear Aunt, what's the problem?"

"Sit down, Thomas. This is a serious matter."

"Oh dear!" he exclaimed innocently, "Was I a few minutes late for dinner? Very rude of me. Maybe it was being drunk last night? Well, I apologise for that. One too many with the boys and ...."

Olivia waved a hand with authority. "Stop drivelling! Where have all my furniture and paintings gone? You've been up there frequently and at odd hours. We caught you out, remember! You suffered a broken arm in the process. You appear to be nothing but a common thief, Thomas!"

"Steady on there, Aunt! That's a bit strong. Yes, I have been disposing of your junk up in the attic but only for your own benefit. It was worm-eaten and discarded because you didn't want it so I got rid of it for a good price on the antiques market. A damn good price considering."

"So why hasn't she seen any of this money?" Charlotte asked enraged. "Come off it, Thomas! You've taken it all without permission, lined your own pocket and set up that tart of a woman in a cottage. I've been there, so don't deny it!"

"Yes," he sneered, "she told me about Batman and Robin disguised as WI women of all things, I had a vision of Cissie in tights but that was rather obscene. There again, a mask would be a blessing in your case."

"Thomas!" shouted Olivia, "Enough insults. You have sold items which don't belong to you. In my vocabulary that spells theft."

Thomas drained his glass. "Dear Aunt! As if I would do anything to hurt you. I was acting on your behalf. You will reap the benefits of the investments I made with the proceeds, it's all quite legal and above board. This house takes a lot to keep up and I know what a proud woman you are. I merely tried to alleviate your financial burden discreetly."

"The woman? Who is she? Someone local?" Olivia thundered, "This could prove scandalous."

"As if I would ever place you in such a position, Aunt!" As Charlotte ground her teeth seeing victory slip away under the suave tongue of her adversary, Thomas continued to wheedle, "As a matter of fact you may know her. She's Uncle Alan's housekeeper. He's gone abroad for a while so I offered her a holiday down here, naturally her assistance in the renovation and sale of the furniture has been invaluable." Turning to Charlotte he quipped, "It's so nice to have someone you can trust."

The old woman nodded. "You see, Charlotte. Innocent until proven guilty is a wise adage! You are far too quick to judge, child. I have known Thomas since he was a boy and I should have known better than to suspect him of doing anything underhand."

Feeling the bile rise in her throat the young woman stood in front of the stubborn, elderly female. "He took the stuff without your knowledge. That is theft, plain and simple. His story of investing money is a lie, where is his proof? Is your bank account overflowing? No. You haven't seen a penny of it!"

A obstinate expression settled on the lined face. "His word is all the proof I need. Leave us. There are matters to be discussed in private."

Charlotte drew herself to full height and walked proudly from the room, but Thomas couldn't resist a parting shot. "Goodnight, old girl. Sorry I'm not the villain you hoped for. No wonder you never made the headlines as a reporter!"

Over her shoulder she smiled and answered softly, "On the contrary, this is just the beginning, old boy! Your past may catch up with you yet."

Striding with a boldness she didn't feel Charlotte made her way to the kitchen and refuge. "Damn! Damn! Damn!" she exploded much to alarm of Mary and Cissie. "He's bloody well got away with it!"

"Easy, lass. Easy now." Price uttered as he followed her into the room. "Sit down and have a cup of tea. The old girl is brainwashed and there's nothing we can do about it."

"If the money isn't there she might sit up and take notice," Charlotte reasoned. "She's bound to ask him where it is, she's not that stupid. She becomes so naive and gullible whenever he opens his mouth. God! I wish Ralph was here to give some moral support."

"Oh yes!" Cissie yelped, "he rang while you were arguing in the lounge so I didn't like to call you out, I thought you were winning! Anyway, he said he'd be back in a day or two."

" Huh!" the young woman snorted, " back to what? He hasn't got a job anymore."

Mary turned pale. "What are you talking about? He's the Estate Manager, his job is safe."

"Not since he resigned and the old girl accepted. Quite a mess, isn't it."

The four sat at the table deep in thought, suddenly Price banged the scrubbed top with his fist. "The woman! His Uncle's housekeeper? Alan Armstrong is a gentleman and from what I've heard about this woman she doesn't fit the part at all. Something's wrong. I must find Alan Armstrong's address and contact him."

A spark of hope dawned in Charlotte's eyes. "Right! He brought Thomas up, didn't he? In Cumbria? Yes! Find his phone number or address Price, and we'll find out who this woman really is."

Cissie laughed. "From what I saw of her she'd be the straw that broke the camel's back! My, My! What a common thing she was."

The company fell silent as the shadow of Thomas Armstrong filled the doorway. He merely stood and gazed at them with sheer malevolence in his face, even the smirk had vanished. After some moments he turned and left as silently as he had materialised.

Nobody spoke. The atmosphere had changed. No more the happy band united against the enemy, just four people who felt cold and numb after being subjected to the most cruel and evil countenance. The devil incarnate who was free to roam the house they lived in.

CHAPTER 15

Disappearances

Charlotte lay awake for hours expecting Thomas to return drunk and triumphant to Glas Fryn and start breaking down doors, hers in particular, but during the waiting she must have fallen asleep. Morning arrived and the sound of rain tonelessly hitting the bedroom window did nothing to cheer, whilst the mirror reflected a less swollen but colourful face.

Skipping breakfast, much to the chagrin of Cissie, Charlotte left the house and headed for Pantmawr. Very little traffic passed her on the road and the village was very quiet. Her first stop was the telephone kiosk. She rang Bill, her old colleague, only to find that he was on holiday. Her second call was a long shot. Directory enquiries. They supplied the number of a Doctor Alan Armstrong in Kendal, Cumbria.

With fingers crossed she dialled the number. He had to be the right one. A young woman answered the phone. "Surgery? Can I help you?"

"Oh! Yes, I hope so. Could I speak to Dr. Armstrong, please?"

"I'm afraid he's out on call at the moment. Would you like to make an appointment?"

"No. I'm not a patient. It's a personal call. When will he be back?"

The disembodied voice became haughty. "He's due back at ten but has surgery until twelve. Can I take a message?"

"Not really," Charlotte answered despondently. "I'll try ......well, some other time."

"Just a minute," the voice snapped, "if it's personal would his housekeeper be of any help?"

"Housekeeper? She's there?"

"Certainly. Shall I put you through to Mrs.Travers?"

Charlotte agreed and waited as the line clicked and

hummed. "Hello?" a thin reedy voice asked, "Can I help you? The Doctor's not here at present."

"Are you Dr. Alan Armstrong's housekeeper?"

"I am. Who are you?"

"Oh," Charlotte laughed without amusement. "I'm ringing on behalf of a relative of Dr. Armstrong. It's....... it's just a social call, to see how he is. He must be back from his travels abroad then. Did he enjoy his trip?"

"Look, Miss, I don't know who you are but ...." Another voice filtered through from the background and a male voice took over.

"Who the devil is this?"

"Dr. Armstrong?" Charlotte asked weakly.

"Yes, yes. I'm going to be late for surgery so you'd better be quick."

"I'm ringing on behalf of Olivia Jones. She's my Great-Aunt and Thomas told her you were abroad for a long time so she asked me to ring for news."

"Good grief!" the voice exclaimed in surprise. "How is the old girl? Glad to hear she's still alive and kicking."

"Very much so, Dr. Armstrong. My name is Charlotte Stone and I'm staying with her. Thomas is too. That's really why I'm phoning you."

"I want nothing to do with that blaggard!" the voice boomed crossly. "I wouldn't even attend his funeral!"

Afraid that the phone would be slammed down, Charlotte rushed her words. "The pity is that he's not dead yet, Doctor. I was hoping you might give me a little information because I think he's taking Olivia for all she's got and I aim to stop him. You see, he told her you were abroad and I had to know whether it was true or not."

"Rubbish ! I haven't been out of the country since I was a student. Many years ago, I can assure you. Why would he tell her that? I can't see the point."

"To cut a long story short, Dr. Armstrong, he's set this woman up in a local cottage and he says she's your housekeeper in need of a holiday. She's blonde, brash and her language is something to be desired. Her accent is Northern. I just wanted to check her out. Obviously another lie which he has concocted."

"Actually, it sounds like Dora Biggins! She worked here for a short time......... Lord, let me think............. oh, yes! I dismissed her about the same time I sent that boy Thomas packing. What are they playing at?"

Charlotte felt elated. "I'm still working on that, but they've sold off a lot of Olivia's antique furniture and paintings. Why did you send him packing, Doctor?"

"Young lady, he was trouble from the day he came here. Lies and deceit which caused no end of trouble, the very opposite to his cousin Ralph. You know Ralph, of course?" There was a muffled voice before he continued, "I must go, emergency. Just be warned, Miss.....er,."

"Stone. Charlotte Stone."

"Just take heed, Miss Stone. He's as crafty as a cartload of monkeys. If I get the chance I'll come down and see Olivia soon, give her my regards."

The line clicked and purred. Charlotte had a little more to go on. Dora Biggins. The woman now had a name.

The village was beginning to burst into life so the young woman slipped into the Post Office before the inevitable queue started building up. A man was being served and judging by the batch of pension books he held it looked like a long wait.

Two women began chatting behind her and Charlotte smiled as they exchanged the usual information about their families then moved on to medical problems, each one trying to outdo the other with bodily mysteries and consequent miracles which confounded the most eminent of surgeons and specialists.

"Of course, my Ted had never been the same since that business up at the House. Jumped up little upstart he is! Treating my Ted like that after all his years up there. She

258

ought to have known better, but NO! Believe that Thomas Armstrong before anyone else. Cissie told me that he can do no wrong in the old girl's her eyes."

"Poor old Ted!" the second voice commiserated. "He was hard done by, we all know that. That old bitch behind the counter is carrying on with him, you know. She tries to be so high and mighty but she's nothing but a common slut!"

"Oh yes, we all know that! He must be using her for some reason. Why else would he bother with that bit of old scrag end!" Both women giggled in unison.

Charlotte turned to face them. "I couldn't help overhearing you. You were talking about Thomas Armstrong. What happened?"

The women's' faces fell in horror. The larger lady found the courage to speak. "You're from the House, aren't you! Ted said that you had a bit of trouble? How is your face, love? It looks terrible."

The other woman nudged her friend. "Shut up, Ada! She's his cousin or something. Sorry, love. We didn't mean any harm."

"On the contrary," Charlotte replied evenly, "I am not his cousin and hate the 'jumped up little upstart'! What did he do?"

"Got my Ted the sack, that's what!" Ada the larger lady answered sharply.

The Postmistress shouted, "Next!"

Charlotte turned to face the caller. "Two recorded, please," then dropping her voice to a whisper she continued, "I expect my mail to be treated with the confidence one expects from SERVANTS of the Post Office. One word to Thomas and your cosy little pensioned job will be on the line, Lady. I understand your living accommodation is included in the package? Am I right?"

The grim face concentrated on the paperwork before speaking in gritty tones, "Fall off your bike, did you? Nasty. You ought to be more careful on our narrow roads."

Passing the money over, Charlotte smiled her sweetest smile and resumed her normal tone. "News travels fast in this place, or are you chasing the Doctor as well? Young, isn't he. Just your cup of tea. I rather think you'd have to drug his tea before he looked at you twice. Never mind, Miss Kemp. Thomas has enough to go around. His mistress in the cottage Eastbridge way obviously doesn't mind sharing him. Thank you. Good morning."

Gloating because the harridan behind the counter was left with mouth gaping, Charlotte waited outside for Ada and her friend. When they emerged they looked delighted.

"What did you say to her? I couldn't quite catch it but it left her speechless for a change!"

"Come on, ladies. Coffee on me."

"Humph!" snorted the larger lady as she snapped her handbag shut. "Something stronger would be better."

"Show me the pub, then. My treat just the same."

The local was not far away. It was austere but quiet. Charlotte brought the drinks and carried them to the table. "Coffee for me and a Stout each as requested. Do you usually frequent this place at eleven in the morning?"

"Only when someone else is paying, love!" the smaller woman laughed.

The large woman took over. "We know who you are. Charlotte Stone. Cissie told us all about you and how you won't stand no messing from the old girl. Good for you, love. About time someone put her in her place! I'm Ada Skinner and this is Beattie. Beattie Barnes. Aren't you the old girl's niece or something?"

"Great niece, yes. Lottie to friends. Did you say your name was Skinner? Are you Ted's wife?"

The larger of the two replied with enthusiasm. "Yes. Ted Skinner the gardener that was. How did you know that?"

Charlotte smiled as she recalled Ted's words about his wife. "I've met Ted twice. He's a character! You said in the Post Office about Thomas getting him the sack? Sorry I overheard you, but I would like to hear the story."

Ada folded her short, fat arms defiantly. "We're not trouble-makers, Miss. If you've met Ted then you'll know that he doesn't hold with gossip."

Charlotte nodded gravely. "Yes. He's a gentleman and that's my problem, you see. I was a journalist before I came here so I've got a nose for the truth. I can usually tell the difference between fact and fiction, truth and gossip. I heard you say in the Post Office that Thomas was involved and would like to know what happened. Cissie was right, Olivia worships him. I don't. If there's any such thing as justice then I want to show Thomas for the true villain he is."

Ada turned to her small friend. "What do you think, Beat? Reckon I can tell her without my Ted giving me hell?"

Beattie nodded. "Things can't get any worse for you and Ted, can they? He lost the most precious thing he ever had. His job. Tell her Ada, I trust her. She's not after gossip, just the truth of the matter. Isn't that right, Miss?"

Nodding gravely, Charlotte qualified her feelings. "I'm trying to make Olivia see what a crook he is. I'd hang him given half the chance."

"Fair enough," Beattie announced. "Go on Ada, give her the rope to hang him with!"

Ada looked immaculate with her permed grey hair in a stiff, unyielding hair style, but her face was lined with worry. "My Ted was gardener up at the House all his working life. No matter what the weather was like off he'd go and see to his precious plants! He grew enough vegetables to supply the House and sell in the local greengrocers, then the money made was used to keep the garden going so that the old lady never laid out a penny for seeds and the like. Anyway, a few years ago that Thomas asked my Ted to move some stuff from the attic.

'Ted told him that he's only take orders from Mrs. Jones herself as she paid his wages. The long and short of it was that Thomas tried to blackmail him. He said that my Ted was making money on the quiet while the old lady had trouble making ends meet.

' My Ted told him he had nothing to hide and still refused to help him. Next thing he was summoned to see Madam. She asked him about the money from the sale of the vegetables and he told her how he used it to buy seeds and tools. Poor old Ted. He stood there while that pip-squeak told her that he'd been lining his own pocket! I tell you, Miss, that is eating my husband alive. He never brought so much as a carrot home to feed his own family even when times were hard. I always used to nag him about caring more for his job than his own family. Mind you! I'm not denying he's brought home the odd rabbit or fish to fill the family crock, but that was just to makes ends meet, like."

Charlotte looked dismayed as she imagined poor Ted Skinner being pitted against Thomas and Olivia. "He couldn't prove anything I suppose? Receipts? The greengrocer?"

Ada stretched her short neck forward menacingly, "Now look here, Miss! In this village we all grew up with one another and have no need of chits of paper. We know who to trust and everyone knows that Ted poured his life and soul into that garden up there!"

"I don't doubt it, Ada." Charlotte responded. "It sounds just like the kind of nasty trick Thomas would stoop to. What did the others say? The Prices'? Cissie? What about the greengrocer, didn't they defend Ted?"

Clutching her handbag like grim death, Ada shook her head. "Oh, they tried, didn't they Beattie? Bob the greengrocer went there but that Thomas reckoned he was in cahoots with Ted anyway, both Price and his daughter said how honest hard-working Ted was and Cissie really went to town because you'll know she's not afraid to speak up. No, not one of them could shake the old girl. She believed that precious Thomas of hers and that was that."

"That's the truth!" Beattie uttered with her head darting forward like a bird, "You may not know it but she's a hard woman. A Tartar! She never had much to do with her own family but that boy can do no wrong!"

"Give Mrs. Jones her due, Beattie," Ada interrupted, "up until that happened she was always fair to Ted. He was always paid on the dot and even had a little extra every Christmas." Folding her hands across her lap whilst still hugging her handbag, she announced proudly, "He even got paid for his summer holiday!"

"Doesn't everybody?" Charlotte asked in amazement.

"Oh no!" both women chorused as Beattie took the lead once more. "There's a lot of places round these parts that can't afford to pay for time off, be it holidays or illness, whatever! Ada's right. Ted had a cushy job until that blighter put his spoke in."

"Well, ladies, you have been an education. I'll try to do something about Ted and ...."

"Hang on, love!" Ada jumped. "He's too old to be working now. I want him to take life easy." She paused as she tried to find the right words. "As upset as he is, I would rather let things be. He couldn't manage to job now, only THINKS he can."

"But his name should be cleared, surely?" Charlotte asked. Both ladies beamed and nodded their agreement. "Then leave it to me, ladies! Justice will be done."

Ada rose and took her hand. "Ta, love. Mind you, if it gets awkward for you don't worry. You have to live with the old dragon."

"I can handle her. Another glass of stout before I go?"

"Might as well, kid!" Beattie laughed, "they'll be getting a stewed cook along with their stewed steak this dinner, but never mind, eh!"

Whilst Charlotte was in the village Glas Fryn was deserted except for Cissie. Mary Price and her father were home in the converted stable block whilst Olivia had gone out to an official luncheon with a local charity organisation. The House was calm and peaceful, even its drabness qualified as elegant antiquity in the morning sun.

The short, plump maidservant hummed and sang as she cleaned all the nooks and crannies in the kitchen. She enjoyed being on her own sometimes even though she was working. Mary was as good as gold, even her father was a kind-hearted gentleman despite his grumpy looks, she mused. Better to her than her own family, if the truth be told.

Still, whenever she could she would still visit her granddaughter. Wanted or not, it was her right. Her pleasure. One day her granddaughter would realise that it was love that counted, not position in life or money. After all was said and done, Cissie contemplated, she was happy. The inhabitants of the House, both upstairs and down, were her 'family'. She had a roof over her head, a little bit of money in the bank and a lovely old place to work in. Yes. She was happy with her lot. The front door banged shut and she smiled and called out.

"Lottie? In the kitchen, lovely girl! I've got the kettle on."

There was no reply, just a clatter of heels and the mumble of voices.

Becoming suspicious she went out to the hall. Cissie felt her colour drain at the sight of the two people before her. "You never had the nerve to bring her to this house!" she gasped in shock.

Thomas laughed harshly. "Oh dear, I thought you would be out. You two have met before, haven't you."

He put his arm around the middle-aged woman besides him. "We have that, Tom. She's one of those nosey old buggers who knocked the door. The fat one."

"Get out of this house!" Cissie ordered outraged. "You have no right here, clear off!"

"Cissie, Cissie, let me explain," Thomas grabbed her arm and ushered her towards the kitchen. "In private, I think." Pushing the stricken maid through the heavy door and pulling it shut he remained on the outside and beckoned to Dora Biggins. "Just a slight hitch. Carry on as planned, we've got ten minutes before they arrive and nobody will be any the wiser."

Lifting her eyes heaven-ward, the woman whispered, "You'd better be right because if we're caught I'm dropping you in it! Hear me?"

"Yes, I hear you! Now go. Into the lounge. Look like the lady of the house, be with you in a few minutes." He slipped through the kitchen door before any further protests wasted precious time.

Cissie was putting her coat on when he entered. "Where do you think you're going?" the man hissed.

"You're up to something and I'm not going to get caught up in it. Lottie should be back soon, she's fit for you!"

"Oh?" Thomas questioned as he leaned against the table with his arms folded. "Fit for me? In which way? I thought she had her claws into Ralph but then he's no prize catch, is he. Just a common farmhand when all's said and done."

Cissie turned to face him, "Estate Manager! You're not fit to lick his boots! You've never done a hard day's work in your life. Just use other people to get everything by lying and cheating, even that slut out there is being used!"

Thomas moved from the table and walked slowly towards the angry woman. "You talk too much! Shut up!"

"Want to hear some more? Ted Skinner suffered through your lies, you tried to rape Lottie but she got the better of you, then you got your hired help to try and put her out of action. It might come out yet, she managed to get the registration of that van. The van you use to steal the old girl's furniture in, no less!"

Thomas moved closer to her, menacingly close. "The truth is spoken in anger, isn't it faithful Cissie. Well, now that we are being honest with one another I can tell you that I'm expecting prospective clients to look over the house and Dora is going to be my 'wife'. Just to keep up appearances, you understand."

"You can't do that! Madam never allow that!"

Thomas sniggered. "Madam will never know until it's too late." Standing directly in front of the frightened servant he continued, "However, you DO know, Cissie. You also clean my room very thoroughly, don't you. Not a speck of dust anywhere, not even INSIDE the drawers! Ever heard that saying 'Curiosity killed the cat', Cissie?"

Shrinking back against the kitchen unit, the plump woman stuttered in her defence. "I never............ never touch........ anything, never,..............never! Anyway, if you .... if you had nothing to hide, then.........then........ " taking a deep breath she shouted, "Get away from me! You're evil! Evil!"

"My brother told me that. Perhaps it's true. He said it just before I put the pillow over his face. He didn't say it again." His cold green eyes stared unblinkingly at his victim.

Spluttering and gasping as her heart thudded like a sledge hammer, Cissie tried to pull away the hands which were clamped around her throat. All the while she thought it was a nightmare, that soon she would wake up and find herself in her cosy room. Where was everyone? She couldn't scream, couldn't breathe. It was getting dark. The pain.

A dull thud echoed through the silent house as Cissie's body slid to the floor. Thomas smiled. She wouldn't gossip again. Like his brother, she could have betrayed him.

At four o'clock Olivia had returned to the house and, much to her disgust, found it empty. 'Where is everybody?' she asked herself out loud. 'Fine state of affairs! I pay them to be here and the first chance they get they're off!'

She went into the lounge and poured herself a large Sherry reasoning that it was the only refreshment available. The telephone rang. Answering under protest she went into the hall and picked up the receiver. "Glas Fryn. Who's calling?"

"Oh," the male voice sighed with regret, "Olivia."

"Ralph! When are you coming back?"

"To what?" Ralph replied evenly. "I resigned, remember?"

"Humph! Gestures are all very well, but they won't feed

you. You are needed back here. Is the funeral over?"

"Tomorrow."

Olivia felt very old and sad. "He was a good man. Arrange a wreath from me, please. How is his wife?"

"Distressed."

"Bring her back with you, Ralph. Just for a week or so."

Unable to keep the surprise out of his voice her replied, "I'll ask her. Are you still selling this property?"

"We'll discuss it. I might have been hasty."

Knowing it was the nearest thing to an apology he would get he agreed. "O.K.. We'll talk when I get back. How is Lottie?"

"Charlotte," Olivia replied pointedly, "is quite well considering her accident. She doesn't look very attractive but seems to gad about well enough."

"Accident? What accident?"

Olivia became impatient, "She fell off a bike! The girl is quite irresponsible at times, but very entertaining despite her obsession with Thomas."

Ralph's voice barked down the line. "I'll come back tomorrow. Straight after the funeral. Until then will you try and keep her occupied?"

Smiling to herself, Olivia remarked, "That is an impossible task! I fail to see why you should want.......... "

"Just do it!" Ralph cut in, then in a calmer tone, "Please, Olivia. It's for her own safety. No time to explain now."

Sighing, the old woman agreed. "I expect a full explanation when you return, it all sounds very strange to me. I assume you will return to your duties in exchange for this daunting task you've set?"

"You blackmailing old harridan! O.K., just keep your part of the bargain."

Chuckling to herself as she replaced the handset, she returned to the lounge and drank another Sherry to celebrate her victory over Ralph Nicholls. Sentiment began to creep into her thoughts as the fiery liquid warmed her being. She went to the bureau and drew out the box which held her engagement ring. Her love had been wasted, extinguished before the flames of passion consumed her. Life was so unfair, it could have been so different if she had married him and bore his children, now all she felt was a distant memory and ....

Olivia Jones stared at the empty box and cried like she had cried so many years ago.......................

Charlotte returned from the village and hear the muffled sounds from the lounge. She found her Great Aunt slumped in a chair with a tear-stained face looking very old and tired. Kneeling besides her she took the mottled hand and stroked it gently. "What's wrong, Aunt? Have you had a turn or something? You look terrible, should I call the Doctor? I'll ask for the old one if you like, I know what you think of Dr. Samuels........ "

"No, no, no!" Olivia protested in a trembling voice. "I'm not ill. Oh, Charlotte! Who would do such a thing?"

"Has someone attacked you, is that it?"

"My ring! My ring has gone! The only thing I had from him, now it's gone." The sobs began anew over the anguish of the loss.

Charlotte turned to see the open bureau and knew the reason for the old woman's distress. Noticing the open box on the floor she picked it up. "Are you sure you didn't drop it or something? Perhaps it's still in the desk somewhere."

"I took the box out from it's usual place and when I opened it the ring had gone! I'm not stupid, child!"

"I wouldn't dare suggest such a thing!" remarked the young woman smiling in an attempt to lift spirits. "Perhaps Price would know something about it. I'll go and ask."

Olivia shook her head. "Nobody there. They're all out. Skive off as soon as my back's turned!"

Taking a deep breath, Charlotte tried to sound patient, "Just stay there and I'll go and make a cup of tea."

"Indeed you won't! You know how I frown on your activities in the kitchen!"

Standing arms akimbo, Charlotte snapped and yelled. "Frown as much as you like! I'm going to make tea.........no ! Better still black coffee. You smell like a distillery my dear, straight-laced Aunt!"

Mary was wiping dishes and looking angry. As the door swung open she didn't look around, just kept on rubbing a plate with vigour. "Oh! Back are you! Really, Cissie. It's not often that Dad and I have time off together so it's really too much to come back to this mess!"

"Before you rub the pattern off that plate it's me, not Cissie." Charlotte quipped. "What's the problem?"

Mary look ashamed. "Oh, dear. Sorry about that. It's just that when Dad and I got back from our cottage there was broken crockery on the floor and the sink had overflowed. We managed to mop it all up but what a mess! Thank God her Ladyship isn't home yet!"

"Wrong again. She is."

"Hell's Bells'!" Mary whispered, "How long? Has she had tea?"

Charlotte shook her head. "Forget it. I'll make her coffee. She's been hitting the bottle rather hard. She said there was nobody in the house when she got home."

Price came through the back door in shirt-sleeves carrying a mop and bucket and had overheard the last sentence. He looked more agitated than Mary. "What's going on around here? Mrs. Jones drinking, Cissie dropping everything and flitting off to God knows where! Dear, dear me. What is wrong with everybody?"

Charlotte saw the anxiety in the old man's face and tried to put things into perspective. "Cissie must have had a message, a phone call or something which made her drop everything and go, she's normally so reliable and careful, isn't she? Perhaps it was her daughter, or granddaughter. As for Olivia, well, she has good cause. Her engagement ring from her first fiancé has gone missing. The poor old thing is upset and seems to have turned to the bottle for solace."

Regaining her composure, Mary spoke in an abrupt tone to her father. "Right, Dad. Lottie will see to the old girl and we'll start the evening meal, that is after you've rung up Cissie's family to see if she's there."

Price looked at his daughter dubiously. "If she's not there?"

"Worry about that when it happens! Go on, Dad." As he left the room Mary turned to Charlotte with a worried expression. "Something's wrong. I feel it. Like you said, Cissie wouldn't go off without a damned good reason. What do you think?"

Busying herself making the coffee, Charlotte was equally concerned. "Any idea where Thomas is? Has he been here?"

"Why?" Mary gasped, "What has he got to do with Cissie?"

"Nothing, Mary!" Charlotte retorted sharply, "Nothing at all. I was just wondering if he knew where she had gone, that's all. I know you and your father were out, Olivia too, so there's only Thomas left."

"Oh, I see." Mary sounded relieved. "As far as I know he left early this morning and I doubt if he's been back here, he doesn't normally return until at least six. That is if he comes home at all."

As Charlotte went towards the door with a laden tray as Price returned to the kitchen looking grim. "Her daughter wasn't much help. She sounded annoyed because I'd rung! I gather she had guests to attend to."

"Typical!" his offspring commented, "Her mother has vanished but that doesn't matter. Oh, no! One must not disturb her busy social life."

"Now, now," Price admonished his daughter. "No need for that, Mary. Come on, we'll start work and hope she turns up. It'll all be something and nothing, I'll be bound. You know what Cissie's like."

"For her sake I hope you're right, Dad."

Charlotte nodded in agreement. "I'll go and sober up Her Ladyship and get her fit for Dinner. Let me know straight away if Cissie walks in that door!"

Plenty of coffee and a hot meal had sobered Olivia up, but once ensconced in the lounge once again she reached for the decanter.

"Do you have to, Aunt?" Charlotte pleaded. "It won't solve any problems. I wonder which concerns you the most? The missing maid or the missing ring! Maybe I should phone the Police Station, they ought to be informed on both counts."

The old woman stubbornly refused. "No! It might be the same problem. Whoever took my ring knew about my hidden cache. Do you understand what I'm saying?"

Suddenly feeling sick with her Aunt's insinuation, Charlotte nodded and joined Olivia with a glass of brandy. Flopping back onto the settee she narrowed her eyes and asked Olivia, "Do you really think Cissie would do such a thing? She may be a gossip, but honest, surely."

"Yes, yes!" Olivia agreed, "Under normal circumstances, yes! It does seem to be rather a co-incidence though. Perhaps Cissie was in dire need of money in a hurry. The point is, dear Charlotte, if the two are connected then I would prefer to wait and see what happens. If we involve the police than poor old Cissie would be in terrible trouble."

Lottie sat up straight in wonderment. "You care! You really care about her, don't you? Despite your most treasured possession going missing you still want Cissie to come home and be absolved."

Olivia let the tears trickle down her lined face. "Of course I care, you silly child!   Cissie has been here for years and never given me any reason to doubt her. Perhaps she didn't take it, perhaps she will be back soon or get a message to us, it must have been something urgent for her to go off without a word. Have you checked her rooms? It's a start."

"Apparently Mary knocked on her door but no reply. She didn't actually go in."

"Well then," Olivia urged, "that's where to start."

At 11pm Thomas returned looking his usual suave, immaculate self and laughed when Olivia told him about Cissie. "Really, Aunt! There's no need to raise a hue and cry for that little busybody! Probably with one of her cronies gossiping and forgetting the time."

"We were just about to call the police, Thomas," Charlotte announced with relish. "Got your alibi ready? Been with Dora Biggins? I hope she's become more reliable over the years. Witnesses have to be reliable, you know."

Olivia looked thunderous. "Watch your tongue, Charlotte. There's no need to drag Thomas into this." Then she hesitated before she turned to ask him, "Dora who? Who is she on about, Thomas?"

Refusing to be drawn to the bait he answered casually, "I told you about her, remember? Uncle Alan's housekeeper? She's staying in a local cottage. Is your memory going, Aunt?"

"Don't be cheeky, Thomas. I do recall and it's very good of you to look after her. Your Uncle would be pleased, I'm sure." Changing the subject quickly she turned to Charlotte, "Did you check Cissie's rooms?"

"Yes, everything is in it's place. Just her raincoat missing off the kitchen coat rack, apparently."

"Not quite the tale of the Mary Celeste, is it!" jeered Thomas.

"Well, if only her coat is missing then Cissie must have gone out suddenly and we'll hear all about it tomorrow I daresay." Olivia concluded as she rose from her chair and tottered to the door, "I'm off to bed. Mary will see to me. Now you two stop fighting, do you hear me? You children are always arguing over something. Goodnight, my chicks, goodnight." They heard her chuckling as she made her way upstairs, her walking stick clattering against the banister rail.

"Stupid old bat!" Thomas laughed. "She's stoned! Well I never. Old Olivia has a human weakness after all."

Charlotte stood up her anger seething and knotting in her stomach. "Alan Armstrong dismissed Dora Biggins years ago and you were involved. I know you are working something on Olivia and I'll find out what it is, Thomas. I promise you I'll find out, even if it kills me."

Smiling as he stared into his glass, he spoke through gritted teeth, his veneer slipping. "Your face doesn't look very pretty at the moment. You should be more careful. Nasty things, accidents. They happen when you least except them."

His tone and demeanour sent a shiver down Charlotte's spine. "You should know. You fell downstairs once, it could happen again when you least expect it. Next time you could be sober and your neck might break. I live in hope."

Charlotte went to her room with all the nerves in her body telling her to run from him whilst she forced herself to walk calmly away. Shutting the bedroom door behind her she realised her body was shaking uncontrollably. He had threatened her, admitted to the 'accident' and she had retaliated. She had laid down the gauntlet. She had always been wary of him but from tonight she would have to be extra vigilant, she would have to be on her guard twenty-four hours a day.

CHAPTER 16

Departures

Unable to sleep through worrying about the missing Cissie, Charlotte got up at three in the morning and went downstairs to the lounge. She would search for that ring, it had to be there somewhere. The state Olivia was in when Charlotte came home preyed on her mind, she could have dropped it or misplaced it then became muddled with the aid of alcohol.

An hour later she had searched and decided her labour was futile and that her Great Aunt was telling the truth, it had been stolen.

"I tell you, I've lost my ring!" a voice shrilled behind her.

Jumping with fright, Charlotte turned to the door saying, "I know, Aunt, I'm just checking .... " Her words went unheeded. A young, attractive woman bustled around the room wearing a calf-length dress of pink satin. She was followed by an old lady who leaned heavily on her walking-stick.

"So you say, Livvy. Now calm down. It will be in the dresser or somewhere." The old woman in black nodded towards a large, mirrored oak dresser which dominated the far side of the room. "You really should be more careful!"

"Mama!" exploded the young Olivia, "you know very well that Annie had been here today. This always happens!"

"How dare you!" shouted the older woman. "Your sister has no use for your fripperies, she works too damned hard to worry about such pretty pieces! She has Eleanor and Mary and in Service, Owain training to be a Groom and only Isobel and Arthur are left. They wouldn't take anything and you know it!"

"Oh, mother!" whined Olivia, "I gave it to Isobel this afternoon. She's such a tom-boy that I thought I should encourage her to be more ladylike. She is fourteen, after all."

Sarah Armstrong smiled. "You can't change what nature had moulded. She'll be off to London next to join her sisters in Service, can you imagine her let loose in a fancy house!" the old woman chuckled. "I can picture it now 'Oh, I'm so sorry Madam. I didn't mean to black-lead the cook as well as the grate!' "

Both women laughed together and Charlotte realised that the young Olivia was quite beautiful. "My little Chicks are growing up fast, Mama. I miss the girls, I really do. Even little Arthur is only a few years off going to work, it's very sad."

"One day you will have children of your own to dote over and realise how much hard work they make! Now, Livvy, let's find that ring before .... " A deep chuckle rose from Sarah's throat and she leaned on her stick for support. "Just..... just.... look, child. On your hand!"

Olivia stared at the opal ring on her left hand. "Oh, dear Lord! To think I accused dear Isobel!"

"Tom-boy she is, but she has her saving graces. Let this be a lesson, my girl! If anything gets misplaced in the future remember to give the benefit of the doubt. It is your duty as a Christian and just this once I will forgive you for taking the Lord's name in vain."

"Yes, Mama." Olivia said as she placed a kiss on her mother's cheek. "I just wish that this engagement ring had turned into a wedding ring. I would have had my children by now," as an afterthought she added, "though not as many as Annie, naturally."

Ignoring the last remark, Sarah sat heavily in a chair. "Yes, my child. We all pay the price. We have lost some men between us, haven't we, husband, brothers, fiancé. All beloved. That's a burden one can never shed, but the love they leave behind is something special."

Brightening and getting up from the chair she tried to hide the tears which threatened to fall, "I'm just a silly old woman, Livvy. You are in danger of becoming an old maid like your other sisters! Get along to .... "

A commotion came from the hall and Annie burst into the room and fled into her mother's arms. "Mam! Mam! They've found her! My Daisy, they've found her!"

Tottering under the impact of her daughter's clutch, the old woman looked towards her youngest daughter, "Well, that's good, isn't it Livvy! Annie love, I told you that.......... "

"No! No!" Annie cried as her cheeks were awash with tears, "she's gravely ill. Do you hear me? Near to death, Mam! Please come! Please help me!"

Charlotte was catapulted back to the present with sickening speed. Had the shock of Annie's news brought her back so suddenly? What had happened to Daisy? Did she live or die? That lovely, radiant girl whose birth she had witnessed so near to death? Olivia. Olivia would know. Olivia had lived through it all. She had meant to ask her before but things kept happening....diverting her from the ....

The door squeaked open and the young woman jumped out of her skin. The ghosts she could handle, but the living...............

"Oh! Lottie, it's you." The wizened face of Price entered the room and quietly closed the door behind him. "I couldn't sleep," he explained, "it doesn't seem right to carry on as usual with Cissie disappearing like that. I thought it might be worth checking around, just in case. When I saw the light under the door I thought it might be burglars or perhaps Thomas. Same difference really!"

"Oh, Price," Charlotte smiled, "You're a tonic."

"Come on," he offered his arm, "let's go to the kitchen and have a cup of tea."

Mary had already brewed with the same excuse as her father. "Cissie's been like a mother to me over the years. I'm very fond of her despite the fact I'm always nagging her."

"She knows that, Mary. That's what is so puzzling." Charlotte sipped her tea and tasted something extra. "Herbs, again?"

Grinning mischievously, Mary nodded. "Don't worry, it will calm us down without doping us!"

Price patted his daughter's hand. "I wish you could make Cissie materialise with your herbs and potions. Do you think we should call the police?"

"Er, no." Charlotte answered. "It may be worse for Cissie if we did. That ring of Olivia's was missing and.............. " the words of her great-grandmother Sarah came back to her *Look, child, on your hand!* . The answer was there. "Hang on, I just thought of something, I'll just pop up and check Olivia."

"Don't bother," Mary sighed, "I put her to bed, remember. She wasn't wearing it."

"How did you know what I was thinking?" Charlotte asked aghast.

"Because she's always 'losing' that ring and finding it on her finger. This time it really has gone. I can't believe Cissie would take it, though. Never in this world."

"So where is she?" Charlotte asked wearily.

They didn't have any answers, any ideas or suggestions. They went to bed hoping that a few hours sleep and the dawn would put a fresh light on the subject or even better, the appearance of the missing maid.

The funeral was well attended and held in a local Kirk. It seemed that the whole village turned out along with all the Estate workers. Ralph was glad to see the service over and returned to the house out of respect and courtesy. Jarvis's widow received the stream of mourners with quiet reserve and relied upon her close friends to cater for their needs.

It was thirty minutes later before Ralph could speak to her alone. They walked out to the garden, away from the murmuring of hushed voices. "Helen, I have to go back now. Will you be alright?"

Nodding, the drawn face looked ashen against the black dress. "Of course, my dear. Thank you for everything. I'll keep you posted about things up here. I expect Olivia will be screaming blue murder by now!"

"That's what it was, Helen. Murder. I'll do my best, but it's difficult. Are you sure you won't come back with me? Olivia would like to see you again."

Inclining her greying head, Helen agreed. "I know. I will pop down in a month or so. She was always very good to us, you know. Did you see the wreath she sent? Very extravagant."

Ralph smiled. "To a Scot, yes! It was her step-son. It's her way."

"Quite. It is appreciated." Helen walked slowly then turned on her heel. "Are you going to tell her? About the Estate I mean. This would seem to be a good time."

"There's too much at stake at the moment, but what you really mean is before someone else tells her? Thomas would really twist that one around."

"He's been burrowing deep, Ralph. My dear Jarvis stumbled on something and paid for it with his life. Don't let it happen to you."

The man stared into the distance, unseeing. "Or anyone else."

Helen shuddered. "Surely he wouldn't harm Olivia? Try and take her for everything she's got, yes, but not physically hurt an old woman?"

Turning to her, his face full of anger he spoke in harsh tones. "It seems that Charlotte has had an 'accident' of some sort. Olivia didn't seem too worried about it, but I think it's a strange co-incidence. Charlotte brings out the worst in him and gets carried away with the past and .... "

Helen was listening attentively, struck by the haunting timbre in his voice. "And? Is she a fanatic history-wise, or what?"

"No. It's just that she's, well.......... " feeling trapped, he didn't know how to explain the person he had become enchanted with. "Lottie has found out who her forbearers were and feels she can relay their experiences with her own."

"I'm not sure I understand!" Helen frowned, "Their lives are on a parallel with hers? How could she know that?"

Ralph clasped the hand of the woman he had come to regard as his family. "Because she sees them, experiences episodes in their lives. It's true, Helen. The only trouble is that she looks haunted because it's taken a hold over her. I have to go back. She's in danger from the past and present."

Kissing him lightly on the cheek she gripped his large, work worn hand tightly. "Go back to her, Ralph. It's beyond me, but whatever Lottie is involved with you are the one to help."

Returning the kiss, a smile broke over his weathered face. "God Bless you, Helen. You never asked too many questions. Jarvis loved you for that."

"Perhaps I will be in Wales soon for a wedding?" the widow happily teased, "Now that's something I would make the effort to come down for!"

Ralph left Scotland behind with a mixture of sorrow and happiness tinged with fear. His fear was not for his own being, but for the woman he had left at the mercy of a cold, calculating killer who would run a man down in cold blood. Yes. Jarvis had been mowed down and left for dead. The police had little evidence and without a single eye-witness they doubted if the culprit would ever be traced. A 'hit-and-run' accident was not an easy crime to solve, but Ralph had the advantage of knowing who was behind the wheel of that lethal car, he had a head-start. Time was both his ally and enemy.

Breakfast at Glas Fryn was served by a drawn-faced Price. Olivia opened her mail in silence whilst Thomas hummed and helped himself to extra food.

Charlotte drank black coffee in order to counteract the drowsiness which dulled her senses. "No news, then?" she asked as she sat next to her Aunt.

"No." Olivia replied curtly as she continued to read her

mail.

"I'll have some coffee, Charlotte." Thomas requested in silky tones.

"Get it yourself."

"Charming!" the young man grinned. "Our fat little friend takes off and everyone wanders around looking shocked and bewildered. We're well rid of her, if you ask me. Nothing but a busybody."

Charlotte got up from the table with cup in hand, walked over to Thomas then threw her coffee over him. She felt immense pleasure at the yell of pain he uttered when the hot liquid made contact with his face. Jumping up and sending his chair toppling backwards the victim grabbed a napkin and wiped his face. "You stupid bitch! You're bloody mad! Mad!"

Laughing hysterically, the tall young woman felt elated. An astounded Olivia spoke in severe tones. "Never have I seen such behaviour under my roof! Have you been drinking, Charlotte?"

"No," she giggled, "but Thomas has!" A fresh peal of laughter bubbled up from the young woman's throat.

Thomas stood immobile. "She'll have to go, Aunt. She might turn on you next. I can arrange things for you."

Charlotte stopped short. "Arrange what, Thomas? My disappearance?"

Olivia clapped her hands. "Enough! You are being silly, girl. You have antagonised Thomas since the day he came here and I think you have become obsessed to the point that you are trying your best to discredit him in my eyes. I think you're jealous of him."

Astounded by the accusation, Charlotte tried to think clearly. This was the moment Thomas had been waiting for. "I think it would be wise for me to leave. I was invited here to do a job, but that job has proved impossible due to you, Aunt. You've hardly been helpful in giving facts where your family are concerned, you even denied my ancestry until I found out for myself. You're right. I am jealous. Jealous of the fact that someone like him can walk into your life and take you for all you've got. His relationship is not even close, so more fool you. You two deserve each other."

As she left the room she could hear Thomas uttering unctuous words which would prevent Olivia from stopping her. He would always win. Charlotte Stone packed her suitcase and glanced around the bedroom. With a sigh she took the silver thimble which had taken her down the corridor of time. It wouldn't be missed by anyone. Shutting the door behind her she whispered, 'Goodbye Annie and Daisy. Goodbye Sarah.'

A rustle made her turn back quickly, but there was nothing in the room. Nothing, that is, except for the strong sweet smell of Lily-of-the-Valley. She rushed to the dressing-table drawers and opened them. The silken underwear lay folded neatly as it had when she first arrived at the house.

Picking up a pastel pink camisole she held it and gasped as it turned to dust in her hands. The particles fell like snow which never reached the ground. Charlotte cried. Her life was falling apart like the old clothes, disintegrating into particles of dust.

Leaving by the back door she said her goodbyes to Mary and Price in the kitchen. Price had unshed tears in his eyes as he spoke with a shaky voice. "Can't you stay, Lottie? He's got his way if you leave this house."

"I know, but I've got a few tricks left. Between you and me I'll be stopping at the Pub in Pantmawr. Once I've booked in I'm going straight to the police station and reporting Cissie as missing."

Mary shook her head, "No! You can't! What about the ring?"

Charlotte smiled at the worried face of her contemporary. "I don't think she took it. Even if she did, her life is worth more than a piece of jewellery. Agreed?" They both nodded. "I'll be in touch. Watch Olivia, the silly old fool is so very naive."

As Charlotte opened the back door Mary rushed to hug her. She spoke quietly, "When Ralph gets back I'll tell him where you are. You could always go and stay in his cottage. I've got the keys. Here, take one just in case."

"Thanks, Mary. I doubt if I'll use it because I've got too much running around to do in Pantmawr. Sgt. Hopkins won't know what's hit him! Still, nice to know there is some kind of sanctuary to bolt to if necessary. Take care. Thomas may turn on you now I'm out of the way."

"Let him try," Mary forced a laugh. "I've got the hockey-stick!"

As she walked through the doorway Charlotte hesitated as the dramatic end to her last 'vision' flashed through her mind. Turning, she wondered if Price would remember the incident. Looking directly at him she asked, "What happened to Daisy?"

His skeletal features became accentuated by the paleness of his skin as he shook his head and dropped into a chair. "What made you ask that?"

"Was she murdered?"

"No! What a terrible thing to ask!" Banging his fist on the table and standing again to full height, his tone became stubborn. "She died of natural causes many years ago. There's no need to rake up the grief of the past, this house has seen enough. Leave well alone, Miss Charlotte. You can hurt people." Abruptly he turned and left the kitchen. The two women were left speechless.

Exchanging puzzled glances, they parted. After Charlotte left Mary found her father in the lounge decanting the sherry. "Dad? What's wrong with you? There was no need to be so sharp."

As he turned there were tears in his eyes. "How could I tell her? Daisy had been kidnapped and kept like an animal for nearly a week. They tried to save her, but within twenty-four hours she died. Murdered? Not quite, but it would have been a quicker death."

Mary put an arm around her father to comfort him. "I see. Did they catch him?"

"That's another story, my girl. Another mystery." Patting his daughter's hand he apologised. "It's the strange business of Cissie going off, now Lottie leaving, it's ....I really shouldn't have spoken to her like that."

"She'll understand, Dad. Lottie doesn't hold grudges."

Nodding, the sad old man agreed. "She's Annie all over again in her ways. Speak her mind, have her fling, but always ready to forgive and forget. Trouble is, she looks the image of Daisy and that is what upset me. I can feel she's in danger. Come on, girl. Let's have a cuppa before the old girl starts because she won't be very sweet tempered, that's for sure."

Booking into the public house in Pantmawr, the Lamb and Fleece, raised many eyebrows. As she climbed the stairs to the guest accommodation she could hear the murmur of questioning voices ripple through the low-ceilinged bar-cum-lounge. Ignoring local reaction she dumped her case and bags in her room, which was quaint and comfortable, then left the hostelry to begin her quest.

Once in the main street she realised that she had no idea where the police station was, but was gratified by the sight of Ted Skinner coming out of the Post Office.

" 'Allo, Miss! You look lost. Can't get lost in a place like this, more's the pity. My Ada seems to know where to find me anytime of the day. She's a tartar!"

Laughing, Charlotte shook her head. "No she's not, Ted Skinner! Can you tell me where the police station is?"

A dry cackle sounded in the old man's throat. "Police station, is it? You gonna get that Armstrong behind bars, are you? I'll 'elp you little lady. I'll 'elp you!"

"This is serious, Ted. Cissie went missing yesterday and I'm worried. Where do I find Sgt. Hopkins?"

The old gardener screwed up his face. "Cissie? Gone missing? That's queer. She wouldn't go anywhere without telling. I don't blame you for being worried, girl. That's queer. Very queer,"

"So were is the station?"

"Hoppy's house is down there on the right. 'E won't be there for some half-'our or so, down at Eastbridge 'e is. Goes every week."

Thanking the old man she went in search of the house. It was a detached square building with a plastic sign over the lintel to denote it's role. Knocking the shabby door she was ushered in by a youth dressed in black.

"Dad's out. Back soon. Do you want to wait in the office?"

"Yes, thank you."

The office turned out the be a bare room with a desk and filing cabinet. The time passed slowly as she sat in the rickety wooden chair waiting, but the policeman's arrival was announced by his loud, booming voice filling the hallway. Within moments he had burst through the door and his large red face looked flustered.

"Ah! Miss Stone! The Black Angel told me that there was a woman waiting. My son. Into this metal music and whatnot! Sorry, but if you've come about that van it's not been traced yet. The number plate tells us it's an imported vehicle, but the owner we traced through records says he sold it for cash. We're still trying though, keeping our eyes peeled. It'll be back, mark my words. Glad to see your face is looking a bit better, yellow and scarred but not so bad."

Standing to her full height she was on an equal par with the large man. "I came about something else. Cissie Jenkins is missing."

The thick, bushy eyebrows raised in surprise, the voice dropped to a hush. "Missing? How long?"

"Since yesterday afternoon."

Looking at his watch he nodded. "Nearly twenty-four hours in my book. Give me the details."

By the time Charlotte told him all she knew the policeman remained sceptical, but promised to make enquiries. His instincts told him that something was wrong and his sincerity was quite moving. He promised to do his best and didn't question her new address.

Returning to the village square she saw Thomas emerge from the Post Office. Much to her disgust he rushed over to her. "Charlotte! I've been sent to find you. There's an emergency."

Amazed at his attitude, Charlotte shrugged and replied icily, "You just thought you'd tell your frustrated old maid first, I suppose! Another little drama which you've thought up? Have you pushed Olivia down the stairs? Has she had a heart attack because she found out you're taking her for all she's got? Crawl back to the sewer, Thomas. I don't believe a word you say, never have."

Not reacting to her accusations and insults, he merely shook his head and sighed. "I'll tell you anyway. Ralph's cottage is on fire. The Fire Brigade from Eastbridge should be there by now, just thought you might want to know."

Shock and panic swept through her body at the image of the burning cottage. She questioned his motives. "You hate him. If it's true you probably set it alight!"

His face remained impassive as he turned away, his right hand swinging his car keys. "Trouble is with you, dear girl," he said over his shoulder, "you can't tell the difference between fact and fantasy anymore."

"Thomas!" she screamed at his back, "wait for me!" Charlotte followed him around the corner and as he opened his car door she tugged his sleeve. "Is it really on fire? Is Ralph back?"

Brushing her off he got into the car. "No. He's not back. I'm not arguing with you anymore. It could be raised to the ground by now."

"Hang on!" the young woman shouted as she ran around to the passenger's door. "Ralph comes before my revulsion for you."

"Charming!" he drawled as they sped off through the

village street at alarming speed. "Where had you been, anyway? The pub said you booked in but nobody in the village seems to have seen you since, I was just about to give up. Olivia told me to find you before you ask."

Nodding, Charlotte felt happier knowing her Great Aunt had sent him. "I've been to the police about Cissie."

"You what!" the driver yelled as the car screeched to a halt. "You stupid little bitch!"

"Why? Because of that precious ring? She's not a thief!"

Red in the face, Thomas flexed his hands on the steering wheel. He spoke quietly and calmly. "We'll see. Let's get to the cottage for now, sort one thing out at a time. I only hope we're not too late."

The car quickly regained its speed as the grim-faced man moved through the gears swiftly. As they passed Glas Fryn's driveway it was a mere blur as they hurtled down the narrow lane at breakneck pace.

As they neared the turning for Ralph's home, Thomas shouted, "Damn! Damn it all!" Passing the junction he careered on towards Eastbridge without explanation.

"What the hell are you playing at, Thomas!" Charlotte demanded between gritted teeth. "You missed the turning!"

"I know! I know! I promise I won't be more than a few minutes. There's something I've got to do." Glancing sideways at his doubting passenger he pleaded innocently, "I really do apologise, old girl, but in the rush to find you I completely forgot something." Taking a right turn at suicidal speed he shook his head. "Just sit tight whilst I pop into the cottage."

"This is highly suspicious, Thomas. One minute you're breaking the land speed record to get to the fire then you decide you've forgotten something from the love nest you've set up. I don't trust you. Let me out. NOW!"

They screeched to a halt outside the place which Charlotte had spied upon the night she was mown down by the van. Thomas did a three point turn and left the engine running as he jumped out of the car. "I promise, just a minute. If you don't believe me then you are free to go. Your door isn't locked."

Bewildered, Charlotte stayed put. Maybe he was genuine this time. She checked her door and it opened as he said it would. She was free to go. He had left the engine running so must have every intention of returning to the car. She scanned the skyline through the windscreen and, to her horror, saw a plume of black smoke hanging over the woodland to the right. It was the direction of Ralph's cottage. He must be telling the truth. Her deep-rooted fear of fire welled up inside her making her feel dizzy and nauseous at the thought of burning, crashing timbers and a home being destroyed.

The minutes ticked by. The cottage was silent and lifeless. The car engine continued to purr away. Where was he? Watching the cloud of black smoke grow with demonic fervour she became impatient and got out of the car. As she walked round the front of the vehicle she noticed the damage on the front bumper along with a cracked headlight and sidelight lens.

She walked to the door of the cottage which was still ajar and gingerly pushed it. It seemed to stick halfway so she shouldered her way into the house calling out. "Thomas! Thomas! Come on! I can see the smoke........."

Something covered her face and the fumes were overwhelming, Charlotte struggled for just a few minutes until the chloroform took effect, then her long, slim body slumped onto the floor with a sickening thud.

"Now what do we do with her?" The large, blonde woman asked as she emerged from the gloomy interior.

Thomas laughed as he tossed the drugged rag to one side. "We'll stick her in the coal shed. Pity she went to the police, but I'll soon nip that in the bud. Lock her in and watch the place. I'll be back later to sort her out."

"Where are you going? Don't leave me in the lurch, Tom!

I'll blow everything if you do, I swear it!"

Stepping over the inert form, the fair-haired young man put his arms around the woman. "Dora, my love! You know how much you mean to me. Have faith, dear girl, have faith! I'm just going to smooth things over. We don't want a hue and cry about this stupid little bitch, do we!"

Her puffy face was sagging with age and worry, the middle-aged woman nodded. "Alright. You've seen me O.K. so far. Just make sure you cover your tracks, Tom. I don't want any bloody coppers round here!"

Once they had dragged Charlotte Stone into the small coal shed and padlocked the door, Thomas left his hostage in the care of Dora knowing she would play her part with uncanny devotion. He had first noticed her criminal tendencies whilst she was housekeeper for his Uncle Alan, it was merely cultivation of an erring soul which led Dora Biggins to follow his every command without question.

She had found his boyhood charm and attention flattering and used her position to take drugs from the doctor's surgery as instructed. It made Thomas Armstrong a small fortune amongst his contemporaries in the public school where thrills were a rarity. It was through Alan Armstrong's compassion that no charges were brought against them, he just ejected them both from his household. That was no punishment for two people who thought him a sentimental fool.

Miss Kemp was just closing for lunch as Thomas arrived. He entered by the back door and she greeted him with enthusiasm. "Twice in one day! I am honoured!" the waxwork face whined.

"Oh, Patricia! It's always a pleasure to be in your company, my dear. I've had such a tiresome morning, you just wouldn't believe it!"

Patting a chair by the empty fireside she giggled like a young girl. "Sit down and I'll make a nice cup of tea. What's been the trouble?"

Taking his place in the old armchair he put his hand to his

brow for effect. "Oh dear, Patricia! If only all women were like you. I have had to deal with that old harridan at Glas Fryn every day of the week and now that stupid niece of hers has done a bunk!"

Filling the kettle at the old Belfast sink, the postmistress was sympathetic. "Good riddance, I say! She's been a thorn in your side all along. As for .... "

"But you don't understand!" Thomas interjected, "Olivia thinks I drove her away. It seems that she went to the police with some crackpot idea of reporting Cissie Jenkins missing and booked into the Lamb of all places! I just feel that she's being too harsh on poor old Cissie who may have wanted to have a few days to herself. After all, what do we know about her private circumstances? Charlotte getting a room in the local pub just rubs Olivia's nose in it, as if her home isn't good enough."

As the kettle spluttered on the gas ring, Miss Kemp sat on the arm of the chair. "Thomas, relax! You are with me now. That silly girl is a nuisance. You should be glad to see the back of her."

"Yes, but.......... " Thomas paused for effect and watched the spinster wait with baited breath, "what about the police? Cissie got on a bus yesterday afternoon and told me that she'd just had enough and leaving! Would the Police believe me? No! As for Charlotte, well, I think it would be better all round if I sent her cases on to her old flat and that would be enough to satisfy any policeman."

As the kettle began to whistle the old maid rose, but not quick enough to avoid Thomas who enveloped her in his arms. It was too much for her to bear. "Leave it to me. I've got contacts, ways and means. Don't you worry, Thomas, my dear. Patricia Kemp will put a stop to any gossip and the antics of that young madam!"

Burying his head into the scrawny neck he muttered, "Oh, God! You are an angel! I knew you would think of something. Leave the tea, I need more comfort than that. The shop is shut for lunch, time enough for us."

Putting up little resistance the Postmistress followed his suggestion, all the more convinced that it was her duty to use her powers to leave Thomas free of the troublesome woman. The woman who insulted her over her own counter. It was time she was out of the way.

CHAPTER 17

Accusations

Ralph arrived home early in the evening after driving non stop from the funeral intending to have a quick shower and a change of clothes before he went over to Glas Fryn. The back door of his cottage was ajar so he went into the kitchen assuming that Mary Price had dropped in to give the place a quick dust before his return, but the only thing that greeted him was silence.

An uncanny silence. No drone of a vacuum cleaner, no sound of anyone moving around, the kitchen empty, just complete silence.

With dread he opened the lounge door. The room had been ransacked along with the study and bedrooms. Every drawer had been pulled out and emptied by scattering their contents in all directions. Cushions had been ripped open and books torn and tossed aside like worthless scraps of paper.

Waiting for the police to arrive he played back messages on the answer phone whilst trying to see if anything was noticeably missing, but it was difficult without being tempted to sift through the debris. There had been only one call of note, that from his brother-in-law. The rest were business contacts either demanding settlement of outstanding bills or requesting orders.

'Ralph,' the message from Brian began, 'I have to go away for a few days, but there are some developments which you should be aware of. The shares for the Scottish venture have dropped dramatically and it has all the symptoms of industrial espionage because the contents of Jarvis's Will seems to have become common knowledge. Just how it had been leaked I'm still trying to find out.

Your dear sister was clearly impressed! Money talks with her as you know. A word of warning, it could look suspicious so watch yourself. Oh! One more thing. A mate of mine is an Estate Agent here in Cardiff, namely Dennis Williams. He told me that a client is trying to sell a large country house near Pantmawr and wondered if I could I tell him something about the area. He wouldn't give specific details, but how many country houses are there in your neck of the woods? I'll ring on Wednesday, should be back by then. Jo has threatened to visit you soon and I doubt if it's anything to do with sisterly love. See you soon.'

Ralph recalled the Last Will and Testament of Jarvis. He had bequeathed his shares to his wife, Helen, with Ralph Nicholls as agent. In plain English he left Ralph, his partner, as the controlling hand in the most successful venture they had risked their life's savings on. The profits were stupendous and split three ways to include Olivia. She was totally ignorant about the wealth their idea and investment had created, was oblivious about the special bank account in her name. As long as Thomas Blake was around she would never know.

The news from his brother-in-law barely had time to sink in before Sgt. Hopkins arrived looking tired and harassed. Accepting a mug of tea he explained, "Because I played merry hell about keeping Pantmawr police house going until my retirement they make sure I take all calls, not that there's that many, mind you! But some days everything happens at once. It started this morning with that young lady from the House and I haven't stopped since. Now this, Mr Nicholls! God in Heaven, what a mess. Never known the like, never!"

"Charlotte came to you this morning? What did she want?"

"Oh! She had some daft idea that Mrs. Jenkins had disappeared but it was all a storm in a teacup. She was seen getting on the bus to Eastbridge yesterday afternoon, had enough of the House I shouldn't wonder! We all know that Mrs. Jones is a tartar to work for."

"Cissie? Missing?"

Placing his mug on the kitchen table, the policeman

nodded. "Like I said, turned out to be nothing to worry about. Then this afternoon some prankster dumped a load of old tyres in the field across the way and set light to them. Fire brigade soon put it out, but I can't see for the life of me what fun they had out of it! Kids! Nothing better to do. Now then, let's see all the damage here."

After surveying the turmoil the rotund policeman radioed through for assistance. It was evident that fingerprints needed to be taken and a detailed examination required.

Ralph felt impatient and surplus to requirements. "Can I leave you to sort things out, Sgt. Hopkins? I can't touch anything before your boys do their job and I really need to go over to Glas Fryn. Mrs. Jones will want to know about the funeral.... you realise that her step-son was buried this morning?"

"Oh," the deep-jowled face fell. "No, sir. I didn't know that. You run along then. I'll take care of things here. Oh! Wait a minute though, we have to know if anything's been stolen and only you can tell us that. Sorry, Ralph. You'll have to stay."

It was almost ten o' clock before Ralph walked through the back door of Glas Fryn to find father and daughter clearing up after Dinner. Mary looked pale and drawn as she welcomed the visitor and offered him a meal which he gratefully accepted. "It will take me ten minutes, so why don't you go and see Mrs. Jones while you're waiting. She's in the lounge feeling sorry for herself. We can catch up on the news after."

Olivia was sitting in an armchair gazing out of the window at the descending darkness. Moving her head very slightly at his entrance she smiled and raised her arm. A glass of brandy and a full decanter were on the table besides her. "Aha! The Fortune-hunter is home! Creeping around my step-son all these years has paid off, hasn't it!"

Walking around to face her he nodded. "So you know about the Will."

"Why did he leave so much to you? More to the point,

where did it come from? He must have been taking all the profit off the Estate for himself, profit which was mine by rights!" Her voice had risen as her grievance was uttered.

Ralph spoke as truthfully as he could, but veiled the facts for her own protection. "If it was from the Estate then yes, it would have been yours. But it wasn't. It was a return on certain investments Jarvis and I made. It's all legal and above board, Jarvis was honest and loyal to you and that's something I shouldn't have to tell you."

Looking crestfallen, the old woman nodded. "Of course! Of course. When Thomas told me about the Will I just thought that it was strange to leave so much money, then I began to wonder....... "

"You mean Thomas suggested the idea of embezzlement! Olivia, ask yourself why he should be interested in Jarvis or his Will. He got hold of the details damned quick!" Pacing the room he continued, "He was hoping there'd be something in it for you so that he could get his filthy hands on it! For God's Sake, Olivia, see him for what he really is, a lair and a cheat!"

Shaking her head, she remained stubborn. "Why is everybody so against him? You've been listening to that little madam! She really hated him. Well, there'll be no more of that!"

"Why?" Ralph asked alarmed.

"Because she's gone. Left this morning."

Leaning forward with his hands resting on the arms of her chair he gritted his teeth. "Where has she gone? Back to the city? Back to her flat?"

"I doubt it. She gave it up when she came here."

"For God's sake, woman! Don't you care? I can't believe you threw her out in the street! You've always been a hard-faced bitch, Olivia, but Charlotte is your own flesh and blood, which is more than I can say for Thomas."

Olivia looked unnerved as she answered meekly, "I know! I know. Oh dear, what a mess! I was dreadful to the child. I should have stopped her, but tempers where up and she was being so nasty to Thomas that I couldn't help myself. Find her, Ralph. Please. Tell her to come home. She belongs here."

The young man nodded. "I'll find her. I just hope it will be in one piece." Frowning at the state of the old woman he asked, "Since when have you started drinking?"

"Since my world turned topsy-turvy! People arguing, going off, things missing! Everything was so simple before...... before ..."

As Ralph left the room her could hear muffled sobs behind him, but he didn't look back. Returning to the kitchen he hastily ate the hot meal provided by Mary whilst Price sat opposite him and explained the situation. "Lottie went this morning, she's staying at The Lamb in Pantmawr. The three of them had a row. On top of that our Cissie went missing yesterday along with Her Ladyship's famous ring and there's no sign of her anywhere, not even at her daughter's. I tell you Ralph, there's something going on. Jarvis's death seems to have started it all off."

Ralph agreed. "My house had been ransacked, there was pure venom in the destruction and ruin of my belongings. The only things actually missing are the files which I kept in my desk. I say the only things, but they could be the most important. When did you last go over there, Mary?"

"I haven't! With all this business about Cissie vanishing into thin air I haven't had chance."

"The key?"

"In my room," Mary went to the door but stopped in her tracks.

"Oh, dear God! I gave it to Lottie this morning, in case she needed somewhere to go. It couldn't be her.......she'd never....... "

"No, she wouldn't." Ralph confirmed. "I think Thomas had a copy made and tried to make it look like a break-in." Pausing, he frowned as he recalled the information in the missing files. "The account records for the Glas Fryn Estate over the past year were taken along with some personal stuff.

To my mind the only person who would be interested is Blake."

Price looked puzzled. "Why should he want them? Facts and figures can't be worth much except to satisfy his curiosity."

"Wrong. They would be essential to sell the place. Lock, stock and barrel as they say."

Both father and daughter looked astounded, the elder recovered first. "How could he do that? Olivia would never agree to it!"

Ralph nodded. "You're right. The fact is that Thomas has the Deeds of the property, she wouldn't know until the deal was completed if he played his cards right. She made him powerful enough to handle all her business interests and that includes possession of the Deeds for this house and the farms."

"This is a nightmare!" Mary gasped, "It couldn't happen! What can we do, Ralph? There must be something?"

"I've got a few ideas," the young man smiled, "but I have to find out where this cottage is that Thomas uses."

Mary threw her hands up in despair. "The only two who knew were Cissie and Lottie." Pausing for thought, her ashen face looked strained as her brow creased. "Funny that. Lottie went out on an old bike to look around the cottage the other evening and on her way back a van tried to run her down, a van which she'd seen there. She was lucky to get away with scrapes and bruises. We had Sgt. Hopkins up here but we haven't heard a word since."

"I can believe it!" Ralph sighed. "He told me that someone had seen Cissie get on a bus yesterday afternoon and was quite happy to leave it at that." Getting up from the table he smiled, "I'm not. I'll go and fetch Lottie then find out what I can about Cissie."

Looking less gloomy, Price nodded. "I'll stay by the 'phone in case there's news of any kind. Thomas hasn't been back since this morning so when he turns up I'll watch him like a hawk."

"Watch Olivia, too. She seems to be turning to the bottle. I'll be back soon with Lottie."

The Lamb and Fleece was quiet. Just a few local men playing dominoes whilst the Landlord wiped glasses behind the bar with meticulous care. Holding a gleaming pint pot to the light he beamed as a customer entered.

"Mr. Nicholls! We haven't seen you in here for a while! Pint of the best?" The rotund man with wispy ginger hair beamed widely as he pulled the pump in response to the nod. "Been away for a few days, we heard. Business or pleasure?"

Taking the brimming glass of clear amber liquid, Ralph sipped before he answered. "Still a good pint, Harry! I went to a funeral. Jarvis. Old man Jones's son. Remember him?"

"Aye. I do that. Soldier through and through. Joined up as a lad he did. Dead, is he? Pity that. Same age as me. Makes you think."

Ralph knew he had to stop the routine philosophising whenever the subject of death was discussed in the pub. "I understand you had a guest book in this morning?"

Scratching his head in bewilderment, the landlord nodded. "Damnedest thing! That young woman from the House booked in this morning and left her bags here, then this afternoon collected her bags and left."

"Didn't she say anything about where she was going?"

"Nope! Didn't even bother coming in herself, just sent the taxi driver in for her bags. I reckon that old Dragon proved too much for her!"

"Did you see Blake around this morning?"

A frown creased the freckled forehead. Leaning over the bar to prevent being heard he spoke quietly like a conspirator in a drama. "I didn't, but they reckon he was visiting the old bird in the Post Office as usual. None of us like him, Mr. Nicholls. Not a single one of us."

"Because of Ted?"

"Not just that," the Barman looked up as the door swung

open, "but speak of the Devil and he appears! Evening, Ted. Ada let you out for a pint before last orders?"

The old gardener shambled in and stood besides Ralph at the bar. "She's not 'arf as busy as her mouth is! Usual, 'arry. Nice to see you back, Mr. Ralph, sir! That girl looks ill to me, time you took 'er in 'and!"

A spark of hope exploded inside Ralph's being like a firework. "You've seen Lottie? Where is she?"

"Dunno where she is now, but she was looking for the police station this morning. They only let ol' Hoppy carry on 'cos he's well in with the Eastbridge lot! Mind you, if it wasn't for 'im we'd be lucky to see a copper. What's the world coming to? I ask you."

"I know she went to the police, Ted, but did you see her after that?"

"Naw! My ol' lady 'ad me fixing the garden fence since then. Prisoner I am! It was 'eaven when your little lady took 'er off for an 'our . She came 'ome well-oiled an' I never 'eard a peep! Even 'er friend Beattie smiled at me!"

Ralph tried to stop the old man rambling. "There's another pint for you if you just answer my questions, Ted. Are you listening?"

The landlord winked as he took the money and Ted stood to attention. "Fire away, Ralph, sir!"

"Lottie spoke to your Ada. Why? When?"

"Well, all I 'eard off my Missus is 'ow that nice young lady from the big 'ouse took 'er and Beattie for a drink. It was only a day or so past, but my Ada reckons that we'll 'ave word from the 'ouse any day now. The girl promised to clear my name, bit late now mind. Shame about that girl. She's got a 'eart of gold, bless her."

"Shame?" Ralph asked concerned, "Why do you say that?"

"Well, I know she 'ad that accident an all that," Ted looked perplexed, "but there's summat else. She's looked like that since I first found 'er in that field. Worried to death, like. Mind you, Cissie Jenkins 'as gone an' that can't help."

Harry the Landlord confirmed the statement. "That's right, but Hoppy was round here earlier and said it was all a hoax. Cissie was seen getting on a bus yesterday."

"Who saw her?" Ralph asked.

Ted Skinner grinned a toothless smile. "Who do you think! Only 'er in the Post Office! I ask yer. Talk about funny."

"Just one more thing, Ted. Someone broke into my place during the last day or so, have you seen anything? Anyone hanging around at odd hours?"

"Bloody 'ell!" stammered the old gardener, "What the 'ell's going on round 'ere? If I saw anyone I'd shoot the buggers!"

Smiling, the Estate Manager nodded. "I reckon you would, Ted. I reckon you would! If you see anything of Lot..... Miss Stone, let me know."

Ralph left them both so fast that Harry and Ted smiled at each other. Ted took his free pint and nodded. "Cheers, 'Arry! I reckon 'e's smitten with the little lady!"

"About time someone caught the lad!" laughed the host as the other regulars looked up in disdain as their game of dominoes was disturbed by the raucous sound.

The private door to the Post Office was opened by the dour spinster. "What do you want at this hour?" she barked.

Jamming his foot in the door, Ralph spoke authoritatively. "I want to ask you a few questions, Miss Kemp. Here or inside. It doesn't matter to me."

"What is it then?" she asked holding the door firmly to prevent the gap widening.

"Your story to the police about Cissie Jenkins. They might believe it but I don't. Thomas Blake put you up to it, didn't he!"

Her face ashen, the woman shook her head vigorously. "I'm a respectable member of the community, Mr. Nicholls. Please remove your foot from the door at once or I will press the alarm bell. The police will be here in moments!"

"No problem, Miss Kemp. Just go ahead." Ralph smiled at

her confused expression. "Then everyone will hear about you and Thomas Blake. Is that what you want, a public announcement of your affair? I doubt if it would please our Mr. Blake. It would cramp his style."

"I refuse to be blackmailed! Now remove your foot from ...."

"Don't put me on the same level as him!" the angry man uttered between clenched teeth. "You gave a statement to the police about Cissie Jenkins. I find it very odd that you were the only person to see her. What did he promise you? Buy a little haven somewhere and live happily ever after?" Seeing the expression of hate on her face he continued, "Oh, yes! He uses people, especially women. Did you know he keeps another woman in a cottage just a few miles away? No? He travels between the both of you, that is in between calling at Glas Fryn and trying it on with Charlotte Stone!"

"Get out! Your lies are wasted on me!"

Putting his hands up in surrender, Ralph tried a different approach. "OK! OK! I can understand your position. He treats you as if you are the only woman in the world. Buys you flowers and small gifts. In return he asks you to do some small favour, just things which a devoted lover would do without question. Am I right?"

Pulling her blouse tight at the neck, the postmistress refused to weaken. "You are outrageous, Mr. Nicholls, and this is becoming ridiculous!"

"The favours get bigger," Ralph persisted, "big enough to place you and your job in jeopardy if the truth came out. He asks you to lie for him, just to keep him out of trouble. Am I still on the right track?"

"This has gone far enough!" the shrill voice screamed.

Taking a gamble, Ralph played his final card. "Did he give you a gift today? An opal and diamond ring?" The woman looked stunned and relaxed her hold on the door. "That ring was stolen," he continued, "Mrs. Olivia Jones had the ring stolen yesterday, the same time Cissie Jenkins went missing.

Go ahead, Miss Kemp. Call the police and I'll explain everything to them, the ring hasn't been reported missing yet."

"Oh, My God!" the spinster stepped back into the hallway staring at her left hand then pulled the ring off, "Here! Here! Take it!"

Playing the situation to the full, Ralph followed her into the hall and took the ring from the scrawny hand. "Now the truth. Two women are missing and if you know anything about Blake you could become the third."

"You mean he would...................... oh, never! I don't really know much." Tears trickled slowly down the powdered face leaving tracks which made her look a pathetic creature. "I intercepted his mail, but never opened anything. He told me to keep back anything Miss Stone sent because she was trying to get him out of Glas Fryn, and yesterday he asked me to say that Mrs. Jenkins got on the bus. Where's the harm in that? I know she's stolen some silver and jewellery, but the old Dragon deserves it if you ask me!"

"Is that what he told you?" Ralph asked enraged. He gripped her wrists and shook her in temper. "Cissie didn't take anything! HE DID!"

Sobbing and nodding her head, the postmistress whined, "I didn't see her, or Miss Stone. I just did as he asked me. Nothing else."

Dropping his voice, the young man kept his grip firm as he demanded, "Keep talking, woman! What happened to Charlotte this morning?"

"He................ he dropped me in Eastbridge and told me to get a taxi and go to the Lamb and Fleece. I had to ask the driver to go into the public house and collect her bags, then go back to Eastbridge and put them in the left luggage office in the Railway Station."

"Didn't you think it was a strange thing to do? You didn't see either woman yet you covered up the tracks! It just doesn't ring true, Miss Kemp."

"Let me go, please! You're hurting me! I promise you it's

the truth. He said that it was just to help them and I believed him."

Releasing her arms, Ralph nodded. "For the moment I'll have to take your word for it. What about the cottages hereabouts? Do you have some sort of record or register of holiday or rented properties?"

Snivelling, the spinster shook her head. "Eastbridge is the main office. They're shut for the weekend now."

Turning to leave, the tall young man squared his shoulders in resolution. "So I'll have to find it by trail and error. This might turn out to be a very serious affair, Miss Kemp. You'd better stay put and lock your doors."

The woman shivered. "Do you really think Thomas is capable of .... well, ... kidnapping?"

"Kidnappers phone or send messages to ask for a ransom. They've had no word at Glas Fryn. Nothing at all."

"Do you mean that......... " the postmistress looked grey. "Oh, Dear God! What have I done?"

Ralph left her and slammed the door behind him. It seemed that the old spinster really didn't think she was doing anything wrong, merely acting in good faith for the man who professed to love her dried up body. Sordid, but understandable perhaps.

"I know Tom 'ad 'er favours, but I'm surprised at you, Mr. Nicholls, sir!" A chuckle accompanied the voice which was familiar.

"Ted! Not poaching this fine evening?"

"Naw. Not tonight. I reckon there's bigger fish to be 'ad, the type that doesn't swim!" Ted wheeled his bicycle round to walk besides Ralph. "You got a job on, finding that lass. Two 'eads are better than one, an' two wheels can go where four can't."

"If you're offering to help, Ted, put that bike in the back of the Land Rover and hop in. Something's badly wrong."

Charlotte opened her eyes but the world was still black.

Was she blind? Oh, dear God, she felt so sick and drowsy. Getting shakily to her feet she put her hands in front of her to hit something solid. It felt like a brick wall. Following it around it measured about 4 foot by 3 with a wooden door. Her hands felt gritty and dirty, she felt along the rough wood of the door for a lock or handle. There was no latch so must be bolted from outside. She kicked and banged the wooden obstruction with the little strength she had, but it merely rattled and withstood her fury. She shouted and yelled until her throat was dry and sore, but all that met her was a deafening silence.

Sliding down the wall to the floor she began to cry. Where was she? What happened? Forcing her mind to think back the last thing she remembered was Ralph's cottage ablaze. Of course, she hadn't actually seen it, but the smoke was black and...................... no! Not a house fire, the acrid smell of rubber burning.

Thomas TOLD her, but she hadn't actually seen it! It was a ruse to get her here. The cottage. She must still be at the cottage. A shed. Her crying turned to laughter as the truth dawned on her. 'I'm locked up in an old shed! Oh, God! Nobody passes this way, only HIM!'

Her tears started afresh as she thought of Thomas. Nobody would miss her, they all thought she'd left Glas Fryn so she could be disposed of without anyone raising an eyebrow. She had played right into his hands, all she could do was sit in the darkness and wait for her murderer to finish the job he'd started......................

Thomas rose from the bed and dressed quickly. "Come on, Dora. It's time we were gone. DORA!" he shouted at the inert form in the bedclothes, "Wake up, you lazy bitch! Get dressed."

The puffy eyes opened slowly. "Got cold feet, Tom? What's the rush all of a sudden?"

Tucking his shirt into his trousers, Thomas yelled, "Just

get up and dress, woman! You know the drill. We got an appointment and the boys will be here any minute."

"Ok!" the plump figure slid out of the bed, "You wanted to come up here, not me! Anyway, everything's packed and ready so what's all the fuss about. By the way, what do we do about 'er?"

"You just pack up what's left and I'll see to the rest."

Clutching her blouse to her ample bosom, the woman blanched. "You're not going to.............. " struggling to say the words she shook her head , "No, Tom. You can't do that!"

Straightening his tie, Thomas glanced out of the window at the sound of an engine. "Stop blubbering, woman! I'm not going to lay a finger on her, now hurry up. The van's here and the sooner we're away the better."

As she ran downstairs, Thomas smiled to himself. Old Dora was becoming a liability. She'd done as she was told up until the last few days, but her moaning was beginning to annoy him. Under pressure she would blow everything. He didn't need her anymore.

Olivia was making life very difficult for the Price family. Mary's patience had worn so thin that she had refused to fetch and carry anymore whilst Price disappeared to Thomas's room to search for any clues he could find.

"Where's your father?" Olivia demanded after ringing the bell for the umpteenth time.

Despite the urge to wrap her apron strings around her employer's throat, Mary put on a calm expression. "He won't be long, he's just checking Cissie's room. She might have left an address or something."

"You did that last night!" Olivia roared. "She's scarpered with my ring! Tell him I want him here at once!"

"Well surely I can.................. " the telephone rang and Mary raced to the hall. "Hello? Yes, this is Glas Fryn. Can I help you? Mr. Nicholls? Sorry, he's not here but if you like ...."

Olivia had followed the housekeeper out and snatched the receiver from Mary with malice. "This is Olivia Jones. Who is calling?" Listening to the answer she changed her attitude with amazing speed. "Helen! My dear girl. How are you? My deepest sympathies, my dear. Very sad."

Mary stood by with her arms folded and ignored the hand which waved her aside. She listened with unashamed brashness. Olivia continued her conversation whilst glaring at her servant. "Yes, my dear. As my maid told you, Ralph isn't here. Is there anything wrong?"

Her expression fell at the reply. "Well, I'm sure that Ralph has complete confidence in me. Rest assured that he will get the message, Helen dear."

Olivia's features grew dark as Jarvis's widow gave her answer. Her final remark confirmed Mary's suspicions. "If he calls I'll tell him to ring you urgently, but I wouldn't hold your breath, my dear. He's obviously not as close to me as he is to you. Goodbye."

Replacing the handset, Olivia turned to Mary. "How dare you listen to my calls! I forbid you to answer the telephone in future. Understood!"

Dipping a curtsey, Mary Price said evenly, "I'll just crawl back to the kitchen now, Ma'am. You know, that place where all the servants congregate and gossip."

Waving her stick, Olivia followed the disappearing employee whilst Mary flung open the kitchen door to find Ralph and Ted Skinner making a cup of tea.

"Well?" Mary demanded. "Any news?"

"That depends, Miss!" Ted replied laughing, "Our lad 'ere putting the fear of God into Miss Kemp was worth seeing!"

As Ralph poured the mugs of tea, Mary clapped her hands in glee before the green baize door burst open behind her. "Huh! What a den of thieves!" Olivia announced continuing to wave her stick. "Pure anarchy - and in my own house! What are you doing here, Skinner?"

Removing his cap with unruffled dignity, the gardener

replied soberly, " 'Aving a cuppa before I goes out into the fine evenin' to poach, Ma'am."

"Out! Out!" yelled the formidable old woman. "How dare you set foot in my house!"

Ralph interceded. "Calm down, Olivia. We're out looking for Cissie and Charlotte and called to see if there was any news. Sit down and try and help instead of acting like an old harridan."

"You could start by telling him about the 'phone call?" Mary urged Olivia.

Dropping into a kitchen chair, Olivia Jones sighed. "It's serious then. Charlotte missing too? Both of them really missing?"

"Yes, Olivia." Ralph nodded gravely. "I'm afraid it's deadly serious."

CHAPTER 18

False Trails

Ralph Nicholls returned Helen Jarvis's call immediately, but an Answer phone gave its automated message to leave name and number after the tone. Slamming the receiver down in frustration, he returned to the kitchen. "Price, if Helen rings back ask her to give you the message. Explain the situation to her. I'm going to see Hopkins and organise a search. Come on, Ted. We've got work to do."

"Fine. I'm used to working at night."

"Wait!" Mary caught Ralph's arm. "We've searched his room but most of his things have gone, except for this." She produced a small notebook from her apron pocket. "There's only names and telephone numbers in it, they can't be important or he'd never have left it, but you never know."

"You dared to search a guest's room?" Olivia started up again. "Mary Price, I'm ashamed of you, girl."

Price stood erect despite his hunched backbone. "I did it. I'm not exactly proud of myself, I've never done such a thing before in my life, but desperate situations call for desperate measures. You can sack me when those two women are back safe and well."

"I was.............." the elderly lady struggled for words. "I expect you're right, under the circumstances .... "

Price put an arm around his daughter. "I know I'm right."

A damp cold was seeping into Charlotte's bones as she paced around the confines of her prison. Even though total darkness fell like a shroud around her, she knew exactly where the walls were and, more importantly, the door. Her shoulders were aching through trying to break through the stout barricade which separated her from freedom. What time was it? Evening or night? How long had it been since the last cracks of daylight had stopped filtering through the gap under the door?

Slipping down to the floor she hugged herself and let the tears fall. Why had she been so stupid as to trust Thomas? What had he done with Cissie? She must have stumbled on something. She had probably been alone in the house and Thomas went back for some reason, poor old Cissie must have seen him up to something. But what? He had already taken everything of value from the attic.

The ring was missing, Olivia's first engagement ring, but that was not of enough value to kidnap two women over. That must have been for his woman, the cheap tarty woman in the cottage. Maybe for Miss Kemp, the postmistress! Giggling to herself, Charlotte began to feel light-headed. Oh, hell! That's what becomes of skipping breakfast, as Olivia would say.

The sound of an engine sobered her up. It was a sound she had heard before, not like a car, more like a van .... of course! The van had returned. Now the Police would spot them and follow it here. It was only a matter of time before she was rescued.

Not for the first time she thought of Ralph. The only person who would have tried to find her was hundreds of miles away. Nobody else knew her ties with the place, her physical contact with the past. Nobody else knew that she could never leave her discovered roots. Annie would survive the ages through her children's children, through herself. Would fate be so unkind as to prevent it?

Voices, heard in the muffled distance, came closer. Their words became louder until they were quite audible and Charlotte listened attentively.

"What the 'ell did you have to do that for?" A rough voice asked.

"Believe me, old boy, that girl could ruin everything! I had to do something. She's been to the Police about that stupid old bat and I didn't know where she'd go next!"

A third male voice, deep and uncouth, joined in. "She's not

a bad looking bit of stuff, Tom! No wonder you grabbed her. I wouldn't mind something like that at my mercy!" Crude laughter endorsed the comment and Charlotte felt her flesh creep.

"Yes," Thomas's cultured voice contrasted with the other two, "well we are not all perverts and rapists. There's bigger things at stake here."

"Hey!" the deep voice boomed, "who are you calling a pervert? Be careful, sunshine, or we might have to make a few phone calls about certain things. You know, fires and dead bodies. Kidnapped women."

The sound of scuffling broke out before a woman's voice shouted, "Lay off, you stupid buggers! We don't want no nosey sods around here, so just cut it out and get packing!"

"Well you get the kettle on, Dora, love! We been doing some very important work for our Lordship here, haven't we, son!"

After some raucous laughter the men dispersed and the captive let out a sigh of relief. Too soon. The sound of the bolts being slid open brought a moment of sheer terror to her soul .

"Awake, are we?" The sound of Thomas' voice came to her as the bright light from a torch shone into her face.

Holding up her arm to hide from the glare, Charlotte stood upright and lunged forward. Her efforts were futile as her body, drained of strength, allowed her captor to grab her and hold her in his arms. He laughed, a deep and sinister sound, then pushed her roughly back against the wall of the coal shed. "It's a pity you didn't play along with me, old girl. Your spirit and my cunning could have made things much easier and far more pleasant. You've only yourself to blame for this mess."

"Lay off me, Thomas! It's you who is in a mess or you wouldn't have to lock me up!"

Dropping the torch he slapped her face hard with the back of his hand then held her throat in a vice-like grip. "You won't be around to know, lady! Like your fat friend. That stupid old bag nearly spoiled everything until I got rid of her."

Choking and pulling at the hands around her throat, Charlotte groaned in agony and felt her life slipping away. Suddenly the grip was released and she fell to the floor coughing and spluttering at his feet.

A raucous female voice was shouting, "Get in there and give us a hand! I thought I'd find you out here messing around with her! Well muggins here is not going to do the dirty work for you anymore, so if you want that money in your pocket you'd better get moving!"

Picking up the torch, Thomas Blake nodded. "You lock up while I see to Fred and Alf."

Charlotte was man-handled back into the coal shed. The door slammed shut and bolts were securely rammed into place. Charlotte slumped against a wall and cried in her prison. Shock, weakness and the knowledge of Cissie's murder were a lethal concoction which would demoralise the most stubborn fighting spirit.

In the quiet, poorly lit lane a loud persistent banging on the door of the Police House woke the household and light began to spill from the windows. The burly Sergeant answered the door wearing his dressing-gown and slippers . "What on earth............................ Mr.Nicholls? What's up, lad? I've only just got to bed. Can't it wait until morning?"

"No. It can't."

"Come in then. Oh! Who have we here? Ted Skinner too? You usually avoid me at nights, this must be serious!"

As they crossed the threshold, the policeman's wife waddled down the stairs in her night attire with a long, grey plait hanging down her back. "What on earth is wrong? Mr. Nicholls? Ted?"

Ralph replied as calmly as he could, "Miss Kemp was lying. Cissie Jenkins was NOT seen getting on any bus and Charlotte Stone has disappeared as well. I think that

Charlotte's in great danger, probably kidnapped."

"Why? That sort of thing doesn't happen in these parts!" the policeman's wife asked puzzled.

"It's something to do with Thomas Blake and his activities."

"Right!" she retorted abruptly. "You go and dress, Hoppy. You two, follow me. We'll have a cup of tea while you're waiting."

When the series of events were unfolded to the Sergeant, he nodded with concern. "Miss Stone never mentioned a cottage that Mr. Blake had. You said that Price found a notebook? Perhaps there's a clue in that. May I see it?"

Handing it over, Ralph felt impatient. "There's just phone numbers, no addresses or anything. He's hardly likely to leave evidence behind, is he!"

"Is Mrs. Jones selling the house?" Mrs. Hopkins asked out of the blue. She had been listening to the three men but remained silent up until now.

"No!" Ralph answered sharply. "What made you ask that?"

Narrowing her eyes, the large woman clasped her hands and rested them on the table. "The day before yesterday at 11.30, just as my friends were leaving our weekly Coffee Morning, a young couple stopped by and asked for directions to Glas Fryn. I told them the way then they asked me about the area. I told them it was a very pleasant place to live, of course. They seemed very nice. It was their last remark which I thought very odd."

"Well?" her husband prompted, "Tell us!"

"I asked them if they were thinking of settling in the area and the man said, 'Perhaps. Only if I am Lord of the Manor and living apart from you serfs'. It was such a stupid and rude thing to say that I dismissed it, until now, of course."

"Serfs, eh!" Ted said as he cackled. "Thass 'ow it used to be. Mind you, the ol' lady would have it the same now given 'alf a chance."

Ralph snapped his fingers. "That's it! Blake was trying to

sell off the house on the quiet. If everyone was out and Cissie the only one there she would be the fly in the ointment! We need to ask Olivia Jones and the Prices' where they were that morning."

"I don't like what you're saying, Ralph," the grave tones of the policeman conveyed deep concern. "Are you sure about the time, my dear?" he asked turning to his wife. "It could be a vital factor."

A scalding look spoke volumes. "Being married to you for years has made me very particular about such things. It was 11.30 I tell you!"

Patting her hand he smiled affectionately. "I should have known better than to ask. In that case, we can assume that Mrs. Jenkins disappearance becomes very suspicious. I think it would be wise to arrange a search of Glas Fryn and the grounds."

Ralph felt impatient. "Sense at last! What about Lottie? She's missing too but I doubt if she's anywhere near Glas Fryn."

"We got to find that ol' cottage, Mr Ralph!" Ted urged. "Leave Hoppy to sort the 'ouse out and we can get on with it."

"So you got some brains after all, Skinner!" the policeman guffawed, "Fair enough. Once I can spare the manpower I'll send some help. What about the old biddy, though? Mrs. Jones won't take kindly to having her house opened up at this time of night."

The Estate Manager knew how difficult Olivia could be so volunteered to call at Glas Fryn to pave the way. Mrs. Hopkins promptly took her coat off the back door peg and insisted she went along. "I can stay with her, keep her calm. I bet I'm the first person to visit the grandest house in Pantmawr wearing her night clothes!"

The shed door opened and two pairs of hands grabbed her arms before roughly pushing her into the cold night air. Sprawling to the ground, Charlotte felt bewildered and totally confused at finding herself outside her prison so suddenly. Her eyes hurt as the light from the cottage window fell upon her, she had been in darkness for so long.

"Fancy a little game, Alf?" a man's voice asked menacingly.

"Give it a rest, Fred. I don't like this at all. He's gone too far taking this one."

Grasping Charlotte's arm with excessive strength, Fred laughed coarsely. "You're getting soft! You were all for running her down last week. Pity you missed, it could have saved us a lot of bother." Cupping her chin in his hand he stared into the frightened face. "I can see the damage, even in this light! Never mind, I'm not fussy."

Trying not to retch at the sight and smell of the face so close to her own, Charlotte summoned up her last ounce of strength and brought her knee up hard and sharp between his legs. An almighty animal yell burst out and he doubled in agony uttering obscenities and nursing his wounded manhood. Any hopes of getting away were quashed when the other man lunged forward and pinned her arms behind her back.

"You alright, Fred?" he asked his suffering partner.

"Aye. Get the bitch trussed before she tries anything else!"

Even though the lights were ablaze, the cottage was deserted. She was pushed and dragged up the stairs skinning her calves on the uncarpeted risers. As they threw her into a bedroom she feared the worse.

The man called Alf held a length of rope and flexed then twisted it around his hands in an intimidating manner. He nodded to a rickety chair in the middle of the room. "Sit there."

Charlotte was almost relieved when he tied her to the chair instead of strangling her until she fully realised her situation. Helpless to defend herself, in a cottage in the middle of nowhere with two men who seemed to find violence a sport, particularly one who now had a personal reason to inflict misery on her. Once she had been securely lashed to the wooden frame the man Alf laughed hideously, took tape out of his pocket to seal her mouth then they both left the room slamming the door behind them.

'Thank God!' her mind said. She felt grateful for the small mercy of the light which Alf had left on, but wondered what their next move would be. Where was Thomas? Why keep me here? Why?

An old alarm clock ticked away on a beside cabinet. It was two in the morning.

At Glas Fryn Price and Mary confirmed their movements on the day Cissie went missing and the mess in the kitchen they came back to. They also confirmed that Olivia and Charlotte were out from early morning until late afternoon.

Olivia was stunned by the invasion of her privacy. "What on earth do you mean? Carry out a search in the middle of the night? It's ridiculous! Cissie ran away, and with my ring I might add!"

Ralph took the item out of his pocket. "This ring?"

"Yes!" Olivia took it feverishly. "Oh, thank goodness it's back. I knew .... " she stopped in the act of placing it on her finger and asked, "and Cissie is still missing?"

Nodding his head in reply, Ralph led her into the lounge and sat her down before telling her the story. "So you see, Olivia, your wonderful and charming Thomas took the ring to play on the emotions of Miss Kemp. How could she refuse to tell a couple of white lies when presented with such an impressive token of his affection."

Olivia sighed. "I am deeply hurt. It really was a most damnable thing to do! He was well aware of the sentiment I attached to this ring." Squaring her shoulders, the fighting spirit returned to the old woman's soul. "So what do you think has happened to Cissie?" Turning to the policeman's wife standing besides her she asked, "Mrs. Hopkins. Is your husband aware of the facts as they now stand?"

"He is, Mrs. Jones. Ralph and Mr. Skinner summoned his help once they found out about Miss Kemp's lies and that's why we think a search of your House and grounds are necessary, with your permission, of course."

"Huh!" the owner of Glas Fryn exclaimed. "With or without my permission is nearer the truth!" Looking the woman up and down she commented acidly, "I suppose it all happened in such a rush that you didn't have time to dress properly? I'm quite surprised to see you in your night attire, Mrs. Hopkins. You always seemed to be respectable when we sat on committees together."

"I wouldn't expect you to understand the obligations of being a policeman's wife, Mrs. Jones. My husband covers a large rural area and has fought tooth and nail to work from Pantmawr instead of being based in Eastbridge where there are many more policemen on call day and night. You'd be surprised how often I'm seen out and about in my dressing-gown if my husband needs support. I'm there besides him whatever the hour. Now, Madam, do you want me to stay and keep you company or shall I go home to my nice warm bed and let them turn the place upside down?"

Ralph chuckled silently. Olivia gave a half-hearted grin before drawing a deep breath and nodding. "My apologies, Mrs. Hopkins. Your role must be very demanding and I respect your loyalty to your husband. He has done his best to stay in the village, that I know. I admire him for his determination. You are a welcome guest and shall be treated as such, whatever you are wearing."

Mrs. Hopkins wasn't quite sure if she'd been complimented or insulted by the last remark, but decided to be gracious enough to accept it as the former. "Thank you. I'll go to the kitchen and get some tea going. It's going to be a long night."

As the Estate Manager turned to leave, Olivia followed him to the door. "Ralph, do you really think something......... well, something terrible has happened to Cissie? Why search here?"

Shrugging his broad shoulders, he answered truthfully. "I really don't know where Cissie is, but they have to start looking somewhere." Pausing, he asked, "Have you seen Thomas since this morning?"

"No. That's not unusual, sometimes he doesn't come back for days. What about Charlotte? If she was here she could tell you about some cottage he rented."

"Exactly, Olivia. Exactly."

The police team arrived at that moment so Ralph made his escape. Olivia was still blind to the gravity of the situation, but maybe that was better than stark reality. Ted Skinner was sitting in the Land Rover with a local map in his hands. "It all looks funny on paper, Mr. Ralph! I'd rather trust memory than this. Can't hardly read 'alf the names."

"The light in here doesn't help, Ted. Why didn't you come into the house to read it?"

"No fear, boy! What did 'er Ladyship say 'bout the ring an' all that?"

"She's agreed to the search, but I don't think she really understands why. As for Thomas, I still think she's a bit soft about him."

"Gawd knows why!" Ted wondered. "Always been trouble, the Blakes. 'E's not even blood I reckon. You are, and so is that girl. It should count for more."

They drove down the crunching gravel drive and turned right away from Pantmawr, away from inhabited areas. The sky was like a black velvet cloak which was studded with twinkling jewels, the moon was bright and the only illumination the men had to help them. It was two o'clock and both knew that the real search had just begun. Amongst the isolated dwellings which were scattered around the intricate system of lanes they hoped to find a missing woman, the task seemed impossible but hope was their spur, sheer determination their momentum.

The cottage was quiet, deathly quiet. As Charlotte sat

316

upright in the chair tied by hands and feet, she fought the urge to close her eyes and drift away. Her arms were numb and pins and needles in her legs were making her nerve ends scream in torment. Not that she could scream. She had been gagged for good measure and the effect was suffocating.

The bedroom door opened and Thomas Blake walked in dressed in a suit, open overcoat and white silk scarf for effect. Carrying a bottle of champagne and two tumblers he staggered slightly as he wove his way towards the prisoner. The grin was particularly ingratiating as he leered at the helpless woman before him.

"What a mess! Coal-dust and all. Not a pretty sight, but there again I doubt if Fred's private parts are looking very healthy at the moment! You got a wallop on you girl, and I speak from experience."

Laughing at his own remarks he sat on the edge of the bed. Placing the glasses on the floor he uncorked the bottle and poured, most of the drink spilling on the carpet. "Well, my dear, it's all signed and sealed now, so there's nothing you can do anymore. Dora made an excellent stooge as Mrs. Blake. The deal was clinched this evening over a wonderful meal. Glas Fryn is history and so is that old battle-axe. Come the morning she'll be kicked out on the road, homeless!" Laughing wholeheartedly he slapped his knee. "Oh, so rude of me!" He leaned over and ripped the tape off Charlotte's face. "There. Is that better? No point screaming. We are miles from anywhere. Fred and Alf have long gone so there's just you and me, old girl."

Her face stinging and mouth dry, Charlotte asked thickly through numbed lips, "Dora? What about Dora?" Perhaps the woman would be able to stop this. It was the only straw she could clutch at.

"Dora?" The look in his eye was strange as he continued to laugh. "She's gone too. Yes." Erupting into fresh laughter he affirmed, "She's gone too! Have a drink? Celebrate with me. Sorry about the glasses, but this place is very basic." As he handed a tumbler to her he stopped short and giggled like a naughty schoolboy. "No hands? Pity! I'd better drink them both."

Wearily rotating her head to ease her aching muscles, Charlotte tried to look unconcerned. "Where has Dora gone? London? Cumbria? Where?"

"Heaven or hell? Who knows!" the mirth continued as the wine flowed.

"Did she go with those men? Fred and ...... the other one?"

"Nosey little bitch, aren't you!" His expression became serious and his tone without banter. "They were well paid and will crawl back to the gutters they came from. That only leaves one loose end." Standing up and walking slowly around her chair he leaned close to her face. "The thorn in my side. Charlotte Stone. What shall I do with you, Miss Charlotte Bloody Stone?"

Charlotte felt sick as the smell of spirits carried on his breath. She shouted back hoarsely, "Stop playing games and get it over with, or maybe you talk your victims to death? Maybe you haven't got the guts to do anything. Oh yes, of course! I've been imprisoned all day, trussed up and gagged, just about weak enough for Thomas Blake to finish off. Makes you feel like a man, does it? It's the nearest you'll ever get to being a man!"

The next moment Charlotte felt as though her head had been knocked off her shoulders, such was the impact of the blow. Just as she tried to hold her head up high in defiance she was struck again from the other side of the face. The world span before her eyes and it seemed an age before her senses stopped reeling. The pain was unbearable, but her stubborn spirit refused to show it.

"You're right." Thomas announced as he sat back on the bed. "But then I discovered very early on that the best way to get rid of someone is by catching them unawares."

"Tell me about it." Charlotte said as she felt her face swelling. If she could keep him talking then there was always hope. She knew that he loved talking about himself most of all.

Thomas then did a surprising thing. He untied her arms and legs and rubbed her hands to bring them back to life. She was grateful that the numbness prevented her from feeling his flesh against hers. "There you are. I'm not a sadist. If you want to hear the story you might as well be comfortable, old girl. Would you like to lie on the bed?"

"No!" she screamed in horror, "I'm alright. Just........ just sit there and ...... and tell me."

Handing her a glass half full of flat champagne, he took off his scarf and overcoat then leaned back on the bed. "Well it all started with my mother, really. She was such a bore! Always blamed me. My brother, my twin brother I should say, well he could do no wrong. She called me a bully. An unintelligent bully."

"Fancy that!" Charlotte muttered to herself, but on seeing his expression change she changed tack. "It must have made life pretty difficult."

Leaning forward, his elbows resting on his thighs, he winked. "I knew you'd understand, dear girl. Well, I soon shut her up. We went for a picnic at a local beauty spot. It only took a little push and dear mother fell."

"Fell?"

"Over a cliff. She lasted a few weeks and I prayed that she wouldn't come round. She didn't."

"But what about your brother? Was he with you when the ......er, accident happened?"

"Of course, leech that he was! That's why I had to shut him up as well. A pillow on the face back at the dormitory and that kept him quiet. I stuck a boiled sweet in his mouth after that and everyone thought he choked to death on that. Simple."

Astonished, Charlotte stared at the man before her. "You did it? Didn't anyone suspect anything?"

"My father did. He came to take me home for the funeral

and asked me what really happened. I told him the truth like a dutiful son should. He had a tricky heart, you see. Conveniently he had a massive heart attack so that saved me a job."

"But you were just a child! You're making it up!" A chill swept through Charlotte which had nothing to do with room temperature.

"Eleven, going on twelve. You're right, just a child. Trouble was that I had an old head on young shoulders, but getting rid of those imbeciles made me feel like a man." He stood up and smiled, walked over to her and began to stroke her hair. "Your lovely, dark hair. It's all knotted." Then he dropped to his knees and caressed her swollen face. "You used to be so pretty. What would Ralph think of you now?"

"Ralph?" Charlotte asked as the name loomed from the distance.

"Yes. Ralph Nicholls. Why him and not me? He's so bloody hopeless he's not even around to help you! Rushed up to the funeral, didn't he? It was a very convenient accident, I should have sent the car repair bill to the funeral director!" A hideous, gurgling laugh issued forth .

Her adrenalin flowed as she pushed her captor away and screamed as hard as she could. Thomas fell back and laughed. As Charlotte stood to escape the room her legs refused to carry her and hurt as weight was placed upon them. Springing to his feet, Thomas hit her across her face again and again until blackness descended and heavenly forces lifted her and carried her bruised and broken body away.

Glas Fryn was a hive of activity as the search got underway. Considering it was nearly three in the morning Olivia was chirpy and thoroughly enjoying the drama on her doorstep. Mary and Price were busy making hot drinks and sandwiches for the handful of policemen who were concentrating on the house. Sergeant Hopkins had arranged for extra men to arrive at dawn to extend the search to the grounds, every inch would be covered systematically.

At 3.30am the Sergeant was called upstairs by a young, white-faced policeman. In an old wardrobe in the attic they found the body of Cissie Jenkins. Confirming her identity, the large, sorrowful Sgt. Hopkins reported the matter to his superior at Eastbridge and the necessary arrangements were made.

As he replaced the receiver he pondered. His grandfather had been involved in a murder enquiry from this house too. History had a nasty habit of repeating itself.

CHAPTER 19

The Eleventh Hour

Cruising along a lane in the Eastbridge direction, Ralph cursed as a vehicle hurtled around the corner ahead of him on the wrong side of the road. Both swerved to avoid collision and Ralph felt the hedge scraping the side of his Land Rover before he managed to stop. In his wing mirror he could see the large van bounce off the bank on the other side of the road before coming to a halt. As he got out the van revved up it's engine and drove away with tyres screeching.

"Damn it!"

Ted Skinner slid into the driver's seat and leaned out of the open door. "I reckon thass the one that 'it our girl! Too dark to see the colour but funny number plates. That be 'im, bet you anything. Got the book?"

"What book?" Ralph asked before he latched on to his companion's train of thought. "The notebook? Hoppy took it off me. Why?"

Tipping his cap back on his sparsely inhabited head, Ted scratched his balding pate. "I've seen that van before, parked up somewheres. Now where was it?" Screwing up his face in concentration he added, "if we 'ad some kind of clue, like something in that book, just something to ring a bell....... "

"For God's sake, Ted, think! We haven't got time to go back to Glas Fryn and wait for Hoppy to ask us the ins and outs!"

"I know that, but there's something............ something back in the past. Some sort of link.... " Pulling his cap well down on his head he sighed. "Aw! I dunno. I'm not used to all this thinking. I could do with a tot, it's cold for my old bones out 'ere. Bit of warm might jog my memory, like. What time is it?"

Ralph half listened while his mind raced. Ted Skinner was

a wily character and on to something, he knew the man too well to put it down to the ramblings of an old codger. "Four just gone. Right. Next turning right is my house. We'll pop in for a minute to replenish your jaded mind, Ted. You'd better come up with something."

It was strange walking into his home knowing that others had been there and rifled through his personal possessions. His comfortable home had been turned into an alien place littered with the debris of a demonic stranger. "Come on in, Ted. Excuse the mess. I think the whisky bottle is still intact."

"Bloody 'Ell!" Ted gasped as he saw the carnage. "Who done this?"

"I've got a good idea. Here. Drink this." Ralph passed a generous measure to the old gardener and phoned Glas Fryn to check if there were any developments. Returning, he gravely broke the latest news. "They've found Cissie's body, Ted. In the attic."

"Oh no!" the old man whispered before gulping his drink. "Give me another, lad. It's 'ard to believe. So you think 'e did it?"

"Blake?" Helping himself to a stiff drink he nodded. "It fits."

Draining his glass he threw it against the wall where it shattered into a myriad pieces. "So where the hell is Lottie! She could be dead too. She could be dead! Dear God! Daisy all over again! Fred Blake killed her and the same thing is happening again. Fred Blake's great-nephew has come back to finish off the last of Annie's family. No wonder Lottie kept going back!"

"What are you goin' on about, lad?" Ted asked puzzled. "Goin' back where?"

"In time, Ted. You found her that morning, remember?"

"Ne'er forget it! Right near where 'er family nigh on got burned to death. Blake you said?" Ted Skinner's old brain started working with the help of an extra libation. "Fred Blake kidnapped Daisy right enough. She 'ad T.B. but when they found 'er she was too far gone. Died a few days later. Old Jim got 'im though! We weren't supposed to know, but I knew. I was there."

Running his hand through his hair, Ralph frowned. "What? What are you going on about, Ted. There's no time to ramble on, we've got to find her. Think hard!"

Ted paused as the information sunk into his mind, then he plonked his glass on the table and announced pleased as punch, "Thass what I'm trying to tell you, lad! That Fred Blake had a cottage hereabouts called Chimneys. Thass where I saw that van! Stands to reason young Thomas would go for that place. Probably been left to him."

Within moments they were heading towards the cottage where Daisy had been found so many years ago.

Lying on the bed, her vision hazy, Charlotte squinted as the man stood over her. "Leave me alone, Thomas. Just go away, please!" Her lips were swollen, her tongue thick in her mouth.

"Who the devil is Thomas?" demanded the voice. The man was fair and bore the features of Thomas but was different in some indefinable way. "You know very well who I am, girl!"

"No, no I don't. What's happening?"

"No pretending, Daisy. Remember seeing me in the hospital? I am your father. Your real father who was banished to some God-forsaken land because of your mother. Oh yes, Annie will suffer just like I did!"

Charlotte could hardly believe it. She was back in the past, assumed to be Daisy and the man before her had to be Fred Blake. It had to be a nightmare. Hallucination. "What are you doing here? Where am I?"

The man talked as though she hadn't spoken. "I set fire to her cottage but she got out! No. There are other ways to break a person. You are her precious child, it will be torture to hear that you've been kidnapped. Annie will suffer as never before."

"You raped her! Suffering enough, surely! Why did you ever come back?"

"To claim what's mine by right. The family fortune. That niece of mine thought she's get the lot, but she will live and die a pauper. Marrying a Nicholls is the ultimate insult! Her drunken father has signed everything over to me, so now there's only blood to spill."

'Emily and David', Charlotte whispered to herself. "So why are you doing this to me? If you've got your family fortune then why don't you just go back?"

Leaning so his face was touching hers he answered quietly, "Because you are MY daughter, not any other man's. I have the power to say if you live or die. Oh yes, I came back for the money but also for revenge."

Struggling for breath, Charlotte raised herself from her prone position on the bed. "James Nicholls is my father, not you! You are a rapist, a cowardly rapist! Nothing on earth will ever make me recognise you as my father!" Without thinking, Charlotte had taken on the role of Daisy.

Grabbing her neck and holding it tight he spoke through clenched teeth, his eyes bulging and wild. "There's too much of your damned mother in you. Annie was always a stubborn bitch and you are the same. I knew she didn't like me. Wouldn't let me near her, but I was too cunning for her!" Releasing his grip he thrust the young woman back onto the bed. "I should have made sure she never woke up again. I got you though. It would break her heart to lose you. Her precious bastard daughter!"

Taking a watch from his waistcoat pocket he became calm again, preoccupied with his scheme. "Time I was off. I've got an appointment at Glas Fryn. In the Summer House. You remember our little fracas there, no doubt. Your family should be frantic about you by now and I will have Annie at my mercy, ready to do anything I ask!"

Fred Blake left the room slamming the door behind him.

Slumping back on the bed and letting the tears fall,

Charlotte wondered if her sanity had left her. She had been talking to a ghost. Fred Blake had met his end in the Summer House at Glas Fryn. Closing her eyes in sheer exhaustion and shutting out the horror she screamed when something cold brushed across her forehead.

Reluctantly opening her swollen eyes expecting the worse, Charlotte was astonished to see her Grandmother's face. "I got here as soon as I could, my dear child. Please forgive me!"

"Forgive?" Charlotte asked barely able to speak.

Annie sat at the bedside in a room which was pink and blurred. Taking a limp hand her grandmother stroked it and smiled serenely. "We'll have you out of here soon. Home is where you should be. Home with your family."

Any attempt at moving her head seemed impossible, so Charlotte lay still and followed Annie with her eyes. "You know who I am?" she whispered.

Annie laughed softly and patted her hand. "As if I wouldn't know my own daughter. It must be the illness. Being out in that coal shed hasn't helped your condition, Daisy." Waving a finger before Charlotte could speak, her grandmother continued, "I know all about it. Caught it off the patients you were nursing from what I can gather. Don't worry, child. They can cure Tuberculosis these days, you'll be well again."

"Where is he? He might come back and he wants to kill us. He's dangerous and .... "

"No," Annie assured her, "Blake has gone. Your father and Sgt. Hopkins will sort him out. Now rest awhile. He's one ghost you can lay to rest, Daisy. Forget him."

Fighting the urge to drift off to sleep, Charlotte tried to think clearly. "No. Fred Blake. He just left."

Annie shook her head. "That was days ago, my child. We have all been praying for you. It looks as though our prayers have been answered judging by your colour. Rest is the only cure for those ailing lungs, rest and my special herbal potion!" A cold butterfly touched her forehead as Annie kissed her. "God Bless you, child."

The vision faded. Charlotte was alone again. Completely alone in the bedroom of the cottage.

Ralph drove down the narrow lane as Ted pointed out the suspect cottage. He kept on going until his companion pointed to an open gate to the left then drove into the field. "Are you sure that's the place, Ted? No lights on and curtains drawn just like any other normal place. No vehicles that I could see."

"Thass the place, alright. Come on, boy. We'll take a closer look. You can put that torch away, we don't want no light showin' us up. I come prepared so just keep behind me."

Ralph was shocked to see Ted with a shotgun in his hands. "Is that mine? You crafty old devil! You really are expecting trouble, aren't you."

Ted Skinner went silently forward with all the stealth and vigour of a younger man. They reached their objective and he motioned to the front door. "Only way in" he whispered, "and out. Shall we......" The sound of an engine drowned his hushed voice and they slipped back under the cover of darkness to watch and listen.

Thomas had returned in his car.

Charlotte drifted in and out of a dreamlike state until she heard the car engine. Did she dream those recent visions of Fred Blake and Annie? Was her imagination working overtime due to the situation she found herself in? The only true fact she could understand was the threat of Thomas Blake and he was back.

With a great effort she got off the bed only to find herself on the floor again. Her legs were so weak, her face throbbing with pain, her arms bruised and swollen, but her spirit was returning. This was her chance to avenge Daisy, avenge Annie. She alone could stop Thomas Blake doing what his Great-Uncle had done, bring grief and misfortune to her family. Ancestors or not, they deserved vengeance.

Crawling to the bottom of the bed she found the bottle

which Thomas had used to celebrate with. Pouring it's remaining contents over her face helped to clear her head, she hardly noticed the sticky patina left on her skin.

Determination coursed through her veins and she heard a door slam shut downstairs. Half walking, half tottering she lunged towards the dressing-table. There was nothing there to use as defence, only the remnants of cheap cosmetics and a pair manicure scissors.

"Charlotte? Are you ready for me?" Thomas entered with a length of rope in his hands, twisting it around his knuckles and grinning. Seeing the empty bed he turned sharply to find her standing behind him. "Oh! Want to play games, eh! I enjoy......."

Charlotte plunged the scissors into his chest and recoiled in horror as he looked at his wound, then her. "My God!" he uttered, "what have you done?"

Footsteps pounded on the stairs and Charlotte realised that Fred and Alf must have returned as well. Picking up the empty bottle she had discarded on the floor behind her she waited until a head came through the door and brought it down with all her strength.

"Bloody 'Ell!" a voice said from the stairs. "'Ands up! I got a gun!" The barrel of a shotgun poked through the doorway and Charlotte fell back against the wall in horror.

Thomas slumped on the floor with an agonising yell before Ted Skinner appeared behind the gun. "At last! Some bugger's got you! Where's the girl, eh?" Without mercy Ted nudged the injured man's chin with the gun barrel.

Sobbing with relief, Charlotte called out, "Here, Ted. I'm here, behind the door."

Looking at the swollen, beaten face streaked with coal dust and tears, Ted Skinner remembered that time so many years ago. "Daisy." he uttered involuntarily. "Just like Daisy. Did 'e do that to you?"

Uncontrollable sobs racked her body as she muttered, "I got him, Ted. I did it for them. I just had to!"

Keeping his gun trained on the groaning culprit, he nodded. "You've laid some ghosts to rest, girl. That you did. 'E ruined my life. 'E took others too. Let 'im rot in 'ell!"

"Ralph?" Charlotte asked weakly, "Is he back?"

"He was," Ted chuckled. "He was."

The world passed out of her vision. Thomas lying against the dressing-table bleeding and groaning, Ted holding a gun, the other man unconscious behind the door. Her Grandmother, Blake, Daisy, all gone. Nothing but empty blackness. Merciful oblivion.

Opening her eyes, Charlotte smiled. It was her bedroom at Glas Fryn. It was daytime. The sun was shinning and the sweet song of birds filtered through an open window. It must have been a nightmare. All those terrible things were a nightmare. Lovingly stroking the patchwork counterpane which her grandmother had made she smiled again. It all seemed so real, though. The ghosts had talked to her. They thought she was Daisy. Poor Daisy............ what had happened to Daisy?

Mary Price came into the room with an armful of bed linen and stopped in her tracks when she saw her patient. "Praise be! You're back with us! How are you feeling, Lottie?"

Trying to speak was painful, but she couldn't remember why. "Sore. How am I here? Didn't I leave this morning?"

Mary dropped the laundry on the floor and sat on the side of the bed. "Four days ago, yes. Can't you remember what happened to you?"

"Yes, well..... some." Charlotte frowned. "I must have gone back and got mixed up........... " Realising that Mary would know nothing of her time travels she changed direction and tried to get things in perspective. "Thomas. I was locked in a shed of some kind. It seemed like days. After that.......... well, I'm not sure."

"Kidnapped you, he did! Terrible things have happened around here. Thank God that you are still alive. We had the

Doctor check you over but since there were no broken bones I told them I could look after you better than any hospital. Didn't want you to wake up amongst strangers, did we."

"What about Cissie? Did he kidnap her too? Was she hurt?"

Mary looked away then decided to tell the truth. "He murdered her. They found her body in an attic wardrobe."

"No! Oh, no!" Charlotte wailed in anger and pain, "Why poor Cissie? I wish to God I'd killed him! I can't remember ...." Realising what she had said she felt sickened by her emotions. "I never thought I would wish anyone dead. It makes me as evil as him. Poor Cissie. Why her? Me I can understand but ...."

"Calm down!" Mary demanded as she tided the bed and tried to divert her patient away from thoughts of Thomas Blake. "To answer your question it seems that Cissie caught him trying to sell this house. She knew too much." Pulling the young woman's face towards her she spoke briskly, "No more now. I have to see to these dressings and if it stings you'll just have to grin and bear it."

A hint of a smile forced it's way through the swollen features. "You're hardly a Florence Nightingale, are you!" A soft giggling gave way to uncontrollable laughter.

Mary knew the shock had to manifest itself in one way or another, so she let the hysterical shrill laughter wear itself out naturally as she prepared the herbal balms on squares of soft lint. Ten minutes later her patient became quiet and tracks of tears flowed down the misshapen cheeks which she bathed and dried. "There. Clean of body and spirit. Do you feel better now?"

"Yes," Charlotte answered truthfully. "I feel as if ...." what a strange thing to do. Laugh. It seems outrageous under the circumstances."

"It's either laugh or cry," Mary stated flatly, "or else store it up and let it turn your mind." As she applied her medication she noticed a visible difference in her patient and thought it worth pushing things along a bit. "Nearly finished. Come on. I think a good soak in a hot bath with do your aching joints some good, especially with my special salts added."

Getting a dressing-gown from the wardrobe, Mary helped the weakened woman out of bed and into the bathroom. "Right, lady! You sit there while I run the water. Four days in bed hasn't helped you look to good." All the while she made sure that Charlotte didn't look in any mirrors.

Ralph had spent the last few days checking the Estate and catching up on his duties. Trying to make order out of chaos in his home was a daunting task, but help arrived in the unexpected form of Ada Skinner. Despite her husband's constant criticism she worked like a demon and had little to say. In two days the place was spotless with just a few items out of place.

"Thank you, Mrs. Skinner." Ralph said sincerely as he placed an envelope in her hands. "A token of my appreciation."

"My pleasure. You got the old cottage looking very nice, for a man that is. Mary Price normally does it, is that right?"

"No. She has the key so she can pop in and check everything whenever I'm away."

"Pity she didn't this time then." came the tart reply.

"Mary had a lot on her mind, Mrs. Skinner." He turned to open the door for her, but she waved a hand to announce she wasn't through.

"I think you got the wrong idea, Mr. Nicholls. We all know the trouble up at the House. Didn't my Ted help you? Yes. We all know. We prayed for her in Church last Sunday."

"For Mary?" he asked puzzled.

"No! For Miss Stone! Even my Ted said she was as good as dead and he's not one for exaggeration. Plain speaking he is. Too plain."

"Well it's all thanks to Mary that she's pulling through. I'd have thought a prayer for the deceased would be more fitting."

"Oh, don't you think we left Cissie Jenkins out, no Sir! Charlotte was mentioned in prayers for the sick, but we said a special one for Cissie. A terrible thing to happen to her."

"Yes," Ralph saw the honest grief on the face and felt humble. "The last few days...... well, I'm sorry. How would you like to come in on a regular basis, Mrs. Skinner? Any day that would suit you."

A delighted look spread over her face. "Ada to you. Tuesdays are best. See you next week." Without further ado she marched through the back door, but stuck her head around it before she left. "You got a visitor, Mr. Nicholls."

Brian was dressed casually and carrying an overnight bag. "Hello! Any room at the Inn?"

"What the hell are you doing here?" Ralph asked in surprise.

"Your sister was very worried about you. She reads the newspapers you know. It was her or me. We tossed a coin and here I am."

Laughing, the Estate Manager clapped his brother-in-law on the back. "I'm glad you won!"

"Right! Now we sorted my accommodation out let's get to the nitty gritty. What's going on? According to the press Olivia is accusing you of mishandling Estate funds, robbing her of all the profits from other investments and trying to take the roof from over her head. Given the normal exaggeration percentage such articles carry you must admit that the matter is serious."

"None of it is true," came the simple reply, "it's her twisted imagination, a distortion of facts. Coffee?"

Kicking his bag in frustration, Brian yelled at his wife's infuriating brother. "Wake up, Ralph! Fate doesn't always shine on the good and honest, you know!"

"Something stronger?" Ralph suggested as he walked out of the kitchen and into the study. "Here, twelve year old malt. Drink it."

Brian did so and refilled his glass before he slumped in a chair. "Who are you protecting? The tall, dark-haired Charlotte?"

Ralph remained standing, drink untouched. "Thomas used Mary Price's key to walk in here and take all the accounts for the Estate and the Scottish venture to boot. Before, or during that time, he kidnapped Lottie, he also presented 'selected sections' and put them before Olivia. She could only reach one conclusion, that I was embezzling funds. The night we found Lottie and took her back to Glas Fryn Olivia said it was all my fault, that I had forced Thomas into such desperate actions in order to reveal the facts. According to the Gospel of Olivia, Charlotte was my accomplice and Thomas merely kept her under lock and key whilst he proved his case against me."

Brian drained his glass and refilled it for a third time. "Goes in for Fantasy does she? Preposterous! What does Lottie have to say about all this?"

"Mary rings me every morning and so far Lottie just drifts in and out of her sleep long enough to take liquids and medication. Most of the time she rants and raves in unknown dreams, a prisoner of her own mind."

"Dear God! Shouldn't she be receiving proper medical care?"

"She was checked over by the paramedics at the scene, but Mary and Dr. Samuel insisted they were the best care available. It's that or admitting her as a patient in a psychiatric ward. On a normal ward she would distress and disturb the other patients. She's not mad, Brian."

Reading the look in his brother-in-law's face he suggested, "Why don't you go and talk to her? Talk her through her nightmare. Love transcends all barriers, so they say!"

"Pointless at the moment. Mary will let me know when she improves, then I'll go round with or without Olivia's permission." Giving Brian a cold stare he added, "and you can stop quoting lines out of all the romance novels ever written."

"Beg your pardon!" Brian replied flippantly, "I've obviously hit home."

Helen Jarvis sat at the desk which had been so recently occupied by her husband. It was sad that there had been no son or daughter to share the loneliness with, no child to carry on where he left off. Their marriage had not been blessed with offspring, but the quality of the love they shared was nonetheless deep and sincere.

The thought of clearing the desk had been daunting, she wondered if she were strong enough to go through the drawers which contained his business dealings and personal mementos, mostly of his Army career to which he was devoted.

A strict disciplinarian in life proved to be borne out in the event of his death as everything had been in order, not a legacy of probate and legal tangles as some widows had. No. The only messy thing about her dear, departed husband had been the manner of his death.

After shedding silent tears which always seemed ready to fall, she dabbed her eyes and squared her shoulders. Ralph had been their son of sorts. From the time he started coming to their home many years ago he had won their hearts.

How her husband had enjoyed the prospect of the visits from the energetic young man with ambitious ideals and strong character. How many times had the two of them sat in this room and argued with zeal about so many different topics? From world-wide affairs to local farming issues. They were friends who respected each other's honesty and forthrightness.

It didn't take long to find the documents she wanted and so, with a final glance at the newspaper article on the desk she packed her bags and rang for a taxi.

Olivia Jones wouldn't know what hit her.

CHAPTER 20

Time for Truth

Price served lunch to his mistress in the morning-room. As he transferred the contents of the tray onto the table he spoke without looking up. "Miss Charlotte is more herself today, Madam. Mary says that in a few days she should be well enough to get out and about again."

Silence descended as Olivia Jones sat at the occasional table and unfolded a napkin with precise movements. The manservant finished his duties and felt his anger rising. For most of his life he had served in this House without commenting on the actions of his lords and masters, done his duty without questioning their motives or actions. It had not been his place to criticise or admonish, until now, that is. He knew that the severe treatment Lottie had suffered from the hand of Thomas Blake was similar to the plight of Daisy at the mercy of Fred Blake. He wondered if the modern woman would survive. Daisy had not.

"Excuse me, Ma'am," he began, "but shouldn't you go up to see her? We are fortunate that she lived through the ordeal."

The large, blue eyes stared at the manservant with horror. "Price! It seems that the disease of the modern generation to speak their mind is catching. How dare you suggest what I should do."

"With all due respect," Price retaliated, "she is your great-niece. Surely you wish her recovery? You haven't even asked about her. She was beaten, locked up, tied up and humiliated. Doesn't that bother you?"

"Really! To be spoken to in such a way is criminal! Go about your duties, man. Run along and leave me in peace to enjoy my lunch."

Giving a deep, gracious bow, the old man nodded. "In that

case, Madam, run along I will. Accept this as formal notice to quit. That goes for my daughter too."

"What will you do for money or a roof over your head?" Olivia smirked, "or have you been dipping into the well too?"

Fuming at the outrageous suggestion, Price turned and walked from the room with his head held high. He ignored the calls for him to return. He would not be humiliated again. Reaching the kitchen he went to his daughter and put his arm around her shoulders. "I've done it. I told her we're off ! Do you approve?"

"Was she just as stubborn about Lottie?"

"As a mule, love. As a mule."

"Then we go. Lottie too. Are you sure Ralph will put us up? That girl still needs a lot of care and attention."

Price smiled. "You think Ralph wouldn't give it?"

Looking glum, the dark-haired young woman nodded. "You're right, Dad. He would do anything for her."

Hugging her close to him, the rheumy eyes filled with moisture. "I know you've always held a candle for him but it's not to be, lass. Not to be. Come on, let's start packing. I'll phone Ralph and tell him what's going on."

Charlotte was stunned to hear that Mary and her father were leaving Glas Fryn. Mary refused to tell her why, just that they could no longer tolerate Olivia's attitude, that she had finally gone too far.

Left alone to rest whilst the Prices' did their packing, Charlotte slid out of bed and tottered towards the door. She opened it and looked down at the empty hallway. All clear. Holding on to the wall for support, then the banister to get down the stairs, it seemed to take an age to reach her goal.

Feeling weak through the simple act of walking she went towards the lounge with her hands forward like a child learning to walk. The room was empty. Leaning against the door jamb to regain her breath, Charlotte turned in the direction of the morning room and the seemingly vast stretch of hall before her. When she finally grasped the door knob and entered the room a look of triumph radiated from her face. 'I made it !' she said, half to herself, half to the startled occupant of the room.

"Who is it?" the familiar sharp tones asked. "Come in properly and show yourself!"

Charlotte used the furniture to make her way towards her Aunt who sitting in the same chair as she was six months ago when she first arrived at this house. The expression on her face was similar too. "Charlotte?" the old woman asked as she screwed up her eyes.

Taking the nearest chair, Charlotte plumped down with sheer exhaustion. "Of course it is. What's the matter with you? Why are you looking at me so funny?"

Trying to regain her composure, Olivia shook her head and picked up the book she had been reading. "No reason. I have nothing to say to you. Please leave me in peace."

"Leave you in peace?" the young woman shrieked then winced as the effort of moving her jaw sent pains shooting through her head. "Price and Mary are leaving and you sit there asking for peace? What's going on around here? I suppose Thomas has something to do with this!"

Dropping the book, Olivia grabbed her walking-stick. "I didn't think you could sink so low! Get out! Go with the others. You are all traitors!" Raising her stick in a threatening fashion she looked formidable.

"What have I done?" Charlotte asked bewildered. "What have I said? Traitors? I just can't.......... "

"Can't what?" Olivia asked as she dropped her arm. "Can't believe you are a murderess? Can't believe you killed him? Well believe this - THOMAS IS DEAD!"

Dumbstruck, Charlotte felt the room spin as the words struck deep in her mind. The vivid nightmare returned. She had attacked him. The scissors. Blood. He had fallen. He must have died. No. It was just a nightmare. She was shaking, her whole body was shaking, a voice was calling her name. A man's voice getting louder and louder .... was he haunting her?

"Lottie! Come on! Wake up. Lottie!"

Opening her eyes in dread she shouted through the pain in her face, her arms, her legs, "No! No! Leave me alone! Please, please........ " Her eyes focused , but it was not the face she feared.

"Come on, Lottie. It's only me. You shouldn't have come downstairs."

"Ralph?" Tears spilled down her face, burning her skin as they fell. "Where have you been? Terrible, terrible things have been happening. I think... I think I killed him. She says I killed Thomas."

"No, Lottie," Ralph said sternly as he gripped her shoulders and shook her gently, "you didn't kill him. Do you hear me?"

"Enough of this!" Olivia's voice commanded. "She's responsible and so are you! You both schemed enough to get rid of him, but I can see through your charade."

"What about her injuries, Olivia?" Ralph asked. "Are they faked too? Just look at her! Take a good long look at the work of your precious Thomas Blake!"

As the words sank in to Charlotte's mind, she gripped the arms of the chair, then got unsteadily to her feet. Gaining her balance and ignoring the aches and pains which made movement so difficult she walked over the other side of the room by supporting herself on the furniture.

Silence felt like a cloak as she gazed at the reflection in the mantle mirror. She saw a woman with bruises around her eyes, a mouth which was swollen and twisted and dressings which covered her cheeks and forehead. Up until this moment she hadn't taken much notice of Mary's administrations, hadn't noticed that talking was painful, hadn't noticed anything much. She had been too busy trying to sort out the nightmare from reality.

Gently touching her cheek, she asked, "Why the

dressings?"

Ralph walked over and answered quietly, "You needed a stitch or two."

Turning around and gazing at her Great Aunt, Charlotte spoke as loudly as she could. "He murdered Cissie. He did this to me. Yet you still protect him. Why? Did you know he pushed his mother off a cliff on purpose? Did you know that he suffocated his twin-brother? Did you know that he confessed it all to his father knowing he had a heart problem? Oh, yes! He was only a child then, but an evil child who was eaten up by jealousy and hate!"

The old woman was shaking her head vigorously. "You're making it all up! He can't even defend himself now."

Walking slowly back across the room to the stubborn woman, Charlotte continued her tirade. "He told me all this because he was going to kill me. He couldn't help crowing about his conquests, he even told me about Cissie but I wasn't sure if he was bluffing to frighten me. Do you know how he got me to the cottage in the first place? By telling me that you sent for me. Ralph's cottage was ablaze and you sent for me! I was locked in a coal shed for so long I didn't know day from night, humiliated by his henchmen then tied to a chair while he told me all about his victims. He did this to me. I had little chance of defending myself. I killed him to avenge the others, I did it for........ " Stopping herself from saying Annie and Daisy she added lamely, "for your sake, Aunt."

"But you didn't kill him, Lottie." Ralph took her arms and turned her round to face him. "That woman did it. The one in the cottage."

"Dora?"

"Yes. He'd hit her and left her for dead in the kitchen, but she'd only passed out. She came upstairs, picked up the shotgun and used it."

"Upstairs? But I was upstairs. I attacked Thomas then another man came up the stairs. I hit him with something, a bottle I think, then Ted appeared. Then.............. "

339

"Then you fainted. Ted dropped the gun to see to you but the other woman picked it up and shot Thomas before old Ted knew what was happening. You didn't kill him, Lottie. You only disabled him, it wasn't a fatal wound. The autopsy confirmed it."

Olivia rose from her chair leaning heavily on her walking stick. Tears trickled down the lined face as she put her hand on Charlotte's arm. "My dear child! I wouldn't listen. I got everything muddled up. I thought you .... oh, dear! Please forgive me?"

The words echoed in Charlotte's head. Annie had said the same to Daisy. Compassion for her Grandmother's sister coursed through her veins, the spirit of mercy was carved on her soul. Lightly kissing the soft cheek, the young woman nodded. "But what about Glas Fryn? He sold it. He told me you'd be out in the street."

"He was right. He had the Deeds and it seems that he had already tried to re-mortgage the property but failed." Falling back heavily into her favourite chair, Olivia reminded Charlotte of the occasion. "Do you recall the day I went to see my Solicitor? I took a taxi because Thomas had failed to keep his promise of a lift."

"I remember." Charlotte replied.

"It was stopped, of course. Thomas just though they'd turned him down, but never knew why or that I found out. I should have had the Deeds back then."

Ralph sighed, his patience wearing thin. "But he managed to sell the whole Estate despite your inside contact! How did he manage that?"

"Humph!" Olivia snorted. "Because my Solicitor had been taken ill and his stand-in didn't consult anyone. Just took it for a straight forward sale. It might have looked odd if Thomas didn't have any other documentation, but it seems he had the accounts to hand and so the Estate was sold in its entirety." Shaking her head, she looked accusingly at Ralph. "You were entrusted with that side of things!"

There was the sound of raised voices coming from the hallway which interrupted their conversation. A woman stormed in carrying a briefcase. Charlotte guessed her age to be around fifty and judging by her austere, tailored suit, a professional person. A stab of jealousy went through her as the intruder kissed Ralph and greeted him warmly.

"Darling, Ralph! Quite a surprise, aren't I!" Turning to Olivia she smiled and stooped to kiss her cheek. "Olivia, my dear, you look well! Don't you remember me?"

The old woman frowned as she tried to place the newcomer, then nodded and clasped the extended hand. "Helen! How lovely to see you. What brings you down her so soon......." At a loss for words, she added, "My deepest sympathies, my dear."

"Thank you. May I sit down? Price is rustling up some tea for us all."

"About time too!" Olivia retorted.

"But he's leaving!" Charlotte snapped feeling ignored by the woman she guessed to be Jarvis's widow. She began to wonder why Ralph had spent so long in Scotland........

Helen felt the enmity and directed her gaze towards the young woman. "You must be Charlotte. So pleased to meet you at last! Ralph has told me all about you, but I gather you usually look quite beautiful. Who did that to you, my dear?"

"Thomas Blake," Ralph supplied, "Need you ask?"

"Yes, Mrs. Jarvis. I am Charlotte Stone and I normally look far more presentable, but we've had some rather harrowing events around here so you'll have to excuse my appearance." Looking up at Ralph she added, "apart from that my brain is functioning so I don't need anyone to speak for me."

"Quite." Helen agreed. "Ralph, go and help Price. Mary is feeding your brother-in-law so she is busy enough."

"Helen!" the Estate Manager uttered, "you can't walk in here and organise everyone like you do back home! Price and Mary have resigned and they were packing when I came in."

Smiling and taking off her coat, Helen Jarvis moved a chair to sit next to Olivia. "Not any more. Go and see for yourself." As the young man left the room she crossed her legs and clasped her hands around her knee. "Now then, I understand you are suing that young gentleman, Olivia. Am I right?"

Anger flooded into Charlotte's face at the statement and she felt compelled to defend him. "You what? You stupid old woman! Can't you see.......... "

"Quiet, Charlotte!" Olivia uttered in a menacing tone. "Keep out of this!" Turning to the woman by her side she hissed, "the same goes for you! Your husband and Ralph cooked up a fine scheme between them. I mean to get to the bottom of it and you'd better keep well out of the way, madam! My advice to you is to go back immediately."

"Not before I've had my cup of tea and sorted you out!" Helen replied casually. "You would look an utter fool if you ever took the thing to Court, an absolute fool."

"How dare you!" the older woman shouted, "Get out of my house! Now!"

"No. Everyone else might be abandoning ship but I've got the lifeboat. Anyway, it's not your house anymore, is it? Giving Thomas Power of Attorney was a bad move, Olivia." Helen looked pleased with herself as well she might since the other two occupants of the room had fallen silent. "Oh, good! I've got your attention at last." Delving into her briefcase she produced documents which she handed to Olivia. "Read these, or would you prefer me to translate?"

Grudgingly, Olivia leafed through them while nodding. "Go ahead. I can read as you talk. It might be quicker."

Helen winked conspiratorially at Charlotte which made the latter feel slightly guilty about her earlier feelings towards the stranger. "Ten years ago you sent young Ralph up to us to learn the trade, so to speak. The art of running an Estate. Correct?"

"You know it is!" snapped the elderly woman who

continued to go through the papers before her.

Helen continued. "It didn't take long for him to realise that the Estate was just about breaking even and had been for years. Am I right, Olivia? You didn't receive much revenue, if any, from our Estate, did you?"

Scanning the pages before her with interest, Olivia Jones answered without thinking. "No. Mr. Jones thought it would be enough to keep his son in a job, earn a decent living and a house to live in. The land was always an asset of course, always something to fall back on."

Helen nodded. "Ralph had an independent viewpoint. He saw the land as a valuable site, an area which could be utilised towards the tourist trade alongside the farming aspects."

"Guards Hyde?" Olivia asked glancing up from the documents, "where is this place?"

"Home to me," Helen responded evenly. "Ralph and my husband invested all they had to make our acres into a Theme Park. On a small scale, I might add. One farm is a working museum whilst the other does all the heavy work. The parkland had been transformed into a nature park, skilfully landscaped whilst retaining the natural beauty of the area. It was a wild idea, Olivia. Quite new at the time and very risky. Thanks to Ralph it has become an established site which is listed in all tourists guides for Scotland. The profits are substantial and growing year by year."

"So I wouldn't look ridiculous taking him to Court!" Olivia laughed triumphantly.

"You would." Helen parried. "Jarvis was your step-son, Ralph your loyal employee. After ploughing some of the profits back into the venture each year they put the remainder into an account in your name. Not bad considering you never put a penny into it!"

"If that's true why the secrecy?" the old woman asked. "I still smell a rat. What good was that money to me if I didn't know it was there?"

Ralph walked in with a tea-tray and placed it on a table. "The rat was Thomas Blake."

"What has he got to do with this?" Charlotte asked totally perplexed by the revelations.

"Because he was doing his best to muscle in on the operation that's why. Remember when you first came here? Thomas denied being in Scotland? He was a ferret as far as money was concerned, he just wouldn't let go once he got the scent. That's why he killed Jarvis. At least, his car did."

"Wild accusations, again, Ralph!" Olivia snorted.

"No. Fact. The police have forensic evidence that his car hit Jarvis. No doubt about it. Shame it's too late to nail him for it, but you can only die once I suppose. Anyway, your special bank account has £50,000 in it Olivia. Now he's dead you have free access to every penny."

"You're a wealthy woman, Olivia." Helen Jarvis confirmed. "Now do you understand all the cloak and dagger stuff? That's why Ralph kept the accounts in his cottage, I should imagine that's why he was burgled. Thomas told you that it was all underhand, that you'd been cheated, isn't that right?"

Olivia's bottom lip trembled. "Yes, he did. I'm so confused by all this nonsense. Thomas always seemed to charming. Such a gentleman. It's hard to think he was scheming all the while. He lost all his family at such a tender age and I was destined to be here for him. All so tragic. I thought that his life was controlled by fate, it's as though a curse had been placed on his family. His Great-Uncle Fredrick was killed in our Summer-House, you know. He was a dreadful man!

'I thought that the past should be laid to rest and I liked his parents very much, such nice people, it was so very sad. I felt obligated to give Thomas every chance to be decent and honest without the stigma of his ancestry. Things like that tend to linger in the memories of folk. The shadows of past crimes. I needed to make it up to him."

Charlotte felt sick. "Fred Blake was responsible for Daisy's death, Aunt. How could you possibly feel guilty about Thomas's forbearers?"

"I just wanted to chase away those shadows, I suppose. Make Glas Fryn happy again like it used to be when I was a young girl. Chattering voices, laughter, noise, a house full of coming and going. I thought my only chance was through Thomas." Her lead lolling back into the wing of the chair she announced, "You just wouldn't understand."

Recalling her travels in time, Charlotte felt humble. "I understand more than you will ever know."

Catching the veiled statement, Olivia sat upright and clapped her hands, "Of course you do! You were the one! I did the right thing after all." She fell silent after the strange performance, but her face beamed with delight and smug satisfaction.

Over the next week the house seemed to be in turmoil. Mary and Price had stayed on once Olivia had sheepishly retracted her wild accusations and promised a substantial increase in salary due to her 'windfall'.

Alan Armstrong arrived for the funeral of his nephew through duty, not compassion. He told Olivia about the trouble he had with Thomas and housekeeper Dora whilst under his roof. "They were taking drugs and selling them, making an illegal fortune out of my practice. I was lucky not to be struck off. I tell you Olivia, I came here not to grieve, but to make sure the beggar's dead! Years ago I made out my Will in favour of Ralph simply because when he came to visit it was as my nephew, not as a fortune hunter."

"If only you'd told me," Olivia said, "perhaps I would have viewed him in a different light."

"Would you have believed me? No, Olivia. Never in a million years."

Ted skinner was called to the House and offered his post as gardener back. His reply was straight forward. "I'm too bloody old now, Missus ! I got a grandson who's learning the ways, I'll tell 'im to start next Monday."

Lottie walked with him to the end of the drive and kissed his cheek in grateful thanks. "You saved my life, Ted. I prayed for Ralph to walk through the door and rescue me, but my white knight never arrived. What did I get? You!"

"Thas where you're wrong, my little lady! Mr. Ralph was the first through the door but you knocked 'im out cold!"

Astonished, Charlotte stuttered, "So he was the ...... I thought .... Good grief ! It never happens like that in the movies, Ted."

Chuckling to himself, his pipe wavering precariously in his mouth, Ted answered dryly, " 'e's 'ardly an Errol Flynn, Miss!"

Sgt. Hopkins had called to see Charlotte and take a statement. She told him all about the kidnapping as her memory of those dark, terrifying hours was returning. Dora Biggins was being tried for manslaughter, but the opinion was that the jury would be lenient in their judgement due to the circumstances. Charlotte promised to appear in Court when the occasion demanded. Miss Kemp, the Postmistress, was last seen by a taxi driver who dropped her at Cardiff Railway Station. She had left the area without a word to a soul. Attempts to trace her proved futile.

The following afternoon was the internment of Thomas Blake. Olivia and Alan Armstrong attended. Following the brief funeral a meeting was called in the dining room of Glas Fryn where Charlotte, Ralph, Helen Jarvis and the Prices' sat around the table whilst Olivia's solicitor held court.

The silence was complete as Olivia indicated for him to begin.

"Mrs. Jones had requested this meeting be held in order to clear up certain events pertaining to the House and Estate of Glas Fryn. You are all aware that the late Thomas Blake sold the entire Estate under false pretences. Under normal circumstances that sale would stand as he was in possession of the Title Deeds and Estate Accounts, not to mention the official qualification to act on behalf of Mrs. Jones.

'However, unknown to the late Mr. Blake there had been one major change to the legal ownership of the property, hence the sale transaction was null and void. On 28th April this year, Mrs. Olivia Jones legally transferred the entire Estate to Miss Charlotte Stone without conditions. In other words, ladies and gentlemen, Thomas Blake no longer had power of proxy.

' Mrs. Olivia Jones was not the owner of the Estate so all the late gentleman's machinations were in vain. I have been instructed to hand the Title Deeds and Estate to Miss Stone in front of the present company who will serve as witnesses to the occasion. Come forward, Miss Stone."

Shocked, Charlotte jumped up and followed her train of thought. "If Thomas Blake wasn't dead then we wouldn't be sitting here now. He would have had the money and scarpered by which time it would have been too late to do anything about it, am I right?"

The Solicitor coughed behind his hand to cover his embarrassment. "Er, well......... one would have recourse to the law, naturally. Our Company were rather..... lax. It would mean tracing Mr Blake and recovering the money, proving .... but we mustn't worry about events which are purely conjecture. Will you........ "

Persisting with her line of reasoning, Charlotte continued. "So the entire Estate would have been tied up with red tape. Glas Fryn empty, land left to nature, employees out of work and their homes, not to mention the minor matter of an old lady and her staff out on the street. Absolutely penniless. Isn't that the probable outcome of your Company's error?"

"If you take the matter to extremes, then your conclusions may have some truth, but I really......... "

Cutting him dead, Charlotte walked over to the man and smiled. "I'll have the Deeds now and you may consider yourself dismissed. Now that I control Glas Fryn I would prefer a more efficient Company to handle my legal affairs."

Wasting no time in collecting his papers after the necessary signatures made the transfer complete, the solicitor left the party without another word.

As he left, Helen Jarvis clapped her hands in delight. "Bravo! Wasn't she marvellous, Ralph?"

He nodded. "Yes. There again, since she's my boss I dare not say anything else!"

A celebration drink was called for by Olivia. Glass in hand she commanded her audience. "Here's to Charlotte. Annie's granddaughter. Glas Fryn will remain in the family for another generation."

A shiver ran through Charlotte as she remembered other ladies who dwelt within these very walls. Sarah Armstrong, Annie, Daisy. The trails and tribulations they had suffered, the joy and despair. No doubt fate had already planned her course, she too would know laughter and tears, but with the courage of her ancestors she was able to face anything.

1995

Charlotte rose from the chair and rubbed her back. Gazing around the refurbished library she recalled the reason why she came to this House. To write a history of Glas Fryn or 'Blue Hill' in English. Well, she didn't get very far by putting pen to paper, but lived through the story instead.

Since that terrible time five years ago when she had faced death, yet clung to life so tenaciously, there had been no more contact with the past. Just one very moving experience a week or so after the event.

In the night she had woken up suddenly. Before her stood Daisy. Looking so alive and beautiful as she smiled and blew a kiss. Then, stepping back slowly, she faded into the shadows of the bedroom waving as her soul returned to eternity.

Knowing that Daisy was saying good-bye, Charlotte had

cried herself back to sleep that night. Despite attempts to see Annie again by wearing the silver thimble, nothing happened. They had left her in peace. She had been saved from the clutches of everlasting sleep. She had survived the evil of the Blake legacy through their love and protection which transcended time. Now she owned Glas Fryn she had become the keeper of the past, the people and events, stories embedded in fabric of the aged stones.

Looking out of the French Doors she could see Ted Skinners' grandson working diligently in the now glorious garden which was alive with colour and the hum of insects. The Summer House had been demolished and a rose-garden planted on the spot. No more shadows.

Olivia was less mobile physically now, but certainly not mentally. The old games room had been opened up and converted to a bed-sitting room for her. Mary Price still ran the house but she now lived in Ralph's cottage with her farmer husband. Her happiness complete, particularly since her father remained at Glas Fryn, retired and living in their old quarters rent free. Much respected and loved by all, he gloried in his knowledge of running a large household with the wisdom of age and experience to dispense at his leisure.

Sgt. Hopkins daughter, Sian, lived in. She was a cheerful, hard-working girl who could turn her hand to anything. Even Olivia laughed at her banter and rarely complained about her work.

As for herself, Charlotte took stock of her present life style. A wonderful old house which had been in her family for generations. Granted, several decades worth of neglect had taken their toll of the purse strings, but time was on her side. An elderly Aunt whose words spilled like acid when the occasion arose, yet turned to honey when the mood suited.

No more ghosts to haunt her.

"Penny for them!" the deep, rich voice came from behind her. She turned to find Ralph Nicholls looking at her intently.

"Oh, nothing really. Just day-dreaming."

A frown creased the furrowed brow as he asked hesitantly, "Day dreaming? Are you sure? Nothing else?"

"Promise! Nothing else. All that stopped with Thomas Blake. Honestly, Ralph! It just never happens anymore."

Taking her into his arms, the man held her close and drank in her scent. "Lilies-of-the-Valley. You always wear the same thing! If you did slip into the past the smell would haunt me!" Kissing her lightly he asked, "Why do you think its stopped?"

Stepping back and smiling, Charlotte answered lightly, "I've just worked that one out. Because I'm happy! I've got a wonderful husband, a beautiful child and my soul is here and now, not being dragged back to other times."

Putting an arm around her shoulder he nodded. "You could be right, Mrs. Nicholls. Best thing Olivia ever did was getting you here in the first place despite all that happened. Come on, let's go and see what our little miracle is up to! Thank God the doctors were wrong all those years ago or we would never have been blessed with our very own Daisy."

Charlotte Nicholls left the library with her husband. In the next month or so their second child would be born and Olivia's wish was coming true. Glas Fryn would ring with the sound of happiness once more. The echoes would reach down the years as memories of Charlotte Anne Armstong and James Nicholls's offspring once filled the house with their happy laughter. Life would deal its hand but the core of the Armstrongs would prove a formidable force that would stand the test of time, stand the test of the past, overcome the test of the future.

On the hall table stood a large, healthy Christmas Cactus alongside a small, silver thimble. The spirit and power of love diminished evil, diminished time and looked on with quiet dignity as the new generation made its mark in the annals of time.

The End

22263800R00205

Printed in Great Britain
by Amazon